A DRY SPELL

Clare Chambers was born in Croydon in 1966 and read English at Oxford. She wrote her first novel, *Uncertain Terms*, during a year in New Zealand, after which she worked as an editor for a London publisher. She married one of her schoolteachers, lives in Kent, and has three small children and no hobbies whatsoever. Her third novel, *Learning to Swim*, won the 1998 Parker Romantic Novel of the Year Award.

Praise for Clare Chambers' previous novels:

'A warm bath of a book – you slip in and just don't want to get out' Victoria Routledge

'Funny and touching . . . very well written, and full of engaging characters' Nina Bawden

'An intelligent escapist read . . . well written and funny' *Express*

'Modern, intelligently observed and highly original' *Daily Mail*

'Delightful' *Sunday Times*

'Lingers in the mind long after it's been put down' *Company*

'A funny book which slips in some acute and painful observations on the side' *The Times*

'To warm the heart and chill it is a rare ability' *Evening Standard*

'A funny and moving story with a great deal of style' *Sunday Telegraph*

'A great read' *Time Out*

By the same author

Uncertain Terms
Back Trouble
Learning to Swim

A DRY SPELL

Clare Chambers

Century · London

Published by Century in 2000

1 3 5 7 9 10 8 6 4 2

This novel is a work of fiction. Names and characters are the product of the author's imagination and any resemblance to actual persons, living or dead, is entirely coincidental

First published in the United Kingdom in 2000 by Century

Random House Group Limited
20 Vauxhall Bridge Road, London SW1V 2SA

Random House Australia (Pty) Limited
20 Alfred Street, Milsons Point, Sydney,
New South Wales 2061, Australia

Random House New Zealand Limited
18 Poland Road, Glenfield
Auckland 10, New Zealand

Random House (Pty) Limited
Endulini, 5a Jubilee Road, Parktown 2193, South Africa

Random House Group Limited Reg. No. 954009

A CIP catalogue record for this book is available from the British Library

Papers used by Random House UK Limited are natural, recyclable products made from wood grown in sustainable forests. The manufacturing processes conform to the environmental regulations of the country of origin

ISBN 0 7126 8408 5

Typeset by SX Composing DTP, Rayleigh, Essex
Printed and bound in Great Britain by
Mackays of Chatham plc, Chatham, Kent

To Peter

MEMO
To: All committee members
From: A.P. Thoday, Chairman, Royal Geographical Society Expeditions and Fieldwork Committee
Date: 20th September 1976

Following the recent tragic events in Algeria involving a party led by one of our members, it has been suggested that aspects of the Society's advice to travellers and expedition leaders be reviewed and updated. Possible areas for discussion at the next meeting (19th October 1976) include: general safety; co-operating with host nations; insurance; legal considerations; unofficial 'blacklists' of hostile nations/regions; consular responsibilities, etc. Revised agenda attached.

I

I

As soon as her son, James, started driving lessons, some months before his eighteenth birthday, Nina Osland sold her car. She knew he would have to have one eventually – modern life without the car was no fun at all, as she was soon to discover – but she was damned if he was going to kill himself in hers.

Unfortunately, the man who answered her advertisement in *Loot*, also a worrier, was buying a car for his seventeen-year-old daughter, reasoning that she would be safer behind a wheel after dark than walking the street – a statistical fallacy. He brought her along for the test drive. She was slim and blonde with a pierced navel displayed in defiance of February weather between the bottom half of a cropped T-shirt and jeans, and large, unnaturally high breasts jammed together by a cruelly wired bra.

She can practically rest her chin on them, Nina thought, handing over the keys to the father, who had just emerged from a rust inspection of the car's undercarriage.

'Do you keep it in the garage?' he asked, squeezing behind the steering wheel and ramming the front seat backwards with the screech of metal on metal.

'Not often,' said Nina, who had decided she wouldn't volunteer prejudicial information – the dodgy catch on the rear seatbelt for example – unless she had to but neither would she lie. The careful deployment of truth and silence was something she had inherited, or perhaps learned, from her diplomat father, and, besides, James had appeared on the doorstep to eavesdrop. His hair was unbrushed and he held a dry Weetabix in one hand. He ate the wretched things on the hoof, leaving flakes like monster dandruff all over the house. She waved him back inside, unwilling to have her sales pitch overheard.

'Do you want to take it for a drive?'

The girl was in the passenger seat. Nina watched her surreptitiously checking her make-up in the mirror on the sun visor. She caught Nina's eye and blushed through a mask of foundation.

'Do you mind?' said the man. 'Just round the block. See how it runs?'

'Go ahead.' I wonder if she's had implants, Nina wondered idly.

'Don't you want to come with me?' the man asked, a little embarrassed. 'I mean, in case I steal it.'

'No, it's okay.' Nina smiled. 'After all you might kidnap me.'

'You think I look more like a kidnapper than a car thief,' he said. 'That's interesting.'

'You don't look much like either,' Nina admitted, observing him properly for the first time. Before he had spoken she had written him off as beneath her interest, but now she bothered to look she could see a tall, balding man in his mid-forties, with tired eyes and a pleasant, decent face. A man who loved his daughter.

'To be honest I'm more worried about getting lost,' he said. 'I might never find my way back.'

'You can take James with you,' said a voice which Nina recognized as hers but which seemed to have come direct from the devil himself. I have seen the future, she thought, as she watched James climb into the back seat behind the girl.

An hour later she was three thousand pounds richer but could take no pleasure from the fact.

❦

It was two months before Nina saw the girl again, and this time she was wearing even less. Nina had already deduced that James had acquired a girlfriend, noticing, for instance, that he was more often out than upstairs playing on his computer, and that he had become much more punctilious about his appearance than his schoolwork. Her heart had heaved in her chest when she saw the tubes of face-wash and spot-cream in the bathroom and caught the aftershock of some new, peppery cologne in the back of her throat. James was also spending more time than ever loitering in the back garden talking on his mobile phone – a phenomenon baffling to Nina as whenever his friends came round they seemed to get along quite happily all evening without ever resorting to speech. Reception was apparently poor inside the house – which contained a normal phone to which he had unrestricted access – so James was obliged instead to pace up and down outside like a water diviner in search of a powerful signal. Sometimes, when it rained, Nina would see him duck into the callbox on the corner of the street for shelter, and emerge minutes later, still talking.

The day Nina caught them in bed together started badly and went downhill. To begin with, a woman claiming to be a Bosnian war widow had knocked on the door asking for a donation of second-hand clothing. Nina had given her a cashmere jumper which had a small moth-hole in one sleeve but which she still occasionally wore. Later, when she went out, Nina found it stuffed in a hedge two gardens down. She took it back home again and restarted her journey with a heart hardened against humanity. She was on her way to perform the melancholy duty of clearing a dead woman's flat so that the council could take possession. Irene Shorrocks, James's grandmother and Nina's comforter and friend, had lived most of her sixty-seven years in East Dulwich and had spent much of the brief interval between retirement and death attending car boot sales. The flat, which grew to resemble a series of walk-in cupboards, was crammed from floor to ceiling with cardboard boxes and black bags of unsorted 'bargains'. Ever since she had named Nina as her executrix, Nina had sent up a nightly prayer for Irene's health and longevity: *Oh God, please let Irene outlive me.*

On this particular morning, as Nina waited for a bus at Crystal Palace, perched on one of the narrow pivoting seats which seemed to have been designed expressly to tip her off into the pile of broken glass at her feet, she felt moved to do a brave and foolish thing. The bus stop had been thoroughly trashed: every pane was broken and every surface sprayed with runic obscenities. The timetable had been ripped out to reveal a fixed notice of apology for its absence. Only a true misanthropist could have devised such a system, Nina was thinking, when she became aware of the sweet, sharp smell of vinegar penetrating the miasma of exhaust. The other person at the stop, a tall, round-shouldered girl in a denim skirt and white slingbacks, was eating chips from the paper, pulling each one into her mouth with plump, painted lips. Nina's stomach gave a loud rumble, which she covered with a sudden burst of throat-clearing. The Bosnian refugee, on top of her other misdeeds, had interrupted Nina's breakfast. In the distance a bus shimmered into view. The girl and Nina swayed forward with one movement to read the number and then back again, disappointed. The chips were as good as finished. The girl screwed up the wrapper, passing it from hand to hand to wipe her greasy fingers, and then, glancing first at Nina, and then at the waste bin not five paces away on the kerb, chucked the whole thing on the floor.

Nina, who would chase a sweet wrapper across the street on a windy day if it fell out of her pocket, was appalled. All right, so there was a fair amount of debris on the pavement already, but really, there was no excuse for apathy on that scale. Images of similar civic outrages rose up before her and she felt her stomach begin to churn with indignation against this invisible army of litter-louts and queue-jumpers, smokers on the underground and defilers of public lavatories. Calm down, she told herself. Don't get involved. But it was no use: various sarcastic turns of phrase were already suggesting themselves.

'It's a long walk to that bin, isn't it?' she said, anger making her voice sound treacherously upper class. The girl was only momentarily taken aback before she advanced on Nina, hissing like a swan, and gave her a terrific shove in the chest which sent her toppling backwards through the missing pane of the bus shelter into the crushed glass on the concrete below. 'Slapper,' was the girl's parting shot as she walked off up the road on her peeling stilettos.

'You want to get down the hospital, get yourself checked out,' the house-clearance man advised, once Nina had explained the reason for her late arrival. He had been sitting in his van outside Irene's eating a bacon roll when she arrived, flustered and sore. There had been no shortage of helpers after the event to pick her up and brush her off and call out the emergency services, but once she had established that her cuts and grazes were superficial she wanted nothing more than to be on her way. When the assembled bystanders realized she was uninjured and reluctant to call the police or exploit the dramatic potential of the incident they lost interest. Someone hailed her a taxi and she made her escape, vowing to resist all future impulses towards heroism.

❦

They were in the darkened sitting room watching a stand-up comedian on the television. There was an empty pizza box along with two bottles of Coke on the coffee table in front of them. James had his arm around her shoulders and they were both slumped well down on the couch, bent-necked, when Nina walked in. He gave the faintest twitch of unease, but otherwise didn't move.

'Oh, Mum, this is Kerry,' he said.

'Hello, Kerry,' said Nina, itching to turn the overhead light on and get a proper look at her. In the bluish glow from the TV she looked more like a ghost than a girl, but she was recognizable as the person who had come to buy the car. Nina could see the studs in her nose and navel glinting.

'Hello,' said Kerry without taking her eyes off the screen.

'She's shy,' James would say later, in her defence. This excuse, intended to mitigate a range of small discourtesies and anti-social habits, cut absolutely no ice with Nina.

The comedian was telling an obscene joke, so Nina decided to stand her ground for a moment in case they thought she was embarrassed. 'I'm not wanting to rush you off,' she said from the doorway, 'but how are you getting Kerry home?' James and his male friends were accustomed to walking vast distances to each other's houses or the pub at any hour of the night, and she didn't want the poor girl with a bare tummy getting a chill or worse.

'Cab,' said James, patiently.

'Well, goodnight then. Nice to have met you,' Nina said to Kerry, not without irony.

I might as well go to bed, she thought. I'm not going to sit out in the kitchen like the family dog. Normally when James brought friends home they didn't lay claim to the sitting room but skulked in his bedroom playing tapes. This departure struck Nina as significant.

It must have been after one o'clock when something woke her. She had fallen asleep sitting up in bed over the *Times* crossword with the light on. Her pen had actually skated across the page leaving a broken line – something she thought only happened in cartoons. She jerked her head up sharply – guiltily even – like someone in a theatre caught napping by the applause.

It must be Kerry leaving, she thought, waiting for the sound of the door, but the house was silent and dark. Then she heard it again: an unfamiliar, female cough. Nina crept on to the landing. James's door was – unusually – closed, a thin blade of light visible along its lower edge. Nina crossed the floor in two strides, knocked once loudly, setting off a frantic scuffling from within the room, and walked in without waiting for a reply.

The two of them were huddled, bare-shouldered under the duvet. Their clothes, which had obviously been shed in some haste, lay in mixed heaps on and around the bed. The only light was from the angle-poise desk lamp, which had been turned to face the wall. They looked so crestfallen that Nina almost felt sorry for them, but then her indignation returned, along with the sense that she'd been made a fool of.

'Not in my house,' she said, pointing at James, and then to Kerry, 'Get dressed. I'll call you a taxi.' She had the grace to step outside while Kerry got out of bed and struggled into her bra and knickers. 'Does your father know you're here?' she added over her shoulder.

'I told him I was staying over with a friend,' came the reply.

'We weren't doing anything, Mum,' said James, in a tone that managed to combine supplication with reproach. 'We were only having a cuddle.'

It's so unfair, Nina thought, having to play the heavy parent all on my own. A great bubble of self-pity stuck in her throat and she withdrew to her bedroom on the pretext of phoning for a cab so that she could give her pillow a few good stiff-armed wallops and compose herself before facing them again.

When she heard the clatter of the car's diesel engine outside Nina came downstairs and pressed a ten-pound note into Kerry's hand. 'That's for the fare,' she explained, as if there could have been any misunderstanding as to its purpose.

'Oh. Right,' said Kerry.

No doubt in her circles that meant 'thank you', thought Nina. James was hovering. He looked as though he might be going to kiss Kerry goodbye, but a glance at his mother, now sitting on the second stair in her tartan dressing gown, made him lose courage. 'I'll call you,' he said instead, and they exchanged meaningful smiles before the door was closed and James had to turn back to face the inquisition.

'Mum.' James opted for the pre-emptive strike. Once Nina got started on one of her lectures she was unstoppable – by the time she was done with him he'd have forgotten what it was he wanted to say. 'I've already told you we weren't doing anything. But even if we were, I'm seventeen, nearly eighteen. I'm old enough to join the army and die for my country' – this was the line he always peddled when lamenting his inability to buy a drink in the pub. 'I'm old enough to get married, to be a father . . .'

'That's precisely what you will be if you carry on like that,' Nina interrupted. 'What are you going to do if she gets pregnant?'

'She won't get pregnant.'

'She might. That's what it's for, in case you hadn't realized.'

'We haven't even had proper sex yet!' James practically shouted.

'Yet?' said Nina in a shrill voice, thinking, what does he mean 'proper'? 'You're planning to, then?'

James mimed banging his head against the banisters. 'What century are you living in, Mum?'

Nina, who considered herself the model of a modern, liberal, emancipated parent, was stung by this. 'It's not sex *per se* I'm worried about,' she said, changing tack. 'I'm not trying to protect your virginity.'

'Too late anyway,' James couldn't resist muttering.

Nina swallowed. 'It's the girl I'm thinking of. You wouldn't be the one saddled with an unwanted pregnancy.' That's it, she thought. This is a feminist issue. 'Apart from anything else, this is my house and I don't want you bringing a procession of girls back here under my nose. It's not as if you've been going out together for any time at all.'

'So how long would we have to be going out for it to be okay?' James wanted to know. He was leaning against the closed front door, in T-shirt and boxers, not having bothered to get properly dressed.

'I . . . I don't know. I haven't got a specific timetable worked out,' said Nina, outmanoeuvred.

'So, basically, as long as we don't do it here, and Kerry doesn't get pregnant, you don't mind?' said James, attempting to tease out the main thread of Nina's tortuous logic.

'No. Yes. I mean I still *mind*, but I know I can't stop you, so I'd rather you at least respect the . . . er . . . sanctity of this house.' No, that wasn't it at all, thought Nina. She didn't give a bugger about the house, and she certainly hadn't meant to convey that she'd be thrilled at the thought of them screwing in potting sheds and in the backs of cars. She felt all her anger dissolve into weary confusion. Perhaps it was cracking my head on the pavement earlier, she thought. It's made my brain go woolly. 'I was assaulted at the bus stop today,' she said. 'On the way to Irene's.'

'What? How come?' said James, glad that the argument

had burnt itself out, and congratulating himself on having escaped so lightly.

'I ticked this girl off for dropping litter and she knocked me backwards into a pile of broken glass.' Nina pulled up one of the wide sleeves of her dressing gown and craned back to inspect the grazes on her shoulder.

'God. Why didn't you say before? Did you call the police?'

'No. It would have made me late for the house-clearance man,' Nina replied. 'As a moral crusade it was a bit half-baked, I'm afraid.'

'Perhaps you should avoid moral crusades – they're obviously bad for your health,' James suggested, with a hint of a smile.

Nina went to pat his cheek – a gesture he hated – and he ducked away, pleased nevertheless that they were friends again. They hardly ever quarrelled.

'Well, goodnight then,' said James, sliding home the bolt on the front door.

'Goodnight,' said Nina, and then half way up the stairs she turned. 'Why don't you invite Kerry to lunch one Sunday so I can meet her properly? I don't want her to think I'm an old dragon.'

James laughed, uneasily. That was exactly what she did think. 'I don't know about lunch. The thing is she doesn't like eating in front of other people. She's not used to sitting around a table and stuff. She'd be embarrassed.'

Of course, thought Nina. You don't get a figure like that by eating normal meals. She probably prefers raiding the fridge at midnight and then sticking two fingers down her throat.

'Not lunch then,' she said. 'Something else.'

'Whatever,' said James in his amiably non-committal way. Nothing would ever come of that little proposal, it was clear.

What a depressing day, Nina thought, as she tossed the *Times* crossword aside and climbed back into bed. On the bedside table, next to the alarm clock and the herbal headache pills was one of the half a dozen items she had salvaged from Irene's flat: the last photograph of Irene's son, Martin, taken through the open window of a Land Rover parked outside the meteorological station in In Salah, Algeria, in 1976. Beside it was a picture of Nina, aged twenty-one, holding James as a six-month-old baby. Their cheeks were touching and Nina was smiling into the camera, with the confidence of someone still young and beautiful enough to outshine an angelic infant. But James was already looking away, his attention caught by something off to the left.

She suddenly felt overwhelmed with grief and nostalgia – for her own lost youth, and for James's babyhood, which was so irretrievably remote now; and because the best of their relationship was in the past. He'd been such an easy baby, so easily comforted. She recalled fleetingly but with perfect clarity the sensation of razor-sharp infant toenails raking her back: James had been a gregarious sleeper and had often crept into bed with her in the middle of the night. It was one of the things that had kept her single. From the moment he was born her vocation had announced itself: James. She would have to be everything to him – mother, father, brother, sister, friend – since everything he lacked was her fault. Once when he was nearly three he had asked if he could have a party for his birthday – he had picked up the concept from a children's television programme. 'How can you have a party, darling?' Nina had said. 'You haven't got any friends.' She hadn't intended the remark to be wounding – he had no friends only because he was still too young for nursery, and Nina knew no one else with young children. But it evidently had been, because the following day when they were out in the car he had said, quite unprompted, and with great dignity, 'The sky is my friend.'

Well, he didn't need the sky any more and pretty soon he wouldn't need her either. These meditations were interrupted by a tap at the door which then opened a fraction. 'I forgot to tell you,' James whispered through the chink. 'There's a message on the answering machine for you.'

'I'll listen to it tomorrow,' Nina replied. She was in a nice warm patch of sheet and couldn't be bothered to move. It was probably something to do with work. Nina had trained as a social worker with Lambeth Council, but was now a guardian ad litem, representing children's interests to the courts in custody disputes. Her clients frequently had out-of-hours crises. Whoever it was could jolly well wait.

'Someone called Hugo,' said James, withdrawing. 'Calling from Australia.'

Nina leapt from the bed as though she'd sat on a scorpion, her heart galloping in her ribs. In her haste, her left foot got tangled in the duvet cover and she fell, striking her face on the corner of the ottoman and dragging the bedclothes on top of her. This is prophetic, she thought, lying stunned on the floor. She put her hand up to her nose and caught the first drops of blood. Even after eighteen years, at a distance of twelve thousand miles, and without raising his hand, Hugo was still an agent of disaster.

2

It was going to be a smacking sort of week. On Monday Harriet had crayoned all over one of her sister's schoolbooks and, when given the mildest reprimand, hurled the book at the fish tank. On Tuesday she had thrown the most spectacular tantrum outside the school gates because Jane had refused to let her walk through the nettle patch at the edge of the playing field. On Wednesday Jane had woken up in a foul mood anyway and it hadn't taken much at all, just a dropped bowl of Weetos – unforgivable, that one really, Jane thought. And today here they were in the doctor's waiting room together because she couldn't leave Harriet with Guy or he'd want to know *why* she was seeing the GP, and Harriet had been running around climbing on and off the chairs and doing that very high-pitched squeal for fifteen minutes now. Half the people waiting were glaring at her, Jane, as though they'd like to tear her heart out if she didn't belt the child soon, and the other half looked as though they might report her to the social services if she did.

The place was punishingly overheated for a spring day, the windows locked and barred, the radiators throbbing. God only knew what diseases were being incubated and circulated around her. Harriet came wheeling towards her, saw her expression and wheeled away again, cannoning into the coffee table, sending a pile of magazines slithering on to the floor. A ripple of tutting and tongue-clicking ran around the waiting room. Beads of sweat began to break out on Jane's brow.

'Harriet, come here,' she said, trying to be both discreet and menacing. 'Go and play with the toys,' she went on, changing her mind, and pointing at the plastic basket of grubby teddy bears and chewed books which comprised the recreation area. Attempts to bribe Harriet to keep still and/or quiet with promises of sweets had failed, as had threats of vague and then specific punishments to be administered later. Jane had tried to restrain her in her arms but, though only three, Harriet was as strong and slippery as a giant fish.

Jane's older daughter, Sophie, now five and at school, had never been like this. She had been a compliant, docile child – inclined to tears, perhaps, but easily comforted. Harriet had shown signs of obstinacy from birth, rejecting all the efforts of her mother and the hordes of professionals and experts in lactation who had been summoned to persuade her to feed from the breast; crying inconsolably every waking minute for the first three months of her life. These early symptoms had now mutated into general defiance, disobedience and a thorough contempt for maternal authority. Jane had only ever wanted girls: she thought they would be gentler, less boisterous than boys, and fondly imagined that life with daughters would be much as depicted in *Little Women* – sitting by the fireside in the evenings embroidering samplers or singing madrigals around the piano. The reality had been a shock and a disappointment. Now she thought boys might not have been such a bad idea. The ones she saw at Harriet's playgroup seemed affectionate, simple creatures, devoted to their mothers.

The old lady beside her, bow-legged and bunioned (Jane was looking at people's feet rather than making eye-contact by this stage), let out a hiss like a punctured tyre as Harriet tripped over her walking stick for the second time. *Crack.* Jane's open palm caught Harriet on the back of the leg with a sound like gunshot. The child collapsed as if she had indeed been felled by a bullet, her wails rending the silence. Right, we're going, thought Jane.

'Jane Bromelow,' said a disembodied voice and an outstretched hand appeared through a hatch, holding her medical notes in their brown cardboard wallet.

Oh God, thought Jane desperately, manhandling the still sobbing Harriet towards the surgery door. As if it's not going to be embarrassing enough, without *this*.

The doctor, a youngish woman she had never seen before,

gave her a wintry smile as Jane dumped Harriet at a small table strewn with more chipped and sticky toys. 'Just sit there for a few minutes,' Jane said.

'What can I do for you –' the doctor glanced at her notes '– Mrs Bromelow?'

Jane looked at the woman's left hand. No wedding ring. She would have liked a married woman doctor ideally; a married woman doctor stuck at home all day with a small child. But that was asking the impossible – even Jane had to accept that.

'Well, I'm probably wasting your time,' Jane said, already abject and apologetic.

The doctor smiled. They all said that, and went on to waste it just the same.

'It's probably not even a medical matter.' She glanced at Harriet, who was now trying to brush the matted hair of a one-armed Barbie doll, and wondered how much of all this she would take in and later repeat. 'It's just that for a while now I seem to have no . . . er . . . libido, if you know what I mean. I seem to have gone right off it,' she finished lamely.

The doctor nodded. 'Are you on the combined pill?'

Jane shook her head.

'Because that can sometimes account for it.'

'Only I'm not,' said Jane.

'Mmm. Are you getting enough sleep? Do the children disturb you?'

'I could always use a bit more sleep. And sometimes they come in, you know, when they've had nightmares. But not all the time.'

'Perhaps you feel inhibited because they might hear you?'

'Maybe.'

'Otherwise relations with your husband are all right?'

'Oh, fine, fine.' Jane pictured Guy, still loyally wearing that horrible pullover she'd knitted him in the early days of their marriage, with a sudden rush of affection.

'Have you talked to him about this?'

'Oh no. I wouldn't want to hurt his feelings. He'd take it personally. And it's not personal. It's not as if I daydream about having sex with other men.' Oh blast, she hadn't meant to say 'sex' in front of Harriet. 'I think he's sort of starting to guess though.'

They had been in bed a few nights previously when Guy had said out of the blue as she was dropping off to sleep, 'Do you have any sexual fantasies?'

This sort of conversation, Jane knew from experience, was likely to be a prelude to a gentle hint that she might like to be a bit more adventurous in that department, and was therefore best headed off.

'Er . . . yes, I suppose so.'

'Go on, tell me.'

'No, no, you'd be shocked.'

'No I wouldn't,' said Guy, suddenly aroused.

You would mate, thought Jane. Because my sexual fantasy is NOT HAVING SEX. But instead she said, 'I think the thing about fantasies is they only work in your head. The minute you try to discuss or enact them they don't work any more.'

'I suppose so,' said Guy. 'But, you know, if there's ever anything you want me to do, I'd do it for you, however weird it seemed.'

'Thank you,' said Jane, kissing him, but failing to reciprocate the offer. 'I'll bear it in mind.' And the discussion had died there.

'Are you happy with your method of contraception?' the doctor inquired. 'Fear of pregnancy can be an inhibiting factor. Perhaps you might like to try something safer?'

Like the libido-reducing pill? thought Jane. 'Maybe,' she said.

'You don't have any psychological problems – any bad experiences with sex in the past that you might need to work through? I could put you in touch with a counsellor.'

'Oh, no, no, I don't think counselling,' Jane said hurriedly. How ever would she fit that in? She couldn't very well take Harriet along. Besides, Jane was a thorough sceptic where that sort of thing was concerned. Even coming to see the GP was a great concession.

'There are these sex therapists,' the doctor was saying, rolling her eyes. She seemed to be having trouble with her contact lenses. 'But they generally like people to come along as a couple. So if you don't feel like involving your husband . . .'

'No, not yet. Perhaps . . .' She was interrupted by a yelp of alarm from the doctor, who shot out of her swivel chair and made a lunge for Harriet, who had abandoned Barbie and had one hand in the washbasin, from which she produced a used speculum. Jane and the doctor exchanged horrified looks as Harriet dropped the instrument back in the bowl with a clatter.

'Here.' The doctor pumped a dollop of antibacterial hand-wash from a dispenser on the side into Harriet's hands and scrubbed them vigorously. 'I'm so sorry about that,' she said faintly, envisioning piles of lawsuits landing on her desk the following morning.

Jane shouldered her bag. 'My fault,' she said. 'Come on, Harriet. I'll think about your suggestions. You've been very helpful,' she lied.

'You could try and experiment with different positions,' was the doctor's final offering before Jane opened the door. 'Women's bodies change after childbirth. Perhaps there's a bit of underlying discomfort that's putting you off.'

'Yes, thank you,' said Jane, now desperate to be on her way.

Different positions, she thought scornfully, as she led Harriet back through a now quiet waiting room. If modern medicine couldn't come up with anything better than that then she'd have to look elsewhere. What a waste of a morning.

'What's a beedo?' Harriet demanded in a loud voice.

'It's a bit like a bidet,' Jane replied, bundling her out of the door on to the street. 'Only different.'

3

On Guy Bromelow's second day at boarding school his mother, Daphne, had received an urgent summons: his PE kit was not complete; could she bring him some white gym shoes, size 4.

She had immediately cancelled her hair appointment and rushed out to the shops in search of a pair, and then driven the forty-odd miles through the Sussex countryside to the school. It was lunchtime when she arrived and the boys were out on the field, hundreds of them, identical in grey and white. One of them, about Guy's age, was loitering near the gate, kicking gravel. Daphne gave an imperious wave and he trotted over obediently. 'Would you give these to Bromelow,' she said, thrusting the green cardboard box into his hands. If she drove like the wind they might be able to fit her in at the salon after all, she was thinking, when the boy said, 'Hello, mother.'

Over the years Guy had often retold this story, against his mother, and he was thinking of it now, sitting in his office looking out across a different school field to where a rounders match was in progress. Every so often he could hear the 'thock' of a good hit and a crescendo of cheering as the batsman approached fourth post, but inside the school, all was quiet. He preferred it like this, when the children and most of the staff had gone home and he could get on with some work.

At the perimeter of the field the council's giant mower, like a combine harvester, was cutting the grass, spilling its rainbow dust behind it. Through the window came the scent of fresh sap. Guy closed his eyes and breathed deeply. He would have to make an announcement in assembly tomorrow: *it is forbidden to throw grass*. When he was a schoolboy grass fights were among the chief pleasures of the summer term – virtually an accredited sport. But now there were angry letters from parents if a child came home with so much as a green smear on his uniform. It was a similar story in winter: *no throwing snowballs, no sliding on the black ice.* Guy was ambivalent about the wisdom of this cosseting. Instinct told him that the elimination of all risk was a vain enterprise where children were concerned, and he rather resented the restrictions to their freedom. On the subject of Children in the abstract he was entirely rational; with regard to his own daughters he was as neurotic as the next parent.

Letters from parents. He had a pile in front of him now to be answered. He moved the ones that were written on lined paper to the top – in his experience the senders of these were more likely to come up to the school to make their point in person if they didn't achieve immediate satisfaction.

Dear Mr Bromelow

I was concerned to learn that my son (Mark 3R) has been asked to produce a project on the subject of DINOSAURS. I am surprised and dismayed that a Church school sees fit to promote a theory which contradicts the teaching of the Bible, and I would prefer it if Mark could be excused from these lessons. Perhaps in the interests of balance he might be allowed to submit a project on GENESIS instead.

Yours sincerely
Eric Sharpearrow

Guy switched on his computer. The school secretary, Mary, typed all his general Dear Parents letters, along with memos, agendas and minutes of meetings, but he didn't like to burden her with the one-offs. Besides he could never quite achieve the necessary fine balance between propitiation and irony when talking into his dictaphone. He began to jab away: he had never learned to type properly, but he could keep up a blistering pace with his two index fingers.

Dear Mr Sharpearrow

Thank you for your letter of March 1st. I am sorry that Mark's class project for this term has been a cause of concern. I'm afraid I can see no conflict between the subject matter and the teaching of the Church of England. If, on consideration, you would still like Mark to be excluded on religious grounds from the lessons in which dinosaurs are mentioned, that is of course your right. However we do not have sufficient staff to supervise individual absentees: he would have to sit outside my office and work independently. After consultation with the class teacher we have agreed that as the dinosaur theme is being taught within a natural-historical rather than a religious context it would not be appropriate for Mark to offer GENESIS as an alternative topic, and we suggest instead REPTILES.

Yours sincerely

G.J. Bromelow

He smiled to himself. He and Jane would laugh about it later.

He saved the document under the name ERIC4: this was not the first piece of correspondence Guy had had with Mr Sharpearrow in the two terms since he had become head teacher. The man always complained as a matter of course whenever the PTA held a raffle or any fund-raising event which involved some element of gambling, and he had been incandescent when one of the pupils had taken the part of God in a school production of the story of Noah's Ark.

The son, Mark, was a nice lad, despite his genes, Guy thought, though horribly oppressed by his father. He never joined in any of the school's extra-curricular activities, was forbidden to go to tea with other children in case somehow polluted, and was not allowed within range of a radio or television. Mind you, Guy was with the father all the way on the last point. Harriet and Sophie watched far too many cartoons, and even Jane, whom Guy had once liked to think of as cerebral, spent most of her evenings slumped dully in front of the TV. He hoped she was in a good mood when he got home, which he tended to do later and later these days.

She didn't greet him on the doorstep with a litany of complaints, exactly, but he could tell from her expression if it had been a good or a bad day. If she made eye-contact that was usually a positive sign; if not it meant she was hassled, distracted and on the point of withdrawing into that distant realm within herself where he could not follow. Sometimes her eyes were red and puffy and that was a bad sign – evidence of a confrontation with Harriet in which the child had emerged the clear victor. And everything was his fault, though Jane never said so.

She hadn't wanted to move. He had applied for his current job as head of a suburban primary school in west London purely for interview experience, but had to his surprise been offered the post along with modest relocation expenses. Jane had cried for two days and he had almost turned it down, but she was a fatalist as well as a martyr. 'It's meant to be,' she said. And so they had sold their small semi-detached house on the south coast, where they had been happy, and where Jane had grown up, and had friends, and a good job with the health service, and where the children had been born, and moved to an equally small but much costlier Victorian semi in Twickenham, five minutes from the school. They were no better off financially, Guy worked much harder and longer and Jane, who was in any case slow to recommend herself to strangers, knew nobody.

Guy glanced down at the photograph of her on his desk, taken in happier times. She was holding Sophie and wearing a soppy, infatuated mother's smile. She didn't often look like that now. A few years of frowning at the children had scored two deep lines between her eyebrows – her laughter lines were faint by comparison. But she was still beautiful, with her red mermaid hair and sea-green eyes, when she remembered to smile. And she had a laugh that could wake the dead – a real lunatic's cackle. It had been what first attracted him to her – even though his own imbecility was its object. Sometimes they surprised themselves by making each other laugh just like they used to, and then it was pure bliss: better than sex. Of which there was, in any case, a dwindling supply. Jane had been acting very strangely lately, decamping to the spare room in the night because she was too hot or too cold or couldn't sleep, and showing no interest whatever in her appearance, slouching around the house in jeans and trainers, when he had offered unlimited funds to buy new clothes. She could be so pretty when she bothered. Then the other night he had come home late from a governors' meeting and found her in the bath with her swimsuit on.

'What are you wearing that for?' he had asked.

She had looked momentarily embarrassed, but then collected herself. 'I always used to want to have a bath in my swimming costume when I was little – just to see what it felt like. But Mum would never let me,' she said, daring him to criticize.

'Oh.' He wasn't going to fall into the trap of siding with a killjoy. 'What does it feel like?'

'Nice.'

He bent over to kiss her and she slid fractionally further under the water, so that he had to stretch forward, straining his back, which was already aching from two hours in one of those excruciating plastic bucket seats. His tie flopped out from his waistband and dipped into the water.

'How has your day been?' he asked, wringing it out.

'Not bad. Harriet nicked a copy of *The Downing Street Years* from the arcade.'

Guy pulled a face. 'We'll have to do something about that child.'

'Her kleptomania?'

'Her taste. How did she manage it, anyway?'

'I was looking for something to give your mother for her birthday; we'd been into every bookshop in town and when we got back to the car I noticed Harriet was carrying this great hardback under one arm. I didn't know which shop she'd taken it from so I couldn't very well return it. I gave her a lecture about stealing of which she understood about one word in ten. Oh and Sophie got Honours in her ballet exam.'

'Did you talk to anyone today?'

She shook her head, pulling the plug out with a plop. 'No

one over the age of five. Not what you'd call a proper conversation.'

'What about the other mums in the playground?' asked Guy. Sophie was in the reception class at his own school; twice a day Jane had the opportunity to join the throng of gossiping women if she so chose.

'They all know each other already. They give me a wide berth, anyway, because of you.'

'Sorry.'

'It's not your fault. I was just saying.'

The sun was setting as Guy switched off his computer, the last of the letters answered and filed. Perhaps he would stop off on the way home and pick up some flowers for Jane and a bottle of wine and they could have a proper chat for once when the girls were in bed. Then he remembered: there was a chance of seeing that comet tonight if the skies were clear. There was no point in spending a fortune on a telescope if you didn't take the trouble to observe that sort of phenomenon. The wine and the chat would have to wait. He locked his office and let himself out through the main reception area. Passing the caretaker's house in the corner of the now empty staff car park he could see the flickering light of the television through the net curtains, and hear the closing music for the early evening news. He would be back in time to read the girls a bedtime story. His heart swelled with love as he pictured their pink, freshly washed faces and shining eyes. He always felt much more indulgent towards them when they were elsewhere. It soon wore off once he got home.

On his way back he ducked into the church adjoining the playing field, where they held the school's carol concerts and harvest festival celebrations. It had become a habit, beginning and ending each day with a prayer. If time was short he might just put his head round the door and call 'Goodnight God'. Twenty years ago, thought Guy, as he pushed open the wooden door and breathed the familiar scent of musty hassocks and wax polish, if you'd told me I'd end up a pillar of the church I'd have laughed in your face. His parents were not religious in the least, though they respected the church in much the same way as they regarded, say, Morris Dancers, as a symbol of a more genteel and picturesque England. He had been confirmed at school with the rest of his year *en masse.* Like prep and cross-country it was compulsory, so the question of faith hadn't arisen. He had had his first semi-mystical experience in the desert when he was twenty-one, and then when Sophie was born, five and a bit years ago, he had felt himself once more in the presence of the miraculous and suddenly discovered a great yearning to believe in God. It was fatherhood which made him look beyond himself to a higher, better Father, who would protect his fragile treasure from all the horrors of the world.

He and Jane had gone along to their local church for Sophie's baptism and had received such a welcome from the congregation – for whom funerals were more common – that they had been easily persuaded to return week after week. He had a subconscious suspicion, never properly exhumed or articulated, that his appointment to this headship had been won on the strength of his – relatively recent – status as a churchgoer. *Applicants must be regular communicant members of the Church of England*, the advertisement had said. That was a tough requirement nowadays; the field would not have been particularly large.

He picked up a copy of the 1662 service book that someone had left in a pew. He preferred this version to the modern one. The more obscure and antiquated the language the better he liked it. The 1980 version was cold by comparison. He turned the tissue-thin pages to the Order for Holy Communion. Here was his favourite bit: *in sure and certain hope of the Resurrection.* He loved that: it was so deliciously non-committal. He unhooked a hassock and knelt down, sending up a puff of dust. His prayers tended to follow the same pattern; brief thanks for the blessings of the day just past, and rather lengthier petitioning for the future health, happiness and safety of his family. Lately though, his devotions had become rather more mechanical than spiritual. When he came to the end of his list of intercessions he would stay on his knees with his eyes closed and ask into the silence, 'Is there anybody there?' For some months now he had not heard any reply.

4

It was in. The letter was in. Jane nearly fainted with embarrassment when she opened the magazine in the newsagent's and saw it there. She had been in to check every week since she'd written, determined not to buy a single issue until she needed to. She had deliberately chosen a down-market weekly for her own protection in the knowledge that no one she knew would ever read it and put two and two together. But now, carrying the thing to the counter, its lurid headlines shrieking of human wretchedness in all its variety, she felt that everyone in the shop must know that she was J.B. of Middx. who had Gone Off It.

She was so distracted that she quite forgot Harriet, who had been sitting at her feet trying to pull the free gifts off the front of the children's comics, and she was out of the door before a wail of alarm brought her up short.

'Don't go without me, Mummy. Someone might take me,' said Harriet in a voice full of reproach, turning Jane's own warning, issued a hundred times a day, neatly against her.

'I wasn't going without you,' Jane lied. 'Don't be silly. Keep up.' And the two of them walked along holding hands for a full minute before Harriet grew bored and peeled off, looking for distractions in shop windows.

Once at home Jane sat Harriet in front of a video of some innocuous cartoons which she had, with amazing prescience, taped the day before, and left her engrossed, inches from the screen, while she retreated to the kitchen to read the agony column.

She made herself a cup of coffee and eased a chocolate biscuit silently from its packet. The sound of rustling would have brought Harriet straight out to investigate. Jane flicked through the magazine to the Problem Page, her face puckering with disdain at the combination of lurid revelation and celebrity tittle-tattle that constituted its principal subject matter. **ABDUCTED BY ALIENS! MY GRAN STOLE MY FIANCÉ! I BORED MY RAPIST TO SLEEP!** The stories seemed to fall into two categories: How I Overcame Disaster, and How Disaster Overcame Me, and there tended to be an element of sexual adventure or misadventure involved. The thought that she, Jane, who was so fastidious about her privacy, should find herself in print alongside this collection of vulgar blabbermouths and self-publicists made her feel thoroughly soiled.

By the time she reached her own letter she had decided that, comparatively speaking, she was problem-free. Her husband did not beat her; she had not caught AIDS from a one-night stand, nor was she pregnant with her brother-in-law's baby. The Agony Aunt clearly did not agree, however, as she had accorded Jane's letter top billing, boxed, in bold type. There was even an accompanying photo of a woman in a silky nightie standing at the end of a bed with one finger up to her cheek and a worried expression on her face. Behind her, half under the covers, was a man looking disappointed.

The letter, which had originally been long and elegantly phrased, was now edited to conform to the publication's rather abrupt style, and read as follows:

Dear Mandy

Since I had kids I've gone right off sex. I love my husband and still find him attractive but I don't enjoy the physical side of things any more. I have tried fantasizing about other men but that doesn't work. It's him I love. I just find sex a chore. I'd rather do the dishes. I'm only 31. Is there something wrong with me?

Yours desperately,

J.B.

Dear J.B.

Yes! But nothing that can't be put right! As a young mum at home with kids it's all too easy to stop thinking of yourself as a sexual being. You love your husband – don't let the spark go out of your marriage. Try to think of ways to bring some romance back into your lives. Surprise your husband with a candlelit supper – or even a candlelit bath! Perhaps a friend or relative could babysit for you while you go away for a night. It's amazing what a change of scene can do. Try to spend as much time and effort on your sex life as you do on the children. Let the housework slide. Watch a romantic movie instead. You owe it to yourselves not to let a small problem grow into a big one. Act now. Good luck!

At the bottom of the page was a list of telephone numbers that anxious readers could call to hear recorded messages offering information and advice on a variety of topics: Rape; HIV; AIDS; Impotence; Herpes; Premature Ejaculation; Abortion. Really, thought Jane, given the great range and diversity of afflictions for which sex was responsible, she might have expected her own stance to be held up and applauded as a model of rational behaviour. But not a bit of it. The professional consensus appeared to be that she was a freak in need of a cure. She rolled the magazine into a tight wad and hurled it like a javelin at the swing bin. It glanced off the lid and came to rest by the back door. A candlelit bath. She quite liked that idea, but only if she could have the bath to herself, of course. She would save it for when Guy was away on one of his conferences.

From the sitting room came the sound of gunshots and violent swearing. Jane hurried in to find that the cartoons had given way, without Harriet appearing to mind, or even notice, to the end of the Quentin Tarantino film which Guy had been intending to save. Jane threw herself at the Off switch, precipitating a shriek of protest from Harriet, which soon turned to furious sobbing. Look at that, thought Jane. She actually does drum her little heels on the ground, just like a child in a comic strip.

'Come on, let's go to the park,' said Jane, attempting the diversionary tactics recommended by all the childcare manuals. It was sunny outside with only a slight breeze. 'We'll feed the ducks.' The crying intensified. 'We might get an ice-cream.' Pathetic, she thought. Craven capitulation.

An hour later they were standing on the wooden bridge over the pond alongside half a dozen other mothers and toddlers, tossing large chunks of sliced loaf into the water, which was beginning to take on the consistency of gazpacho. A couple of bloated ducks skulked in the reeds at the bank, trying to dodge the missiles. Harriet was eating one of the crusts. She wouldn't touch bread at home. 'Look,' she said. 'There's a kiss in the sky.'

Jane looked up. Two aeroplane trails had chalked a white X against the blue. It's really not so bad, she thought. This was one of her favourite places – about the only good discovery she had made since they moved. There was the narrow pond, which ran the length of the park – a mass of dropped litter and coagulated bread at one end, but green and glassy at the other, with lily pads and the odd freckled fish. There were tennis courts, unused all year round apart from the few weeks after Wimbledon when they were booked up from dawn to dusk; the children's play area which had enticing yet safe equipment, and a café, at which Jane and Harriet were regular visitors.

It was to the playground that the two of them now made their way, Harriet at a run, Jane following at a more dignified pace. Half an hour on the swings, half an hour in the café, fifteen-minute tantrum, home, twenty minutes' colouring, pick up Sophie, forty-five minutes in the garden if I'm lucky and it's fine, sponge painting if it's not, then Guy will be home. Jane parcelled out the rest of the day in her mind; it was the only way to get through it. Every minute had to be accounted for and planned in advance. The moment Jane slackened off and let her attention wander Harriet would switch via boredom to downright aggression. She'd been caught that way too often.

There were only half a dozen other children in the playground. It was easy to keep an eye on Harriet. I could almost have brought a book, thought Jane, though she hadn't so much as picked up a book in months. Reading was just another of those pleasures associated with her previous, childfree life, which she had given up. There was no necessity for this, but Jane felt that, in the absence of overpowering maternal feelings, self-sacrifice was the one area where she could really shine. She had given up her job, her home town, her friends, her hobbies, going out, singing in the choir, smoking and finally reading. No one would be able to blame her selfishness when Harriet finally went to the bad, as she one day surely would.

Jane looked around for somewhere to sit – not so close to the swings that Harriet would be encouraged to keep coming over and pestering her, but near enough to intercept her if she suddenly took off. The bench by the horse-chestnut was the ideal spot – Jane requiring partial sun and partial shade like a tender plant – but next to it, too close not to be acknowledged, was a woman lying on a rug beside a sleeping baby. The woman was wearing a long black skirt and matted jumper, even though it was the sort of early spring day when an optimist might chance short sleeves. Her long dark hair, which was swept up into a bulldog clip was thickly streaked with grey. An old mother or a young granny perhaps, Jane thought, though her demeanour wasn't what Jane would have called grandparental. She was lying on her stomach reading the paper, a can of lager at her side and a smouldering cigarette in the hand furthest from the baby. How irresponsible, thought Jane, a reformed smoker, at the same time experiencing a pinprick of envy. Harriet would never have slept so conveniently at that age. The moment you tried to ease her towards the horizontal her eyes would have snapped open and she'd have been shrieking. As if reading Jane's mind, Harriet, who had climbed unassisted into one of the kiddies' swings, began clamouring to be pushed.

Jane waved her assent and hurried over before the shouting turned to screaming. She gave the swing a few good, hard shoves and, when Harriet was safely airborne, made a dash for the kiosk. Something had given her a thirst. While the youth behind the counter poured her tea she read the advertisements on the cork board in the window.

FOR SALE: Birdcage, cot mattress and Ford Fiesta wing mirror (left). £10 the lot.

The owner must have extraordinary faith in coincidence to imagine that somewhere out there was a buyer in need of all three, thought Jane, smiling to herself. She glanced back at Harriet who had almost come to a standstill and was gearing up for another yell. She paid for her tea and fished the teabag out with a plastic stirring rod, leaving a pattern of drops across the counter to the bin. The polystyrene cup was rather too wide to hold its shape properly and kept threatening to fold itself into a spout and tip boiling liquid over her. I'll bring a flask next time, she thought, calculating what that would save her in 50ps over the course of a season, when she noticed that the grey-haired woman with the baby was on her feet, hands on hips, looking impatient.

'Will!' the woman called. The baby at her feet stirred. '*Will*!' This time more loudly. 'Where are you?'

Definitely a mother, Jane decided. That combination of exasperation and guilt in the tone was unmistakable. Besides, she had a gold stud in her nose, and she didn't look nearly so grey from the front, quite dark in fact, and not that much older than Jane herself. She approached Jane, who was half way across the playground, tea in hand.

'Have you seen a little boy – three years old, with dark hair and a red T-shirt,' she said, not actually looking at Jane, but casting anxiously around her and then glancing back at the baby, still dozing on the blanket.

'He's not in the kiosk. Do you want me to watch the baby while you look for him?' She wouldn't have dreamed of leaving her own child with a stranger, but that didn't prevent her from making the offer, which was gratefully accepted.

'Would you mind? I won't be long. He always does this,' the woman added, taking off at a long-legged sprint for the gate.

Well, if he always does it, why didn't you take the precaution of keeping an eye on him? Jane thought, glancing automatically at Harriet before sitting down on the grass side of the baby. The shade had moved and a small drop of sunlight rested on his cheek. Jane positioned herself to cast a shadow across his face. 'Don't want you to burn,' she whispered.

Harriet, bored in her motionless swing and scenting fresh drama, clambered out and came running over.

'Don't wake him and don't touch,' Jane hissed, as the little girl dropped to her knees millimetres from the baby's head, making him twitch violently and open his eyes.

'He's awake already!' cried Harriet in delight.

'Ssh!' said Jane as the baby blinked and gave a few little bleats. 'Look what you've done. Go and play.'

'Can I hold him?' said Harriet, patting him rather forcefully on the top of the head.

'No. Leave him alone and he might go back to sleep.' The woman will probably come back and find him bawling and accuse me of shaking him or something, Jane thought. 'Harriet, go and play and I'll buy you an ice-cream when the lady gets back,' she pleaded.

Harriet ignored her, bending over the baby until her fringe tickled his face, at which point he seized a good handful of hair and gave it a hard yank. Harriet screamed, inadvertently headbutting the baby, who started to wail. Oh Godalmighty, thought Jane, hysterically. Now he's going to have a broken nose or a bloody great egg on his head. She pushed Harriet away. 'Go away or you won't get an ice-cream. Ever again,' she half-shouted, picking up the baby and trying to pacify him and examine him for damage at the same time. Harriet finally obliged, taking advantage of Jane's inability to chase after her, by performing dangerous stunts on the roundabout. The baby didn't look too injured, but his face was so red and contorted with crying that it was hard to tell. Don't come back yet, don't come back yet, Jane silently urged the absent mother. Not until I've got him quiet.

She struggled to her feet, holding the baby to her shoulder and rocking from one foot to the other, humming frantically. After a few minutes of this the cries subsided to a whimper, but the moment Jane relaxed he tensed up and opened his mouth again. He was surprisingly heavy for such a little chap, and hot too – Jane could feel rivulets of sweat trickling down her side under her shirt. She kept up the rocking and the inane humming, all the while trying to fix Harriet with a glare sufficiently menacing to stop her jumping on and off the moving roundabout. Ten minutes passed. Jane's arms grew leaden. When she ventured to adjust the child's position she saw he was asleep, tears sparkling on his eyelashes like dew on a web. She eased herself down on to the blanket, and having accomplished that without rousing him, dared to lay him beside her in the spot he had not long ago occupied.

She wiped her damp fringe from her forehead with the back of her hand and plucked at her shirt. There was a damp patch on the front, whether from perspiration or infant dribble Jane couldn't tell.

Harriet was on the seesaw now. She had made a friend and the two of them were being pumped up and down by the other child's mother. The source of Harriet's sociability and confidence was a complete mystery to Jane. She allowed herself to relax and glance at the newspaper beside her. The cryptic crossword was half filled in, the margins of the paper littered with doodles and anagrams. It was years since Jane had done a crossword. Giving up newspapers was another of those small, frequently unnecessary sacrifices which had become a habit. She had never had enough time to read them when there were two children around all day, and it frustrated her to see them piling up, unread, clogging up first the coffee table and then the bin. She didn't miss them. All that war and famine and child abuse. Better not to know. Nevertheless, crosswords seemed to inhabit a different, purer world. And you never lost the knack: it was like riding a bike. Jane picked up the pen. Five down. Well, that was *Goblin Market* for a start. And that long one would have to be *Housemaid's Knee.* Quite forgetting herself, Jane started to fill in the clues, ticking them off as she went. The woman had left her handbag on the blanket, half open, which seemed to Jane to betray a reckless faith in human nature. But then one would hardly trust someone to look after a baby in preference to a wallet.

Harriet came running over, her cheeks bulging with sweets that she had evidently extorted from her friend on the seesaw. 'I want to go home now.'

Jane filled in the last clue. *Limoges*. 'Well, we can't.' Harriet *never, ever* wanted to go home. Jane usually had to prise her fingers one by one from the bars of the climbing frame and carry her, kicking, to the car. 'We've got to wait for the lady to come back.' Jane glanced at her watch. She'd been gone more than twenty minutes. She obviously can't find him, thought Jane, her heart starting to thump. Maybe he's fallen in the pond; maybe someone's snatched him. What if she comes back without him, distraught? She dropped the pen she'd been holding as though it were a bloodstained knife. What if she comes back without him, distraught, and finds that I've been sitting here casually *doing her crossword*. What can I have been thinking of?

'I. Want. To. Go. Home. Now,' said Harriet, stamping her foot at every syllable.

Jane ignored this. A brilliant idea struck her. She removed the outside cover of *The Times* and put it in her pocket, and had just refolded the whole paper into a neat rectangle when the woman reappeared, in no great hurry and hand in hand with a dark-haired boy of about Harriet's age. Jane scrambled to her feet, smiling with relief.

'I finally caught up with him right down by the other gate,' said the woman, making no apology for having kept Jane waiting. 'I think you and I will have to have a little talk when we get home,' she addressed her son mildly.

A little talk? thought Jane. A little wallop, more like.

The woman picked up her handbag from the blanket and ferreted for her cigarettes. She put one in her mouth before turning the packet on Jane. 'Do you smoke?'

'No. It's bad for you, apparently,' said Jane drily.

The woman affected surprise. 'Now they tell us,' she said, tossing the unlit cigarette into the bin beside the bench.

'Well, I'm glad you found him,' said Jane, looking around for Harriet who was now trying to walk up the helter-skelter.

'Yes, so am I,' said the woman. 'Up to a point. Thanks for watching the baby,' she added as an afterthought, as Jane turned away.

'Come on, hometime,' Jane called to Harriet, who had

now reached the platform at the top of the helter-skelter and was barring the way down to a growing queue of impatient children. The little girl, a moment ago demanding to leave, now gave Jane one of her mutinous stares. It was an expression familiar to Jane, an especially hostile one which heralded the start of a lengthy confrontation which would involve, though not necessarily end in tears – not always Harriet's.

'Well, I'm going. Bye,' Jane called. She had tried this bluffing routine before but it seldom worked, and more frequently resulted in a humiliating climbdown on her part, but she was damned if she was going to shin up the slippery bit of the helter-skelter and smack Harriet in front of all those other mums. Especially someone whose baby she had just been minding. I bet she doesn't smack her kids, thought Jane. Just lets them run riot.

It was only when she was through the gate that she allowed herself to look over her shoulder. Harriet had come down from the helter-skelter but was not following, indeed, she had her back to Jane and seemed oblivious to her departure. Blast. Now she would either have to sit and wait until she noticed, or whip up a temper and storm back to fetch her. Jane felt more weary than angry, and decided to wait by the hedge, out of sight, but still watching.

Maintaining continuous surveillance through a foot of woody privet was not easy and required some dodging and weaving on Jane's part. She was just thinking what a very undignified figure she would cut if she happened to bump into anyone she knew, and how fortunate it was that she was relatively new to the area, when a voice said, 'You haven't lost yours now, have you?' and the black-and-grey haired woman appeared as if from nowhere, with the blanket over her shoulder, somehow managing to carry the baby, hold her son's hand and eat an ice-cream all at the same time.

'Ha-ha. No,' Jane said, straightening up, embarrassed. But the woman had moved on, oblivious.

In the meantime, after a few minutes of pushing an empty swing Harriet appeared to remember her mother's existence and came running towards the gate. Jane watched as the child's face crumpled with panic, as though just about to melt, and she experienced a moment of cruel gratification swiftly followed by shame and guilt.

'Here I am. I told you to come, didn't I?' she said, stepping out from behind the hedge before Harriet had a chance to start crying.

An unbelievable result, thought Jane, as Harriet scuffed along beside her. Out of the park without a tantrum *or* an ice-cream. And she felt a great surge of maternal self-confidence. A hearse was passing by slowly as they reached the road. Its roof was decked with pastel-coloured flowers, packed together like so many screwed-up tissues.

'Mummy, look at that beautiful car,' said Harriet, pointing. 'Can I go in one like that one day?'

Over my dead body, thought Jane, dropping down to Harriet's level and hugging her tightly.

5

Hello, Nina. This is Hugo Etchells calling from Australia. I tracked you down through the University magazine and international directory inquiries. I was just phoning to say that I'm coming back to the UK this summer. For good. As soon as I can tie up a few loose ends here. I thought it would be nice to meet up again and talk about Old Times. I won't be needing accommodation or anything like that. I'm sorry you're not there. I might try you again nearer the time. My number's Sydney 969 9278 if you want it, but there's no need for you to call back.

Good, thought Nina. Then I won't. She didn't even bother to take down the number before she pressed the erase button, but against her will she had already memorized it. Sydney 969 9278; the more she tried to forget it, the deeper it lodged. *I won't be requiring accommodation.* Nina didn't like that line. The very fact that he'd mentioned the subject showed that he must have considered her even briefly as a source of hospitality, and that struck her as presumptuous after so many years of silence. *For good.* She didn't like that line either. If it was just a holiday or business trip a meeting could easily be avoided, though Nina was hard pressed to imagine what sort of business Hugo would be engaged in – drug running, perhaps?

But if he was coming back to England to live after sixteen, seventeen years, he would have all the time in the world to pursue old acquaintances, and the thing about Hugo was his absolute determination in the face of any resistance. If she expressed enthusiasm and delight and put herself out to meet him, he wouldn't show up; if she hedged and made excuses he would be on to her like a pack of hounds. She would come back from work one day and find him camped on the doorstep, overnight bag in hand; or in the sitting room, running an appraising eye over her possessions, and cross-examining James.

James. She felt her throat constrict with fear. If Hugo ever met James the cat would really be out of the bag. She had always thought it no more than a possibility that when Irene was safely dead and beyond harm, and James was old enough to understand the value of a certain type of lie, she would sit him down and tell him everything. Now, thanks to Hugo, it looked as though this long-deferred moment had finally arrived.

6

In 1974 Nina had enrolled as a geography student at University College, London. She had spent the previous seven years at boarding school so the idea of 'leaving home' held no particular delights or fears. Her father was in the diplomatic service, and during her childhood had held posts in half a dozen different countries, the most recent of which was Kenya. By the age of eighteen Nina was well travelled, but rootless.

She was offered a shared room in a hall of residence in Camden Town. Her room-mate, a girl called Barbara who was studying politics, was in the habit of bringing her boyfriend back for the night when she imagined Nina to be asleep. After enduring the sound of this furtive coupling for a fortnight or so, Nina complained to the accommodation office and was moved to a much smaller single cell in a block off Oxford Street. From her window she could see open-topped buses packed with tourists; she gave her address as 'Off Park Lane'; Selfridges was her corner shop.

Nina was a natural extrovert, but her reserves of sociability had been somewhat depleted by the false start in Camden Town. She had made an effort to be friendly there and met some promising people. Even Barbara, when not screwing, had been pleasant enough company. Now, several miles away, she debated the wisdom of demanding a single room. At times it had the aura of solitary confinement. The corridor into which she had moved was lively enough: there often seemed to be a party in progress in one or other of the cells, Pink Floyd and Yes reverberating through the walls in the early hours, making the leaves of her Yukka plant quiver. But cliques form quickly and Nina had so far not been invited to join in.

She even resorted to the unusual measure of making an

overseas call to her parents to whinge.

'Cheer up, darling,' said her mother, breezily, in response to Nina's lamentations. 'It's always hard at first. You know what we're like when we first move. It's just a question of gritting your teeth and breaking the ice.'

Breaking the ice. Nina had an image of herself wielding her smile like a pick-axe. The next day she had summoned up the courage to knock on her neighbour's door and introduce herself. She had not actually seen the occupant coming or going, but had noticed a light under the door at night. In response to her gentle tap there came a faint scuffling noise and then the prickly silence of someone pretending to be out, and Nina had slunk back to her room, humiliated, vowing to make no more gestures of friendship.

For the next few days she tried, in spite of herself, to catch a glimpse of the reclusive inhabitant by bursting out of her room whenever she heard footsteps in the hall, often surprising someone emerging innocently from the bathroom, but she never caught anyone entering or leaving. She began to wonder whether she had imagined the scuffling noise, and to suspect the room was vacant, but then one morning there appeared a mysterious note tacked to the door. YOU'RE DEAD, BREAD! it announced in angry capitals. From this Nina deduced, intuitively, that her neighbour was male. Later that day she noticed that someone had appended, in minute letters, the reply *Bread is risen!*, but of the subject of this bizarre correspondence there remained no sign.

Fortunately Nina's isolation proved to be only temporary. Her hall-mates were an amiable bunch, well able to assimilate a newcomer, especially one who was attractive and charming and ready to have fun. After only a week in solitary Nina was initiated into party life by a knock at the door as she was getting into bed. She pulled her dress back on hastily, embarrassed to have been caught going to sleep at such an early hour – it was well before midnight – and threw the door open. Two girls, one of whom she'd nodded at on the stairs as she was dragging her suitcase up all four flights, and a boy she recognized from the Geog. Soc. disco she'd attended last week, with her Camden friends, stood outside holding bottles of Newcastle Brown. The unfamiliar one of the girls who had long red hair parted in the middle, and large white front teeth, also parted in the middle, said in a cheerful voice, 'We're having a party.'

'Oh?' said Nina, with one of her ice-pick smiles. 'Where?'

'Here,' said the boy, pretending to take a step into the room, and they had all laughed. He was good-looking in an open, unthreatening sort of way, with blond hair and very blue eyes.

'No,' said the other girl, who had one hand hooked into the boy's waistband. 'I thought if we all open our doors, we can drift in and out. I'm over there.' She pointed across the hall to a dimly lit cubbyhole in which several bodies lay slumped on cushions, hardly moving. It all looked rather more horizontal than the parties Nina was used to, but she realized that to be stand-offish now would condemn her to terms of her own company. And besides, there were those blue eyes.

'Okay,' said Nina. 'I haven't got any drink, or anything, though.'

'That's all right,' said the red-haired girl. 'We've stocked up. I'm Fee, by the way. This is Martin and Jean.'

Jean had stepped past her and was inspecting Nina's record collection which was still lying on the floor like a spread deck of cards. 'Hey, can we take this one?' she said, picking out a Velvet Underground LP. 'I love it. It's so mellow.' She was wearing a long cheesecloth dress with tiny bells around the hem, and had bare feet and a silver ring on her middle toe. She moved on from the records, browsing unhurriedly through Nina's few possessions. 'Oh, you've got a twelve-string guitar,' she said, pausing beside the instrument which was resting on a stand with a college scarf around its neck. She ran her thumb across the strings. 'Can you play?'

'Not much,' Nina admitted. She wasn't about to be tricked into giving a recital. 'Blackbird' and 'The House of the Rising Sun' were the beginning and end of her repertoire. 'It's more of a clothes horse really.'

'Martin can, can't you, Martin?' said Jean, smirking up at him.

'Three chords,' said Martin, 'and I'm working on B7.'

'Are you coming then?' said Fee from the doorway. She was trying to conduct a conversation across the hall with one of the prone bodies at the same time.

'Er, yes, I just need to sort myself out,' said Nina, conscious that she wasn't wearing any knickers and that this was no way to set off to a party.

'So where have you been hiding for the last few weeks?' Jean asked, when they had finally joined the smokers in the darkened cell across the corridor. Nina explained about Barbara's creaking bedsprings and her successful petition to the accommodation office. 'It didn't occur to me that I might have to share,' she said. 'I'd sort of taken it for granted that I'd have my own place.'

'Martin's sharing with two other people,' said Fee.

'One of them doesn't speak any English,' said Martin, 'and he's *always* in.'

'If you'd got your act together earlier you could have been living in this corridor,' said Jean.

You mean *instead of me*, Nina thought.

'Well, I'm always in the wrong place at the wrong time,' said Martin, smiling at Nina.

'We didn't realize your room was empty all that time,' said Fee. 'We thought there must be another weirdo living opposite.' They all laughed.

'Have you met your neighbour?' Jean asked, accepting a joint from the person beside her, and passing it on to Nina, who took a cautious drag. She had never smoked dope before and wasn't sure what to expect. She didn't want to start seeing snakes or thinking she could fly in front of a roomful of strangers. All the same, none of the others present looked as though they were tripping wildly; on the contrary a couple of them – a very hairy-faced bloke and his girlfriend – seemed to have nodded off. In the event her first joint did nothing more than give her a sore throat: subsequent experiences were more successful, but she never bothered to cultivate or seek her own supply.

'I knocked on the door but there was no reply,' she said. 'In what way is he a weirdo?'

Jean shrugged. 'I don't know. His reputation preceded him. He's in his second year here, but he'd already done two years at Oxford.'

'Cambridge,' someone corrected her.

She wafted her hand dismissively. 'He got sent down for selling acid, I think,' she went on.

'No. I heard he got pissed one night and crapped on the bonnet of some professor's car,' said the hairy individual who was roused momentarily from his slumber. This was greeted with gales of laughter from the company.

'There aren't any cars in Cambridge,' said Martin. 'It must have been a bike.'

'You're just guessing,' said a blonde girl in the corner, who had been silent, apparently comatose, until this point. 'Ziggy told me that she knew someone who was at Oxford at the same time as him and she said he was accused of raping this fresher. Apparently the college authorities wanted to hush it up and the girl agreed not to go to the police as long as he was thrown out.'

'So, to summarize,' said Nina, who was forming a less and less favourable picture of the character beyond her bedroom wall, 'my neighbour is an ex-Oxbridge drug-peddling rapist with loose bowels.' This was received with more laughter. 'Why do people call him Bread?' she went on.

'I think his friends must call him that, if he's got any,' Jean said. 'He makes his own.'

'Friends?' asked Nina.

'Bread. He fancies himself as a bit of a chef.'

'God,' said Nina. 'Worse and worse.'

'I tell you, he's completely mad,' said hairy face. 'But a genius.'

'Of course,' said Nina, drily, catching Martin's eye. She was beginning to twig that they were winding her up.

'I should just point out that nobody here has actually met him,' Martin said, taking the joint from Jean.

'I have,' said Jean indignantly. She struggled to her feet to change the music, her bare feet getting caught up in the tassels of her dress. There was the rasp of needle on vinyl as she yanked the record-player's arm up. Nina glanced fearfully at her Velvet Underground LP, which Jean was dragging from its sleeve, fingers and thumbs all over it. 'I went into the TV room the other night to ask them to turn the sound down a bit and he was in there on his own watching *The Sky at Night*,' Jean went on.

'What did he say?' Fee wanted to know.

'He didn't say anything. He just sort of grunted, and turned the sound down; and when I went back a while later he was still there, sitting right up close to the screen.'

'He didn't try and rape you, then, or sell you acid?' said Martin.

'No,' she admitted. 'But then he wasn't exactly, like, friendly either.'

The music started and she stood swaying dreamily beside the loudspeaker, letting her long dark hair swing down across her face. 'Listen to this bit, everyone,' she suddenly commanded, putting one hand up, and they all kept still and paid attention dutifully to an unremarkable couple of bars of guitar music while Jean closed her eyes with an expression of rapture. 'That's exquisite, that is,' she said, coming back down to earth. 'I'm going to play it again.'

Rape and pillage, thought Nina, when the party had finally dispersed and she had changed back into her nightdress and climbed drowsily into bed. I don't believe a word of it. But she reached over and locked her door for the first time, just in case.

7

Jane removed her shoes on the threshold to reveal a broad ladder on the instep of her tights. The blob of nail varnish with which she had attempted to halt its progress had now fused the fabric to her heel. Guy and the girls were already inside, shoeless. Jane had gone back out to the car for the bag of toys and the present. Her in-laws always subjected them to this humiliation, as if they were naughty children who had just come in from making mud-pies in the garden, or as if the place were a mosque, or something. A shrine to the god of Wilton double twist at £39.99 a yard, thought Jane, trying to peel the sticky tights from the sole of her foot and sending the ladder racing further up her ankle. Guy's parents themselves were not obliged to parade around in their socks, but wore what Mrs Bromelow called House Shoes: hers were a pair of elasticated, red sateen slippers which snapped shut like clams when not occupied.

Family visits to Guy's parents were rare, and dreaded by both Guy and Jane as occasions when all the deficiencies in their approach to child-rearing and discipline were cruelly exposed. The combination of pale carpets, spindly antique tables and precious ornaments ranged at about knee level, seemed to make the children more than usually clumsy and boisterous. Jane would spend the whole day scolding and apologizing and scrubbing at spills. There was nothing for the girls to do, of course, and nothing that might conceivably entertain them was ever provided. The loft was full of Guy's and his brother's old toys – all in mint condition, naturally – and these items were often alluded to but never produced in case they got damaged in the course of play. Quite what circumstance they were being preserved for was never made clear. There would be a long, tedious, sit-down lunch to negotiate, perhaps with some elderly, childless guest in attendance. Guy's parents were the world's slowest eaters: Jane would have almost finished before the last person was served, and be obliged to make one sprout last fifteen minutes. All her concentration would in any case be required to keep Harriet and, to a lesser extent, Sophie, chair-bound.

It was by mutual agreement that this ordeal was confined to Boxing Day or other significant anniversaries. Otherwise the senior Bromelows tended to visit their son at his own house, where tensions were more easily disguised. Today's break with tradition was caused by Guy's mother having sprained her ankle in the garden a few days before her birthday. Around the door Jane could just see the injured limb, minus its red slipperette, bound in crepe bandage, resting on a tapestry footstool.

'Absolutely excruciating,' the invalid was saying. 'Worse than childbirth.'

Jane, who had had rather difficult labours, was inclined to take umbrage at this. 'Hello, Daphne. Happy birthday,' she said, walking into the sitting room and handing Guy's mother some roses and a wrapped present – the copy of *The Downing Street Years* that Harriet had pinched from the arcade.

'Oh. Thank you so much.' Having ascertained from its shape and weight that it was a book Mrs Bromelow laid it aside unopened. Guy was standing with his back to the unlit fire, rocking on his heels and trying to urge his daughters to kiss Granny hello. Although she showed no other sign of affection towards them, she demanded this act of homage at each meeting.

'Go on,' Guy said, pushing them gently in the middle of their backs. They shuffled reluctantly in the direction of their grandmother's corrugated cheek.

'Hello, Sophie. Hello, Harriet,' said Mrs Bromelow, acknowledging their grudging kisses. 'Mind Granny's foot.'

'Now don't let me forget. I've something for you,' she said, a moment later, addressing Guy. 'You know we inherited most of Aunt Muriel's things?'

'Oh yes?' said Guy, hope fluttering.

'Well, some of it just doesn't look right here. So I thought you could take the dogs. Do you remember – they used to sit either side of her front door?'

Guy's face fell: he did remember. 'Oh, right. Thanks.'

'Anyway, do take them; I've put them in the downstairs cloakroom for the present, but they need a good home. Go and have a look at them, Jane.'

As she passed, Guy gave her a grimace, which said, 'Be prepared', and she felt a surge of happiness, as she always did when he fell back on one of their private codes to exclude his parents or some other hostile element. He understood her so well. Inside the cloakroom, in which a small bowl of shrivelled pot-pourri was competing with the full might of a plug-in air freshener, a pair of three-foot china alsatians sat guarding the lavatory. Jane almost laughed. It was quite the most unnecessary and undesirable gift she had ever received. And there was so much of them: their absence (for Jane had no intention of keeping them) next time Guy's parents came to visit, would be hard to overlook.

'Big, aren't they?' said Guy on her return.

'Yes.' She feigned confusion. 'I couldn't work out where you were supposed to put the loo roll.'

Mrs Bromelow gave Jane a wintry smile to let her know that her sarcasm had been noted, but not appreciated.

In the corner her husband was pouring sherry from a crystal decanter. The smell reminded Jane of college tutorials with the Dean, of après-funeral drinks, of other Sunday lunches with her in-laws, of everything dreary.

'Here you are, girls.' Jane dropped the bag of toys and they pounced on it eagerly. 'Don't just tip it all on to the floor,' she said, as Harriet pulled out a long packet of felt-tipped pens, upside down, and they cascaded over the blond carpet. In her armchair, Mrs Bromelow stiffened as if she could already see graffiti on the walls.

'Well, cheers,' said Mr Bromelow, when they were all holding their sherries. 'Good to see you all.'

'Happy birthday,' said Guy, tilting his glass towards his mother.

'I want a drink,' said Harriet.

'So do I,' said Sophie.

'What's the little word you've forgotten?' said their grandmother, frowning.

'NOW,' said Harriet.

'Please,' said Sophie.

Mr Bromelow squatted beside the drinks cabinet and produced from among the port and single malts an ancient and half-empty bottle of bitter lemon. When he twisted the cap there was only the feeblest hiss.

'I don't want that,' said Harriet.

'You'll like it,' Jane promised. 'It's fizzy.' Or was, she thought.

'When does Harriet start nursery or playgroup or whatever they call it?' Mrs Bromelow wanted to know. Jane could map her train of thought precisely. It went Harriet – rudeness – discipline – school.

'She's already started. Two mornings a week,' said Guy.

'Soon be off your hands, Jane,' said his mother, encouragingly. Jane resented the implication that she couldn't wait to be rid of her own daughter – the more so since it was true. 'Then what will you do with yourself?'

'I haven't really thought,' Jane lied. In truth she thought of little else; she imagined herself being pampered in one of those health clubs for the idle rich, or turning out pen and ink drawings of local parish churches, doing a second degree in some subject far removed from her own specialism: nursing studies. Linguistics, perhaps, or philosophy: something that would sweep her away from the material world of Coco Pops and Barbie dolls and nits and up into the rarefied realm of pure theory. 'The school day is so short. There aren't many jobs that would fit in.' There was no point in elaborating as Mrs Bromelow was already on her foot and, with the aid of a pair of Great War-style crutches, hopping towards the hallway. Jane had momentarily forgotten that conversational elephant trap that her mother-in-law liked to lay: ask a question and then leave the room. Jane walked into it every time.

'Garden's looking nice,' said Guy, taking a few steps towards the French windows. Out on the lawn stood a wheelbarrow of box-clippings – evidence of work in progress.

'Plum tree's diseased,' said his father. 'Needs chopping down. Perhaps you'll give us a hand after lunch.'

'Of course,' said Guy, who had no time for such chores in his own home, and barely got around to cutting the grass.

'And there's a little concreting job I've been saving for you,' Mr Bromelow laughed jovially.

Don't know why he bothers to put on clean clothes to come here, Jane thought. Don't know why he doesn't just come in his overalls.

From the kitchen came the sound of pan lids crashing. Jane ventured in to help. Mrs Bromelow was standing at the hob on one leg, skimming fat from a spitting pan of roast lamb.

'Can I do anything?' Jane asked. Her mother-in-law looked at Jane's white silk blouse. 'No dear. Just get everyone sitting down.' As well as her House Shoes, she was wearing what Jane took to be a House Dress – once smart and evidently expensive but now frayed at collar and cuffs and coming apart under the armpit. It was what she always wore indoors, unless company was expected, in which case she would disappear upstairs and change into one of several navy suits. Jane longed for her to be caught out by an unexpected visitor, but this would never happen: the Bromelows didn't mix with the sort of people who dropped in. Jane watched her forking eight roast potatoes into a serving dish. Guy's mother was a good cook, but portions were miserly. Jane had meant to suggest to Guy that they stopped at a service station on the way down for a pre-lunch snack, but time had been short and Guy would sooner starve than be late for his parents so she had kept her mouth shut. And, besides, the implied criticism would wound him. Not that he didn't enjoy a good moan about them himself now and then, but when Jane pitched in with her own observations he tended to go quiet.

'Oh there you are, Stilton,' said Mrs Bromelow to a fat spaniel who waddled in at that moment, and made straight for

Jane, sneezing violently. That's right, Jane thought. We all have to take our shoes off, while the dog is allowed to spray his germs all over the kitchen. He always greeted her with enthusiasm, as if he could scent the one dog-hater in the crowd and was bent on converting her. Usually he'd come bounding in from the garden, mid-shit, and throw himself at her, but he was a bit subdued today, his breath sounding even more laboured than usual. He collapsed at her feet, chest rattling, and gazed up at her with a pool of slime in the corner of each eye.

'I think it's emphysema,' said Mrs Bromelow, peeling a piece of lamb from the bone and letting the dog eat it from her fingers.

Jane watched her wipe the slobber from her hand on Stilton's straggly coat before turning back to make the gravy. 'I'll tell the others to sit down,' she said, feeling suddenly queasy.

'So how's school?' asked Mr Bromelow, when they were all finally seated. The table was set with white linen and the best crystal and china – the stuff that didn't go in the dishwasher, so half the afternoon would be spent washing up. Jane watched her father-in-law carve two minute slices of lamb from the joint and lay them on a plate beside one small roast potato, and was about to say that Harriet would have no broccoli, thank you, when she realized that the plate was destined for her. Really, it was inconceivable how Guy and his brother had managed to reach six foot on such rations, she thought. It must have been all that boarding-school stodge: bread pudding and gypsy tart.

'Not too bad,' said Guy. 'We've got an inspection coming up.' He didn't bother to go into details; his career was something of a disappointment to them. Mr Bromelow had reached the rank of brigadier in Her Majesty's Armed Forces. Whole rows of grown men had had to salute him as he passed. Ticking off under-elevens seemed very small beer by comparison and not altogether a job for a man. And if he didn't actually have a class to teach, what on earth did he find to do all day?

'One of the children brought in some frogspawn a month ago,' Guy was saying, at the same time trying to feed Harriet, who was having trouble manipulating the heavy silver cutlery. 'We've got this nature area behind the caretaker's house, with a pond and wild flowers. So then all the other kids started bringing jam jars of the stuff to school and now the whole pond is like jelly. We're going to have a plague of frogs in a few months' time.'

'Is that true, Daddy?' asked Sophie, suspiciously. She was used to Guy spinning her a yarn.

'Do frogs bite?' Harriet wanted to know.

'No, they stick their tongues out like this,' said Guy, pulling a face and waiting for her to copy him. As she opened her mouth he went to pop in a piece of carrot, but she was too quick for him and snapped her teeth shut so that it fell untasted on to the creamy white napery between them.

'The chair of governors is retiring,' said Jane, feeling that this, if anything, was the sort of information Guy's parents were after, not tales of children and frogs.

'Oh really?' said Mrs Bromelow. 'The one you like?'

'Yes. The woman who appointed me. I hope her successor is as nice. Now that school governors have so much power it's vital to get on with your chair.'

A vision of Guy, conversing gaily with an elegant Chesterfield, rose up before Jane's eyes.

'This is bisgusting,' said Harriet, loudly, laying down her fork.

'*Dis*gusting not *bis*gusting,' Guy corrected her. 'How many times?'

'It's delicious,' said Jane, firmly. Her own plate was empty but her stomach still felt cavernous and unfilled. She would be forced to hang over the children's plates like a buzzard, clearing up their leavings. The rest of the joint stood steaming on the sideboard, prompting her to a fantasy of second helpings, but she knew that any minute now it would be borne away to the kitchen, never to reappear. It was a mystery to Jane where such leftovers ended up. She couldn't see Daphne mincing it up for rissoles, somehow. She glared at Stilton, comatose beneath the sideboard. Privately she suspected him of being the beneficiary of her unassuaged hunger.

'Sit up, Harriet, and eat your dinner or there'll be no pudding,' said her grandmother severely. 'Does she always fidget this much?' Harriet, bored with adult conversation, had slid down on her seat so that the top of her head was now level with the table. Every so often she would fling out a foot to try and kick Sophie, jogging the gate-leg and setting the plates and glasses jangling.

'Oh, fidgeting's the least of her vices,' said Jane.

Mrs Bromelow pursed her lips.

'Quite,' said Guy. 'Only the other day she pinched something from one of the shops in town. What was it?' he went on, ignoring agonized signals from his wife. Fortunately his memory for details was poor. 'I forget now, but I think it proves that a life of crime has begun.'

'Well, I should think half of the children I see going around the supermarket will end up in Borstal. The mothers don't seem to have any control.'

'Supermarkets and children don't mix,' Guy agreed, trying to make the conversation more general, and less obviously about their own children.

'Well, I think modern parents have got it all wrong,' said Mrs Bromelow, as if Jane and Guy could conceivably be some other breed, and therefore not take what followed personally. 'They've read all this rubbish by sociologists and they're afraid if they tell a child off it'll end up repressed or some silly nonsense. When I had you we didn't have any books. We just got on with it.'

Not have books? thought Jane. What period of prehistory could Daphne possibly be referring to? It was only here that she was made to feel like a caricature of a slack, liberal mother. The rest of the time she worried that she was rather too short-tempered and free with her slaps – indeed something of a tyrant.

'Any news of William and Caroline?' Guy asked. William was Guy's younger brother. He did something on Wall Street: Jane had never grasped precisely what, and neither, she suspected, had her mother-in-law, but it seemed to hold true for Daphne that the less she understood, the more impressed she was. His phenomenal wealth and success were often discussed at the Bromelow table, and Jane found herself disliking this mythical William for being so evidently and unfairly the favourite son. The real William was, in fact, perfectly amiable and on the few occasions when they'd met Jane had enjoyed his company. His wife, Caroline, on the other hand, was, in Jane's view, snobbish, materialistic and humourless – therefore a natural ally of Mrs Bromelow.

'I spoke to him the other day. He said he'd received your birthday card,' Guy's mother replied.

Guy, unaware that he had ever sent one, shot Jane a grateful glance. 'Oh. Right.' Although he had always got along fine with William their worlds no longer converged. They weren't great letter writers – it just wasn't something busy men did. And Guy wasn't a great phoner either. In his experience a ringing phone usually heralded trouble: complaints from parents, problems with pupils or staff, imminent visits by inspectors, or, at home, unwanted guests. As a result they tended to exchange news of each other via their parents, with the odd call at Christmas or New Year to say hello, and the even less frequent visit.

'It's terribly sad. He was telling me their last go at IVF was unsuccessful so they've got to go through it all again.'

'Oh dear,' said Jane, a small, mean corner of her soul rejoicing at their misfortune. Fertility was the only area in which she and Guy outperformed them: as soon as Caroline conceived, their one advantage would be lost.

'So unfair,' Mrs Bromelow went on. 'They'd make such marvellous parents.'

'Yes, they would,' said Guy, generously. Jane, inferring from the previous remark that her mother-in-law considered her to have been undeservedly blessed, remained tight-lipped.

While Mrs Bromelow collected the plates and brought in a bowl of trifle from the kitchen her husband took the opportunity to move the conversation away from the subject of child-rearing – something that had never interested him in theory or practice. Instead he began a long and involved tale about the laziness and uncouthness of the decorators who had just finished work on the guest bathroom. This was a familiar theme: Guy's parents' house was large and in a state of perpetual refurbishment. Jane could recall many afternoons before the children were born when visits to the Bromelows would entail driving miles into the Sussex countryside to track down a rare shade of quarry tile, or some bespoke doorknobs.

'He brought his twelve-year-old son along as plumber's mate, if you please,' Mr Bromelow said, a vein throbbing in his temple. 'It wasn't even the school holidays. When were the holidays?' he asked Guy. This digression was interrupted by a distant ringing.

'Someone go and see who that is,' ordered Mrs Bromelow, laying a scant tablespoon of trifle in a bowl and passing it to Jane. 'I can't go.'

Guy glanced at her foot. 'No, of course not,' he said, standing up.

'In this dress.'

'Oh, I see what you mean.' He left the room, closely followed by Harriet and Sophie, who seized the chance to slip down from the table.

'How's your house coming along?' Mr Bromelow turned on Jane. 'Done much to it yet?'

'No. Not so's you'd notice,' she replied. They had only been in the place seven months. There were piles of boxes in the spare room still to be unpacked. She couldn't think what they contained – no one seemed to be missing anything. She was half tempted to take the whole lot down to the tip unexamined. The only room they had tackled was the loft conversion, which had been abandoned by the previous owners before it came to putting in a staircase, and had to be reached by means of a flimsy ladder. But it had carpet and electric light and shelves and skylight windows through which Guy could examine the heavens with his telescope, so he had appropriated the room as his study, and would retreat there to work or stargaze as the mood took him. When the need for privacy became overwhelming he would pull the ladder up after him.

The rest of the house was much as they'd found it: not to their taste, exactly, but too recently decorated to be redone on anything but frivolous aesthetic grounds. At present it was what Guy called 'Suburban Grand' with plush carpets and brass fittings and flowery wallpaper with contrasting borders everywhere. Ideally Jane favoured more austere surroundings: white walls and bare boards, perhaps, or rough sisal carpets which would skin the legs of anyone who dared to slide down the stairs.

'Well, it's perfectly adequate for your purposes, isn't it?' said Mrs Bromelow, as if there were other purposes less humble than merely living in the house to which they might one day aspire.

'Anyway,' Jane said. 'Now spring's here we'll live in the garden.' As she said this a few fat raindrops hit the French windows, and there was an ominous roll of thunder. 'There goes the concreting,' she added, in as neutral a tone as possible.

'Oh, it'll keep,' said Guy's father. 'Till next time.'

The meal proceeded a while in silence, Jane shaving minute layers of sponge and custard from her trifle to make it last. 'What can Guy be doing all this time?' his mother asked. 'Do you think he's been kidnapped?'

'Shall I go and find him – and the girls?' Jane volunteered.

'No,' Mrs Bromelow replied. 'Let's enjoy the peace while it lasts.'

Harriet and Sophie came panting in, giggling. They had been trying to play pony rides with Stilton, who had wedged himself under the telephone table in the hall and refused to come out.

'Where's Daddy?' asked Jane, lifting Harriet back on to her chair.

'Talking to a man and a lady,' said Sophie.

'What about?'

'God.'

'Jehovah's Witnesses!' said Mrs Bromelow in horror, flinging down her napkin. 'If he shows the slightest interest we shall never be rid of them. I hope to God he hasn't taken any of their literature.'

'Oh, he'll be there for hours, politely debating with them,' said Jane, whose doorstep technique for seeing off unwanted callers of all types was more abrupt: a cheerful, but utterly inflexible 'No thank you', followed immediately by withdrawal of eye-contact and then a slow smooth closing of the door. It was hesitancy which was fatal in these situations. Only a few weeks ago someone had called selling a little laminated sign to put in the front window which read: **No free newspapers or door-to-door salesmen!** Guy had bought one, of course, to be nice. 'Isn't that rather like sawing through the branch you're sitting on?' he'd said to the man.

A moment later Guy himself reappeared, tract in hand.

'Oh you *haven't*,' said his mother.

'You took your time,' said Jane. 'Don't tell me they've converted you.'

'I think they might have done – to atheism,' said Guy, with a troubled frown, taking his place at the table and failing to join in with the burst of laughter that greeted this remark.

'You're very quiet,' said Jane on the way home. The children were asleep in the back, heads lolling, exhausted by the two-hour tramp through the West Sussex countryside which Guy's mother had suggested as a means of prolonging the life of her furniture. Naturally she herself had stayed at home, warm and dry, to rest her foot. The china alsatians were in the boot, wrapped in coats to stop them clanking together. Guy was driving, as usual. They had stopped for Jane to pick up some chips and she was full now, and happy. Guy hadn't wanted anything to eat: visits to his parents always took away his appetite.

'I was just thinking about those Jehovah's Witnesses,' he said. The copy of *Watchtower* was sticking out of the glove compartment, where it would remain for several weeks, unread, before being thrown out with the old crisp packets and lolly sticks. When he had opened the door to a smiling, well-dressed, middle-aged couple, he had taken them for friends of his parents – neighbours locked out of their house, perhaps – and had treated them to one of his lip-splitting PR smiles. When they had whipped out a pamphlet and asked him if he didn't think that there was a lot of misery and wretchedness in the world, he realized his mistake, but the moment for slamming the door was past, and they had him there, squirming like a worm on a hook.

'I am a Christian myself,' Guy had said, politely, hoping they would take the hint and push off in search of the heathen, but this seemed only to encourage them.

'Are you?' said the man, still holding out the pamphlet. 'That's very good to hear. Because so few people are nowadays. It's a tragedy that so many people still haven't taken Jesus into their hearts. Wouldn't you agree?'

Guy sensed a trap. 'I can't help feeling that it's a matter of conscience for every individual, rather than an idea that can be sold on the doorstep like dusters,' he said. 'Perhaps that's because I don't share your sense of urgency.'

The man affected astonishment. 'There is every reason for urgency. Salvation is an urgent business.' He offered Guy the pamphlet. 'You might find this useful. It answers some of the questions people like yourself ask.'

'No thanks,' said Guy. 'I prefer to go straight to the Bible itself if I need help with any . . . er . . . spiritual dilemmas.' This wasn't entirely true. Guy hardly ever picked up a Bible, unless he happened to be reading in church, and didn't find it particularly helpful in strengthening his faith. Rather the contrary, in fact. The deeper he probed, the less he understood.

'That's very wise,' the man was saying. 'Because the Bible

is after all the Word of God. And there's no arguing with that, is there?'

'We-e-ell . . .' said Guy, feeling more heretical by the second.

Sophie and Harriet, meanwhile, tired of tormenting Stilton, had tried to push their way between Guy's legs to get a look at the callers.

'Don't do that,' he remonstrated, trying to hold them back with one foot.

The man gave them an indulgent smile.

'I don't like that man,' said Harriet loudly, from behind Guy's knees. 'I don't like his trousers.'

The smile intensified. 'Do take this,' he said to Guy. 'It explains things far better than I ever could.' There was no way Guy could avoid taking the proffered leaflet, short of putting his hands behind his back. 'Perhaps when you've had a chance to read it we could come back and discuss it?'

'Well, unfortunately, I don't actually live here,' said Guy, pouncing on this chance of escape. 'I'm just visiting my parents.' He was beginning to tire of this exchange now, imagining his waiting trifle. If he hadn't confessed to being a Christian, and thus committed himself to displaying a degree of tolerance and decorum, he would have told them to bugger off by now. Instead, they had parted on the politest of terms, but the encounter had left Guy rattled, with graver doubts than ever.

'You haven't really stopped believing in God, have you?' said Jane, beside him, trying to pick up the travel news on the car radio. As far as the horizon the traffic on their side of the motorway was stationary, red tail lights glowing through a pall of exhaust.

'I don't know. Not just like that. It's been coming on for a while.'

'You've never mentioned it before.'

'I think it started when I took this headship. The moment faith became part of my job description it began to wear off.'

'Well, I'm sure He still believes in you, anyway,' said Jane, giving up on the radio and giving his leg a gentle squeeze. He smiled at her, surprised. She didn't often touch him nowadays. He was suddenly struck with the suspicion that she was really only looking for somewhere to wipe her greasy fingers, but dismissed this as unworthy.

'What if I ended up a rampant non-believer?' he pondered aloud. 'Would I have to resign?'

'Absolutely not,' said Jane, removing her hand. She had an unwelcome vision of the four of them on the street, homeless, those unsorted boxes from the spare room on the back of a cart like the rest of their belongings. 'They asked for a practising Christian. So just keep practising.'

'I haven't quite descended to that level of hypocrisy,' Guy retorted. 'Anyway, it's not as if I've lost my faith altogether. It's more like migraine – I get these sudden, blinding attacks of atheism which take a while to wear off.'

'It's that telescope,' said Jane. 'You thought you'd be able to see Him.'

'I knew you'd work the telescope into things,' said Guy. A recent bone of contention was the amount of time Guy spent holed up in the loft.

'I'm only joking,' said Jane. 'Perhaps you should have a word with the Rector?'

'Oh no. I couldn't bother him with something like that.'

'Why ever not? It's his job. He'd probably be delighted to be approached on a matter of faith, instead of being asked for favours by people all the time.'

'Talking about it doesn't help. I told you: it's like migraine. Just thinking about it can set it off.'

'Sorry,' said Jane.

'I didn't mean talking to *you* doesn't help. It does. You're the only person who understands me. There's nothing we couldn't say to each other, is there?'

Jane gave his knee another squeeze, and smiled at him, without committing herself to agreement with this dangerous proposition.

Later that evening, as they prepared for bed, Guy watched Jane collect her nightclothes and disappear with them into the bathroom. He used to enjoy watching her undress: he still found her beautiful even after, what was it? eight years and two kids. But she seemed to be shyer now than when he'd met her, and a much sterner critic of her physical imperfections – to which Guy himself was oblivious. When she returned she was wearing one of the pretty silk nightdresses he had bought her over the years and which she normally shunned in favour of a baggy T-shirt with dogs on, or that shroud-thing which she wore *with knickers*. This was a good sign. But when he came out of the bathroom, having washed with optimistic thoroughness, he found Harriet curled up on the landing, crying.

'What's the matter?' he said, nearly falling over her. 'Why are you out of bed?'

'I'm very sad,' she said.

'Why?'

'Because I want to sleep in your bed.'

'Why do you want to sleep in our bed, darling?'

'Because I'm very sad.'

He picked her up and she twined her arms and legs around him. 'Come on. Back to your room. I'll tuck you in.'

'But I'm scared.'

'What of?'

'My dream. The lamb ate me.'

Guy couldn't help laughing. Harriet's nightmares always featured the most improbable predators. 'No. You ate the lamb. At Granny's, remember?'

By the time he had settled Harriet back in bed, peeling her fingers from his neck, and watched her arrange her legions of cuddly toys according to her own arcane system, Jane's reading light had gone off, and when he finally got back to bed she was already asleep, or pretending to be.

8

Nina was shaking so violently that someone on the Northern Line actually offered her a seat. It was the rush hour and she was on her way to observe a case conference about a new client: a seven-year-old whom the local authority had removed from his father and stepmother and placed with foster-parents. This affair was unlikely to be resolved without tears, but it was in her domestic rather than professional capacity that Nina was now distressed.

James, who had been travelling with her, had got off the train at Charing Cross, on his way to a lecture at the London School of Economics, quite unaware of her condition.

'You should wear a jacket and tie,' she'd said, when he came down for breakfast that morning in jeans and a sports shirt. 'First impressions are really important.'

'It's just some A-level lectures, not an interview,' he replied, tipping cornflakes into a bowl with one hand and posting bread into the toaster with the other. 'Anyway, they've already offered me a place.'

'It doesn't matter,' said Nina. 'You can never be too smartly dressed.'

'I'm not wearing a tie. I'll look a complete dork.'

'No you won't. I bet everyone else will have come in suits and you'll stick out a mile.' Nina mashed a peppermint teabag against the side of her mug and then flipped it into the bin.

'I'm only going to be sitting in an auditorium – completely anonymously. No one is going to give a toss what I'm wearing.'

'So you won't mind dressing up as a dork then.'

'Stop nagging,' he crunched, through a mouthful of cereal. 'If it's the sort of place that discriminates against people in jeans I don't want to go there anyway.'

'Oh, you are so unintelligent sometimes,' snapped Nina. 'Don't you realize that universities are deeply conservative places. What they want are people with original minds who behave conventionally.'

'Look, it's just a one-off course for sixth-formers. I doubt if I'll even set eyes on a tutor. I promise you if everyone else is in suits I'll wear a striped blazer and a boater for the rest of the year if it'll make you happy.'

'No, that would be eccentric,' said Nina. 'What time does it start?'

'Nine-thirty. But that's just the preliminary waffle. I don't need to get there till ten.'

Nina rolled her eyes towards the heavens. 'Why not just be on time for once? If you leave with me now you can make it by nine-thirty.' She rinsed her mug and left it on the side to drain. James had finished his cornflakes and was spreading marmalade on his toast in an unhurried manner. 'You are such a worrier. It's me who's going to be late, not you, and I'm not worried.'

'You are me,' said Nina cryptically. He shook his head, but they did in the end leave the house together, Nina rather later than she would have liked; James rather earlier. He had come through the age of embarrassment and didn't insist she walk fifty yards ahead on the other side of the road as he used to, although he did put on his dark glasses the moment they were out of doors even though the day was cloudy. And when his mobile phone rang, as it invariably did whenever he ventured into a public place, he dropped back a few paces. If it wasn't a phone it was a Walkman, Nina thought. He always had to have something trilling in his ears. She indulged him by walking on, but couldn't help herself tuning into his end of the conversation.

'Hi . . . No, I'm on my way there now . . . Oh, I dunno, about half three . . . if it's boring I'll leave earlier . . . (Nina bridled at that). Okay . . . I'll come to your house . . . you too.' He caught her up, slightly pink in the face. 'That was Kerry. I won't be in for a meal tonight.'

'Okay,' said Nina, wondering what she was going to do with all that lamb she'd taken out of the freezer. She would have to get into the habit of cooking for one. This wasn't the first time it had happened. 'When you don't eat at home, where do you eat?' she asked.

'At Kerry's,' said James. 'Where else?'

'Who cooks? Her mother?' She hadn't forgotten that James had failed to take up her offer to have the girl round to dinner one night.

'No. Bob usually. Her mother doesn't live with them.'

'Bob?'

'Kerry's dad.'

'And all three of you sit down and eat together?'

'Four. She's got a younger brother, too.'

'Around the table?'

James was starting to weary of this line of questioning. 'No. In front of the telly. Why?'

'I was just wondering,' said Nina, as they reached the underground station. 'No reason.' She had an image of the four of them cross-legged on one of those L-shaped sofas, plates of something microwaveable steaming on their laps, *Coronation Street* or something else James never watched, roaring away on a huge TV screen, and managed to feel both superior and jealous.

'What does her father do?'

'He's a copper.'

'Oh.' Nina just refrained from asking his rank.

'I know what you're doing,' said James, as they rode down the escalator. 'You're trying to find out all about them so you can put them in a little box with a label on. I bet you're dying to know what sort of carpet they've got in the lounge.'

'Don't be silly,' said Nina, thinking, *they call it a lounge, do they?* 'I'm just interested. You don't volunteer any information, so I have to ask.' What she really wanted to know was why they always went to Kerry's house rather than her own, but she could guess the answer. Bob, the laughing policeman, was evidently a much more congenial host, not given to barging into people's bedrooms and turfing them out of bed.

Tooting Bec station was even more crowded than usual. The platform was already packed and the escalators kept delivering fresh bodies into the crush. The bus strike, Nina remembered. Another good idea of yours, James was muttering. It's all right for him, head and shoulders above the crush, Nina thought. I'll be wedged under someone's armpit. A train swept in, faces and limbs squashed against the glass like a vision of hell. The doors opened and half a dozen people fell out through each opening into the crowd, then attempted to fight their way back on. Those in the middle carriages hadn't a hope of getting out. They were going to the West End, like it or not.

Two more trains came through full. On the third there were spaces and Nina and James allowed themselves to be herded through the doors. The heat inside was intense, as was the smell – a combination of last night's garlic and musty suits. Most of the passengers had their eyes closed as a defence against the indignity of it all. As the train lurched out of the station the people in the aisles swayed and clutched at each other. There wasn't sufficient foot-space to stumble. James put a hand up to catch one of the straps, and it was then that Nina, beside him, holding on to the back pocket of his jeans for support, noticed it. There, in the small depression in the crook of his arm was a puncture mark: the hole left by a hypodermic syringe. Nina's eyes began to smart and there was a pounding in her ears of waves crashing on rocks. As the train hurtled into a tunnel and everything went black she recognized the signs of an impending panic attack, something she had not suffered from since that experience in the desert half a lifetime ago. It was all just as before – shortness of breath, a constriction around the throat and chest, an agonizing pain down one arm, tingling fingers and an overwhelming sense of doom.

'I'm off then,' said James, as they reached Charing Cross. He squeezed past her, not noticing her glassy-eyed stare. 'I'll be late. Don't wait up.' And he was through the doors and swallowed up by the crowd before she could catch her breath.

'Do you want to sit down?' A young woman, suited and lacquered for the City, stood up and pointed at her empty seat. Nina nodded and sank into it gratefully, her hands clenched around her bag. She could feel her heart thumping: a maddened bird in the cage of her ribs. Deep Breaths, she told herself, closing her eyes and trying to visualize something soothing: green meadows, a stream, turquoise sky, pure white clouds. When she looked up they were at Tottenham Court Road. Staring at her from a poster on the opposite wall was a pale and wasted youth with black shadows under his eyes. DRUGS, it said. FIRST YOU LOSE YOUR MONEY. THEN YOUR LOOKS. THEN YOUR FRIENDS. THEN YOUR LIFE.

Nina staggered to her feet and on to the platform, clawing her way through the crowds as if swimming through treacle, and up, up from the heat and stench of that infernal pit into the open air.

James sat in the canteen at LSE eating a plate of lamb curry, cauliflower cheese and chips and enjoying a sense of contentment he couldn't quite source. The woman behind the counter at the servery had kept ladling food on to his plate as if the sooner she'd emptied her tins the quicker she could go home. James had had to restrain her from topping the whole lot off with a piece of cod. He had taken his tray to an empty table as he was half-expecting Kerry to call and felt self-conscious talking on the phone in crowded public places. In any case, he wouldn't be able to make himself heard above the clamour of conversation from the two hundred or so other sixth-formers also attending the course, every one of them tie-less, except for that one poor loser in a grey suit.

University was going to be all right, he decided. The academics who had addressed the various lectures he had attended in the morning were all encouragingly normal; some even showed traces of humour. There would be enormous helpings of simple food, cheap beer, and, if he got organized, a room of his own in the heart of London to which he could bring Kerry. At the thought of Kerry, James went to check his back pocket to reassure himself that the letter from the clinic was still there. His face broke into a smile; *that* was the origin of that feeling of self-satisfaction that had been with him all day. Tonight he and Kerry were going to have Unsafe Sex for the first time, and no slimy, squeaking bit of rubber was going to come between them. James swallowed a mouthful of lamb: a bad choice, curry. He would have to remember to buy some extra minty chewing gum later.

'Is anyone sitting here?' Greysuit was hovering at the edge of the table, tray in hand. A domed meniscus of custard quivered above the rim of his bowl. His plate was also dangerously awash with gravy. James shook his head as neutrally as possible. He didn't want to offer the bloke any grounds for starting a conversation. Greysuit lowered his tray thankfully and then retreated, returning with a wad of paper serviettes with which he attempted to contain the spillage. It was rather a tight squeeze between the tables; after some apologizing and chair-shifting Greysuit finally installed himself. James watched his discomfiture with sympathy. And that was how Mum would have had me dressed, he thought. Really, she had no idea. A half-smile died on his lips, for suddenly there was his mother, standing in the doorway, scanning the faces before her with that funny, short-sighted frown of hers. It was too late to duck – she'd seen him and was making her way towards him, tucking chairs back under tables as she approached.

Nina stood in the doorway of the refectory trying to pick James out in the crowd. Oh good, she thought, as she finally caught sight of him, he's found a friend. Once when he was small, not more than five or six, she had gone up to his school to spy on him, and had spotted him standing at the far end of the playground all alone, while the rest of the children ran around together, laughing and having fun. She'd hurried away, her stomach churning, and from that moment on had made a point of asking a series of his classmates back to play. Those with glasses or speech impediments were her favourites.

When she had emerged from the subway at the corner of Tottenham Court Road she had stood, clutching at the kerbside railings, dazed by the noise of the traffic, trying to fight off the sense of paranoia that had assailed her in the underground. If only I was at home I would know what to do, she thought. If there was only someone I could ring. Irene – until recently a fount of sympathy and wise counsel on the subject of her grandson – was no longer a possibility. She considered and dismissed several close friends. No: this wasn't something she particularly wanted anyone to know about – especially people who would be certain to meet James at a later date and judge him according to this lapse. My son, the heroin addict, she would say, introducing him. There was James himself, of course. He could be contacted on his mobile, but this wasn't an inquiry that Nina cared to conduct over the phone. He might hang up; he might not come home. An ungenerous thought came into her head: *It's that Girl.* Then she remembered. She had Kerry's number in her diary. James had grudgingly passed it on when the two of them had started going out. For emergencies only, he had warned. She would call and ask to speak to Mr Whatwashis-name? If his daughter was involved he had a right to know.

Inside the telephone box was a montage of stickers and postcards offering to cater for sexual depravity in all its forms. *Corporal Punishment, Whips and Fetters*, one promised. That's what happens when society starts to break down, thought Nina. When there's no respect for authority. You even have to pay someone to beat you. She foraged in her bag for her diary. In the booth next to her a man in overalls was taking down all the cards, painstakingly scraping off the stickers with a knife. By nightfall a fresh outbreak would have taken their place. He gave Nina a weary smile through the glass.

She found Kerry's number at last under G. For girlfriend, perhaps? What was their surname? She had written it down on the registration document when she'd sold them her car. No. Like so much lately it was quite beyond retrieval.

'Yes?' The phone was picked up immediately, before it had even rung at Nina's end.

'Oh!' said Nina, taken aback. 'Is that Mr . . . er . . .' – she almost called him 'Mr Bob' – '. . . Kerry's father?'

'Yes. Hello, James's mother.'

'Oh. How did you know it was me?'

'I recognized your voice.'

'Goodness.' Nina gave a nervous laugh. 'We've hardly spoken.'

'It's very distinctive.'

'Oh.' She was thoroughly wrong-footed now. The conversation had taken a flippant turn which didn't suit her purposes at all. 'I'm ringing because I'm afraid I've just discovered something rather alarming about James, and it may have implications for Kerry.' Now that he'd mentioned her voice she was bound to be self-conscious. It sounded plummy and artificial even to her ears.

'Really?' said Mr Bob, not joking any more.

'I think he's been injecting drugs.' There. She felt better already, just for having told someone. Simply saying the words seemed to give her the measure of the problem. There was a silence. 'Hello?' said Nina.

'Are you sure?' came the reply. 'That seems very unlikely to me, though of course you know him better than I do.'

'Well, I would have said it was unlikely myself.'

'I mean, they don't even smoke. Kerry does a lot of dance and sports – she's very against that sort of thing.'

'Well, yes, so is James, ostensibly. But perhaps that's just what they tell us. I mean, that's what they would say, isn't it?' Nina was feeling less sure of her diagnosis by the second. What if there was some innocent explanation? James would be furious with her for interfering. Mr Bob would think her a neurotic.

'Have you spoken to James?'

'No. I've just this minute found out. I saw the puncture marks on his arm this morning.' There had in fact only been the one, but Nina was prone to exaggeration in moments of self-doubt.

'Ah. Would you like me to talk to him?'

'No, no, I didn't want to drag you into this,' she said, then thought: yes I did.

'Oh that's all right. Drag away.'

'I didn't know who to tell – and I thought you'd probably have some experience of this sort of thing.'

'No. I'm very law-abiding, I'm afraid. It's an occupational hazard.'

'I didn't mean . . .'

'I know. I'm joking.'

'Oh.' Again Nina had a sense of the conversation slipping away from her. 'Right. Well, I suppose the only thing for it is to confront James.'

'Yes. I'll have a word with Kerry, too, just for reassurance. It's a question of choosing the right moment. Perhaps you'll let me know how you get on.'

'Of course.' The right moment be damned. Her motto was: Do it Now.

'There's the question of money, too,' said Mr Bob.

Nina wasn't listening. Her attention had been caught by one of the sex adverts on the wall above her head. The illustration was a bit fuzzy – a result of repeated photocopying – but it seemed to involve a girl in bondage gear and a golden retriever. Were there no limits?

'I'm sorry?' she said, standing on tiptoe to get a better look. It wasn't as bad as she'd feared: someone had in fact stuck a Guide Dogs for the Blind sticker over the girl's crotch.

'If he had a heroin habit he would need money.'

'I suppose I could check his account,' she said. 'I'll do that now.' She didn't relish the idea of snooping through his belongings, but her experiences with some of her clients had taught her that once children started on drugs they became crafty and devious. You had to fight guile with guile.

'Well, I hope your anxiety turns out to have been unnecessary,' Mr Bob was saying, attempting in the politest way to terminate the conversation. Nina took the hint and said goodbye, asking in passing if the car was still behaving. She wondered whether in a spirit of friendly co-operation she ought to mention the faulty rear seatbelt, but decided not to put herself at even greater disadvantage. Nina, whose telephone manner was usually so brisk and controlled, didn't feel she had acquitted herself particularly well.

She turned back to the tube and then changed her mind and hailed a taxi instead. It would cost a small fortune to get all the way back to Tooting, but she could always forgo some other luxury: this was potentially a matter of life and death.

James's room was, as usual, in a state of chaos and decomposition. Nina threw open the windows to let out the smell of trainers. She had replaced his hardbacked chair with a stool to prevent him using it as a clothes horse. Instead he now stuffed his clothes under one side of the bed, or threw them in the direction of the laundry basket to lie where they fell. On his bedside table were the ossified remains of a satsuma and half a cheese sandwich, dried to the texture of a loofah. Nina gathered up these and the four mouldy coffee-mugs from among the dead flies on the window sill and dumped them in the kitchen before beginning the hunt for his building society book. After a lengthy search, which inevitably evolved into a tidying up job, she finally spotted it, tucked into a perspex box of computer disks. Locked. He probably had the key on him, Nina thought, shaking the box in frustration. In fact it turned out to be sitting on top of the computer console – the only uncluttered surface in the room.

Nina picked it up to reveal a key-shaped stencil in the dust. The account book yielded up just the information Nina had feared: two recent withdrawals of one hundred pounds. It would have taken him a month of Saturdays in the supermarket to earn such a sum. The blood rose up in her cheeks in a hot tide of indignation. How had her handsome, intelligent, considerate son been reduced to this? She telephoned for another taxi with trembling hands.

❦

'What are you doing here?' asked James, standing up as his mother approached, not out of courtesy, but from a desire to waylay her and hustle her off somewhere more private. She had one of those carrying school-mistressy voices and a high embarrassment threshold: in his experience the two often went together.

'I must talk to you,' she said, more agitated than he'd ever seen her.

Bad news, he thought. Something's happened to Kerry. He abandoned his lunch unfinished and led her out of the refectory into one of the corridors. Nina grabbed his wrist and twisted it round so that the crook of his elbow was exposed. 'What's that?' she said, indicating the needle mark.

He looked at her with a combination of astonishment and dismay. She must have X-ray vision, he thought. She can penetrate brick and stone. 'If I tell you, you'll only be upset. Why do you keep trying to find out things you don't want to know?'

'You've been injecting drugs,' Nina said. 'I wasn't born yesterday, you know. I have worked with addicts before.'

James gaped. 'Mum. Have you gone mad?' He lowered his voice and said, rather fast and without looking at her, 'If you must know I had a blood test so that Kerry and I can have sex without using a johnny. She's had one too and they're both negative, so we know we're okay. And she's on the pill so you don't need to worry about her getting pregnant. Satisfied?'

'But . . . but . . .' Nina was completely taken aback. 'What about all the money you've been drawing out?'

'What money?'

'The two hundred pounds missing from your account.'

'Have you been going through my things?' he demanded, red in the face with anger.

'Yes. What about the money?' I've gone too far, thought Nina, cringing. James was more uptight than she had ever seen him. That was exactly it: he was both Up and Tight like an overpumped balloon. Any second now he might explode.

'I used some of it to pay my phone bill and I bought Kerry a gold chain for her birthday,' he said, when he had contained his fury. 'You are totally out of order, Mum. That book was in a locked box. I don't go looking in your handbag.'

'I've got no secrets,' Nina replied. 'In my handbag.'

'No life you mean,' James muttered, and then regretted it as he saw the frown gather on his mother's forehead.

'So if you've nothing to be ashamed of, why lock the book away?'

'Because I knew you'd think it was extravagant to spend a hundred quid on Kerry.'

Well it is, thought Nina. 'It's your money,' she managed. The relief which ought to have accompanied his explanation had not quite materialized. Instead she felt hot and bothered: James had obviously been engaged in free-range sex for some time, or why have a test? She herself had missed an important meeting without giving any warning; she had stooped to breaking and entering; she had revealed herself to be paranoid and naïve.

'And this is what happens when I try to act responsibly,' James said, palms up, addressing an imaginary third person – a recent habit which Nina found intensely irritating.

'So tell me again. You've never taken drugs.'

'No. Have you?'

Nina hesitated, contemplating a blatant lie. It had been different in the mid-seventies when she was at university. Everyone smoked dope: you were considered deviant if you didn't.

'Only marijuana. I never took acid or anything.' How quickly he had turned the tables. Here she was justifying something she had done eighteen, nineteen years ago.

'I don't believe it,' said James. 'You?' He couldn't quite absorb the image of his mother, who was so straight, as a dope-smoking hippie. He had seen her and his father in their panoramic college photo, so he knew what she had looked like then. But as with all old photos he couldn't believe that the subjects, those hairy men in tight shirts and flares, and women with centre partings and lank hair and platform boots, weren't just got up that way for the picture. They were surely smiling because they *knew* how freakish they looked. 'What was it like?'

'Nothing special. Anyway, it was different then,' said Nina. This wasn't what she had trekked back and forth across London to discuss. She had always wanted to be the sort of parent who was unafraid of difficult questions, who would be able to explain the facts of life on demand without a blush; who would not be evasive or embarrassed. What a vain endeavour that had proved. Perhaps since they were both in semi-confessional mood now was the time.

'I can't believe you're my mother sometimes,' James said, shaking his head. It wasn't clear from the tone of his voice whether this was a compliment or not.

'Well, believe it,' said Nina. That much, at least, was not in dispute. 'I'm sorry I went through your things,' she went on. 'I do trust you really.'

'Good. Can I go and finish my cold lunch now?'

'No,' said Nina. 'Let's find somewhere quiet where we can sit down. There's something important I want to tell you.'

9

Early in Nina's first term at UCL there was a residential field trip for first year geography students. They could choose one of two possible destinations – the Yorkshire Dales or the Forest of Dean – and were expected to devise their own research project. Equipment was provided and members of the faculty were on hand to offer advice and suggestions, but individuals were encouraged to work as independently as possible. Nina, whose school holidays had always been spent in whatever foreign country her father currently had a posting, had seen very little of England, and therefore approached this with a tourist's enthusiasm.

'When are you going to wear a bikini in Yorkshire in October?' Jean demanded, watching Nina packing her case on the morning of their departure. Jean had by way of luggage a small rucksack, of the size that might serve Nina as a handbag, containing underwear, spare jeans and jumper, toothbrush, tobacco pouch and a copy of the *I Ching*.

'I don't know. I thought there might be somewhere to swim,' Nina said, pulling the bikini out, along with several pairs of tights, with which it was now entangled.

'And what the hell's that?' Jean pounced on a circle of elasticated plastic with a lace trim.

'It's a bath hat,' said Nina, suddenly losing confidence in her domestic habits. 'You know, to keep your hair from getting wet.'

'A *bath hat*,' said Jean gleefully. 'I thought it was a pair of incontinence pants. You haven't got a bedjacket and slippers in there as well, have you?'

'No,' said Nina, who had in fact packed a pair of slippers *and* a dressing gown.

'You're going to have to carry that case from the station, you know,' Jean went on, closing it up and testing its weight.

'I think you'd better take everything out and start again.'

But Nina had been adamant that she couldn't do without half her wardrobe, her felt hat, platform boots with the silver stars, hairdryer, sponge bag, file-paper, camera, and all three volumes of *Gormenghast*. 'I speed read,' she explained, when Jean raised her eyebrows.

'I just speed,' Jean replied.

There was another reason for Nina's excitement and careful preparations: Martin. After that first meeting at the corridor party, she had decided calmly and rationally that he was The One, and that a swift transfer of affection from Jean to herself was urgently required. This wasn't as callous as it sounds: it was by no means established that Jean and Martin were a couple. Jean was usually draped over him, but Nina soon realized that she was like that with everybody, Nina included. They couldn't even have a chat without Jean gripping Nina's arm or pawing the front of her clothes. And Jean would never sit on a chair when there was an empty lap available; every time Nina went into the Academical Bar Jean seemed to be snogging someone or other.

'Are Jean and Martin actually going out?' Nina asked Fee, as casually as possible, when they were alone.

'Yes they are,' said Fee, 'but not heavily.'

So it was that while the other twenty-nine students hiked the two miles from the railway station to the hostel in the pouring rain with their rucksacks on their backs, Nina hitched a lift on a tractor, which took her luggage right up to the door.

The hostel had draughty single-sex dormitories with creaking iron bunk-beds and grey army blankets. The girls fought like eight-year-olds for the top bunks. There was curling lino on the floor and bathrooms without locks, and water which ran hot for the first thirty seconds and then switched directly to freezing. Downstairs was a recreation room with trestles and chairs, a dartboard but no darts, bar billiards, a ping-pong table and some chewed bats with shreds of pimpled rubber flapping against the plywood. Food was prepared by the resident staff in a huge kitchen where there was an enamel trough for washing up and, perversely, no shortage of hot water.

The nearest pub was two miles away, but the walk from the station had put people off and evenings tended to be spent in the hostel. The far-sighted had brought drink from home, and although this didn't outlast the first night, there developed a convivial bar-room atmosphere of smoking, card-playing and conversation. This generally centred around an ongoing billiards tournament and table-rugby, a variation of ping-pong played with the perished bats and a dented ball which bounced unpredictably. The food was execrable, creating an instant bond between those forced to experience it. For her first packed lunch Jean was given a spam sandwich and a hard-boiled egg with a blue-grey yolk. Nina, who had pretended to be a vegetarian to avoid the previous night's corned beef hash, had a sandwich made from an egg of the same vintage as Jean's, and a whole, raw, green pepper.

'What am I supposed to do with this?' she asked, unwrapping it and holding it up by the stalk. She, Martin and Jean were sitting on top of the limestone pavement at Malham Cove, eating a picnic in the driving rain. They were now so wet that any attempt to seek shelter was pointless, and besides, there was no shelter to be found on the exposed plateau.

'Do they expect me to eat it like an apple?' she asked, twirling it between finger and thumb.

'Save it,' Jean advised. 'You might be glad of it later. It could be curried marrow again tonight.'

Nina pulled a face. 'I wonder what they'll give me tomorrow lunchtime. An aubergine, perhaps.'

They had spent the morning measuring clints and grykes on the limestone pavement. In the afternoon Nina was planning to analyse the soil impaction on the pathway. She wasn't quite sure what she was going to do with all this data, meticulously collected and recorded. Every morning she would set off laden with equipment – clinometers, rulers, ranging rods, soil augers, quadrants – and return having reduced some feature of the landscape to a column of figures, without having any hypothesis in mind to which they might relate. Her tutor had not been particularly forthcoming. 'Look up some of the articles on your reading list; get inspired,' he'd advised, from his easy chair, before they'd left. 'I'm not going to spoonfeed you.'

'Here, give me that pepper,' said Martin, who was trying to smoke a limp roll-up in the rain. 'I think I've found a use for it.' He cut the stalk and seeds out with a knife and made a hole in the rounded end through which he threaded his cigarette so that only the filter protruded. 'There,' he said, putting it to his lips like a trumpet. 'An all-weather smoking shield.'

The general dissatisfaction with the catering was not entirely the whingeing of pampered youth. On the third night Nina was woken in the early hours by the sound of breaking glass followed by violent retching. Jean, in the next bunk, had wasted crucial seconds hunting for her torch which she had knocked on to the floor and smashed in the search. She had not quite made it to the door before throwing up over herself and the lino.

Nina, still half-asleep and confused, climbed out of bed and hurried over, fragments of shattered torch embedding themselves in her bare feet. Jean was doubled over by the wall, moaning and spitting. 'I'm dying,' she said, clutching her stomach. The sour smell of vomit made Nina gag. 'Don't move. I'll get a cloth,' she gasped, escaping on to the landing, where she took some gulps of fresh air. By the time she had helped Jean to mop herself up, and supplied her with a clean T-shirt, and a bucket from the kitchen, the rest of the dormitory was awake, several of them complaining of griping guts and nausea. 'It's just the smell,' said Nina, throwing open a window to admit a rush of foggy autumn air. She climbed back into bed, tucking the bristly blanket around her, and glanced at her watch. Three hours till dawn. As her head touched the pillow there came the sound of footsteps thundering down the landing from the men's dormitory, and the slam of the toilet door, and, as if that was the signal everyone had been waiting for, there was a sudden stampede.

The lights were thrown on, and all around Nina people were writhing and groaning on their beds or puking uninhibitedly in the communal bucket.

By morning the scale of the calamity was apparent and the culprit identified. Only those few, like Nina and Martin, who had had the macaroni cheese the night before were unaffected. The shepherd's pie was roundly condemned. Several people claimed to have detected a peculiar taste at the time, then backtracked as soon as the others began to rail at them for having said nothing. The invalids spent the day in bed, sipping water and comparing symptoms and degrees of affliction, vomiting intermittently and queuing outside the toilets.

Nina, with no such excuse to keep her in bed, had planned to return to Malham to finish her study of footpath erosion and to collect some soil samples. But on her way out of the dormitory, where she had been saying goodbye to a wan-faced Jean, she bumped into Martin, who was on the same errand.

'Wait a minute,' he said. 'I won't be long.' She watched him approach the sickbed where Jean was lying propped up on several of the miserly, underfilled pillows. Nina had just donated her own, and tucked the blankets around her tightly as if, she thought later, to prevent her from getting up. Martin smoothed the hair from Jean's forehead and squeezed her hand.

'Have fun,' she said, weakly, closing her eyes and turning her head away.

'Do you want to come and help me with my research?' Martin asked when they were outside.

'All right,' said Nina, pleased with this turn of events. 'Where are we going?'

'I thought I might hitch to Ribblesdale. Do some work on the three peaks. Have you got some decent shoes? We might have to do a bit of walking.'

Nina lifted a booted foot for his inspection. 'I don't mind walking.' In truth the sight and smell of all those poor sickly wretches in the hostel had made her feel better, fitter, more vigorous than ever. She felt, irrationally, that it wasn't pure chance that they'd been spared. It was destiny. 'Do we need any equipment?' she asked.

'No, no,' said Martin. 'Just ourselves.'

'In what sense could this be called research, exactly?' Nina asked later as they sat outside a pub in Austwick, sipping Guinness and admiring the scenery. It was a crisp October morning, warm in the sun, cold in the shade, with the smell of wet grass and woodsmoke in the air.

'Well,' said Martin, offering her a peanut. 'What we're engaged in here is a bit of environmental perception.'

'Oh? Meaning?'

'We look at the landscape and respond to it. Either positively or negatively, depending on our personal experiences, cultural background, education, etc. etc.'

'Is that all?'

'Yup.'

'It doesn't sound very scientific.'

'This is the way geography's going now. The quantitative revolution is over.'

'Is it?' said Nina, who wasn't aware it had even begun.

Martin nodded. 'It's no use reducing everything to formulae and devising models and systems any more. That sort of geography is . . . history.' He gave a sudden burst of laughter at his own joke.

Nina looked at him through narrowed eyes, wondering whether he was making fun of her.

'Come on, drink up. Another pub, another view, another valuable contribution to my dissertation.' He emptied his glass and pulled her to her feet. They hitched a ride in the back of a farm truck as far as Ingleton and then walked up to Thornton Force to see the falls, which Nina declared to be 'very nice'. Martin made a great show of writing this observation down.

'You're not getting much of a range of opinion here, are

you?' said Nina. As she led the way her boot slipped from under her on a mossy tree root and she stumbled. Martin caught her elbow and held her up until she was steady – and for a few seconds after that.

'It's not a survey. It's only your response I'm interested in.'

'You're making me blush,' said Nina. 'And I'm not the blushing type – too thick-skinned.'

'Perhaps it's all the confidence they dish out at those posh girls' schools,' said Martin, squinting at her.

'How do you know I went to a posh girls' school?' asked Nina, indignantly. 'I never said that, did I?'

Martin laughed. 'Only every time you open your mouth.'

'What's that supposed to mean?' said Nina, her cut-glass accent wavering slightly. This was the first time someone she actually knew had made fun of her voice, though on occasions she had noticed shop assistants and other functionaries sniggering. At school all the girls had spoken properly; so did the sorts of people her parents entertained from the embassy – even the foreigners. Especially the foreigners.

'It's just an observation, not a criticism,' said Martin. 'Please don't take offence.'

'None taken, I assure you,' said Nina, listening to her own pronunciation to see what other clues it could possibly be yielding.

'Do you want to walk behind the waterfall?' Martin asked, looking doubtfully at Nina's suede coat. 'Since we're here.'

'Is it necessary for your research?' she asked.

'No. But we're going to get wet either way.' He pointed back the way they had come at a lowering anvil-shaped cloud which was advancing across the expanse of clear sky towards them. As he spoke a gust of wind blew along the river valley, whipping the dead leaves up off the path in violent copper eddies, and bringing down still more from the branches above. Before the storm cloud was overhead the first flurry of raindrops fell, as if miraculously from the blue; there was a distant, low growl and suddenly it was as if a great black curtain had been drawn across the sun. 'Quick,' said Martin, making a dash for the shelter of a broad oak which grew on the bank alongside the path. There was a brilliant flash followed a second later by an explosive thunderclap.

'Not under a tree,' said Nina, as water started to pelt down with the force of a tropical monsoon. 'Not in a storm.'

'Where then?'

'Behind the waterfall.'

By the time they had slithered and scrambled across the rocks to the relative shelter of the overhang the path had become a running channel of mud and the splash of the waterfall had turned into a roar.

'Oh!' gasped Nina, flicking wet hair from her eyes. 'Next time I go on a field trip, remind me to choose somewhere hot and dry.'

❧

At Ingleton they found a pub with a log fire and sat in front of it, steaming, while they waited for their food to arrive. Nina tried to rub her hair dry on the roller towel in the Ladies. The drenching had made her skin look clear and dewy, though the ends of her fingers were shrivelled as if she had spent too long in the bath. She hung her dripping suede coat over the back of a chair where it created a puddle on the floorboards and presently began to give off a smell which Martin identified as 'beast'.

They had cowered under the waterfall until it became so swollen by rain that they were in danger of being knocked off the ledge. Wading back along the path had seemed the only option. When they at last reached the pub the rain running down Nina's neck had met up with the water being drawn up her jeans – the fabric acting as a wick. If she had been in any company but Martin's this would have prompted energetic complaint, but somehow, today, she could see the funny side of her predicament. Even when he gave her a playful shove and she had stepped up to her knee in a brimming pothole, she had laughed while she was swearing at him.

'I can't help feeling guilty,' she said, as their meal was

ferried to the table. 'Enjoying myself while the others are in bed, ill.' This was not entirely true: it was guilt at what she might go on to do which was troubling her. She broke her roll into little pieces and scattered them on the surface of her soup.

'I don't,' said Martin. 'I'm just glad it's not me. I hate being sick more than anything else.'

'Perhaps we should take something back for Jean,' Nina suggested. 'To show we've been thinking of her. Perhaps something that's made locally.'

'Wensleydale?' said Martin.

'I meant pottery. Or jewellery.'

They spent the afternoon browsing around the craft shops in Ingleton, all pretence at fieldwork abandoned. Nina, who liked to spend, and was in any case infected by the holiday spirit, bought a key ring, some argyll socks, a leather bookmark, and an embroidered sleeve patch of the Pennine Way.

'What are you going to do with that?' Martin inquired. 'Sew it on to your Girl Guide's uniform?'

'I always envied other children who had these on their anoraks,' said Nina. 'My mother said they were vulgar. They didn't sell them in the sorts of places I went on holiday anyway.'

'Such as?'

'Oh, Hong Kong, Singapore, Mombasa, you know.'

'Not really, no,' said Martin, whose family holidays had been spent in a caravan in Shanklin.

'It wasn't much fun stuck in some embassy compound. There were never any other children to play with,' said Nina, spinning a carousel of earrings beside the till while the assistant wrapped her purchases in tissue paper. 'That's nice,' she added, pointing to a gold St Christopher beneath the glass top of the counter. 'My father gave me one the first time I went on an aeroplane on my own. I used to wear it whenever I was travelling, but we had a break-in and it got stolen with all the rest of the valuables. I don't know whether Jean's got one, do you?' she added, conscious that it was, after all, Jean they were supposed to be shopping for.

Martin shook his head. 'I can't even remember whether she's got pierced ears.'

Oh really? thought Nina, encouraged by this admission.

'Here we are. This'll do,' said Martin, picking up an eight-ounce bar of Kendal Mint Cake, which didn't strike Nina as a terribly romantic gift. More the sort of thing you'd buy your granny. Better and better. 'She'll need building up when she's got her appetite back,' he went on, digging in his pocket for some change.

Nina left him to pay and continued on up the street, looking in the shop windows and grimacing at her bedraggled reflection. She was looking covetously at an earthenware coffee pot and wondering whether she would be able to get it home in one piece in her suitcase when Martin caught her up, slightly red in the face.

'Here,' he said, handing her a small box. 'A souvenir of today.'

It was the gold St Christopher. 'Oh, Martin, that's so kind of you,' cried Nina, delightedly. 'But when I said all that just now about losing mine, I didn't mean you to . . .'

'It was such a tragic story, I couldn't help myself,' said Martin, smiling at the effect of his attack of generosity.

'I'm going to put it on right now,' said Nina, gently disentangling the fragile chain. Martin lifted her hair free of her collar while she fastened the clasp and let the medallion drop down inside her jumper to rest coolly against her skin. 'I won't take it off and leave it lying around like the last one,' she promised. 'I'll wear it all the time. Even in the bath.' Martin raised his eyes at the thought of Nina in the bath. 'I feel luckier already,' she went on. 'Watch me get us a lift,' and she set off up the street with her thumb up and her arm stuck out into the traffic.

They walked four miles before someone picked them up. The sun had set suddenly in a blazing reef of pink clouds and the sky was now navy blue. The only light came from the window of a distant farmhouse and the occasional sweep of headlamps.

'Why isn't anyone stopping?' Nina demanded, pressing herself into the bramble hedge as another car roared past. She was slightly rattled because she had hoped Martin might try and kiss her once they were away from the town, but it didn't look as if he was going to, and now a van was pulling up and that was that.

'Kettlewell any good to you?' the driver said, cranking the window down.

Martin nodded. 'Good enough.' He held the door open for Nina to climb in.

'Shove the dog over the back,' the man said, indicating the sleeping Jack Russell on the bench seat beside him. Nina put out a tentative hand and the dog began to growl, curling up his black lips. 'Stop your moaning,' said the man, scooping the creature up in one hand and dumping him behind the seat on top of some lengths of copper piping and bags of tools.

Martin explained where they were staying. 'I can run you to the door no problem,' said the driver, but as they approached the turn-off to the hostel Martin signalled for him to stop. 'Just here will do.'

'What did you do that for?' Nina asked, as they stood on the grass verge watching the van's red tail lights weaving into the distance. There was still half a mile or so to walk.

Martin set off. 'Because I wanted to kiss you,' he said over his shoulder. 'And I didn't want to do it right outside the front door.'

'Oh,' said Nina, momentarily lost for words. Then, '*Wanted*?' she called after him.

He turned and they stood facing each other, twenty paces apart as if in a duel. It was so dark she couldn't make out the expression on his face, and when they started to walk towards each other it seemed to take a long time before they met in the middle. As Martin kissed her Nina felt something hard pressing against her stomach through the thickness of their coats. 'Blimey,' she thought, and when they finally broke apart Martin said, 'Excuse me,' rummaged in his pocket, and brought out the gift-wrapped bar of Kendal Mint Cake, crumpled and crushed beyond redemption.

10

Jane was in the park again, trying to walk off an ugly row with Harriet – the culmination of a stultifying day of sponge painting, flash cards and Lego. It had started so well, in the kitchen making shortbread, although Harriet would keep sneezing all over the mixing bowl, trying to eat slab margarine straight from the packet, and being generally unhygienic. But the biscuits had been finished, cooked and pretty much eaten by ten-thirty and there was still the rest of the day to be filled.

In spite of her best intentions to humour the child, play with her, keep her occupied and head off confrontations before they could escalate, a quarrel had blown up from nowhere. Jane had ventured to suggest that Harriet help her to tidy up the Lego before starting a new game. Harriet had refused, and pretty soon unfriendly words were being exchanged. It had ended, as usual, with a smack. Harriet had hit back – not an uncommon occurrence – but made worse this time by the fact that Jane was kneeling and the blow therefore caught her in the face.

'You horrible little child!' Jane had said at one point.

'You make me horrible!' Harriet blubbered, before running upstairs. She descended some time later holding a pair of scissors and a bald Barbie, and suffered Jane's remorseful hugs with her usual frigidity.

Someone had left a copy of the local paper on the counter at the kiosk. Jane glanced at the front page as she stood waiting to be served. Harriet was tearing around the playground outside, chasing pigeons, and setting the empty swings rattling.

BOY, 9, KEPT CHAINED LIKE DOG, ran the headline. This was the latest detail in an emerging saga Jane had been following on the regional news. Apparently a woman and her young son had been found living in conditions of unspeakable squalor, in an ordinary suburban house not two miles away, alongside half a dozen feral cats and the decomposing corpse of the woman's mother. The boy, who was unable to read, write, or speak coherently, had never been to school – a fact which had evaded all the relevant authorities. He had not, it seemed, been out of doors much at all in the preceding three years. The neighbours on either side had noticed nothing amiss.

Jane shuddered as she read the most recent revelations: the child had been found with a peculiar fungus growing on his skin caused by a chronic lack of sunlight. He had occasionally been let out to play in the back garden – a wilderness, the neighbours conceded, but then horticulture isn't everyone's thing – but only at night. The rest of the time he spent chained on a longish leash to the banisters, except when his mother made her fortnightly excursion to the dole office and the local supermarket, during which time he would be shut in the cupboard under the stairs. The matter was now in the hands of the social services, and arrangements were being made to try and rehabilitate mother and son together. Both had demonstrated genuine distress at the possibility of separation.

Jane tutted out loud. Right under our noses, she thought, taking her place at the front of the queue.

'How much to put a card in the window?' she asked the man behind the counter, raising her voice to compete with the roar of the chip fryer.

He flashed his fingers at her a few times. 'Fifty pence for one week.'

She slid her card and coin across the counter towards him. It read: *FOR SALE: pair of china alsatians, perfect condition, 110cms high. Any offers?* She and Guy had spent an enjoyable half-hour the previous night debating the wording of such an advertisement. Guy had originally been dubious about getting rid of the things altogether, fearing the inevitable parental inquisition, though he was as adamant as Jane that they were not having them on display. Even in a self-mocking, post-modern, 'so-bad-it's-good' capacity it was unthinkable. His natural inclination had been to stow them out of sight somewhere so that they could be retrieved in an emergency. Jane had demanded to know what sort of emergency he had in mind – the sudden arrival of the risen Auntie Muriel, perhaps?

'You could take them to school,' she had suggested, mischievously. 'They could go in the Smokers' Room.'

'As a deterrent, you mean?' said Guy. Only two members of his staff of twenty smoked. The other eighteen had voted to make the main common room a smoke-free zone, but still somewhere had to be provided for the pariahs to indulge their craving. It was thought to be undignified, and moreover a bad example to the children, for them to skulk outside, so a dingy cell of a storeroom had been given over for the purpose. Even this compromise didn't satisfy some of the eighteen, who resented yielding up valuable cupboard space for the pursuit of a vice. 'No, I don't think so,' Guy said to Jane. 'It's cramped enough in there as it is.' But at home as at school storage was at a premium, especially since the loft had become Guy's observatory.

Jane had finally swung things her way on ecological grounds. It was irresponsible to hoard something they didn't use and waste the planet's precious resources: tat should be circulated – that way, less of it would be produced.

The man in the kiosk took Jane's coin and shunted the card back to her and indicated that she should find a space on the board. She chose a slot in the FOR SALE section, noting the insalubrious character of the surrounding company. Really, she had never seen such creative spelling. Would anyone conceivably want their CV typed by someone who thought professional had two fs? And who on earth would trust a childminder capable of producing such a deranged script?

Moses basket, car-seat (0–6 months) and pram for sale. Never been used, ran one advertisement which caught Jane's eye. What tragedy lay concealed behind those few words? she was wondering, when her attention was drawn to a neatly written card – quite different in style from the desperate petitions for work or money alongside. A blush rose up into her cheeks as she read: *Would the red-haired woman who kindly looked after my baby here last Thursday when my son ran off please call me as a matter of urgency. Many thanks. Erica.* This was followed by a local telephone number.

Jane's first reaction was to step back sharply and guiltily from the noticeboard. What can she possibly want? Jane thought, casting her mind back to the previous Thursday and immediately assuming the worst. The baby had gone on to fall into a coma or develop brain damage, that was it. Harriet had clonked him on the head. She remembered it clearly now. Oh God.

She reread the message and began to calm down. Surely the woman wouldn't have used the word 'kindly' in such circumstances. Unless it was a trap: after all, who would respond to an appeal that said, *Will the redhead who injured my baby last week please get in touch*? Don't be ridiculous, Jane told herself. It was just a tiny bump. It hadn't even left a mark. I don't have to ring. I could quite easily not have come back to the park today, or ever, she thought, knowing all along that she would ring, and soon. Both her curiosity and her conscience were troubled – a formidable combination.

She allowed Harriet a scant half-hour on the swings and then lured her home with the promise of television in the afternoon. As soon as the child was settled in front of a School Science programme on magnetism, for eleven-to fourteen-year-olds, Jane shut herself in the kitchen and dialled the number that she had scribbled down on the palm of her hand. The click of an answering machine coming to life took Jane by surprise. She hadn't planned what to say and hated the thought of her improvised burblings being caught on tape. She was about to hang up when a voice said 'Hold on', over the top of the recorded message, and then 'Damn this bastard thing'; there was some more mechanical whirring and the high-pitched whistle of feedback, before the machine was finally disabled. 'Sorry,' said the voice. 'Are you still there?'

'Yes,' said Jane, recognizing the woman's Scottish accent.

'I saw your card in the café window. It was me who looked after your baby.'

'Oh, I'm so glad you've rung,' came the reply. 'You've no idea.'

'Is he all right?' stammered Jane.

'Who?'

'The baby.'

'Yes, fine. Why?' The woman sounded puzzled.

'No reason,' said Jane, almost laughing with relief.

'No. What I'm after is my newspaper.'

'Oh!' In her anxiety about the boy's health Jane had completely forgotten that business with the crossword.

'You took my newspaper. Or at least the front cover. I'm sure you had your reasons, but I need it back. Have you still got it?'

'I . . .' Jane had only a split second to decide whether to own up and explain or carry off a strenuous denial. Either way she was doomed: this Erica would think her a lunatic or a liar. 'I'm sorry,' said Jane, coming down marginally on the side of lunacy, 'you're going to think I'm a bit odd. I did take the cover, and it'll be in a bin somewhere here. I could probably fish it out if you need it, but it might be a bit gooey.'

'I don't care how gooey it is,' said Erica briskly. 'I wrote a telephone number in the margin and forgot to transfer it to my diary. And when I came back from the park and went to make the call the page was gone. So if you wouldn't mind going through your bins . . .'

'Of course,' said Jane, meekly. 'I'll do it now.' She laid the receiver down and hurried out to the back of the house where the dustbins stood, their lids balanced on top of bags of compressed rubbish. It was the day before they were due to be emptied, and an additional heap of plastic sacks had accumulated beside them, bloated and waterlogged from last night's rain. She couldn't understand how the four of them managed to generate so much trash. One day, she promised herself, she would investigate recycling. She selected a bag, estimating it to date from approximately the previous Thursday and pulled it open at the neck, reeling back from the smell of rotten food. There was the folded piece of newspaper, a corner of it just visible beneath a pile of old teabags, half a mouldy cucumber, a chicken carcase, and a layer of rice.

Jane was just about to put her hand into the bag to try and tweak the page free, when she noticed to her horror that what she had taken to be rice – which, come to think of it, they hadn't had for months – was in fact a mound of maggots. She dropped the edge of the bag in disgust; the contents duly subsided and resettled, burying the newspaper even further in the heaving, maggoty sludge. Jane dashed back into the kitchen, casting around for a suitable implement, all the while imagining the woman on the other end of the line, drumming her fingers in impatience. Finally, in her haste, she tipped the contents of the knife drawer out on to the draining board and seized from among the tangled metal a pair of barbecue tongs. With these she managed to extract several fragments of paper from the pulp but they had disintegrated too far for any text to be legible. Nevertheless she carried them at tongs' length into the kitchen.

'I'm so sorry,' she said into the receiver. 'It's all dissolved. It would take a forensic pathologist to get anything off here.'

'Bugger,' said Erica. 'It was a number to ring for cheap standby flights. Oh well.'

'I'm not a habitual thief,' said Jane, feeling that some plea of mitigation was necessary. 'I only took it because I'd pretty much finished your crossword while you were away, and I suddenly thought it would look a bit callous, if you really had lost your little boy. So I took the outside pages and stuffed them in my bag. It was totally out of character.'

'Ha.' Jane could hear her grin. 'That's the most pathetic excuse I've ever heard: it must be true.'

'I can only apologize,' Jane said.

'Ah well. Never mind. It can't be helped. No real harm done.'

'No,' said Jane, thinking of her barbecue tongs, which were going straight in the bin the minute she put the phone down.

'I've given up smoking, by the way,' said the woman, suddenly. 'After your sarcastic remarks.'

What's that to me? thought Jane, who couldn't remember having made any sarcastic remarks on that or any other subject. Instead she said, 'I'm glad I've done something useful. Goodbye.' As soon as she had hung up, Jane resealed the maggoty bag and then washed her hands under scalding water, scrubbing and scrubbing them until they felt raw and clean.

When Guy came home from his school open evening, with a pounding headache, his face stiff from two hours of smiling, he found the ground floor of the house in a state of confusion.

Having fed and bathed the girls, read them a story and put them to bed on her own Jane had set about tidying away their clutter from the living room so that the space could be reclaimed for an hour or so of civilized relaxation. Once this was done she had hit upon the idea of rearranging the furniture to make the room look bigger, but whichever way she tried it one of the armchairs always ended up adjacent to the television, and effectively redundant. She had then tried removing the spare chair altogether, putting it in a corner of the dining room, which was seldom used except on Sundays, or for entertaining of which they did little.

It was while standing by the French windows looking out at the twilit garden which was beginning to show patches of spring colour, that Jane was struck with the idea that this really was much the nicer of the two rooms and was wasted in its current role. It would make altogether better sense to swap the contents over so that the general living area overlooked the garden rather than the street and the row of Victorian semis opposite. Gripped by sudden enthusiasm for change, Jane had dragged the dining table into the hallway, scoring some deep grooves into its legs as she negotiated the door frame, and effectively blocked the progress of any further traffic. Realizing that she would have to create some space in the former sitting room, she had begun to shift some of the bulkier items – the couch, the bureau, out into the hall where they ran up against the table creating a gridlock.

By the time Guy put his key in the door, tired and tense and longing to sit down, both rooms had been evacuated and the contents stacked in two pyramids at the bottom of the stairs, each one blocking the other from its destination. Indeed the front door itself would only open a foot or so before coming to rest against the video cabinet, so Guy had been forced to insinuate himself through the gap sideways, briefcase first.

'What's going on?' he asked in dismay, looking across to the empty sitting room where Jane stood, imprisoned. She had just been thinking how easy it would all have been if only their hall had one of those revolving floors like the stage at the National Theatre.

'Oh, you're back,' she said. 'I've got myself into a bit of a pickle.' On occasions like this when she required deliverance from a predicament of her own making she tended to revert to the language of childhood. In normal circumstances Guy was happy to collude with this pretence of female helplessness, but tonight he was exhausted, and the modest fantasy he had been entertaining on the way home, of unwinding in front of the TV, wine glass in one hand, wife in the other, now lay in smithereens.

'I was just swapping the rooms over,' Jane explained.

'Any particular reason?' asked Guy, taking off his jacket and hanging it over a standard lamp, which now stood between him and the coat hooks. He could just see the television, there at the bottom of the heap. There were ten minutes until the News.

'I thought it would be better. But it was a two-man job, really.'

Now suddenly I'm to blame for not having been here! thought Guy. 'Well, in that case why didn't you wait until there were two men available to do it?' he said patiently. He didn't want to get into an argument. He just wanted the television and a chair within range of a plug socket, soon.

'It was the inspiration of the moment,' said Jane. 'I think we just need to pass things across to each other,' she went on, as if they were discussing a bag of groceries rather than a three-piece suite.

It took eight minutes, under Guy's management, to restore order to the ground floor. The furniture was returned to its original positions and the changeover deferred to another day. 'Have you eaten?' he asked, as the last chair was shunted back into place. He was hoping that the answer would be No and that there might be something tasty simmering on the stove, although this wasn't their usual arrangement if he was late.

'Yes,' said Jane. 'I had a Chicken Dinosaur with the girls.'

A chicken dinosaur? thought Guy, wondering what Mr Sharpearrow would think of this.

'I could make you something,' Jane added, without much conviction.

'No, it's all right.' On those evenings when he wasn't back in time to eat with the whole family he was supposed to take care of himself. He glanced at his watch. Two minutes until the News. 'I'll grab something,' he said, forgetting that it was the day before Jane shopped and that provisions would be low. In any case she had become so parsimonious lately that there was never much in the cupboards in the way of slack. Every item seemed to have its designated place in the week's menu, so that it was impossible to knock up, say, a poached egg, without compromising some future meal. Miraculously there was a wedge of cheddar in the door of the fridge. Guy took it, an apple and a couple of paracetamol back into the sitting room. He would have to encourage Jane to be less thrifty with the groceries. Not now, though, because there was only one minute to the News and he didn't want to get into a discussion about money or anything else until it was over. As usual the remote control gadget was missing. In a state of mounting frustration, Guy located it down the side of the couch, pulling out a handful of Lego in the process. As the dying notes of the theme tune gave way to the first chime of Big Ben, Jane came in with her cup of tea and sat down.

'*New wave of terror closes down city*,' read the announcer in a melodramatic voice.

'Harriet hates me,' said Jane.

Guy sagged in his chair. They had had this conversation, or variations of it, a thousand times and he had no wish to rehearse it now. 'No she doesn't. She's just a three-year-old. They're like that.' He tried to keep the tone light and sympathetic. With any luck he could head this one off before it developed into a full counselling session.

'She slapped me round the face today.'

'Why?' asked Guy, keeping one eye on the television. The cameras roved across a deserted station concourse. Another bomb hoax. His finger hovered over the volume switch as he considered whether he might get away with turning the sound up a fraction.

'Because I smacked her. It's a long story.' She started to tell it, nevertheless, with her usual gabbled delivery. Guy nodded occasionally to signify interest, at the same time as trying to tune in to the news report which had moved on to cover the atrocities in the former Yugoslavia. There on their doorstep a country was tearing itself apart, neighbour against neighbour. The village from which the war correspondent was sending his report of a massacre of Muslim families looked much like those he and Jane had driven through on a touring holiday before the children were born.

He looked sharply back to Jane whose mouth was still opening and shutting. It was harder than he'd imagined, listening to two conversations at once. Those people who did simultaneous translations at the UN and other international summits really earned their money, he was thinking, as he caught up with Jane. She seemed to have moved on from Harriet and was relating some incident concerning the theft of a newspaper, a woman with a missing baby, and some maggots.

'She must have thought I was mad,' she finished. 'Anyway, I've chucked out the barbecue tongs.'

Guy let the remark pass. There was no way he was going to untangle that one without admitting he hadn't been paying attention.

'She's so aggressive?' Jane went on.

'Who?' said Guy, still trying to picture the maggot woman.

'*Harriet*,' said Jane, impatiently. 'And she never shows me any affection. Even when she's hurt herself she doesn't want a cuddle.'

'Not everyone likes physical contact,' said Guy, without taking his eyes off the screen. His finger came to rest on the volume switch and he eased the sound up infinitesimally. There was an item on about rising crime and delinquency among under-twelves. Another excuse to bash primary schools; he could see it coming. Sure enough some member of the Right was wheeled on to deliver the usual lecture about family values and the evil of sixties-style trendy teaching methods, while a representative of the Left blamed unemployment and government cuts in services. The headmaster of an inner-city junior school, an excessively nervous, twitching individual, was invited to add his comments. It was hard to imagine him as the victorious candidate in any interview line-up. Where do they find them? Guy wondered. Fortunately Jane seemed to have gone quiet. He looked over at her and saw that she was resting her chin on one hand, and that her eyes had that foggy, pre-tears expression.

'What's the matter, darling?'

She shook her head and a tear rolled off her eyelashes on to her cheek. She knocked it away with a flat hand. 'Nothing. You're not listening.'

'I am, I am,' he said, flustered. 'It's just that there was this thing on about schools' – he pointed at the television – 'and I got distracted.'

'Who can I talk to about things, if not you?' she said miserably.

'You *can* talk to me.' He hit the off switch and there was a pop as the screen went blank. Now he would never know whether or not grape skins offered any protection against cancer. 'Talk away,' he said, in what he fancied to be a tone likely to encourage confidences.

The phone rang. 'That'll be your mother,' said Jane, as she always did, with only about fifty per cent accuracy.

'That is the most futile comment I've ever heard,' said Guy, standing up. 'The fact is, we don't know who it is until we answer it.'

'No, no, I'll get it,' said Jane, who was nearer the door. Guy heard her pick up the receiver in the kitchen and say 'Yes?' in a brusque voice which gave way to something softer and more polite, indicating to Guy that it was not a close friend. 'Oh really? . . . Yes, he has mentioned you actually . . . I'll just get him.'

She came back into the room with the self-satisfied expression of someone with news to relate.

'Well, who is it?' said Guy.

'The infamous Hugo Etchells,' Jane replied. 'He's coming home.'

II

When Jane was fifteen a French student called Séverine arrived at her school on a year's secondment from university in Lille, to hold conversation classes. She had long, black, corkscrew curls, tied back with a scrap of lace, wore a leather jacket and tasselled skirts and smelled of tobacco and incense and perfume unavailable in Worthing. In the summer she exposed, without embarrassment, legs and armpits untouched by a razor. Occasionally her long-haired boyfriend would come over to visit for the weekend and whisk her away from the school gates on his motorbike in a cloud of exhaust and cigarette smoke. She brought copies of *Paris Match* for the girls to read and discuss – a tantalizing combination of gruesome photographs and impenetrable French journalese. Celebrity gossip rubbed shoulders with close-ups of victims of gangland executions and fatal car crashes; the lessons were never dull.

Séverine seemed to take a liking to Jane, and often lent her additional reading matter – *Les Fleurs du Mal*, or *Thérèse Desqueyroux* – with which Jane struggled, dictionary in hand. Jane reciprocated this attention by trying to imitate Séverine's loopy, continental handwriting, and wearing knee-length whiskery sweaters, and smudged black eyeliner, and smoking out of her bedroom window. This last pursuit was curtailed when her mother leaned out of the window one day to shake out a duster and saw that the guttering was full of butts. Until this point Jane had wasted much of her precious youth trying to comb, blow-dry and iron her Pre-Raphaelite curls straight. Now she let them dry naturally into ringlets and tied them back, like Séverine, into a loose, low ponytail. (As soon as she had children, of course, all the curl would fall out and she would spend even more time and money trying to restore it.)

One afternoon the subject under discussion was marriage:

pour ou contre. The consensus seemed to be that it was an outmoded convention designed to protect male interests and had no relevance in modern society. The debate had more or less ground to a halt when Jane, who often found herself in these lessons venturing opinions that weren't really hers, but were dictated by the vocabulary at her disposal, said, 'I'm going to marry for money.' It was just a silence-filler, quite untrue to Jane's character: at fifteen she had no great interest in either money or marriage. Séverine turned on her, fixing her with smoky eyes, and pointing a blunt fingernail, and like a gypsy laying a curse, said, 'No. You will marry a poor man for love. And you will struggle.'

Of course the few men Jane went out with and thought herself in love with at university in Canterbury were poor: students were always broke – it went without saying. They wore horrible coats from Oxfam, and lived on beer and kebabs and shivered in unheated rooms, and worked all summer just to get their bank balance back up to zero again.

Then, when Jane started work as an administrative officer for the NHS, in a community unit back in Sussex, most of the other staff had been women, and she would have been happy to set eyes on an eligible man between Monday and Friday, rich or poor. She was living in a house in Brighton at this time, with an old friend she had known since nursery school – Suzanne – who commuted to a job at a London advertising agency. Having grown up in the area, their circle of friends was quite large, and weekends would be spent shuttling between wine bars, restaurants, and dinner parties. Suzanne was usually in the process of falling in or out of love with some man or other, apparently favouring relationships of violent intensity but brief duration, and Jane was often called upon to provide emotional support, or diversionary entertainment during these many crises. Even as a child Suzanne had preferred quantity to quality, Jane remembered; she had had six imaginary friends to Jane's one.

It was in the aftermath of one of these parties – held to give Suzanne an excuse to invite her latest quarry, a minor aristocrat who had just lost his fortune in a casino – that Jane met Guy. It wasn't love at first sight, exactly, but he certainly made an impression: it wasn't every day Jane found a naked man leaping around in the kitchen. He had come along as a friend of a friend of one of Suzanne's cast-offs, but he had arrived late when the flat was already heaving, and Jane hadn't come into his orbit. If he hadn't got drunk and missed the last train and dossed down on Suzanne's floor under a pile of coats they might never have met at all.

Although Jane was used to Suzanne's habits by now, she was nevertheless taken aback when she came downstairs the next morning to find a strange man in the kitchen, wearing her own tartan dressing gown and trying to light the electric hob with a match. He was tall – at least six foot, and built like a rugby player. His dark hair was short and sleek at the back, like moles' fur, longer and scruffier on top.

'Hello,' he said, looking up. He was hungover and unshaven, but good-looking in an accidental sort of way. Jane wondered how she had failed to notice him the night before. 'I'm trying to make bacon and eggs, but I can't get the cooker to light. There's obviously a knack to it.' He struck a second match towards himself and the burning head flew off and buried itself in the tartan fleece which began to smoulder. He tried to brush it off but it was already melting through the material. He gave a cry of pain as it reached bare skin, tore off the dressing gown, and jumped up and down on it, goose-flesh naked in the grey kitchen, while Jane stood looking on, laughing in astonishment.

'That's my dressing gown you're . . . not wearing,' she pointed out at last, handing him a PVC apron which was hanging on the back of the door. He tied it round his waist, though it was a little late for modesty by this time and in any case the backless red PVC looked even kinkier. He picked up the matches. '*Little Devils*?' he said, reading the name on the box. 'Little bastards, more like.'

'May I?' Jane reached past him and flicked a switch and the electric ring began to glow orange.

'Ah.' He looked sheepish, and then, remembering his manners, held out his right hand. 'I'm Guy, by the way.'

'Jane,' said Jane, and they shook hands. 'You wouldn't be the gambling aristocrat?' she asked, feeling sure he wasn't.

'I'm afraid not,' said Guy. 'Do I look like one?'

'No,' said Jane, taking in his bizarre state of undress. 'You look like a right idiot.' And they grinned at each other, and at the absurdity of their starting to fall in love like this, in a kitchen, surrounded by empty bottles and full ashtrays and the detritus of a party at which they hadn't even met.

After breakfast they cleared up the house and went for a walk along Brighton beach. They threw stones into the freezing February surf and ate chips on the pier and Guy wasted a pocketful of change in the amusement arcade, just to prove that he could gamble with the best of them, if required. The cold wind blew away Guy's hangover and whipped the party smoke from Jane's hair and they came back with raw red faces and earache, but tingling in every fibre. In the evening they tried to make some mulled wine without a recipe, but it was peppery and disgusting, and the more sugar and lemon peel and cinnamon they threw in the worse it tasted, and the funnier they found it. Suzanne came in and asked Guy to help shift a chest of drawers in her room, as she'd lost an earring behind it. While he was upstairs Jane put the sitting room clock back by half an hour so that he would miss his train again. And this time there was no question of him sleeping under coats on Suzanne's floor.

12

Tap tap tap, went the new boy's shoes along the corridor. His grandmother had hammered in the metal heel reinforcers the night before, as soon as she'd finished sewing Cash's name-tapes into his uniform.

The tapping stopped outside the classroom and Guy looked up from the page of *Ecce Romani!* to see the door open and the housemaster usher in a short, plump boy with red cheeks and spectacles thick as paperweights.

Mr Granger, the Latin master, paused in the act of writing out a grid of noun endings on the blackboard, and said, half turning, but still keeping the chalk in contact with the board, 'This must be Etchells. *Salve Etchelle.*' He pointed at the empty desk next to Guy. '*Sede prope Bromelovium.*' The housemaster withdrew, his mission accomplished. There were some sniggers as Etchells looked blank and didn't move, the red of his cheeks deepening a shade. 'Translation: sit next to Bromelow.' This was greeted with more sycophantic laughter.

Guy, remembering his own first week and the humiliation of having no plimsolls for gym, gave the newcomer an encouraging smile and nodded towards the seat beside him. He was already starting to feel sorry for the poor thing, imagining the torments that were sure to follow. Short, fat, half-blind, and saddled with the name *Eggshells*. Indeed he did rather resemble Humpty Dumpty as he tapped his way across the classroom towards Guy and squeezed into the vacant seat. The illustration in Guy's hardback *Mother Goose*, now suddenly recalled, showed Humpty Dumpty lying at the bottom of a wall in pieces, the fragment containing his face frozen in an expression of shock. When his mother had explained it was just an egg, Guy, aged four, had said, 'Why did someone think horses would be able to mend it?'

The Latin master, leading a chant of '*puella, puellam, puellae, puellae, puella*', took a pale green exercise book from his drawer and slapped it on the new boy's desk. On the front were four ruled lines in a box. 'Name, form, house, subject,' he said, breaking into the middle of his chant without any variation in tone.

Guy watched the boy produce an ancient, chubby fountain pen – just like the one Guy's father used for what he called his 'paperwork' – from his blazer pocket, and shake it violently before filling in the box in writing so minute as to be barely legible:

Hugo Blanchard Etchells
1G
Cranmer
Latin

The houses were all named after famous martyrs. The school motto, embroidered on the blazer badge, was *Ad astra per aspera*: 'through strife to the stars'.

Mr Granger gestured to Guy to wait behind at the end of the lesson. 'Keep an eye on Etchells, will you?' he said, gathering up a pile of books and stowing them in a scuffed briefcase. 'Show him the ropes.'

Guy had an image of the thick white ropes hanging from the wallbars in the gym where Miles Henderson had been made to stand on a stool with his head in a noose. He knew why *he* had been chosen to watch over Etchells-not-Eggshells. Because he was the tallest in the class, and popular too: not someone who was picked on. 'He might be feeling a bit lost. His mother's just died, poor fellow. That's just between ourselves.' He snapped the jaws of the briefcase together and a little puff of chalk dust escaped. 'Good lad.'

And while I'm standing here listening to you, They've probably got him already, Guy thought. There was no sign of him in the common room or the playground. Guy finally tracked him down at the furthermost corner of the field where he was beheading mushrooms with a stick.

'We're not supposed to come right to the fence,' said Guy, as kindly as possible.

'Why not?' said Etchells, pausing momentarily before resuming his attack on the mushrooms. 'What's the point of putting the fence there then?' He had a strange accent which Guy didn't recognize.

'I don't know. It's the rules.'

Etchells looked disgusted. 'What a stupid place this is.'

'Mmm,' said Guy, non-committally.

'I was supposed to be going to Winchester, but my father lost a packet last year so I've got to come to this dump instead.'

'Where are you from?' asked Guy. 'You don't sound English.'

'South Africa. My father's got a farm out there. But my grandparents are in Cheltenham. And my mother now.'

'Oh,' said Guy, confused. Perhaps Mr Granger had misinformed him.

'She's buried there, I mean,' Etchells went on. 'But she always wanted me to go to school in England. And I'd rather be where she is, dead, than where my father is alive, if you see what I mean.' He gave a short bark of laughter, which confirmed Guy's suspicion that he wasn't joking.

'What did she die of?' asked Guy, who was interested in other people's tragedies.

'A car crash.' Etchells felt in his inside blazer pocket and produced a small colour photograph which he handed carefully to Guy. It showed a dark-haired woman in a pink suit and sunglasses. She was sitting on a five-bar gate and smiling at the camera. Guy nodded sympathetically and handed it back. Across the grass he could see some of his friends kicking a ball around, and wished he was with them, instead of looking after this sad podge.

'Do you want to play football?' he asked, thinking even as he said it that he'd be hopeless; they'd have to put him in goal.

'No thanks,' said Etchells. 'I hate football. I hate all sport.'

Ungrateful too, thought Guy. 'Fair enough,' he said.

'You don't have to stay and talk to me just because you've been told to,' said Etchells, poking the earth with a twig. 'I don't mind being on my own. I'm used to it.' He looked up at Guy through his thick spectacles. They were so powerful that his face behind them was reduced to a fraction of its width, as though someone had taken a bite out of each temple.

'It's all right,' said Guy, embarrassed. In the distance a bell rang for end of break and they joined the general drift back towards the building. They would be the last to cross the playground, and very probably late for the next lesson. As they came closer Guy could see one of Them, the worst one, Michaelson, standing just inside the doorway, watching their approach.

'Not that way,' said Guy, pulling Etchells's sleeve and tacking off towards the library.

'Why? We need to go in there,' Etchells protested.

'Michaelson's there,' Guy whispered, with his head down. 'Don't look!' he hissed, as Etchells stared at the figure in the shadows. 'It's best not to walk past him.'

'Not walk past him? Why the hell not?' demanded Etchells, his cheeks reddening with indignation.

'It's best to keep out of his way. He'll only start taking it out on you,' Guy advised, but Etchells was already striding towards the door on his short, fat legs, his metal heels ringing on the concrete.

'Excuse me,' he said to Michaelson, who had moved to block his way in. Michaelson didn't move. 'I said "excuse me",' Etchells repeated a little louder. Guy tacked off round the other side of the library, muttering to himself, 'Stupid idiot. Serves him bloody well right.' As he reached the cloisters he heard Etchells roar 'EXCUSE ME!' in a voice that was audible all over the school. Guy sprinted round the back way in time to see several classroom doors open and alarmed teachers emerging. Michaelson was forced to retreat and Etchells, flustered but victorious, stepped over the threshold.

Guy was simultaneously elated and dismayed. The trouncing of Michaelson was something he would have given a lot to witness, but poor old Etchells was now done for. It would take all Guy's vigilance to keep him from some terrible retribution. Guy wasn't sure he was up to it: he had devoted much energy to the art of avoiding intimidation, and now here he was attached to someone bent on making himself conspicuous.

It didn't take Them long to catch up with Etchells. Guy had tried his best, but he couldn't shadow him every minute of the day, and the moron hadn't a clue when it came to self-preservation. If someone had left a blazer or bag on a bench where he wanted to sit down, well, Etchells would just dump it on the floor and sit down. If he knew all the answers in class, which he generally did, his hand would be the first up, whoosh, every time. And when one of the masters said, 'Right, if no one owns up, the whole class will be on litter duty,' Etchells would grass *immediately*. 'It was Otterwell, sir.' Really, he had no idea.

A week or so after this incident Guy had to spend his morning break in the chemistry lab, sweeping up the broken glass from a rack of test-tubes he had accidentally knocked off one of the benches on his way out. The science teacher had hauled him back by the collar of his blazer and handed him a broom before he had a chance to apprehend Etchells and tell him to wait. By the time the job was done the bell was already ringing to signal the start of the next lesson, but Etchells failed to show up, and the desk beside Guy remained ominously unoccupied.

Guy's sense of unease turned to anxiety when there was no sign of Etchells at lunch: he liked his food and would not willingly have missed a meal. Guy bolted his plate of ox-heart and cabbage, nearly gagging on the string that held the shrunken parcel together, and then, forgetting he had rugby practice, set off to find him. A tour of the obvious places – the sick bay, the field, the cadets' hut, the back of the cricket pavilion, the wheelie bins where they had found that poor bastard, whatshisname, sitting amongst the garbage – all yielded nothing. Finally, as a last resort, Guy tried the toilets, though he had instructed Etchells never, ever, to go in there alone at break time. He pushed open the door and a gust from the open windows caught it and flung it hard back against the side of the urinals with a crash. There didn't seem to be anyone about, but one of the doors was closed.

'Etchells?' he hissed.

'Bromelow? I'm in here,' came the familiar accented voice from the occupied cubicle. 'They've got my clothes.'

'What do you mean?'

'They've taken my clothes. You'll have to find me some.'

'What are you wearing?'

'My shoes and socks.'

Guy was seized with pity. He could imagine Etchells's flabby form, clad only in shoes and socks, perched on the toilet seat, helplessly awaiting rescue.

'Are you, you know, all right?'

'They didn't beat me up if that's what you mean,' said the voice.

'Don't worry, Hugo.' He had never used his Christian name before, and couldn't think what had prompted him to do so then. 'I'll get you some clothes.' If only you weren't so fat, you could have borrowed some of mine, he couldn't help thinking.

'Guy,' said Hugo as he was leaving.

'Yes?'

'Would you mind shutting the window. It's a bit cold.'

It was while engaged on this errand that Guy came across most of Hugo's clothing, screwed up and stuffed on top of the cistern in one of the empty cubicles. He climbed on to the toilet seat and retrieved it, brushing off the dust and cobwebs as best he could. Hugo's trousers were still missing – in a bin somewhere, no doubt. 'Here.' He shoved the bundle under the locked door.

'Don't look!' yelped Hugo.

'I'm not,' Guy protested. 'Look at what?'

'Me. Nothing,' Hugo mumbled. And then, 'They've

taken the photograph. It's not in my blazer pocket.' Guy could hear the fury in Hugo's voice beginning to dissolve into self-pity. Any minute now he'd be in tears.

'Wait. I'll find it.' He dived back into the cubicle where he'd turned up the clothes: there it was on the floor, face down in a pool of – well, best not to think about it. Guy picked it up and wiped it on the roller towel beside the basin. The edges looked a bit soggy and stained, but the image was still intact. He passed it under the door and felt Hugo take it gently from his fingers.

'I'll go and find you some more trousers now, okay,' said Guy, but there was no reply.

It was only later that evening as they were undressing for bed that Guy discovered what it was Hugo hadn't wanted him to see. Through a gap in the curtains dividing their beds he caught a glimpse of Hugo's bare back before he pulled on his pyjama jacket. They had drawn all over him with a black marker pen: dotted lines, like a butcher's diagram of a pig, showing the different cuts of meat.

Hugo was more inclined to take Guy's advice after that, though he retained a dangerously sociopathic streak. It wasn't that he went looking for trouble, but he seemed to lack the ability to read situations correctly, and couldn't scent confrontation until he was in the thick of it. He was by far the cleverest boy in the class, but made no attempt to disguise it, in fact became openly impatient with the others for not keeping up. Guy, on the other hand, who had no problem with academic work, made sure his achievements were less ostentatious.

Being with Hugo put Guy in mind of trips to the park with his parents' plump, aggressive Jack Russell, Porky. One could never quite relax in case he suddenly decided to take on a Dobermann or a couple of alsatians. Guy couldn't count the times his father had had to wade into the middle of some affray and beat off half a dozen vicious dogs to rescue that unrepentant mutt. That was how it was with Hugo – you got no thanks for imperilling yourself. He was loyal like a dog too; having latched on to Guy he showed no inclination to exert himself to make other friends. If Guy was otherwise occupied he was just as happy on his own, digging up worms from the margins of the field or conducting bizarre experiments with equipment filched from the labs. One lunchtime Guy found him in his favourite spot, as far from the school building as possible, in the out-of-bounds area between the sports pitches and the fence, holding one of the lenses they'd been using in physics to study parallax, above a pile of dried skeleton leaves. A white dot of winter sun was focused on the centre of the leaf, which presently began to smoulder and then burst into flames.

'What are you doing?' Guy asked.

'Just practising,' said Hugo. 'For when I burn this place to the ground, and everyone in it.'

'Oh?' said Guy, somewhat slighted by this remark.

'Not you, of course,' Hugo conceded. 'Everyone but you.'

'You'll need more than a lens and some dead leaves,' Guy laughed, trying to lighten the tone. Hugo's fantasies often involved an element of violence, like slipping some deadly toadstools into the school mince, or dispatching his enemies with an icicle through the heart. Guy knew better than to say 'Go on then: you wouldn't dare.'

'I know,' Hugo said seriously. 'I'd need petrol, or some other inflammable solvent.'

Fortunately for the other five hundred or so pupils and masters, Hugo's dreams of arson didn't translate into reality: the following term he had so far outstripped his classmates in academic performance that he was moved up a year. And soon after that his father enjoyed a reversal of whatever financial predicament had put Winchester out of their reach, and Hugo was duly transferred to that establishment, and vanished, temporarily at least, from Guy's life.

13

There were dozens of books about sex in the reference section of the library – how to do it better, more interestingly, everything you ever wanted to know about it, but nothing at all about giving it up. The fact that all this information and advice was to be found in the Health section troubled Jane. The inference that she was the one who was sick, while the exhibitionists, sadomasochists and reckless experimenters, whose case histories she had just been reading, were normal, fit and flourishing, was galling in the extreme.

She hadn't always felt this way: there was a time, at the beginning of any new relationship, and particularly when she had first met Guy, when sex had seemed like a Good Thing and she had been quite the enthusiast. But her pregnancies had subtly changed her attitude to her own body – she had fallen out of love with herself, even if Guy hadn't. Once her reproductive duty was done she couldn't help feeling that further, purely recreational sex was an irrelevance – an imposition, even, when she was so tired and so put upon. Unfortunately Guy didn't seem to be similarly disposed, and Jane's increasing physical aloofness, far from discouraging him, only seemed to have made her more desirable. There were avoidance tactics, of course: going to bed considerably earlier or later than Guy, or making allusions to migraines, exhaustion or protracted and heavy periods usually did the trick. As an absolute last resort she might engineer a mini-quarrel before bedtime. There was generally plenty of material. For example, his unilateral offer to put up this long-lost friend, Hugo, for an indefinite period over the summer.

'He can sleep in the spare room,' Guy had said, dismissing her look of outrage.

'We haven't got a *spare* room,' she replied. 'It's a room full of boxes. In constant use. What's wrong with a hotel?'

'Well, they're expensive for any length of time.'

'How long is he staying, for God's sake?'

'I don't know. Until he finds a place. I felt sorry for him. His contract at the university hasn't been renewed, his wife's kicked him out . . .'

'You could have consulted me first. From what you've told me about him he sounds a completely undesirable house guest. His wife may have had good reasons.'

'All right, all right. Next time he phones I'll tell him to doss down on the Embankment.'

The Hugo affair wasn't entirely resolved by that little exchange, but it had got her out of having sex.

Jane often wondered whether her problem might have resolved itself early on if only there had been someone she could have talked to about it. Guy himself, who was her confidant and adviser in most matters, was out of the question. The one time she had experimented with sexual honesty and told him she sometimes wrote the weekly shopping list in her head while they were making love had been a terrible mistake which she was forced to retract immediately and pass off as a joke. Her parents, dead for some years, would never have been contenders for a heart-to-heart on this subject. And her oldest friend, Suzanne, who was frequently on the end of Jane's bellyachings about the children or the in-laws, was far too indiscreet for this sort of confession, and was in any case a nymphomaniac and unlikely to empathize. Only the other day Suzanne had phoned to invite her to what Jane misheard as a 'Laundry Party', but which turned out to be a 'Lingerie Party'. Once this error was cleared up it hadn't cost Jane a pang to invent a prior engagement. She could well imagine the minute shreds of scratchy lace which they would be encouraged to snigger over and ultimately buy. 'Besides,' she'd added, testing the water, 'it's like asking a teetotaller to a wine-tasting.' Suzanne had evidently taken this as further evidence of Jane's self-deprecating style of humour, as she had merely guffawed, and said, 'Yeah. Right.'

It was a shame that she had to refuse really, thought Jane, because they hardly saw one another now. Suzanne was single, with a career in the City and plenty of money; there wasn't much common ground between them any more. Bars, clubs and restaurants were Suzanne's natural habitat – all places where Jane felt uncomfortable nowadays. She found herself oppressed by crowds and noise, shocked and humbled by the prices at the establishments Suzanne considered reasonable, and overwhelmed by the heat and racket of nightclubs. It was in any case hard to pin Suzanne down in advance. She had this irritating tendency, Jane had noticed, to avoid committing herself to a date until the very last minute, in the hope that something more promising might arise in the meantime. On the rare occasions she did venture into the suburbs to visit she would fawn over the children for five minutes, shower them with sweets and presents, introduce them to some boisterous new game, whip them up into a frenzy of hyperactivity and exhibitionism, and then collapse into an armchair with a bottle of wine and wonder why they wouldn't silently melt away to bed and leave the grown-ups to get drunk. Whenever the two women made their farewells they professed vehement envy for the other's lifestyle.

'You're so lucky, Jane,' Suzanne would say, climbing into her new, red sports car. 'You've got it all sorted out: husband, kids, house, garden. And' – complacently checking her appearance in the driver's mirror – 'I'm just an old maid.'

'I wish I had a fraction of your freedom,' Jane would reply. 'I bet you have such a brilliant time at Christmas with the children, opening their stockings at the crack of dawn.'

'Yes we do, but that's only one day a year!'

In spite of these protestations each woman felt a sense of relief to return to her own existence. We're a modern fable, Jane thought. Town mouse and country mouse rewritten. She'd always found it an oddly unsatisfying story, though it was a favourite with the girls. With most of those Improving Tales the protagonists tended to learn a valuable lesson from their experience, but in this case the mice returned home with all their prejudices reinforced.

This train of thought led Jane away from the reference section of the library and towards the children's lending area, where she picked out a couple of books each for Harriet and Sophie for the week ahead. She was heartily sick of the selection they had at home; she could almost recite them in her sleep. Sometimes just to enliven proceedings Jane would attempt to abridge them as she went along, or replace the odd word with a nonsensical alternative, just to see if anyone would notice, but the girls caught her out every time, and were most indignant at any tampering with the original. Jane looked forward to introducing them to proper books, books full of incident and plot and reversals of fortune, with just the occasional line drawing, and cliffhangers at the end of each chapter. Something like *The Silver Sword* or the *Narnia* stories which she had enjoyed as a child. But that was all still years away.

She didn't linger in adult lending. Aside from the fact that she no longer had the time or concentration for reading, it would be just like the Health section. She would be made to feel a freak and an outsider. Even a cursory glance at the jackets and the blurbs was enough to tell her that Sex was king here. Desire, Pursuit, Conquest, Fulfilment, The End: the same old story in a thousand different guises. Jane picked out *The Joy of Woks* from the Cookery shelf instead. She would do a stir-fry tonight. Strip down that chicken carcase and use up those old vegetables in the bottom of the fridge before they went any softer.

At the desk someone had left a pile of books on the counter. The top one caught Jane's eye: *My Brilliant Career* by Miles Franklin. It had been her favourite novel as a teenager – a turning point, really, in her relationship with literature. She couldn't count the number of times she'd read it, or the number of people she had bought copies for over the years. Whenever she came across one in a second-hand shop she would buy it because she couldn't bear to think of it stuck on a shelf unread. She would have called Sophie Sybylla, after the heroine, if Guy hadn't vetoed it in the strongest possible terms. The other books on the pile were two crime novels of the mortuary-slab tendency, an Iris Murdoch, and a DIY manual. Jane was just thinking what a bizarre and eclectic brew this was, and trying to put an age and sex to the imagined reader, when a dark-haired woman in jeans and a suede jacket slapped a copy of *A Beginner's Guide to Astronomy* on the pile and said, in a familiar but not instantly placeable voice, 'It's you again.'

Jane looked up and gave a false smile of recognition. The face rang a bell, but a distant, muffled one. Out of context like this Jane had no hope of identifying her. One of the mothers from church, perhaps, or school? Or just someone who worked at the bank?

'You haven't a clue who I am, have you?' said the woman, through a mouthful of nicotine chewing gum, and then Jane remembered that Scottish accent and was able to reply, 'Yes. Erica. But you look different.' It was the hair, Jane realized. Now worn long and loose, it hid all that grey that had been exposed when swept up. But this wasn't something that could be offered in mitigation. The woman was rummaging in her bag for her ticket while the girl behind the desk waited with the barcode scanner poised.

'Where's your baby?' asked Jane, looking round for the pushchair.

'Oh, my husband's over,' Erica said, emptying her bag out on the counter. This struck Jane as a peculiar remark. Over what? 'Oh, where is this bloody ticket? I've only had it a week.'

'Are you interested in astronomy?' Jane asked, looking at the topmost volume. 'My husband's turned our loft into a sort of observatory.'

'Really?' Erica started on her wallet, picking out and discarding the contents, piece by piece. A queue was forming behind them. 'Mine's just bought me a star for my birthday, so I thought I'd better look it up.'

'Bought it from whom?' Jane asked. It had never occurred to her that bits of the cosmos might be for sale.

'Not *bought* it exactly. Had it named after me. Somewhere out there is a ball of burning gas called Erica Crowe.' She laughed.

Jane could sense the queue starting to fidget. Sighs of

impatience rippled along its length, and one old man slammed his book down and walked out in disgust. Erica waved everyone past her, scooping her mound of trash along to the end of the counter. 'I'm determined to find this card,' she said to Jane, whose *Joy of Woks* was being scanned and stamped. 'I'm going on holiday tomorrow and I've got to have something to read or I'll go mad.'

'You can put them on my ticket if you want,' said Jane, wanting to make amends for the stolen newspaper, and scenting a potential convert to Miles Franklin. 'If you promise to return them on time.' She laughed, to indicate that she was only joking, which she wasn't, of course. The state of Erica's handbag and her inability to keep tabs on a library card for more than a week didn't give Jane great hopes.

'Really? That's kind,' said Erica, pushing the pile towards the librarian, who looked rather sceptical at this arrangement. 'Now when are these due back?' she went on, checking the front flap. 'May 11th. How on earth am I going to remember that?' she said, as though the invention of diaries and calendars had entirely passed her by. Jane's heart sank. 'Of course!' Erica smote her forehead. 'It's Salvador Dali's birthday.'

I'm going to regret this, thought Jane, already totting up the possible fines in her head.

14

Nina was in her room plagiarizing whole paragraphs of *Topophilia* for an essay due in the following day. Smoke bloomed from a patchouli joss-stick on the desk, a cigarette smouldered in the ashtray and a pleasant fog settled around her shoulders as she worked. Every so often she would get up and put a new LP on the record-player. She always wrote to music: the task took longer but felt less of a chore, and besides, if you didn't have your own record on you ended up listening to somebody else's through the wall instead. She couldn't work in the library; the sight of all those heads bent over books, and the sound of scratching pens and discreet throat-clearing made her fidget. And in any case she could never find the books she needed: they were either out on loan or down in the stacks somewhere, awaiting excavation. She was in a hurry this evening because Martin and some of the people from his house in Cromwell Road were doing a long-distance pub-crawl from the George in Southwark to the Prospect of Whitby, and she was hoping to intercept them somewhere along the route. As it was now ten o'clock and they had earlier hinted that the itinerary was open to last-minute alterations, her chances of finding them were slim. I'll just finish this page, then I'll go, she bribed herself. Her handwriting expanded across the page, as this thought solidified.

It was a month since the field trip to that damp, disease-ridden hostel in Yorkshire, and Nina and Martin were now firmly on the scene as a couple. She couldn't quite believe how well Jean had taken it, and how little criticism they had attracted for sneaking around behind her back while she was in bed, sick. 'No worries. I've never been into that whole jealousy/possession thing,' Jean had said. Nina wasn't entirely convinced by this and similar declarations, but she was grateful nevertheless. She was sure she wouldn't have been nearly so magnanimous in Jean's place. As she made it quite clear to Martin, she, herself, *was* into that whole jealousy/possession thing, so he needn't get any ideas.

Nina threw down her pen. There. By means of some transparent waffling her essay had limped on to its fourth side. She had earned a rest. Sitting cross-legged on her chair with a cushion in the small of her back had deadened her lower legs, and she winced as she flexed her ankles and felt the blood seething back into the veins. As she pulled on her coat and plucked her keys from the desk it occurred to her that she hadn't eaten since breakfast. She remembered a natural yoghurt in the fridge that was hers and some bread that wasn't. Perhaps she would pinch a slice or two and have some toast, just to line the stomach. It was surprising how often she could get to the end of a day without having eaten anything substantial. What was that French saying about not living on love and fresh water?

Nina pushed open the door of her room to be greeted by a tantalizing smell of cooking: garlic, rosemary, wine, toasted cheese, something sharp and citrus. She felt dizzy with hunger. That natural yoghurt would never do. She made her way towards the source of the smell, breathing deeply. Normally the communal kitchen stank of tinned tomato soup, or Lemon Vim if the cleaner had been round. This was something quite different. What was going on in there was *cuisine*.

On the table was a single place setting: two knives, two forks, a glass of wine and a white linen napkin. A half-empty bottle of red wine was open on the work surface which was cluttered with used pans, bowls, chopping board and implements. A wide shallow pan simmered on the stove. Beyond the streaked glass of the oven door and lit by a greasy bulb sat a soufflé, perfectly risen and golden and high as a chef's hat. There was no one about so Nina approached the stove to have a better look at the contents of the pan, which turned out to be joints of some sort of poultry in a syrupy sauce with shallots and mushrooms. The liquid had almost all evaporated and was starting to crackle as though it might soon stick. Nina was just wondering whether she ought to give it a stir when a voice behind her said, 'Don't open the oven. Please,' and she leapt away as if she'd been burnt.

The speaker was a man of around Nina's age, with shoulder-length wavy hair and thick glasses. He was on the plump side, with a paunch that strained against his shirt buttons and rested on the waistband of droopy flared jeans. His lips were full and wet-looking. He was holding a white, fine china plate. 'It's just that the souffle will sink,' he went on. 'It's got another . . .' he checked his watch '. . . minute and a half to go.' He took Nina's place at the stove, fractionally adjusting the heat under the pan and agitating the contents gently. *Bread*, thought Nina, her heart beating a little faster.

'I wasn't going to open the oven, actually,' she said, taking courage from the fact that he didn't look anything like as malevolent as his reputation. 'I was just worried that your chicken was going to burn.'

'It's duck,' the stranger corrected her. 'I'm trying to get it to caramelize. I've never tried this recipe before – it's one I've adapted, so I don't know how it will turn out.' He had a South African accent, as thick as clotted cream. He turned on the hot tap and held his plate under the jet of scalding water for half a minute before wiping it dry.

'Well, it smells very nice,' Nina admitted, retrieving her yoghurt from the fridge. Someone had punctured the foil lid, and the sell-by date had elapsed some days ago. She wavered for a moment and then dropped it in the bin.

'Best place for it,' said Bread, opening the oven door to release a rush of hot, cheese-scented air. He carried the monstrous, trembling soufflé to the table, his pendulous lower lip pegged between his teeth.

'I think we're neighbours, aren't we?' said Nina, without taking her eyes off the dish.

'Are we? Which side?'

'Left. West. Number Sixteen,' said Nina.

'Oh, it's you who plays the loud music then,' said Bread, without appearing to be joking. He hovered awkwardly by the table, waiting for her to go.

'Someone left a note on your door which said, "You're dead",' she mused.

'Well, his optimism was unwarranted, as you can see.' The soufflé was beginning to sag. 'Oh damn. Look – are you hungry?' he said, almost accusingly.

Nina hesitated. It was a filthy night: the idea of traipsing the streets in search of Martin and the others was looking less and less attractive. In fact, now she came to think of it, she couldn't understand the point of a pub-crawl. No sooner were you comfortably installed, beer in hand, than you were being urged to drink up and herded out into the cold again.

'I'm starving,' she admitted, throwing her coat off.

'Well, go and find yourself a plate and a knife and fork and you can have some of this. And a glass if you want wine. You don't mind if I start, do you? Only timing's everything.'

Congratulating herself on this coup, Nina turned up a chipped plate and some scratched cutlery in one of the cupboards, while her companion helped himself to a large spoonful of soufflé. Wait until I tell the others, she was thinking. Breaking bread with Bread, notorious rapist and drug-pusher. She rinsed a smeared tumbler at the sink.

'This looks yummy,' she said, when she was finally seated and served. Bread did not look especially pleased with her choice of compliment. 'Ten o'clock's an odd time to be eating, if you don't mind my saying,' she went on, less confidently. 'Do you always eat late?'

'Only because it means I get the kitchen to myself. Usually.'

'Oh.' There was a silence as they carried on eating. Nina finished her wine and accepted a refill. Taken on an empty stomach it made her feel instantly euphoric and flushed. 'Is that why they call you Bread? Because of the cooking?'

'I thought so,' said Bread. 'But apparently it's because my head looks like a loaf.' Now that he'd pointed it out Nina couldn't help noticing that it was rather square. There was something doughy about his complexion, too. 'My name's Hugo,' he added as an afterthought, dividing the last piece of soufflé between them.

'I'm Nina,' said Nina, pleased to have moved the relationship on a millimetre or two. 'Why did your friend want to kill you?'

'I can't remember,' said Hugo with his mouth full. 'I often seem to have that effect on people.' He put the empty dish with the pile of used pots on the worktop and turned the heat out under the pan. He tasted the sauce with a wooden spoon and then ground pepper furiously over the duck before bringing the whole lot to the table. He gave Nina the breast joint and himself the leg and then spooned some of the sticky glaze on top. Nina dug her fork into the crispy skin and the whole thing came away in one piece. 'You know,' she said, nibbling one corner and letting the flavours explode on her tongue, 'you aren't a bit like I imagined.'

Hugo, who was pulling bone from flesh with his fingers, looked baffled at the idea that he should have figured in Nina's imagination at all.

'You hear such conflicting reports.'

'And which of these reports do you believe?' Hugo asked, helping himself to more wine. 'The one about my conviction for arson. Or is it GBH? Am I a transsexual this week or a Neo-Nazi? I can never remember.'

Nina laughed. 'They say you're a good cook,' she said. 'And a genius. It's not all bad, you see.'

'And what do you think?' She could sense him beginning to thaw.

'Well, I'd obviously need some more evidence before I decide you're a genius, but they didn't exaggerate about the cooking. Hugo – do you mind if I call you Hugo? – this is the most delicious meal I've ever had. Honestly.'

'Really?' said Hugo, looking momentarily animated. 'You don't think I've overdone the cardamom?'

'Absolutely not,' said Nina, who wasn't even sure what it was. A relative of the pappadom, perhaps?

'Well. I think it needs some work. I'm still ambivalent about the black treacle,' said Hugo, his brows furrowing.

Nina burst out laughing. He was surely having her on. But he didn't join in; he merely looked bewildered. 'I'm glad you like it anyway,' he said finally. 'I wouldn't normally offer someone a meal that was still at the experimental stage.'

'But I sort of gatecrashed my way in.'

'Yes.'

'But you don't mind now.'

'No.'

'In fact you're secretly pleased that you asked me to stay,' she went on, determined to wring some banter out of him.

'Your input has been useful,' he conceded.

Nina's laugh pealed out again. Really, he had no idea how comical he sounded. She'd never met anyone so useless at flirting and so immune to her charms.

'Why do you hide away in your room so much?' she asked. 'I mean, I'm out and about all the time and I've never seen you.'

'To avoid having to make conversation with all the other assholes out there. Since we're speaking plainly,' said Hugo, giving her a brief smile before gathering up the plates. 'Would you like some Brie?'

Nina nodded. 'But they might not all be assholes. Some of them are, I admit. But some are really nice. You could be missing out.'

'That's a risk I'm prepared to take.' Hugo produced an oozing triangle of Brie from a wicker box on the side. 'Anyway, I'm not *hiding*. My friends know where to find me.'

'Most of the people on this corridor are pretty much like me,' Nina went on, feeling bound to defend them. 'And you like me, don't you?' she wheedled, accepting a fresh plate.

'It's a bit early to have formed an opinion,' replied Hugo, seriously. He was peeling a very ripe pear with a small fruit knife and the juice was running over his hands. 'I don't dislike you. Here.' He passed her a pear-half on the end of the blade and Nina fumbled it with slippery fingers. 'I once sat up until three in the morning waiting for a pear to ripen,' he mused.

'Was it worth it?' asked Nina.

'I didn't have much else to do in those days. At boarding school.'

'I went to boarding school, too,' said Nina, throwing herself on this speck of common ground. 'Did you like it?'

'No. I hated it. Until the very end when it started to get better. Did you?'

'Yes, I was very happy, actually,' Nina confessed, almost guiltily. In the presence of strange and troubled souls like Hugo she couldn't help feeling that her unafflicted upbringing and tendency to enjoy herself were deficiencies which needed explaining. 'The girls were nice, the teachers were nice. I'm afraid I missed out on all those character-building experiences like canings and homesickness and bullying. It's probably why I've got no personality.'

'I was never homesick,' said Hugo, entirely failing to come to the defence of her personality. 'Holidays were even worse than term-times.'

'Why? Didn't you get on with your parents?'

'My mother died when I was ten. My father and I didn't make a very good job of consoling each other. "If only it had been you instead," I think he said.'

'Oh my God,' said Nina. 'That's appalling.'

'I probably said the same thing to him first. I certainly thought it.'

'I'm so sorry,' said Nina. 'Did he ever hit you or anything?'

'No. He threw things at me occasionally. Books and the odd bottle. But fortunately he was rather a poor shot. It was more neglect, really. He just didn't want me and didn't know what to do with me.'

'Weren't there any other relatives you could stay with?' asked Nina. She had finished eating now and without any discussion they started to clear away the plates. She wasn't sure if this was the sort of subject that could be pursued over the washing-up, but he didn't seem to mind her questions, and, besides, he never asked any of her, so she couldn't offer any personal revelations in return.

'My mother's parents live in Cheltenham and there was an aunt in Portsmouth. I used to be passed around like a Christmas present nobody wants. But sooner or later I'd have to go home to the old man.'

'Which was where?' Nina asked.

'South Africa,' said Hugo, adding a few more dollops of cream to his accent.

'Of course,' said Nina. 'Silly me.' She ran hot water into the sink and started to wash up with an ancient, balding plastic brush. 'I always hated the journey home. Sitting in transit lounges on my own,' she went on, having ransacked her memory in vain for any childhood traumas.

Hugo nodded agreement as he wiped the dishes and replaced them in the only one of the cupboards with a padlock, but he didn't ask her where she was from or exhibit any curiosity about her life at all.

'What's your subject?' she asked, at last, when it was clear he wasn't going to come up with a question.

'Geography,' said Hugo, locking the last of the pots in the cupboard and pocketing the key.

'Same as me. But you're in the second year?' said Nina, thinking that she might have tapped a useful source of lecture notes.

Hugo nodded. They had finished clearing up now and stood loitering by the empty table. Nina certainly had no wish to return to her essay, and Hugo didn't look as though he was in a tearing hurry to be gone. 'Have you any idea what you'll do next?' she asked. She herself hadn't a clue about careers.

'I thought I might go back to my room and drink brandy,' said Hugo, misunderstanding her. 'If you want to come.'

'Well . . .' Perhaps this was how he lured his victims back to his lair, Nina thought. Perhaps everything I've heard about him is true. Presently curiosity overcame all her scruples. 'Why not?' she said. It would give her a chance to have a good snoop around. 'Actually, when I said what are you going to do next I meant after university,' she said as they walked back down the corridor to Hugo's room. 'You could be a chef.'

Hugo pulled a face. 'I don't like taking orders,' he said. 'No, I'm intending to be a perpetual student. I'll do a PhD on some aspect of desert morphology, extended over many years.' He unlocked his door and pushed it open. The room was still dark and the bedclothes were twisted up and trailing on to the floor as if he had fallen out of bed. He drew the curtains against the rain and hit a switch.

A single, unshaded lightbulb gave out a sickly yellow light. A bin in the corner was piled high with flattened beer cans and empty wine bottles, and there was a musty masculine smell of unwashed clothes. A winged armchair in black padded vinyl faced out of the window, its back to the room. The walls were bare, apart from a cork noticeboard above the desk to which a couple of scrolls of paper were attached with a single drawing pin. Against the longest wall were some precarious bookshelves made of planks supported at each end by bricks and sagging in the middle under the weight of hundreds of books. Nina inspected the titles with growing astonishment. No wonder she could never find any decent books in the library – they were all here. 'Isn't there a limit on borrowing?' she asked, as Hugo kicked a few odd shoes and crumpled items of clothing under the bed and straightened the sheets.

'I've got more than one ticket,' he replied, cryptically.

Oh really? thought Nina, adding FORGER to the list of allegations against him. At least she would know where to bring her reading list in future.

From a cardboard box beneath the desk Hugo produced a bottle of Courvoisier and a pair of dusty goblets into which he poured two huge measures.

'Do you think there's a geography of women?' Nina asked casually.

Hugo laughed. 'I've done that essay,' he said. 'I've got it somewhere.' He dragged a box file from under the desk and thumbed through the papers until he found it. 'Here.' He handed her a dozen pages, densely covered in the most minute handwriting Nina had ever seen. 'You can borrow it if you like.'

'Are you sure? That will really get me out of trouble,' said Nina, taking it from him gratefully. If she didn't hang around here too long she could copy it out before she went to bed.

She rolled it up and tucked it in the pocket of her smock. 'What's in it for you, though?'

'Oh don't worry, I'll call in the favour sooner or later,' said Hugo, handing her a brandy glass. 'I always do.' He spun the black vinyl armchair round so that it faced into the room and offered it to Nina, who sat in it, cross-legged, holding her drink in her lap, while Hugo sat on the floor leaning against the end of the bed. He took out a crushed packet of Camels and a lighter from his back pocket and tossed them up to her.

'Do you know Martin Shorrocks?' she asked, thinking that now might be a good time to invoke her absent boyfriend, just to make it quite clear that she was unavailable. Not that Hugo had shown any interest in that direction, it had to be said. He hadn't even committed himself to liking her yet. And she was certainly in no danger from herself: physically he was only just the right side of repulsive. That wet lower lip . . .

'He's your boyfriend,' said Hugo, neutrally.

'Yes. How did you know?'

'I've seen you together. And heard you.' He glanced at the party wall.

Nina was annoyed to find herself blushing. 'We were supposed to be going on a pub-crawl tonight,' she said, throwing back the Camels. 'A whole load of us. You could have come.'

Hugo shook his head. 'No thanks. I always feel like a performing bear or something when I'm in a crowd of strangers. As if I've got to cavort around and entertain people and make a pratt of myself – which I usually do.'

'I wish I had an older brother like you,' said Nina, impulsively, and then wondered what on earth had prompted her to say it.

Hugo gave a cheerless laugh. 'Women often say that to me. It's a way of letting me know I'm Not Their Type.' His bitten nails scrabbled at the cigarette box. 'Then when they get to know me better they realize they wouldn't even want me for a brother. You wait.'

'I didn't mean it like that,' said Nina, mortified that her compliment had been interpreted so shrewdly. She took a sip of brandy. There was no way she was going to finish it without being ill. She'd never liked spirits. Hugo was already helping himself to more. She could pretend to knock it over by accident, but he'd probably just give her a refill. It was better to own up. 'I don't like this,' she said.

Hugo shrugged and took it from her, tipping it into his own glass. 'I thought you were struggling.'

'It's all right on Christmas pudding,' she said. 'I should be going, anyway. I've got an essay to copy.' She stood up and patted her pocket.

'Let me know if you need help deciphering my writing,' said Hugo, from the floor. 'I'm told it's easier if you use a magnifying glass.'

Nina was hunting for her keys. 'I definitely had them when we were eating,' she said. 'I was on my way out.' She checked her coat pockets, and felt her way around the hem in case they had fallen into the lining. Hugo offered to make a quick inspection of the kitchen, but returned shaking his head. 'They must be in here,' Nina insisted, peering under the bed. In Hugo's spartan living quarters there were only so many places to look, and these were soon exhausted.

'Damn.' Nina stood in the middle of the floor, hands on hips. Now she would have to trek over to Martin's place in Kensington in the middle of this typhoon on the offchance that he was there. It would be pointless trying Jean across the hall: she only slept in her own bed as an absolute last resort.

'You can stay here if you like,' said Hugo. 'I'll sleep on the chair.'

'Oh no, thanks, really,' said Nina. 'I'll get the night bus to Cromwell Road. It's no problem.' Even as she spoke there was a machine-gun clatter of hail on the window.

'I won't molest you. In spite of what you may have heard,' said Hugo, wearily. 'You're not that gorgeous.'

'I haven't heard anything,' Nina retorted, too quickly. 'I'm not scared of you.' Her heart was pounding. She'd have to stay now, if only to prove that she held no brief for college tittle-tattle.

'So stay then.'
'All right, I will.'

When Nina awoke the following morning, it was still dark and it took her a moment or two to remember where she was. Her dress, which she was relieved to find she was still wearing, was twisted tightly round her; there was a great bolt of fabric under one armpit, and the imprint of one of her cuff buttons on her cheek. Through the gloom she could make out the slumped figure of Hugo, half out of the armchair, his arms flung out like a dead man's. She ran her tongue over unbrushed teeth. There was a foul taste in her mouth. She tried smelling her breath by huffing into her cupped hands: empty cigarette box with a hint of onion. Unravelling herself from the bedding she slipped out into the empty hallway, the click of the door causing Hugo to stir in his sleep and edge an inch or two further over the lip of the chair.

In the bathroom Nina splashed cold water over her face and rinsed her mouth. The unforgiving fluorescent light made her skin look pale and blotchy. The button imprint was still visible and a spot glowed on her chin. *Not that gorgeous*, she thought, raking her fingers through knotted hair.

Back in the bedroom she found Hugo examining his broken spectacles. His creeping progress towards the floor had accelerated dramatically during Nina's absence and he had woken up to the sickening crunch of glass and wire and a jarring pain in the rear.

'I wish they'd make these things more robust,' said the Falstaffian Hugo, in an aggrieved tone, waggling the mangled frames. 'I found your keys, by the way.'

'Oh? Where?'

'Down the side of the chair. I must have been lying on them all night.'

You're lying all right, thought Nina. That was the first place I looked. But she said nothing, and returned to her room, baffled by the whole encounter.

When she came to copy out Hugo's essay on the geography of women she found it completely impenetrable. It inferred a vast body of background knowledge, which in Nina's case was entirely lacking, and was peppered with footnotes and long quotations from unpublished theses and allusions to texts and authorities she'd never heard of. There was no way in the world she would be able to pass it off as her own. In the margins the tutor had occasionally pencilled in *Absolutely!* or other affirmatives, and at the bottom of the last page was the comment: *Excellent. Can I borrow this?* Evidently not *everything* people said about Hugo was unfounded.

15

In the spring of 1976 Guy came across Nina through his involvement with a student production of *The Two Gentlemen of Verona* at University College, but it was some months before their paths crossed again, with such disastrous consequences for all concerned.

At that time Guy was doing his postgraduate year in primary teaching at the Institute of Education, a step his parents regarded as only marginally preferable to dropping out altogether.

'I can't understand why you are choosing to throw away a perfectly creditable degree in Economics,' his mother had written in one of her fortnightly letters. His decision had evidently rattled her: she had gone on to a third side of Basildon Bond. 'You will never be well off. You won't be able to support a wife and family. You won't be able to afford to give your children the education you had.'

Well, amen to that, Guy thought. Although he had not suffered unduly at school himself, he had seen plenty of others who had. In fact it was recalling his teachers' botched efforts to make little men of them that had set him on this path in the first place. Already he could see that there had to be a better way to bring up boys: no son of his was going to endure the sort of cruelty that poor old Etchells and others like him had put up with.

Guy had originally considered the idea of secondary teaching as a career, but soon dismissed it. He had observed that people went into it because they enjoyed and wanted to use their subject, and if they didn't already dislike children, they soon grew to. Those who went into primary teaching did so because they liked children. It was in this camp that Guy felt he belonged. He wasn't quite sure where this feeling had come from. As his mother pointed out, he didn't even *know* any children, apart from that family back home with all those little girls in headscarves, and he'd never shown much interest in *them*. But Guy had a natural affinity with underdogs: he could recall quite clearly the bitterness of being punished unfairly, and the futility of competing with a preferred younger brother. As a teacher he would never stoop to favouritism.

Guy's participation in *The Two Gentlemen of Verona* was one of those accidents born of his good nature. A friend who was studying organic chemistry at UCL had been cast as Launce in a college production and was in desperate need of a dog. Guy, who had no interest in amateur drama, and wouldn't have dreamed of setting foot on stage himself, had immediately volunteered the services of his parents' elderly labrador, Bones – the successor to the delinquent Porky – who had seemed to meet all the necessary criteria. He was even-tempered, a little sleepy if anything, good with strangers and unlikely to suffer from stage-fright. Guy, ignoring the STRICTLY NO PETS clause in his rental agreement, had brought him up on the train from Sussex and installed him in his lodgings a week before the performance.

Bones's brief was to enter with Launce and sit quietly at his feet for the duration of a longish soliloquy, while Guy stood by in the wings to offer silent encouragement. Bones carried this off without a hitch at his audition for the first and last time. At the first rehearsal he stood up and wandered off into the wings, tail wagging, as soon as Launce opened his mouth. On the second attempt he stayed put, thanks to furious offstage gestures from Guy, but barked throughout the entire soliloquy. One of the cast suggested tethering him to a stake, beside which a pile of Good Boy Choc Drops could be placed by a member of the crew during the blackout. Again, Bones proved too ingenious for them, bolting the chocolates within seconds and then barking furiously for more.

It was at this point that Launce, who was beginning to resent having to play the stooge to such a shocking upstager, suggested slipping Bones a mogadon before the show to make him drowsy. Guy refused to contemplate dog-tampering of any kind. The opening night loomed, and there was talk of firing him from the show. Finally it had gone to a ballot of the cast, resulting in the rout of the anti-dog lobby. Guy, who was by now fed up with his role as agent, and had heard more than he cared to of *The Two Gentlemen of Verona*, had in fact voted against, and would have been glad to withdraw him there and then. But the victors were jubilant: Bones had become a sort of mascot, and his anarchic behaviour on stage was for many the highlight of the play.

Guy arrived a little late for the first performance – though in plenty of time for Bones's scene – having been caught up in an altercation with his landlord, who had turned up unannounced on the pretext of fixing a washer on the bathtap. In fact he was checking for unofficial tenants: it was not unknown for eight students to share a flat intended and priced for four. Guy had to pretend that Bones, who was looking thoroughly at home, curled up on the sofa, was a stray who had that minute wandered in off the street, and was about to be sent packing. The landlord had looked sceptical, and on discovering half a dozen tins of Chum in the kitchen had threatened to evict the pair of them without notice. 'And you can kiss your deposit goodbye as well,' he had said, wagging his finger. Ugly words had then been exchanged, and Bones, roused from his customary torpor by the sight of his master being harangued, had jumped up and snapped at the landlord's outstretched hand, just missing flesh and bone, but leaving a row of puncture marks in the sleeve of his leather jacket. With threats of magistrates and extermination orders ringing in his ears, Guy had fled from the scene, a by now thoroughly over-excited dog bounding along at his heels.

When the pair arrived at the Collegiate Theatre they found the play under way and the rest of the cast in a state of dejection and disarray. The girl playing Silvia – a plump blonde called Jean who had tried and failed to pick Guy up on their first meeting – had been struck down by laryngitis. There was no question of her being able to muddle through – after a few croaks her voice had given out entirely. There were no understudies, and not nearly enough time for anyone to learn the part from scratch. A compromise had finally been reached, in the form of Jean's friend, Nina. She would stand in the wings and read the part of Silvia, projecting her voice as best she could, while Jean, on stage, mimed along to the words. The two of them had been practising their lip-synchronization all day, but the effect would nevertheless be that of a badly dubbed film. Guy couldn't help feeling relieved at the news. The quality of the production was now mortally compromised: the heat was off Bones.

Leaving the dog in the dressing room to be fussed over by his admirers Guy crept into the back of the auditorium. There was Jean, centre-stage, mugging away for all she was worth, while an unfamiliar voice issued from the wings. From a distance the result was not too disconcerting, but those in the front seats would find themselves unable to concentrate on anything else but the frequent discrepancies in Silvia's miming.

What a ropy, third-rate production of a ropy, third-rate play, he was thinking. People falling instantly in and out of love; a girl dressing herself up as a boy to win back her lover by sheer devotion. Oh, yes, *that* would work, thought Guy. And as for the so-called comedy: not a joke in sight. But if you dared to point that out to any of this lot you were labelled a Philistine and an ignoramus. And now thanks to his own generosity in coming to the aid of a friend he would probably find himself homeless and fifty pounds out of pocket.

This was the turn Guy's thoughts were taking when he took up his position in the wings ready for Bones's entrance, and caught sight of Nina across the other side of the stage, huddled inside an afghan coat, reading the part of Silvia in her head-girl's voice, by the light of a bicycle headlamp. She was small and slim, with waist-length blonde hair and delicate features. Now that's more like it, he thought. Shame they hadn't cast her in the part to begin with. It was much easier to imagine Valentine and Proteus fighting over her than over that scary Jean. Suddenly he didn't feel so hostile towards

Launce for getting him involved, fifty pounds didn't seem such a huge fortune, and even old Shakespeare had his moments.

'Ready,' said Launce, beside him, taking the end of Bones's lead and patting the packet of Good Boy Choc Drops in his pocket.

Guy nodded. 'Break a leg.'

'I'll break all his bloody legs if he cocks it up this time,' Launce whispered back as he stepped on to the stage. In the blackout Guy could hear the pitter-patter of chocolate buttons on wood, followed by the sound of eager chomping. The lights came up to reveal Launce sitting on a crate and Bones licking the floorboards at this feet.

'*When a man's servant shall play the cur with him,*' began Launce, in what he imagined to be a West Country accent. Bones, having cleaned all trace of chocolate from the floor stood up, blinking into the spotlight, and, giving an experimental bark, wandered around the back of the stage looking for seconds.

'Sit!' Guy whispered, making furious hand signals. Launce pressed on in a slightly louder, tenser voice. Bones, meanwhile, appeared from behind the crate, sat down, and with one leg up against his ear began to lick himself ostentatiously. There were a few titters from the audience: the first of the evening. 'Stop it!' Guy hissed. 'Bones!' The dog refused to look at him. Opposite Guy, Nina had one hand over her nose and mouth and was starting to shake. Launce, encouraged by the audience's laughter, and mistaking its cause, began to throw himself into the part with more vigour, berating the dog enthusiastically and now and then giving it a reproving prod with the toe of his boot. Bones, tired of this sort of unscripted harassment, was on his feet again in no time and heading for the downstage exit. Finding his progress checked by his chain which was attached to the crate he stopped short, a roll of fat bulging over his collar, gave a couple of short barks and began to drag the crate offstage behind him. Launce, realizing he was about to lose his set, quickly sat down on it, nearly garrotting the dog, at which point there was a loud splintering sound, and Bones rocketed out of sight behind the curtain to a round of applause from the audience.

Launce struggled on, raising his voice to drown the last of the clappers, while Bones, who had now disappeared around the back of the cyclorama, still trailing his chain, could be heard rattling and clanking like the theatre ghost and howling each time he became snagged on a piece of scenery.

Guy caught up with the dog on the far side of the wings, being petted by Nina.

'You're fired!' he said, pointing an accusing finger at him.

'That's a shame,' said Nina. 'He got the biggest applause of the evening.' She tickled the thick fur of Bones's throat, while Guy disentangled the piece of splintered crate from the end of the leash.

'I'd better take him out before he does any more damage,' said Guy, noticing that beneath the afghan coat Nina was wearing a tie-dyed T-shirt and no bra.

'Make sure he's back in time for his curtain call,' said Nina. They exchanged smiles in the darkness.

'Are you doing anything afterwards? Are you coming for a drink? Shall we get a drink?' Guy rehearsed as he walked down Gordon Street with Bones trotting along at his side. He'd never been any good at chatting up women – a flaw he put down to his years of incarceration in a boys' boarding school. There had been parties at the local youth club back home, during the holidays, but Guy had always been one of the envious bystanders who lined the walls during the slow numbers, watching other more confident blokes claim the prettiest girls. Then when he'd gone to university he'd suddenly met a new breed of woman, who didn't wait to be asked, and no effort had been required on his part at all. In the last three years he'd never been short of girlfriends, but he'd never felt especially infatuated with any of them. Instead of being attracted to the sort of woman who did all the running, he found he preferred the other sort – who had to be chased and won over, but who might in the end refuse to be caught, and were therefore best avoided. Human nature was so perverse.

By the time he had walked a few times around the block and found a suitable alleyway for Bones to do his business, Guy had almost talked himself into a confident and masterful frame of mind. But when he reached the theatre he found the play had ended, the cast and crew gone and the theatre in darkness. The following night when he reported for duty Jean was back in full voice, there was no sign of Nina, and Bones had been dropped from the cast and replaced by a stuffed Airedale from Camden Market. He never did catch up with Nina. It was left to coincidence, that blind puppeteer, to bring them together.

16

'Why are you driving slowly, Mummy?' asked Harriet, from the back seat.

'Because I'm following someone,' said Jane, distractedly.

'Who are you following?'

'A lady. You don't know her.'

'Why are you following a lady?'

'Because I want to see where she lives. Oh damn!' The lights at the pedestrian crossing turned to red and Jane pulled up sharply, drumming her fingers on the wheel as an old woman pushing a zimmer frame advanced, inch by inch, across the road.

'Damn is a rude word,' said Harriet solemnly.

'Yes, it is. Don't ever say it,' said Jane.

'I want a grape. Can I have a grape?' Harriet rustled one of the plastic shopping bags on the seat beside her.

'No, they're not washed. Leave that shopping alone,' snapped Jane. Harriet had already nibbled both ends off the French stick so that would be stale by teatime.

'What car is she in?'

'Who?'

'The lady.'

'She isn't in a car. She's walking.' Jane could see her in the distance, turning down a side road, pushing her buggy. I'm going to lose her now, she thought. As the elderly woman set the front wheels of her zimmer on the kerb Jane put her foot down and the car leapt forward and stalled. Jane yanked the gearstick into neutral and revved the engine aggressively before lurching off again.

'Why are you driving fast, Mummy?'

'Because I want to catch up with this lady before she disappears into one of the houses,' Jane explained, impatiently, taking the corner too early and clipping the kerb with a jolt.

'Why did you do that, Mummy?' asked Harriet.

'I didn't mean to,' Jane spluttered. 'Look, it's very difficult to drive when you keep asking me questions all the time.' There she was, about half way down the road trying to drag her buggy up a short flight of steps to her front door. Jane, still some distance away, pulled over and watched her let herself in. As soon as the door was shut Jane drove slowly past, checking the number of the house. It was a redbrick Victorian cottage, with a tiny front garden, occupied by two dustbins and an overgrown hedge. On the porch was a bicycle minus its wheels and a broken umbrella like a dead crow on a stick. The downstairs curtains were closed and there was a vase of wilted flowers between them and the glass. The front gate swung from one hinge.

'What are you looking for, Mummy?'

'Nothing. I've found it,' said Jane. 'We can go home now.' She had been thinking about Erica Crowe on and off ever since that meeting at the library. Thinking that she seemed an interesting person whom she would like to know better. And then when the first letter from the library had arrived, requesting the immediate return of the six overdue titles Erica had put on her ticket, Jane had started to feel slightly less warm towards her, but rather more urgently inclined to bump into her again and issue a curt reminder. Jane had caught sight of her once the previous week, but too far in the distance for pursuit to be dignified or even feasible. Jane had been on foot at the time and burdened with empties for the bottle bank. Later she had taken the car out and cruised the streets close to the sighting, on the offchance. And she'd been back to the park at every available opportunity sometimes with Harriet, sometimes alone, but with no success. At the back of her mind, unexamined, lay the thought: all this for a few library books? Really? Then today on the way back from the supermarket, thinking about Erica again, Jane had seen her emerging from the off-licence with a box of beers on the bottom of the pushchair. As if I'd made her appear, Jane thought.

It was a couple of days before Jane worked up the courage

to knock on her door. She had contemplated forwarding the letter from the library, anonymously and with no further explanation, and hoping that did the trick. But something stopped her. Nosiness or politeness, or something stranger. In the event she took Harriet along for moral support. Although the presence of small children could often complicate a simple situation, very occasionally the reverse was true.

The front room curtains were still closed when Jane and Harriet made their way up the steps, and the wilted flowers were now crisp and dead. At the slightest touch they would disintegrate all over the floor, thought Jane, who would never let things get to that stage, even supposing anyone were to buy her flowers.

Without waiting to be told, Harriet pressed the bell which promptly stuck, and a continuous, angry buzzing sounded deep in the house.

'Look what you've done!' said Jane, swatting her hand away, as the door was thrown open. Erica, in a headscarf and paint-smeared overalls, stepped past them without a word and gave the bell-push a sharp tap with a wooden mallet which she then replaced just inside the house. 'Come in,' she said. 'I'm up a ladder.'

'Well, I was only . . .' Jane began, but Harriet, who needed no further persuasion, had already marched indoors and vanished into the front room, from which the sound of a television issued.

'Do you mind if I finish this ceiling?' Erica called over her shoulder. 'I've only got a corner left to do, and I don't want the brush to go hard.' Through the kitchen door Jane could see work surfaces cluttered with what looked like a week's unwashed dishes and pans, all protected by swags of clear polythene dustsheets. 'We had a bit of a flood last week,' Erica went on, climbing back up the ladder and applying white emulsion with a fat brush to a nicotine-coloured patch of ceiling. 'One of the boys let the bath overflow and the water came right through into here. It was dripping off the light fitting. So I thought I'd better cover up the stains.' She pointed at the door, through which Harriet had disappeared moments before. 'Why don't you make yourself at home? I'll be finished in a second.'

Jane, who hadn't advanced much beyond the doormat, picked her way down the hall, which was littered with baby toys, shoes, crayons, and pieces of model railway. On a nest of tables in the corner a dusty telephone shared the space with a full nappy sack, a rack of red bills, two pieces of toast with an infant-sized bite missing from each piece, and a baby's bottle on its side dripping milk on to the rug below. Jane stood it up and started to dab at the wet patch with a tissue. She couldn't leave it – you had to treat that formula milk immediately or it would reek of sick.

'Oh, don't worry about that,' said Erica, coming down from the ladder and tossing the brush into a pail of water at her feet. She pulled the scarf off and twisted her hair round and round into a knot at the back of her head, where it seemed to stick without the aid of pins. A diamond stud glinted at the side of her small, straight nose. Her eyes were ringed with yesterday's make-up. She unzipped her overalls to reveal a pair of tartan pyjamas. 'Oh,' she said, zipping them up again. 'I forgot I hadn't dressed.'

She pushed open the sitting room door, meeting some resistance from a pile of newspapers and magazines. The room was dark, the curtains still closed, but Erica made no move to open them. In a high chair, in the bluish light of the television, the baby that Jane had minded in the park had fallen asleep face down on the food tray. On the couch beside Harriet, a boy of eight or so, also in pyjamas, was watching a daytime chat show and eating tortilla chips from a huge drum on his lap.

'This is Gregory. He's ill,' Erica explained. Gregory gave Jane a smile full of crisps. 'I thought you'd gone quiet,' she said to the slumped baby, extricating him from his harness and laying him on the couch where he twitched and drew his knees up to his chest a few times before relaxing back into sleep. 'I'd offer you a cup of tea, but the kettle's buried somewhere under the dustsheets. There are some beers in the shed.'

'Oh, no,' said Jane, who was still trying to get accustomed to the semi-darkness. 'I don't want anything to drink.' She didn't like beer much at the best of times, which this wasn't.

'I know why you're here,' said Erica. 'It's those sodding library books. How much do I owe you?'

'Nothing,' said Jane, dragging her eyes from the television screen, where an uncomfortable-looking man was being berated by his wife and mistress, to cheers from the studio audience. 'I thought I ought to remind you, that's all. In case you'd forgotten. I'm starting to get letters.'

'Oh God, sorry. I've got such a shocking memory. I think it's genetic. My mother's completely ga-ga, and she's only sixty-five.'

Jane smiled uncertainly. She wasn't sure if this was a joke. 'They'll be here somewhere,' Erica was saying. 'Under something. Except perhaps the astronomy book. I think my husband might have taken that one back.'

'To the library?' said Jane.

'No, to Kuwait.'

'*Kuwait?*'

'Yes, he works for a construction company out there. Perhaps if I put the light on we might be able to find the books,' Erica went on, as if suggesting something controversial.

'Shall I open the curtains?' Jane offered. She was beginning to find the gloom unnerving. 'It's quite a nice day out there.'

Erica nodded. Jane twitched the curtains apart and the shrivelled flowers collapsed into powder on the window sill, leaving a few dead stalks in the vase. The sudden burst of sunlight through windows densely stippled with fingerprints revealed the full extent of the room's disorder. Newspapers, magazines and piles of laundry lay on every chair. Like the hallway, the carpet was strewn with toys and pens, and a pack of cards that had evidently been flung up in the air. Between the television and the couch was a trail of crushed crisps, and every horizontal surface was furry with dust. The wallpaper behind the couch where the children were sitting had been torn off in ragged strips, like a row of stalagmites.

'Daylight's very unforgiving, isn't it?' said Erica, surveying the scene with a critical eye.

'Well . . .' said Jane, wondering what sort of lighting arrangement could possibly flatter such a room. No wonder she kept the curtains closed.

'Oh, who's done that?' Erica suddenly said, noticing the peeled wallpaper for the first time. Without taking his eyes off the TV, Greg solemnly raised a hand.

'You idiot. What did you do that for? Look at it!'

'You said I could.'

'I did not!'

'You said this was the next room we were going to decorate.'

'Yes it is. *Eventually*. Not today, you great pudding.'

Jane couldn't help laughing. Really, perhaps her own kids weren't so bad after all.

'She helped,' said Gregory, pointing at Harriet.

'What?' said Jane.

'Don't tell tales,' said Erica, simultaneously.

'I want to go and play upstairs,' said Harriet, sliding off the couch.

'Did you pull some of that wallpaper off?' Jane demanded.

'He said it was allowed,' Harriet retorted. Not a glimmer of contrition, thought Jane, preparing herself for a good rant.

'Please,' said Erica, holding her hands up. 'It doesn't matter. You go up into the boys' room and find some toys, darling,' she said to Harriet, who skipped off, delightedly.

'And don't make a mess,' Jane called after her automatically, and then blushed, as Erica gave a sardonic laugh. On the TV the chat show was giving way to a commercial break. *Coming Next*, flashed a message across the screen, *the man who lost everything through his addiction to jelly!*

'Oh, do turn that thing off.' Gregory hit the remote button and the screen gave a pop and went blank. 'And put some clothes on,' she added, as he slouched out of the room.

'I'm fed up with all these jobs,' was his parting shot.

Jane and Erica turned to each other and shrugged, in a gesture of solidarity, at the trials of motherhood. 'What's the time?' asked Erica, looking at Jane's watch. 'Eleven. I think I will have that beer after all. What about you?'

Jane opened her mouth to refuse, then changed her mind. She wasn't driving anywhere; Sophie could be picked up on foot. 'Okay, why not?'

❦

'So has your husband worked abroad for long?' asked Jane when Erica had returned from the garden shed with four bottles of lager, and cleared a space either side of the baby for them to sit down. The library books had been temporarily forgotten.

'Eight months. He's got another ten to go.'

'Don't you miss him?' Jane tried to imagine how much, or whether, she would miss Guy, and whether there might be something to be said for enjoying the financial and social advantages of marriage without having to accommodate the habits of a husband. No, life would be intolerable without Guy. Even at such moments of disloyalty she was struck by how much she did love him.

'I miss him more at weekends,' Erica said, after some thought. 'Though I can't say I sit around pining. We could have gone with him, but it didn't seem worth uprooting for such a short time. Will's just got settled in at the playgroup, and Greg's happy at school. We thought it would be best not to disturb their education.' From above their heads came the loud electronic music of a computer game. 'Anyway, I like it here.'

'Your phone bill must be huge. Do you ring each other much?'

'Once a week he calls me from the office. And we've got a fax so we send messages quite often. It's not as bad as all that. It must be worse for him.'

'Yes.' Jane had no clear image of Kuwait. She pictured skyscrapers, and faceless, modern industrial estates. And sand. She took a sip of her lager. Such a bitter, dirty taste. Erica was already well down her second bottle. It was just like giving up sugar in coffee. You had to persevere.

'Are you married?' said Erica.

Jane nodded. 'He's head of the primary school down the road.'

'Oh, that's your husband, is it? He'll know Gregory then. He must like kids.'

'Other people's. No, that's not fair. He's good with the girls, when he's not too tired. Well, it's easy to be good with Sophie.' She lowered her voice. 'We're both at a bit of a loss with Harriet. They prefer him anyway.'

'I don't think I've ever spoken to him,' said Erica, thinking with her head on one side. 'He's not been there long, has he?'

Jane shook her head. 'Nine months. How come I haven't seen you at school then? I'm up there twice a day, taking and fetching, and I've never noticed you.'

'I don't go up there much. Greg walks home now with a couple of his friends. There's no roads to cross. I sometimes drive in the morning if it's raining, and just tip him out at the gate.'

'That's very brave of you – letting him go on his own. I think Guy and I will still be escorting the girls when they're twenty.'

'I'm not a great worrier,' Erica admitted, her hand straying instinctively to the baby's tummy, rising and falling between them.

No, thought Jane. It was fully consistent with losing library books and drinking before lunchtime and leaving old nappies and pieces of toast in close proximity. This wasn't the house of an obsessive.

'What's this for?' Harriet asked, walking in holding a rusty mousetrap, primed with a lump of hard, cracked cheddar.

'Whoops,' said Erica, retrieving it. 'Was that on the landing? Sorry. Just a little local infestation. Nothing major.' She tapped the cheese with a crayon from the floor and the trap sprang shut, snapping the crayon in half. Jane went white.

'I want one of those,' said Harriet, impressed.

'Perhaps we'd better go and look for those library books,' Erica remembered. 'Come on, kids, there's a prize for anyone who finds them.'

'Only don't go hunting through things, Harriet,' said Jane, finishing her beer with a shudder of distaste. Who knew what other hazards might be lurking out of sight? 'Just see if you can see them, without touching.' She followed Erica up the stairs, casting an anxious glance at the baby on the couch as she left. What if he woke up and rolled off?

Most of the landing was occupied by a life-sized model dalek with two towels draped over its metal arms. 'I made that for them,' said Erica. 'But as they've never seen *Doctor Who* they don't really know what it is. It's become a sort of clothes horse now.' The carpet beneath their feet was randomly striped with masking tape. 'That's just there to mark the squeaky floorboards,' Erica explained, seeing Jane's expression. 'So I don't wake the baby.' On the wall at the top of the stairs was a framed black and white photograph of fishing nets on a breakwater, and another of a man running away from the camera across a vast expanse of sand at low tide.

'They're nice,' said Jane. They were the first things she'd seen in the place which she could admire with any sincerity.

'Oh thanks. I took them,' said Erica, pausing in the act of rummaging through a carrier bag hanging from the banisters.

'Really?' said Jane, amazed to discover that an aesthetic sense could flourish amidst so much chaos. 'You're a photographer?'

'Non-practising,' said Erica. 'I don't have time any more. And my dark room's about to be converted into a nursery.' She pointed at a closed door next to the bathroom.

'Well, there's always that one-hour place down by the station,' said Jane, smiling.

Erica nodded. 'Thanks. I'll bear it in mind.'

'And this is yours, is it?' said Jane to Gregory, who had forced open the door of the box room for her inspection. A pair of bunk-beds stood against the window blocking out much of the light. A chest of drawers and a brimming toy trunk occupied the rest of the floor space that was not already ankle deep in cars, trains, books, naked action men, and crushed jigsaw boxes from which the contents had slithered and merged. There was scarcely room to put a foot to the floor. 'Mine and my brother's,' said Gregory, wading to the edge of the bed, where Harriet was dangling upside down from the ladder.

'Do you sleep in the top bunk?' Jane went on, conversationally. It was hard to think of anything else to say about the room which wasn't expressive of shock or disapproval.

Gregory appeared to find her suggestion highly amusing. 'Of course not, silly. It's much too messy. I have to sleep on the couch downstairs.'

'Oh,' said Jane. Now she came to think of it there had been a sleeping bag on the couch downstairs. She had taken it for an appurtenance of his illness.

'Which means I'm not allowed to get up in the night in case I set off the burglar alarm,' he went on.

'Found them!' came Erica's voice from the master bedroom. Through the doorway Jane could just see the corner of a double bed and beside it an exercise bike hung with clothes.

'What if you need to go to the loo?' asked Jane, who was finding Gregory's revelations rather exhilarating.

'I just have to hold it,' Gregory explained, crossing his legs and adopting a pinched expression.

'What about your brother, Bill . . . Billy? Where does he sleep?'

'Will. He starts off there.' He pointed to a small depression in the pile of teddies on the bottom bunk. 'But he always ends up in Mum's bed,' he said in a scornful voice. 'When my dad comes home for ever we're going to get a bigger house and I'll have my own room and Will and Yorrick can share.'

Yorrick, thought Jane. Good grief! What sort of person would name their baby after a skull?

'They're all here, I think,' said Erica, reappearing with a pile of books. 'Except the one that's gone to Kuwait. I'll have that one transferred to my ticket so the fines come to me.' She turned to Gregory. 'Get some clothes on. We've got to go and get Will. Put them over your pyjamas if it's quicker.'

'Would you like me to stay here with the children while

you go?' Jane suggested. 'You don't want to take him out if he's ill.' Privately she doubted there was anything much wrong with him. His appetite was certainly hearty enough.

'Really?' Erica brightened at the prospect. 'I'll do the library business on the way back. I'll have to go like this. No time to change,' she said, rolling up the trailing legs of the overalls and forcing her feet into a pair of laced-up trainers. She dropped the books into a rucksack and clumped down the stairs, swiping a bunch of keys from the window ledge at the bottom. 'This is the second time you've minded my children for me,' she said over her shoulder as she left. 'And I don't even know your name.'

'I don't recognize the name,' said Guy, later that evening, as he stood at the kitchen sink scrubbing at a casserole dish. Jane was drying up. 'Gregory Crowe. Well, if I haven't run into him it means he must be an average sort of kid.'

'I can assure you he isn't,' Jane laughed. 'You've never seen such a set-up. Talk about chaos.'

'Did she seem embarrassed when you told her I was your husband?'

'No. Not in the least. I don't think she's capable of embarrassment. Oh, I've just remembered something else. There was a piece of light flex just hanging from the children's bedroom ceiling. Nothing on the end of it – completely uninsulated.' She reached past Guy to put away a glass and he seized her with warm soapy hands, making her squirm. 'You smell beery,' he said, when they'd kissed.

'That's because I had one today.'

'But you don't drink beer. You hate it.'

'I used to,' said Jane. 'But it's not too late to change.'

17

There was one occasion during his first year at university when Guy had taken a small bag of dirty clothes home for the weekend. His mother had thrown them in the machine with a very bad grace. 'The dog doesn't bring me his washing, you know,' she'd said, frostily. Of course when it came to his brother's turn a few years later, William would regularly bring back a vast trunk full of foul-smelling socks and begrimed sports kits, and return with them freshly laundered.

Today, though, Guy was doing his washing in the basement of the intercollegiate hall near his flat. The coin slot in one of the dryers had jammed in the On position, offering those in the know unlimited free rides. As so often, Guy had forgotten to bring a book with him and was forced to sit and stare at his clothes cartwheeling around behind the glass door, and listen to the drone of the machine and the clank of metal fastenings against the drum. The cycle only lasted fifteen minutes before it had to be restarted, and a full load took at least an hour to dry. Other people's laundry hung suspended from rows of wooden poles above his head, or sat in damp piles on the benches. The air was heavy with water vapour and the pungent smell of wet clothes. Ghostly trails of steam floated just below the ceiling and condensation streamed down the windowless walls. Guy had read every word on all six sides of his box of Daz when he heard the metallic footsteps descending the stairs. The sound of Blakeys on stone always made him think of Hugo and his reinforced school shoes, but before that train of thought had had a chance to gather momentum, the door opened and there before him, ten years older, a few stone heavier, and carrying an empty suitcase, stood Hugo himself.

The moment of recognition hit Hugo slightly later, but he was the first to recover. 'Guy! *Hello!*' He dropped the suitcase and gave Guy the benefit of a joint-cracking handshake.

'Hugo. I knew it was you before you even came through the door. You're the only person I know who has metal heels.'

'What are you doing in this stinking basement?' Hugo asked. He seemed genuinely delighted to see Guy. 'You don't live in this building, do you?'

Guy shook his head. 'Not that far away. I'm at the Institute.'

Hugo raised his eyebrows. 'You're going to teach?'

'Supposedly. Where are you?'

'UCL. Third year.'

Guy looked puzzled. 'Third? Have you lost a couple of years somewhere?'

'Yes. I wasted them at Cambridge. Anyway.' He didn't seem inclined to dwell on this.

'I'm surprised I haven't bumped into you before. We must haunt the same square mile.'

'I don't get out much,' said Hugo, dragging various items of clothing from the wooden poles above his head and tossing them into his open suitcase.

'Do you ever eat at SOAS? It's got the best canteen in London. Dirt cheap.'

Hugo gave a condescending smile. 'Well, maybe. Do you know that Free House in Bloomsbury Way? It's got the best beer in London.'

Guy knew it, and was about to cite others of a similar calibre, when Hugo carried on. 'I'm going there tonight. Do you want to come?'

'Well.' The thought of an evening with Hugo did not fill Guy with enthusiasm, but he'd hesitated too long now and no ready excuse had sprung to his lips. 'Yeah, okay, why not?'

'Great.' Hugo forced the lid of his suitcase down and snapped the catches shut. 'I'll see you there about nine.' And he was off up the stairs, sparks leaping from his metal heels.

'Nine,' said Guy to the diminishing gap in the doorway. He was regretting it already. He had nothing to say to Hugo.

It was always interesting to re-meet old acquaintances, but an exchange of hellos and what-are-you-up-tos more than satisfied his curiosity. What would they talk about for two hours? They couldn't reminisce about school indefinitely, and, besides, the memories weren't especially flattering to Hugo. Well, it was only one evening; he wouldn't be making a habit of it.

The drying machine switched itself off and Guy watched his clothes collapse against the bottom of the drum. He had let it run too long: the handle was hot to the touch and when he opened the door he could smell scorched lint.

Guy spotted him straight away. It was a weekday evening and the pub was nearly empty. There were a couple of squaddies getting drunk at the bar, and a group of office workers feeding the juke-box. Hugo was sitting at one of the round tables in the middle of the room with his back to the door. His watch lay on the table beside a row of foamy pint glasses, recently drained. Guy was ten minutes late; he'd been unable to find his wallet as he was leaving and had turned his room upside down to no avail. He had nothing but a handful of coins, and was tempted to stay at home, but decided it would be marginally worse to stand Hugo up with no explanation, than to arrive empty-handed and scrounge. In any case he would be bound to bump into him again – in Dillons, or the Union bar or somewhere – and then his excuse would sound all the lamer for not being fresh. Guy hated apologizing, which was a shame, as he so often found himself in situations for which it was the only remedy.

'Sorry I'm late,' he said, dragging a stool up to the table. 'Have you been here long?'

'An hour and ten minutes,' said Hugo, with more than a hint of reproach. He picked up his watch and strapped it back on to his wrist.

'I thought you said nine. You did say nine.'

'Well, whatever,' said Hugo, refusing to acknowledge his

mistake. He indicated the empty glasses. 'You've got some catching up to do.'

'I'm a bit stuck for cash,' said Guy. 'That's why I was late – ten minutes late, I mean. I've lost my wallet. I'll pay you back.'

'That's all right,' said Hugo, patting his trouser pocket. 'You can pay next time.'

'Okay,' said Guy, wondering how he was going to wriggle out of a second meeting now that he was indebted. He watched Hugo lurch unsteadily towards the bar and position himself directly between the two squaddies, effectively halting their conversation. One of them made an obscene gesture behind Hugo's back. 'Faggot,' Guy lip-read. Oh God, he thought. Trouble already.

Hugo returned, oblivious, slopping bitter from two glasses. 'Cheers,' he said.

'Yes. Cheers,' Guy replied. There was a silence while they both took a long draught. 'So how's your family?' he went on. He'd never met any of them – there were grandparents and a despised father, he remembered – but it was something to say.

'All dead,' said Hugo, cheerfully. 'I'm an orphan at last.'

'Oh,' said Guy, who had not expected the death toll to be quite so high. 'I'm sorry.'

'I'm not,' said Hugo. 'I didn't even go to my father's funeral. Apparently there wasn't a wet eye in the house.' He lit a cigarette and slung the packet across to Guy. The ashtray was already full of butts. Hugo leaned across to the next table and swapped it for an empty one.

'You never made it up, then?'

Hugo shook his head. 'No. There was no deathbed reconciliation, I'm afraid. Not for lack of opportunity, I have to say. He took an awfully long time to die.'

'What from?'

'Cirrhosis of the liver.' He raised his glass. 'I'll drink to that.'

Guy smiled. 'Did he leave you anything?'

'His debts,' said Hugo. 'The farm had to be sold to pay

them off. I got the change. And his car. Very useful, given that it's in Johannesburg. And I don't drive.'

'So you've got no living relatives at all? How weird.'

'There are some very distant ones I've never met. We don't communicate. I don't even know where they live. No, I'm a lone, lorn creature all right,' he said, complacently. 'Can you drive?' he added, as an afterthought.

'Yes,' said Guy, wondering for an insane moment whether Hugo was going to offer him the use of the South African car. 'But there's no point in London, is there? There's nowhere to park it.'

Having learned the answer, Hugo didn't bother to pursue the subject. He finished his pint and stood up. 'Same again?'

'Okay. Or we could move on.' He could see that Hugo was quite drunk already. The squaddies had cast unfriendly glances in their direction more than once.

'No, let's stay,' said Hugo. 'They know me here.'

'All right. Suits me.' Guy shrugged. Without money of his own he couldn't very well insist.

The pub had started to fill up with new arrivals and Guy watched with a sense of unease as Hugo joined the scrum at the bar. In spite of his professed intimacy with the staff Hugo seemed to have trouble getting served, and it was a while before he returned with two pint glasses, one less full than the other, and a sopping wet sleeve.

'Stupid tart jogged my elbow,' he said belligerently. He started to pull packets of crisps and nuts from various pockets, like a magician producing doves.

'Yes, well, never mind, eh?' said Guy, who was beginning to find Hugo a less than soothing companion. 'You're in the third year now, then? Doing what? Maths, I bet. Or physics.'

'Geography, actually. Please don't say "that's not a real subject".'

'I wouldn't dream of it. Being an economist myself.'

'Ah.'

'So what are you going to do next year?'

'A PhD. If I get a first.'

'Is that on the cards, then?'

Guy remembered that as an eleven-year-old Hugo had had no time for false, or any other sort of modesty.

Hugo nodded. 'Unless I have a brainstorm. It's a cushy life, academia, don't you think?'

'Not my branch of it,' said Guy, through a mouthful of peanuts.

'No, well. Teaching. What a horrible thought. You must have enjoyed your schooldays more than I did.'

'I wasn't unhappy,' Guy admitted. 'But then I wasn't sad to leave either. You were going to burn the place down, I remember. You must have had a change of heart.'

'Not at all,' said Hugo. 'Just a failure of nerve. My heart was quite committed.'

'Anyway, I'm not going to be teaching teenage arsonists. I've opted for the little ones.'

Hugo rolled his eyes and shuddered. 'Worse and worse. Don't they all want to cling on to you and sit on your knee?'

Guy nodded. 'And they twine themselves round your legs like cats,' he said, laughing to see Hugo's expression of revulsion.

'What sort of teacher will you be, I wonder? Wackford Squeers or Mr Chips?'

'I'll be one of those long-haired inner-city progressives my parents are always ranting about. Abolishing uniforms and exams and corporal punishment.'

Hugo laughed, drunkenly, though Guy had only been half-joking. He had every intention of keeping his hair long. And he would certainly never use the cane on a child. The thought sickened him.

'You'll have to play the guitar in assembly,' Hugo warned. 'And wipe up lots of vomit.'

'I know. I've been practising,' said Guy. 'The guitar, not the wiping.'

'And you'll be starting this September, will you?' asked Hugo, tipping a crisp packet into his open mouth and gagging as the last few shards caught in the back of his throat.

'If I get a job.'

'Got anything planned for the summer?' he went on, casually.

'No, not really,' said Guy. 'Looking for work or preparing lessons, mostly, I suppose.'

'You don't fancy a free trip somewhere hot?'

'Er . . . I'm not sure,' said Guy warily. 'Where?'

'I'm running a field trip to Algeria in July,' said Hugo. 'Doing research on sand dunes for my PhD. I'm going with another chap and a girl I share a flat with. They're geographers too. Only we need another driver,' he wheedled. 'Since I can't.'

'Ah.' He'd done it again – allowed himself to hesitate when all that was required was an outright refusal. 'I don't think so. I wouldn't know the others. It would be awkward.'

'No – it would be good. People always behave better with strangers. They argue less. I was going to advertise for an outsider for that very reason.'

'But I don't know anything about sand dunes. I'd be no help at all.'

'That's all right. It's only measuring, taking readings – elementary stuff. It's the interpretation that's difficult, and I'll be doing that.'

'How are you getting there?'

'Land Rover. They're very pleasant to drive, I'm told. I'm aiming for In Salah, on the Great Western Erg.'

Guy pulled a face. 'Do you need visas and stuff? Isn't Algeria at war with Morocco at the moment?'

'Not officially. Anyway, it's all been approved by the Algerian government. We're doing them a favour. Basically it's impossible to build efficient road and rail systems across the Sahara because they keep getting engulfed by sand dunes. No one's done any really prolonged research on dune initiation. If we can discover how they start, and their patterns of movement, we can predict their behaviour.'

Guy nodded. Four people in a Land Rover in the middle of the Sahara counting grains of sand, or whatever Hugo intended. It sounded like a vision of hell. 'I think I'll be pretty tied up over the summer, finding a job and somewhere to live. Otherwise . . .'

'Well,' said Hugo. 'Think about it.' He pushed a beer mat across to Guy. 'Give me your address and number and I'll let you have more details when I've got them. I'm still grubbing around for sponsorship at the moment. You're no good at fund-raising, I suppose?' he added, as if Guy was already part of the team.

'No. Absolutely crap,' said Guy decisively. He produced a chewed biro from his jacket pocket and wrote his details on the beer mat which was slightly damp and spongy, and watched Hugo tuck it into the pocket of his jeans. Guy didn't invite Hugo to reciprocate, but he did, anyway.

'Thanks,' said Guy. He could now send Hugo the money he owed him for the beers rather than get drawn into another night out. Hugo pushed his wallet across the table. 'Get another round in while I'm in the bog,' he said, standing up abruptly and knocking the table into Guy so that his glass clashed against his teeth. Hugo's unsteady progress did not pass unnoticed by the squaddies, who waited until Guy was at the bar ordering drinks before exchanging a nod and following Hugo into the Gents. Something about their purposeful stride filled Guy with dread. Oh shit, he thought, abandoning the drinks. It must be my destiny to rescue Hugo Etchells from toilets. He pushed open the door just in time to see Hugo hit the floor, his glasses flying off and skidding across the wet tiles. The look of astonishment on his face was rapidly replaced by one of intense pain as he registered the blow to his jaw that had sent him sprawling. He instinctively curled up and covered his head as one of the squaddies followed up with a hard kick. Guy never did find out whether they had intended robbery, rape or murder, or whether this was just a recreational beating, because at this point the outer door swung open to admit two of the office crowd, one of whom was about six foot six and built like a bouncer. The squaddies seemed to lose interest in performing in front of an audience and, turning abruptly away from Hugo, who was still wedged under the basin in a foetal position, they sauntered out again, giving Guy the benefit of a leering smile.

'Is he all right?' the bouncer-type asked, as Guy helped Hugo to his feet and rinsed his glasses under the tap.

'They nearly broke my fucking jaw!' said Hugo in a thick voice, full of outrage and incomprehension. He ran his fingers along the lower part of his face to check that it was all still there. One cheek bulged as if he'd just had a wisdom tooth removed, and the skin was fiery red. There would be a spectacular bruise there in the morning, thought Guy. On the back of Hugo's head, where he'd fallen against the water-pipe, was a walnut-sized lump.

'Animals,' said the smaller one sympathetically.

Guy dried Hugo's glasses on the edge of a soiled roller towel and handed them back.

'And my shins,' muttered Hugo, pulling up his trouser leg to take a look at the site of impact of the squaddie's boot.

'Come on, you're okay,' said Guy, nodding to the two witnesses to indicate that the situation was now under control. 'Let's go, shall we?'

'What about that last drink?' Hugo protested.

'You can't have it. You might be concussed.' He urged Hugo out of the crowded pub, carving a path to the exit with an outstretched arm. In the Strand a cold drizzle was falling, making the pavement greasy, and releasing the smell of urine from the gutters. A red Routemaster shimmered to a halt at the traffic light beside them. 'I'm hungry. Shall we go to Veeraswamy's?' Hugo suggested, as Guy took a step towards the platform.

'No. This is our bus. You'll have to come with me because I haven't got any money,' Guy said, impatiently. He wanted nothing more than to be back home. There was half a packet of bacon in the fridge which he could have on toast with mustard. His stomach gave a volcanic rumble at the thought of it.

They sat downstairs on the long seats, watching the blurred lights of the West End through the rain-streaked windows, the cold, damp air whipping at their ankles. Hugo seemed to fall into a trance, swaying gently with the rhythm of the bus, his eyes half-closed, then half way along Piccadilly he suddenly said, 'I'm going to be sick', in a voice loud enough to bring the conductor out of his lair. 'Not in here, you're not,' he said, yanking on the bell wire above his head. '*Off!*' As the bus slowed down Guy and Hugo stumbled off the platform on to the slippery pavement. 'There's a bin here,' said Guy, pointing ten yards up the street.

'No, it's all right. I feel better now,' said Hugo, momentarily regaining his balance, before doubling over and bringing up a torrent of watery vomit in the darkened doorway of Fortnum & Mason's.

Guy felt his stomach lurch, and turned away, trying not to hear the heaving and splattering that continued behind him. Hugo straightened up, slack-jawed, groaning with relief, and Guy dared to look. Little threads of saliva stretched from his wet chin to the front of his jacket. He had tried to contain the flood with his hands and now they were dripping and foul. He held them out in front of him like alien objects. Guy felt in his pocket for a handkerchief, finally producing a compressed ball of used, dried tissue the texture of pumice. He passed it over apologetically, and Hugo grimaced before rolling it around his hands. Then he brushed his sleeve across his watering eyes and blinked hard. 'It must be that blow to the head,' he said at last. 'Those bastards could have killed me.'

They probably would have done if I hadn't come in, thought Guy. But don't thank me. 'Have you got enough money for a taxi?' he asked. 'Perhaps you'd better go home to bed.'

Hugo nodded. 'You're right. I'll go and sleep off my concussion.' He thrust a hand out into the road and within seconds a black taxi had detached itself from the herd and pulled up alongside them.

'Is there anyone there to keep an eye on you, in case you go into a coma or something?' said Guy over the clattering engine, praying the answer would be yes. The last thing he wanted to do was put Hugo to bed and play nursemaid all night.

'Yes, don't worry. My friends are used to looking after me.' He settled himself in the back of the cab.

I bet, thought Guy.

'Well, that was fun,' said Hugo, through the open window, apparently without irony. 'We must do it again some time.' And then the taxi sped off, leaving Guy alone on the pavement to the realization that in his haste to be rid of Hugo he had forgotten to borrow his fare, and that he would now have to walk all the way back to Kensington in the rain.

Nina and Martin were still up watching the late film on Martin's black and white portable TV when Hugo returned. Nina had cooked goulash and their half-full plates were still on the coffee table next to an empty wine bottle and a full ashtray. The meat had been tough and rubbery and neither of them had had the stamina to finish it. 'I must have bought the wrong bit of the cow,' said Nina. 'I thought it was cheap. There are probably softer bits.'

'The rice was all right,' Martin was saying, kindly, when he heard a taxi pull up outside and a second later the sound of someone holding the front doorbell down.

'Hurry up,' called Hugo through the letter-box. 'I haven't got enough money for the fare.' Nina and Martin had no money either, which was why they had stayed in with the TV and the cheap beef, but Hugo had no patience for Martin's measured explanation. 'There must be some in the house somewhere,' he snapped. Finally Nina had resorted to opening the pay phone in the hall and paying the driver off in ten-pence pieces. They had promised themselves they wouldn't do this: the money was supposed to be there to meet the bill.

'What happened to you?' Nina asked, when Hugo was back indoors, in the light.

He put his hand to his jaw. 'I was set upon by two thugs in the Princess Louise. Out of the blue,' he said solemnly. Nina and Martin glanced at each other. It wasn't the first time something like this had happened 'out of the blue'.

'You stink of puke, if you don't mind my saying so,' said Martin.

'Well, it's not surprising. I've got a serious head injury.' And Hugo bent over and parted the hair on the back of his head so they could inspect his lump. 'Anyway,' he added. 'It wasn't a completely disastrous evening. I think I've found our Fourth Man.'

18

'. . . Nineteen, twenty, *coming*, ready or not,' came the sing-song voice from upstairs. Erica and Jane were drinking tea in Jane's sitting room while the four older children played hide and seek somewhere, out of sight. Baby Yorrick was propped fatly on the floor, supported by cushions, and twitching his arms in the direction of an activity cube, which he kept kicking out of reach. Every so often he would slowly sink forward, and Erica would stretch out her foot to intercept him before his forehead hit the carpet.

The two women had bumped into each other twice since Jane had called at the house a fortnight earlier – once in the supermarket and once at the school – though neither meeting could be called accidental, since both had involved a degree of contrivance on Jane's part. Erica had made some remark about doing her shopping on a Monday morning, which Jane had remembered and followed up. They had nearly collided in the frozen food aisle. Will was standing in the well of the trolley, in an exact rendition of the pose illustrated on the handle and marked with an unambiguous X. Harriet was lashed into the seat, squirming, and whining loudly. It had not been practical for the two women to do more than exchange hellos and sympathetic grimaces before ploughing on. Since then Jane had walked down Erica's road a couple of times though it was a cul-de-sac and therefore not strictly *on the way* to anywhere. And then today it was pouring, and Jane knew Erica was likely to turn up in the car to fetch Gregory, so she had loitered with a rather puzzled Sophie and Harriet near the Juniors' entrance, in the hope of running into her again. All of which behaviour, Jane admitted to herself, was uncharacteristic and weird and not unlike the symptoms of infatuation. This thought had been brought before her again when, on finally seeing Erica emerge from a dented estate car in the rain without an umbrella and with two coatless children, Jane had felt her heart give one sudden syncopated lurch.

'These spring showers catch a lot of people out,' Jane said, as they drew level. It had poured relentlessly since dawn.

Erica gave a quick, wide smile. 'My umbrella's broken,' she said, zipping the baby tightly inside her own jacket. 'I used it for something else.'

Jane remembered the dead-crow-on-a-stick on the doorstep. 'Walloping the mice?' she inquired. Something about Erica suggested she wouldn't be the sort to take offence at this.

'No, no, nothing violent. Unblocking a drain, I think.' She beckoned urgently to Gregory, who was sauntering through the rain towards them. 'I'd offer you a lift,' she went on. 'But I can't fit you all in.'

'That's okay,' said Jane. 'We're dressed for a monsoon.' And they were – in raincoats, hoods, boots, and a huge golf umbrella which obstructed the full width of the path. Whatever she lacked in emotional resilience, Jane felt that in the practical matters of motherhood she more than compensated. 'But come back for tea anyway. If you're not too busy.'

'You keep an orderly house,' Erica said, absent-mindedly stroking the petals of the artificial flower arrangement on the coffee table. It was looking considerably less orderly since Erica and her children had arrived. The boys had brought several different games down from Sophie's room and abandoned them half-assembled on the floor. Will had wet himself with excitement and was now running around in a pair of Harriet's Minnie Mouse knickers while his trousers soaked in the bathroom sink.

'I bet you're the sort of woman who keeps change in the car for parking meters, and aspirin and plasters and spare tights in your handbag.'

Jane laughed. She hadn't thought of carrying spare tights, but she would now.

'If these flowers were in my house they'd have artificial greenfly,' Erica went on.

'I feel more sane if things are tidy,' Jane explained, fighting the impulse to clear away the toys from the floor before the children had finished with them. 'Perhaps that's just the delusion of a madwoman.'

'Do you feel mad? I don't. I always think it's everybody else who's mad,' said Erica, standing up to inspect the framed photographs on the wall. There were half a dozen studio portraits of the girls from babyhood up to the present, and a picture of Guy behind his desk at work. He was wearing his reading glasses – which he never otherwise used – to make himself look mature and learned, but someone had obviously cracked a joke seconds earlier as he had an unforced and most unheadmasterly grin on his face. Jane was very fond of that picture. The mantelpiece was three deep in still more photographs of Harriet and Sophie, in christening robes or party dresses, or on the beach.

'I've hardly got any of the boys,' Erica said, her inspection complete. 'Which is a bit ironic really. I was quite good when Greg was little. But I wasn't so diligent when Will came along. And poor old Yorrick. I think I've got one picture of him with his hand in front of his face. I bet you've got all those baby books filled in, haven't you? First tooth, first word, first tantrum, first hangover.'

Jane admitted that she had. 'I like to get things down in black and white before I forget them. Then when I'm old and sad I can dig out all the albums and remember.' From above their heads came the sound of squeaking bedsprings and several pairs of feet hitting the floor. Jane was at the bottom of the stairs in a trice. 'Not on the beds, please,' she called in a much milder tone than she was accustomed to use on Sophie and Harriet when unobserved.

'There are no pictures of you here,' said Erica, when Jane returned.

'Well, that's because it's always me behind the camera,'

Jane replied. 'Anyway, I don't particularly like looking at myself these days.'

'Same here,' said Erica. 'In fact I think there's a horrible old witch living behind all the mirrors in our house. And I'm the only one who can see her.' She tugged a hank of greying hair from behind one ear and pouted at herself in the mirror above the mantelpiece. 'God, it's even worse here without the dust.'

'There is one of me somewhere,' said Jane, plucking an oval silver frame from the back row of the collection. It was a photo of her and Guy, taken pre-children, looking young and happy.

'That's nice. That's not a wedding photo, is it?'

'No. A funeral actually,' said Jane. 'I know it sounds awful, but it was my grandfather's funeral and my aunt brought her camera along to take pictures of the rest of the family while they were all together. It's the best picture we've got of the two of us. Much better than our wedding photos.'

'You're looking very cheerful,' Erica pointed out. 'Did you stand to inherit?'

'No. But you know how you always get the giggles at funerals,' said Jane.

'I met Neil at a crematorium,' Erica mused. 'We're second cousins. I inherited £5,000 and picked up a husband. That was a good day's work for me.'

Sophie appeared in the doorway, her hands behind her back, head on one side in the pose of a supplicant. 'Can we have a biscuit?' she wheedled. The others had evidently nominated her as the most likely to succeed in this quest. Normally she would know better than to ask so soon before tea.

'Yes, all right,' said Jane, sensing that at Erica's the boys probably had the run of the larder. 'Take the tin up with you. But don't go mad.'

'Sound advice,' Erica nodded, as Sophie scampered out to the kitchen. 'I do envy you having daughters,' she went on. 'I always wanted boys because I thought they'd be easier and I'd be able to foster the cult of the mother and be adored like a Sicilian. But when I was pregnant for the third time I started to hanker after a girl. I think it's the names. I could name a whole convent of girls. But it wasn't to be.'

Jane glanced at Yorrick, as if he might be eavesdropping and feeling slighted. Until now she had always felt superstitious about articulating, or even thinking too hard about any such dissatisfactions, preferring to let them fester unexamined. 'I only ever wanted girls,' she said. 'Only with me it turned out to be a case of "Be careful what you wish for". Now I wish I had a son.'

'Really?' said Erica, interested.

Jane leant forward. The urge to confide was too strong. 'It's Harriet,' she said, out of the corner of her mouth. 'We don't get on. She is actually a Fiend in Human Form.'

Erica looked dubious. 'From a short acquaintance I'd say she was only averagely fiendish. She's three, isn't she? I mean, look at Will. He's a little savage.'

'But he's an affectionate savage,' said Jane. 'He'll hold your hand and cuddle you. Harriet won't let me touch her. She hates me.'

'Some children don't like being touched. Some adults too,' said Erica.

Well, that was true, Jane agreed. Guy had said much the same thing not long ago – with her in mind probably.

'I suppose what I'm really saying is . . .' Jane lowered her voice, conscious that she was about to break a taboo, '. . . I *prefer* Sophie. I can't help it. She's just . . . nicer.' There, she'd done it: said the unspeakable. 'I've never told anyone this before. Not even Guy,' she went on, quailing at the thought of Erica's disapproval. 'It's such a terrible thing to say. Like cursing the Holy Spirit or something.'

'I'm sure you're not alone,' Erica said finally, though without, Jane noticed, admitting to similar tendencies. 'And anyway, it's only temporary. When she's five she'll be as sweet as an angel and you'll forget you ever felt like this.'

'Or she'll be at school all day and I won't notice it so much,' said Jane. She didn't feel optimistic about the prospect of change. Harriet's personality had seemed stamped on her from birth. The moment of bonding – the two-way surge of tenderness, which she'd experienced when Sophie was a few hours old – still hadn't happened.

'Shall I put the kettle back on?' asked Erica, whose cup was empty.

'Yes. Sorry, I'll do it,' said Jane, opening the sitting room door and almost falling over Harriet, who was standing just outside dressed in the Witch's costume Jane had made last Hallowe'en. Someone had attempted to crayon her face green.

'Oh!' Jane gasped, reeling backwards, wondering how long she had been there and how much she could possibly have heard or understood.

'We've been doing face paints,' said Harriet. 'Can you do me a black tooth?' Her heart still hammering, Jane took the black pastel and smeared it on one of Harriet's tiny front teeth. 'Don't lick it off. It's not good for you.'

'Will I die?' asked Harriet, who was becoming keenly interested in death and brought it up at any opportunity, however tangential. Only the other day she had asked Jane during the minute's silence in church whether Jane would die before her. She had seemed much relieved when Jane promised to try.

'No, of course you won't.'

'When are they going?' Harriet added loudly.

'Soon,' said Erica, joining them in the hallway. She had picked up Yorrick who was starting to grizzle. 'Tell the boys they've got five minutes,' she instructed Harriet, who scampered back upstairs, delighted to be the bearer of bad news.

'We're out of milk,' said Jane, after a quick glance in the fridge. 'I'll nip to the garage. It won't take me two minutes.'

'Don't bother. I'll take it black,' said Erica. 'Or better still, forget the tea.' Jane felt her spirits sag. In a short while Erica would leave, having made no further arrangement to meet and it would be up to Jane to skulk and contrive if she was to see her again. She didn't feel she'd made an especially good impression; chances to shine didn't tend to arise in the course of normal conversation. She felt an urgent and irrational need to detain Erica.

'No, no. Don't go yet. I'll need more milk for breakfast anyway. Two minutes,' she said. And she was out of the door before Erica could protest.

❦

Guy decided to leave the after-school drink-up early. He'd had a headache since lunchtime and could feel a rawness in his throat which heralded the start of a cold. There had been inspectors crawling over the place all week, interviewing staff and observing lessons and rifling through the children's work and shaking their heads over his strategic planning file and racking their brains for something negative to say about the place. In particular there had been one supercilious bastard to whom Guy had taken an instant and fully reciprocated dislike. He had described Guy's leadership style, to his face, as 'somewhat informal and idiosyncratic, but satisfactory'. Guy looked forward to further condescension when the written report was delivered. Everybody else was equally exhausted and demoralized, and desperate to get home; he'd laid on drinks and nibbles in the staff room but no one had the energy to celebrate with any conviction. And then to make matters worse, this afternoon Guy had come out of his office and slipped on a frog. He had half crushed its back legs underfoot as he skidded on the lino. Guy, who couldn't even kill a spider, had had to hop back into his office with it still hanging from his heel and finish it off properly, and then wrap it in tissues and hide it at the bottom of the bin. When he emerged again a few minutes later, pale and nauseous, he found six more frogs in the corridor, and was wondering what makeshift frog-catching equipment might be had from the caretaker's stores, when there was a commotion in the nearest classroom and thirty pupils and their teacher erupted through the doorway.

'Don't tell me,' he said. 'Frogs.' They were everywhere: on the tables, on the window ledges, in the toilets, hundreds of them, wherever you looked. Around the school other doors opened and shut, as classes prepared to evacuate. Clearly the new wildlife reserve behind the caretaker's house was suffering from an amphibious population explosion which natural predators had been unable to staunch. That was what happened when you tried to kick-start your own ecosystem. In the end he'd rung the fire bell and got everyone out on the playground while the pest control people had gone in. What a day!

The rain had stopped by the time he picked up his overcoat and said goodbye to the caretaker, but when he opened the car door there was an inch of water swilling around under the pedals. As he reversed out of his space he could hear more water slopping back and forth somewhere in the undercarriage. Another job for the weekend. If only he'd walked to school instead of driven today, Jane, not he, would have discovered it and had to deal with it. He slowed down as he passed the church, his conscience pricking him as he recalled the previous Sunday's sermon. The curate had spoken movingly on the subject of Doubt: 'On the journey of Faith, Doubt may well be a regular fellow-traveller. Rather like a garrulous companion who attaches himself to you uninvited, he may interrupt your concentration, and distract you from enjoying the scenery. You wish he'd go away and leave you in peace. But if you keep strictly to the path you intended, without stopping or changing direction, even though you may no longer have any heart for the journey, and find it tedious, one day you will look around and notice he's given up and is no longer by your side.'

Guy had stopped to talk to the curate after the service. 'I'm having just the experience you describe,' he said.

'And yet here you are coming to church,' said the curate. 'Which is exactly the right thing to do.'

Perhaps Jane had been right when she'd said, 'Just keep practising.'

'You can ask God for help, you know,' the curate went on. 'Even if you feel He isn't there. It's often at times like these that He reveals Himself most unexpectedly.' So Guy had slipped back into the church and prayed: Please, Father, give me a sign.

He had promised himself he would observe a daily act of prayer, and now, here he was, only five days into the regime and already taking a day off. He was too busy imagining himself indoors, enjoying a quiet lie-down with a hot toddy and a couple of those knockout painkillers Jane took for her periods. But as he pulled into the drive and switched off the engine he heard a noise from inside the house that was both familiar and strange: the whimpering of a young baby. He was momentarily transported back to those first few months after Harriet's birth, when the sound of his key in the latch each evening seemed to trigger a full six hours of inconsolable screaming. None of the strategies recommended by the childcare manuals had provided any relief. He had an enduring image of Jane, standing in the bay window of their old house, jigging Harriet up and down in her arms, both their faces red and bloated with crying.

The noise had stopped by the time Guy opened the front door. 'Hello,' he called, then stopped, as a small boy emerged from the downstairs loo, pulling up a pair of pink lacy pants. He looked at Guy in alarm and scuttled into the dining room, closing the door behind him. Guy took off his coat and slung it on the banisters – an annoying habit that Jane was trying to break – and dumped his briefcase in the hall before putting his head round the sitting room door. On the couch a woman he'd never seen before was breastfeeding a fat, bald baby. They both had their eyes closed as if fast asleep. Guy retreated, experiencing a sudden loss of confidence that he was in the right house, but, no, the furniture was his, and there was even a picture of him on the wall with that goofy expression on his face. He made his way upstairs, stepping over pieces of broken biscuit and crayon stumps as he went. A small witch, whom he recognized as Harriet, came panting past him on the landing. 'Who's that downstairs? Where's Mummy?' he asked.

'I'm a naughty witch and I'm going to turn you into a frog,' she replied, giving him a gap-toothed leer, then thundered back downstairs, grinding biscuit into the carpet at every step.

Guy shook his head. He'd had quite enough of frogs for one day. He went into the bathroom in search of some tablets; the pressure behind his eyes was intolerable. In the sink a pair of boy's jeans lay leaking navy dye into the surrounding water. As usual a couple of naked dolls were floating belly-up in the bidet. There didn't seem to be a glass to hand, so Guy choked back the dry tablets which sat like pebbles half way down his gullet. He wondered whether he ought to go back downstairs and introduce himself – and inquire after his wife – instead of skulking around like a burglar in his own house, but he didn't feel the least bit inclined to be sociable. Perhaps he would just lie down on the bed and fall asleep, and when he woke up his headache and the houseful of strangers would be gone.

In the bedroom Guy drew the curtains and pulled off his tie. He saw with some irritation that the contents of the laundry basket in the corner had been strewn over the carpet; most uncharacteristic of Jane. He kicked the clothes into a heap and started to change out of his suit. He had just taken off his trousers and was draping them neatly over a hanger when he noticed that the lid of the Ali Baba basket was moving – rising up, in fact – and a second later a boy's forehead and eyes appeared over the rim.

'Shhh!' hissed the boy. 'I'm hiding.' And then his eyes widened with the shock of recognizing the half-undressed figure of his headmaster and he dropped back into the basket with the lid on top of him.

Slightly dazed, Guy reeled out on to the landing and scrambled into the loft, pulling up the ladder behind him.

When Jane came back with the milk the car was in the driveway, but Erica claimed not to have seen or heard Guy. 'We have been dozing over this feed,' she admitted, when Will came crashing in, saying, 'There's a man upstairs with not much clothes on.' And before either of them could reply, Gregory had appeared in the doorway with a look of panic and confusion on his face, adding, 'Yes. And it's *Mr Bromelow in his pants.*' The laughter that greeted this remark only seemed to deepen his bewilderment.

❦

'You could have warned me,' Guy complained later, when the visitors had departed and the house was restored to order. 'I suppose that story will be all over the playground on Monday.'

'I didn't know you'd be coming back early,' Jane replied. She was still laughing over it hours later. 'Didn't it occur to you to say hello to Erica when you first came in?'

'It was the end of a long day,' said Guy. 'Who is she, anyway?'

'My friend,' said Jane, with a hint of defensiveness. 'She's my friend.'

'How can she be? I've never even heard of her.'

'You don't listen, that's why. I've known her months. Well, two months.' Now, with hindsight, Jane considered their friendship to date from that very first encounter in the park. Looking back she was able to invest it with tremendous significance. The near catastrophe of a lost child; the providential theft of a newspaper: she could see them for what they were now – the first links in a chain binding her and Erica together, a chain growing longer and stronger every day.

19

A little less than a month after his meeting with Hugo, Guy was woken in the early hours by the telephone. He twitched awake, heart hammering, and then lay there hoping that someone else would get it, or that it would stop ringing: there was no heating in the flat and Guy hadn't the slightest intention of leaving his warm bed. But whoever it was was prepared to hang on, and after a minute or so, Guy caved in and stumbled downstairs, shivering and worried, now, that, having committed himself to being awake and cold, he would be too late, and the caller would hang up, unrebuked.

'Yes?' he said into the receiver, without bothering to conceal his irritation.

'Am I speaking to Mr Guy Bromelow?' said a brisk, unfamiliar voice.

'Yes,' said Guy, moderating his tone a little.

The caller introduced himself as a police officer. 'Do you know someone called Hugo Blanchard Etchells?'

'Ye-e-es,' said Guy, uneasily, wondering what this admission would lead to.

'Only we've got him down here at St Thomas's Hospital, Casualty. He's been in an accident, and we'd like someone to take him home. We're not going to be charging him,' he added, which made Guy's heart sink.

'Is he all right?' he asked. 'What happened?'

'He's not injured, just a bit scratched. He was going the wrong way through the Kingsway tunnel in a shopping trolley when he was struck by a moped.' The police officer related this without a snigger. 'We suspect he's under the influence of drugs.'

'Oh,' said Guy, nonplussed. 'Look, I hardly know him. How did you get my number?'

'It was written on a beer mat in his pocket. He said to call you.'

'All right, I'll be along as soon as I can.' And before he could stop himself he even said 'Thanks'. As he hung up he caught sight of himself in the glass of the front door, naked and goose-pimpled. Thank you for waking me in the middle of the night so I can trek half way across London to bail Hugo out of some mess of his own making, he thought crossly, pulling on yesterday's clothes and pocketing the pile of change and crumpled notes on the bedside cabinet. He'd had no intention of seeing Hugo again. He had sent him a cheque to repay that night in the pub and had been quietly relieved when there was no follow-up. The matter of the desert trip had apparently been forgotten, or, as Guy suspected, had collapsed early in the planning process.

When Guy arrived at Casualty and inquired at the desk, he was directed to one of the curtained cubicles. Hugo was sitting on the examination bed, legs dangling, a peaceful, vacant expression on his face. He was wearing a hospital gown and his socks. A policeman was slumped in the only chair, passing an empty styrofoam cup from hand to hand. He sprang up as Guy entered.

'Oh, good. You're here at last.'

Guy bridled at that, and was about to expound on the difficulties of crossing London in the early hours, but the policeman cut him off, saying, 'You can take him home now.' He turned to Hugo. 'Don't do it again, mate. It could be a bus next time.'

'Buses aren't allowed through the underpass,' Hugo pointed out, and then went into convulsions of silent laughter.

'Look, you're lucky we're not charging you,' the policeman snapped, riled by Hugo's ingratitude and general insubordination. 'What's he on?' he demanded, addressing Guy in the same tone.

'I've no idea,' said Guy, aggrieved at the way he was being treated as some sort of accomplice.

'Possession of drugs is an offence, you know.'

Behind his back Hugo held up his hands and turned them over, then flapped his hospital gown to indicate that he was clean. 'He's lucky we're not charging him,' the policeman said again, before ducking between the curtains. Guy could hear him telling someone, a nurse, presumably, that he was leaving. 'The next of kin's arrived,' he said.

I am not his next of kin! Guy wanted to shout. He is nothing to do with me!

Still laughing, Hugo slid down off the bed and reached for his clothes. As he slipped off his gown Guy saw that the whole of one side from shoulder to hip was grazed and sticky with ointment.

'What about the other bloke, on the moped?' Guy asked, catching up with the policeman outside. 'Is he okay?'

'Well, he's discharged himself. The bike's damaged though. That'll be an interesting one for the insurance company.' Over his shoulder Guy could see Hugo silhouetted against the curtain, hopping about trying to put his trousers on. 'I'm off then.'

'Righto. Thanks.' He'd done it again, before he could stop himself. Really, he cursed, was there no limit to his grovelling? It was Hugo's fault. The sheer tactlessness of the bloke made you swing to the other extreme.

Hugo, entirely unabashed by his brush with death and the forces of law and order, presently joined Guy in the waiting room, buttoning a torn shirt one-handed. He plucked at the fabric on his injured side. 'It's sticking to me,' he complained. 'You'd think they'd have given me a dressing or something.'

'Perhaps you only get the basic one-star service if the wound is self-inflicted,' said Guy.

'No chance of a ride home in an ambulance, then?' asked Hugo. He looked at Guy with puzzled, bloodshot eyes for a moment, then said, 'What are you doing here, anyway?'

'I've been asking myself the same question,' said Guy frostily. The fact that he had selflessly turned out on this errand of mercy appeared to have gone unacknowledged by all. 'The police called and asked me to pick you up. Apparently you had my number in your pocket.'

'That's right,' said Hugo, pleased to have remembered something relevant. 'I told them you were my next of kin so that they'd ring you if I died. Otherwise you'd have been wondering why you never heard from me.'

'That was very thoughtful of you,' said Guy, his sarcasm quite wasted on Hugo, who beamed at him. Guy steered him towards the exit. 'Are you going to tell me what happened, then?'

Hugo's brow furrowed. He spoke with great concentration, counting off each stage of the story on his fingers. 'We were in someone's flat smoking skunkweed. Quite strong stuff, actually. In fact I'm a little bit stoned. Can you tell? Er . . . oh, yes, we decided to go for a walk. Someone found a shopping trolley in Southampton Row. I got in it – don't know why. Childish really. They pushed me down the middle of the road right into the tunnel under the Aldwych. In the wrong direction. Those trolleys can go quite fast downhill. Er . . . I could see this bike headlamp coming towards me so I sort of jumped out, and the trolley kept going and hit the bike. Someone called an ambulance. The others just legged it as soon as they heard the sirens. Bastards.'

'So apart from that graze are you injured?'

'I don't think so. They did some X-rays.'

They had reached Waterloo station by now. Hugo kept widening his eyes and blinking at the lights. Occasionally he would catch hold of Guy's elbow and squeeze it tightly. 'It's never affected me like this before,' he kept saying. And then, 'Have I just said that?'

Guy looked at his watch. It was five past three. 'There'll be no tubes. Do you feel up to getting the bus?'

Hugo looked mutinous. 'No. Perhaps I'll just hang around here till morning. I'll find somewhere to lie down. It might have worn off by then.'

'Don't be ridiculous,' said Guy. Hugo was the sort of person who could get into a punch-up in the British Library, or Harrods food hall – there was no way he'd survive a night among the dossers and winos at Waterloo. 'I've got enough for a taxi. Come on,' he said, trying to quell a sudden upsurge of that odd combination of exasperation and pity which Hugo always managed to provoke.

Hugo plodded meekly a few paces behind Guy all the way to the taxi rank where a row of cabs stood empty, their drivers a few feet away in a group, chatting and smoking. One of them, seeing Guy and Hugo hovering, gave them a nod and flicked his unextinguished cigarette into the gutter before climbing back into his cab. Guy couldn't remember Hugo's address, and neither, to begin with, could Hugo: he could only think of his previous place in North Row. Just as Guy was about to surrender and offer Hugo a bed in his own flat for what remained of the night, Hugo's memory returned, and the taxi sped off across the bridge into the deserted heart of London. Hugo seemed to fall into a stupor on the journey, and Guy was able to close his eyes himself, and calculate how much sleep he might be able to snatch before morning. He wasn't even tired now; that was the trouble. But he would be later, in class. And he was being observed today.

'Oy, we're here.' Hugo was rapping on the glass partition. Guy opened his eyes with a start as the driver braked hard. He followed Hugo out and passed next week's beer money through the taxi window. He would have to walk home: that meant three hours' sleep, maximum. Hugo's building was in darkness. He produced a key from his back pocket, but it didn't fit the lock. He looked at it, mystified.

'Are you sure this is the right house?' Guy asked urgently, as Hugo jabbed the bell and pounded on the door with his fist.

'Yes. Right house, wrong key.' He opened the letter-box with a flat hand and yelled 'Wakey wakey!' through the slot. A light at the top of the house came on and a moment later there was the sound of unhurried feet on the stairs.

I'll see him safely indoors, thought Guy, and that's it. Goodbye. If he rings, I'm out. If he writes, I've moved.

The door opened and Nina stood there, in a man's white T-shirt, her long hair rumpled from sleep. She had a grumpy expression on her face, which gave way to surprise as she saw

Guy standing in the shadows. Hugo patted her on the shoulder as he passed. 'Put the kettle on. I'm parched,' he said.

'Hello,' said Nina, ignoring Hugo and looking at Guy. 'You're the man with the performing dog.'

'You're the woman with . . .' but Guy couldn't think of anything funny or even accurate to say. He hadn't forgotten her face. It, and the rest of her, had figured in many of his daydreams.

'Oh, Nina,' called Hugo from deep within the house. 'This is Guy. He's coming on the desert trip with us. Aren't you, Guy?'

'Is he?' said Nina, smiling. 'He doesn't look terribly convinced.'

'Oh,' said Guy, shaking himself up. This was the moment. There would be other bad decisions, of course. But this was the one that would echo down the years, so that even as an old man he would remember standing there on the threshold, saying, 'Yes. I'm coming. It's all decided.'

20

Jane lay in bed watching the luminous hands of the clock stretch the minutes into hours, and experiencing a growing sense of kinship with all those other people in the world outside who were awake while others slept. Shift-workers and nursing mothers and jet-lagged travellers and fellow insomniacs and the man in the 24-hour garage round the corner who was always on the telephone whenever you tried to pay. Beside her Guy was sleeping peacefully, one hand under his cheek like a child. He'd been up in the loft until late, raking the heavens with his telescope. Looking for God, Jane supposed. Insomnia was generally more his department: worrying about work, chewing over some confrontation, making lists for the morning. Since giving up her job she'd been free of all that. Her anxieties about the children weren't the sort to interrupt sleep. They were vast, cosmic, unspecific fears, not niggling little matters which required any action on her part. She resisted the temptation to prod Guy awake, as he would take it as an invitation to make love, and that was the last thing she wanted, though it might have induced the necessary weariness to send her off. Instead she slipped out of bed, as stealthily as possible. Guy was much more apt to share his insomnia by thrashing from side to side and, if that failed to rouse her, by switching on his reading light.

Jane felt for her dressing gown in the wardrobe, setting the metal hangers jangling. It was old now and balding in places, and still had a scorched patch on the front from that match-head. Guy hated it because it made her look like a bag lady, and was always offering to buy her a new one – something silky and semi-transparent and dry-clean only, no thank you. She checked the girls before going downstairs. Sophie had climbed in with Harriet; their faces were side by side on the pillow, and the dim glow from the comfort light gave them a grey, ghostly look. Like the Princes in the Tower, Jane thought, and then shivered at her morbid imagination. She watched them for a moment or two to reassure herself that the bedclothes were rising and falling, and then withdrew hastily as Harriet started to stir. She didn't want to wake them; they looked so lovely asleep. So trusting and defenceless and ignorant of all the horrors of the world. She wished she could sustain these tender feelings throughout the day: they usually evaporated over breakfast.

It was Erica, or rather the thought of her, that was keeping Jane awake. It had been exactly the same on the last two occasions. Her pleasure in Erica's company had swiftly been replaced by agitation and depression: agitation that she, Jane, had failed to acquit herself as a dazzling and entertaining companion, and depression that there was no knowing when or if she might have another chance. It was most perplexing. None of Jane's other friends induced this sort of response. It would never occur to her to wonder whether Suzanne, for instance, found her witty and amusing, and it wouldn't trouble Jane if six months passed between meetings. The last time Jane had felt like this was over a boy called Trevor whom she had met on holiday in Cornwall, aged fifteen. He had taken her phone number but not given his own, and the feelings of impatience and anxiety with which she fretted away the days waiting for him to call, now, at a distance of sixteen years, seemed horribly familiar. She had had no way of contacting him. His surname was Smith and he came from Cheshunt; that was all she knew. He had phoned, eventually. Despair turned to euphoria. They had arranged to meet on the steps outside the National Gallery but, again, she hadn't the confidence to ask for his number. He didn't turn up, of course, and she was plunged back into that abyss of despair whose depths were only emphasized by the feeble glimmer of hope that he might soon ring and explain. It was the hope that was hardest to bear: once that had perished, recovery was possible.

Downstairs Jane stood in the kitchen making a cup of tea, feeling the chill from the tiled floor boring into the soles of her feet, and flinching from the roar of the kettle in the silence. Perhaps I'm turning into a lesbian, Jane thought. Perhaps it's oestrogen depletion or something. She reined in this fantastical line of reasoning. No. You either were or you weren't, and she wasn't. She tried to imagine what it would be like to kiss Erica, and felt her face automatically pucker into a grimace – it was like the first grapefruit segment of the morning. No, she had no impulses in that direction, no physical interest in Erica at all.

In the sitting room Jane switched on one of the small table lamps, resisting her usual impulse to rearrange the furniture in the quest for more floor space. She sat on the couch, her bare feet tucked underneath her, listening to the heartbeat of the house: the hum of the fridge, the twanging pipes, the breath of the wind through the kitchen vent. She thought of Gregory, lying on his own couch, unable to move for fear of setting off the burglar alarm, and wondered whether Erica was asleep, Will and Yorrick tucked in beside her, or up and pacing the floor, already on the first nicotine chew of the day.

She closed her eyes and allowed herself to rehearse the daydream that had been keeping her awake earlier. As a fantasy it was pretty unambitious, even she could see that. Not the sort of thing to feature in those anthologies of female erotica which Suzanne was always reading. It involved her and Erica of course. They were in a cabin somewhere, near a lake or a river. For some reason there were no children around. This was a flaw as far as Jane was concerned. Unless the plot was feasible it was impossible to get really engrossed; she'd have to work on that bit. They had been for a long walk through the woods and had returned, tired, to the cabin, which was warm and clean and tastefully furnished and free of clutter. They had eaten, and were now sitting at opposite ends of a long couch, finishing a bottle of wine and reading their separate books. Between them on the seat was a large box of chocolates, which they would kick back and forth to one another. They didn't converse; there was nothing to be said. Just at the moment when Jane was starting to feel drowsy, Erica closed her book and said she was going to bed.

Through an open doorway was another room, containing twin beds made up with white linen sheets. When Jane returned from the bathroom – for even in her fantasies she would not let herself go to bed without cleaning her teeth – Erica was already in bed. Just before she turned the light out Erica reached across the gap and squeezed Jane's hand and a look of complete understanding passed between them. Then they dropped hands, and turned over, and Jane slept, dreamless and undisturbed all night, the deepest and most refreshing sleep of her life.

Jane sat up with a start. She had dozed off right there on the couch with her teacup in her lap.

'Are you all right?' said the voice that had woken her. She scrambled to the bottom of the stairs. Guy was leaning over the banisters, a worried look on his face.

'I couldn't sleep,' she whispered back. 'I didn't want to disturb you.' Now she was properly awake and unfolded from her warm patch in the armchair she realized how cold it was in the unheated sitting room. Her bones felt brittle with cold.

'Neither could I,' said Guy – his standard response, even though she'd listened to him snoring away for hours. 'Are you coming back to bed?'

She nodded and climbed the stairs.

'I'll hold on to you,' Guy offered, throwing back the duvet and then recoiling from her frozen limbs. 'Aargh. Keep away. You're like a corpse.'

'I'm sorry,' said Jane, through chattering teeth. 'I can't help it.'

After a second or two he relented. 'Come on, then. I'll try and thaw you out,' he said, pulling her towards him and wincing at the touch of her skinny arms: dry winter branches rimed with frost.

21

'No.' Hugo was emphatic. 'No, no, no.' A vein was throbbing in his temple and his face was an even deeper shade of red than usual.

I shouldn't have asked his advice, Nina was thinking. I should have just gone ahead and done it.

They were sitting in the roof garden at Biba, where Nina had a Saturday job. She was wearing a huge pair of dark glasses and a floppy straw hat to keep off the sun. Hugo was just sweltering. It was going to be in the nineties again.

'Don't even *think* about it. How am I going to replace Martin at this short notice? Four is the absolute minimum. It was only by a sheer fluke that I managed to persuade Guy to come at the last minute.'

It was me that persuaded him, not you, you fool, thought Nina, but instead she said, 'I didn't say Martin shouldn't come. I just said I want to break up with him before we go. If I do it now he might be over it by the time we leave.'

'In ten days? Are you mad? He'll be a blubbering wreck and you know it. What sort of atmosphere is that going to create? It'll be horrendous. No. I absolutely forbid it.' Hugo mopped his brow.

'I don't need your permission to split up with my own boyfriend,' Nina said, indignantly, beating off a wasp.

'So why did you ask me then?' Hugo demanded. He pressed his cold beer glass against one cheek then the other. The sweat patches under his arms had spread and merged with the one at his chest.

'Because . . . because I'm polite and considerate,' said Nina.

'Well, good. So *be* polite and considerate and don't do anything until we get back. Six weeks isn't going to make any difference.'

'It is to me. Especially now I've admitted to you that I've gone off him. I'll be playing the part of his girlfriend in bad faith, and you'll know it.' Nina fanned herself with her hat. She had hitched up her long skirt so that her legs might catch the sun, but they had now started to tingle.

'Oh come on, it's not as if you hate the bloke,' said Hugo.

'No, of course not. I'm very fond of him. But . . . but he's so annoying sometimes.'

'You're not seeing someone else, are you?' asked Hugo, squinting at her under his hand.

'No. Nothing like that. I just want to be free.'

'Did this suddenly come on last night?' Hugo wanted to know.

'No, no. It's been sort of dawning on me for weeks.'

'Well, why didn't you do something about it weeks ago? It's too late now.'

'Because I didn't realize it was happening. I didn't wake up one morning and think, uh-oh, I don't love Martin any more. It crept up on me.' Nina finished her bottle of Coke and glanced at her watch. Her lunch-break was nearly over.

'Look, Nina.' Hugo mastered his impatience. 'You've no idea how much effort I've put into arranging this trip. It's not like a holiday that you can put off and do some other time. My PhD depends on this research. I wanted you and Martin to come because you're my friends and I thought we'd have a laugh. And because Martin can drive, of course. If I'd known you weren't solid as a rock I wouldn't even have considered asking you. But it's done now and we're going and you'll just have to put up with his annoying little ways for a few more weeks.'

Nina gave a mutinous sigh but didn't raise any further objections. Encouraged by this, Hugo pressed on. 'Anyway, after a week of being cooped up in the Land Rover we'll all be getting on each other's nerves.'

'Well, two out of three of you are on mine already,' Nina retorted. 'And we haven't even set off yet.'

Hugo ignored this remark. 'So we'll just have to be extra tolerant and co-operative. Exercise a bit of give and take.'

Nina lifted her sunglasses above her eyebrows to give Hugo the full benefit of her best sardonic look.

'All right,' he conceded. 'Let's keep it simple. You lot give and I'll take.'

II

22

They spent the first night at Nemours, just south of Paris. Guy had been instructed to present himself at Hugo's at 6 a.m. on the 1st of July with his passport and luggage, which was to be kept to a minimum. There had been one preliminary planning meeting in the Princess Louise at which Guy and Martin had been introduced, and duties and responsibilities allocated by Hugo. The division of labour was as follows: compilation tapes for the journey: Martin. First aid kit: Nina. International driving licences: Guy. Provisions, equipment, maps, tickets, visas, sponsorship, insurance, everything else: Hugo.

'You're a born delegator, aren't you, Hugo?' Nina had observed.

When Guy arrived the hallway was already full of boxes and bags, access to the stairs was blocked and the front door was trapped open. There were tents, sleeping bags, a primus stove, pots and pans, several plastic canisters for water, ranging rods, anemometers, shovels and picks and other equipment borrowed from the Geography Department at UCL, ex-army camp-beds, Nina's guitar and hundreds of packets and tins of non-perishable and unenticing food. Martin had started carrying the heavier items out to the Land Rover, which was double-parked outside. Attached to the front bumper was a large plastic tiger, which Hugo had stolen from the forecourt of an Esso garage.

'These boxes fit nicely on the roof-rack,' Martin said, on his fourth trip. 'All the loose stuff can go inside. What do you reckon?'

'Oh, yes, whatever you think,' Guy replied. Left to himself he would have put the lighter stuff up on the roof and the heavy boxes inside, but he wasn't going to start asserting himself this early in the trip. He was just the spare driver, the makeweight.

'What's in here?' he asked, pointing to a large cardboard box with the royal warrant on the side. Hugo was coming down the stairs, a pair of John Lennon-style round sunglasses balanced on his forehead, above his regular spectacles. He was holding a clipboard. 'Oh, didn't I tell you I managed to get sponsorship from Tate & Lyle? Well, that's it.'

Guy opened the box. Inside were forty-eight tins of golden syrup. 'Useful,' he said, closing it again.

'We're not actually taking them with us, are we?' asked Martin, staggering past with a huge drum of powdered milk.

'I thought they might come in handy as presents – you know, for helpful border guards and friendly Tuaregs,' said Hugo.

Guy pulled a face. 'I thought cigarettes were the international currency of bribery – not syrup.'

'We're not giving our fags away,' said Hugo, horrified. 'Which reminds me, we must get our duty-free limit on the boat or we'll be reduced to smoking donkey dung.' He climbed over the barricade of luggage to where Guy was still standing holding his rucksack and a football in a string bag.

'What's that?' he asked.

'It's a football, Hugo,' Martin explained patiently.

'I thought we could just kick it around if we get bored,' said Guy. Hugo raised his eyes to heaven and wrote *Kickball* on his list and then ticked it off methodically.

From the basement came the sound of water draining from a bath, and then a door opened and Nina came padding up the stairs in a towel, leaving a trail of damp footprints on the lino.

Hugo looked at his watch and sighed theatrically. Nina gave the three men a winning smile. 'I had to,' she said. 'It might be the last wash I have for six weeks.'

It took an hour to pack, according to Martin's method, and then half way to Ramsgate, after the Land Rover had nearly blown over in the crosswind on the A2, it had taken another hour to repack. Hugo had wanted to know whose bright idea it was to put the heavy stuff on the roof.

'Guy and I discussed it and thought it would be best,' said Martin, in what Guy thought was a rather free interpretation of their exchange on the subject. He made no attempt to contradict him, though. He didn't want to give Martin any grounds for disliking him. Yet. He'd just been reading an account of a canoeing trip down the Zambezi. The author recommended keeping a diary as a means of palliating petty grievances. It afforded the writer a little relief without wrecking the atmosphere. It was essential, he said, to maintain an illusion of co-operation, not to backbite or split into factions. Guy had packed a notebook and pen with this in mind.

'I feel a bit of a fraud,' he said to Nina on the ferry, while Martin and Hugo were off buying duty-frees. 'I'm not even a geographer. I don't know what use I'm going to be when we get there.'

'That's all right,' said Nina, laying down a worn copy of *A Glastonbury Romance*. 'He specifically wanted a non-specialist. That way he knows you won't steal his research.'

'It wouldn't have occurred to me,' said Guy.

'Well, it occurred to Hugo,' said Nina. 'Because that's what he'd do.'

'Have you known him long?' Guy asked.

'About a year and a half. Though it feels longer. We were neighbours for my first year, but he was such a recluse it was a while before I bumped into him. You were at school together, weren't you?'

'Briefly. Until he was promoted.'

'What was he like?'

'Well.' Guy didn't want to be disloyal, but then swapping confidences with Nina was, after all, what he'd come for. 'Clever, but bullied. He tended to get up people's noses.'

'So he hasn't changed, then?'

'No,' Guy admitted with a laugh. 'He blends in better as an adult, for some reason. He was like an old man at school, but he seems to be getting younger with the passing years.

Wait till we're middle-aged – he'll be skipping around in short trousers.'

'What an unpleasant thought,' said Nina, as the object of this prediction squeezed between the closely packed tables and chairs of the bar to where they were sitting. He was carrying eight hundred Marlboro and a bottle of Johnny Walker.

'You won't be able to take that into Algeria,' said Guy, pointing at the whisky.

Hugo gave a short laugh. 'Don't worry. This won't even get me to Naples.'

Martin returned a moment later with a copy of *The Times* and settled down to do the crossword, assisted by Hugo.

'Can't you tear that bit out and let me read the rest of the news?' asked Nina, who found cryptic crosswords deeply threatening.

'No,' said Martin. 'It has to be attached.'

'Why?'

'It's an aesthetic thing. Isn't that right, Hugo?'

Hugo nodded. 'I'm afraid so.'

'Well, just show me the front page,' she pleaded. Martin unfolded the paper. BRITAIN SWELTERS IN THE DROUGHT, announced the headline. Alongside it was a photograph of the parched, cracked bed of a reservoir. 'Wait a minute,' Martin said, looking at the date. 'This is yesterday's paper.' He threw it across to her in disgust. 'Here, it's yours.'

'What difference does that make?'

'I can't be bothered doing a crossword if I know the answers have already been published,' he said. 'It just takes the edge off it.' Hugo nodded agreement again.

Nina appealed to Guy. 'Is this a bloke thing? Are you like them?'

'No,' said Guy. 'I'm too thick. I'm just here to drive the Land Rover and dig latrines.'

There was a thunderstorm that night at Nemours, accompanied by torrential rain, so Guy's skills with the shovel were not wasted. He spent most of the evening digging a trench and soakaway around the perimeter of the tent to prevent a flood, while Nina and Martin inspected the swollen river, which marked the boundary of the campsite. Hugo squatted under the canvas, cooking stew on the primus stove while trying not to set light to the tentflaps. It was the first rain they'd seen in weeks, but the novelty soon wore off, even so. The groundsheet was quickly smeared with muddy footprints, which would in turn be transferred to the sleeping bags. There was no bar or café on site – even the toilets were of the primitive hole-in-the-floor variety – so after supper they walked into town in search of entertainment, and fetched up at a small bar with waterlogged tables and chairs out on the pavement. Hugo had brought a travel Scrabble set, but no one could be persuaded to give him a game.

'I'm not playing with you. You cheat,' said Nina.

'I don't. I just happen to know lots of words that aren't in the dictionary.'

Inside a group of local youths were playing a noisy game of table football. They glanced up as the four entered, then looked away again, uninterested. Behind the bar the patron, a big man in a tight paisley shirt, was smoking and watching the television which blared from a bracket on the wall.

'You've got A-level French, Nina. You go and get the drinks,' Martin suggested, unzipping his waterproof and hanging it over the back of a plastic stacking chair, of the sort to be found in church halls and cheerless municipal buildings.

'What does that prove?' Nina protested. 'That I've read Racine. It doesn't mean I can make myself understood.'

'I'll go,' said Hugo, who spoke French with a confidence that was wholly unwarranted. Before he'd moved though, the patron tore his gaze from the television screen and said, 'Oui?' Presently, after Hugo had gabbled their order, and Nina had reinterpreted it for the benefit of the bemused patron, three beers in long-stemmed glasses and a pernod and cassis were secured, and Martin proposed a toast 'to the holiday'.

'It is *not* a holiday,' Hugo corrected him.

'It is for me,' said Martin. 'I've never been abroad before.'

The others were amazed. Impressed, even. 'Not even for a day trip?' asked Guy, who had spent some of his early childhood in army houses in Germany and Cyprus and had taken foreign holidays for granted.

'Never,' said Martin. 'We always went to the Isle of Wight. Except for one very exciting year when we went to Swanage.'

This soon led the others to try and trump Martin's contribution with still more shocking admissions of inexperience.

'I've never been to a football match,' said Hugo, with some pride.

'Well, neither have I,' said Nina. 'So no points there.'

'I've never been in a fight,' said Guy. 'Though I've had to get people out of them occasionally,' he added, looking at Hugo.

Martin admitted that he had been beaten up outside a youth club in south London as a teenager, and that he'd thumped a few people in the playground in his time. They already knew about Hugo's record.

'I've never stolen anything,' Nina said.

'Are you including petty pilfering?' asked Hugo.

'Yes, of course!'

'Oh,' said Hugo.

'You must have lifted the odd sweet from Woolworths when no one was looking,' said Guy.

'No. Really. I've never taken anything that didn't belong to me.'

'Yes you have. Me,' said Martin.

Nina laughed, and even looked a little embarrassed. 'That doesn't count.'

'I've never seen a dead body,' said Hugo, as if this was a matter of some regret.

'For God's sake, Hugo. Who has?' said Nina, nonplussed by the turn his thoughts had taken.

'I don't know. They wouldn't let me see my mother, because I was too young and she was such a mess. And then my father died in Johannesburg so I was too late to see him as well.'

This remark was followed by an uncomfortable silence. Finally, to steer conversation back on to firmer ground, Guy said, 'I've never had a one-night stand.'

'Is that on moral grounds, or for lack of opportunity?' Nina inquired.

Guy just laughed, non-committally, enjoying her curiosity.

Hugo, who had been staring at the floor, looked up suddenly. 'Oh, I can beat that. Yes, I think I've got the winning ticket.' The others looked at him expectantly. 'I've never kissed a girl,' he said, allowing the emphasis to fall ambiguously. This was greeted with even more embarrassment than his previous outburst about his parents' bodies. Hugo, who liked to disconcert people, even at his own expense, looked suitably gratified.

It was Nina who came to the rescue. 'Well, neither have I,' she said, and then leant across the table and kissed Hugo firmly but not passionately on the lips.

'Have you noticed,' said Martin, keeping the tone light, 'that Nina hasn't admitted to having done anything interesting.'

'I know,' she sighed. 'I've led a very sheltered life.'

'There's nothing wrong with that,' said Guy, who was starting not to enjoy the game. He had never been able to work up much excitement over other people's secrets. 'Shelters have a lot to recommend them.'

Later, back in the tent, Guy found himself alone with Nina again for a moment, while Hugo and Martin were still performing their ablutions in the shower block. He had hurried with this in mind. A torch had been suspended from the overhead pole providing a narrow cone of light, in which Nina sat, brushing knots out of her hair.

'That was a nice thing you did, kissing Hugo,' said Guy, sitting half in and half out of the tent to remove his boots.

'Martin didn't think so,' she replied, tugging her brush viciously through the tangles. 'He said it was patronizing.'

'Oh, he was probably just jealous,' said Guy.

'That's what I said.'

'Is he the jealous type, then?' Guy asked, in as conversational a tone as possible.

Nina put her head forward and started to brush her hair upside down so that Guy could no longer see her face. 'It's hard to say,' she said. 'I haven't put him to the test. Yet.'

23

Guy's diary: Annecy, 2nd July 1976
Thunderstorms seem to be following us across Europe. I can't help taking it personally. According to the map we are camped at the foot of the Alps, though it might as well be Clapham Common: outside all is grey. Hugo is in a bad mood because Martin has just admitted he's claustrophobic and doesn't want to go through the Mont Blanc tunnel, which means an unplanned detour over the St Bernard pass. Nina is trying to give Martin a pep talk. Hugo is swearing. 'You should have declared any disabilities at the outset,' I think he said at one point. Perhaps I'll stick my oar in and pretend to be afraid of heights.

Rapallo, 3rd July
In spite of gentle hints from me, Martin drove us over the Grand St Bernard pass in top gear with his foot on the brake, to the smell of burning rubber. About half way down, when I could see we were going to be doing the rest of the journey without brake blocks – if we didn't plunge over an Alp first – I begged to be allowed to drive. Martin got a bit shirty, but I'd weighed things up carefully and decided I'd rather be unpopular than dead. Anyway he let me take over, and just as we reached Rapallo the sun came out so everyone cheered up and the tense atmosphere was forgotten. I didn't want to humiliate him: I just wanted to live. He and Nina sat in the back playing cards for most of the journey, or talking – too quietly for me to overhear – while Hugo sat next to me reading the map and giving directions. He's a good navigator, to give credit where it's due, and he's planned this itinerary to the last detail. You can hardly stop for a shit without booking it in advance. The compilation tapes provided by Martin have been played end to end since we left London and we are all now heartily sick of every track. If I hear Albatross *one more time I won't be responsible for my actions.*

We reached the campsite late in the afternoon. There was a market on the quayside, so Nina bought some fresh mackerel which we had, fried, for dinner with salty bread and some warm beer from the back of the Land Rover. Hugo was right about the Johnny Walker.

Naples, 4th July
Hugo was cracking the whip as usual, wanting to be on the road all day, but the rest of us mutinied, and just before lunchtime we turned off the road, through some conifers and scrubby grass, to the beach for a swim. Martin brought the football and the two of us headed it to each other for a while, watched by Nina. Hugo, who doesn't like to be caught enjoying any tourist activity, dragged all the maps out and pretended to be studying the route, squatting in the sun like a great, sweaty Buddha. I drank a whole bottle of Coke at lunchtime and then stupidly went for a swim and got the most lethal attack of cramp. If Martin hadn't realized that I wasn't just waving at them all for fun, and swum out to rescue me when he did I'm pretty sure I'd have drowned.

'Thanks, mate,' I said, as soon as we were back in shallow water and I'd caught my breath, and he just gave me a crooked smile. 'I nearly died,' I explained to Nina and Hugo, who were still sitting on their towels, reading, where we'd left them, and didn't seem to appreciate the gravity of the situation.

Hugo was unmoved. 'I wonder if we'd have been allowed to claim your duty-free allowance on the way home?' he said.

Then Martin said, very nonchalantly, that he was going for a walk, and did Nina want to go with him. She said, 'Not really', so he shrugged and strode off into the trees, and then Hugo raised his eyebrows at Nina, and she said, 'Oh, all right' – but not to Martin, who was out of earshot by this time – and ran after him. I thought this was pretty weird but I didn't want to ask Hugo what it was all about, so I started bouncing the ball on one foot. I'd got up to sixty-six – a new personal best – when Hugo suddenly said, 'She's going to dump him when we get home,' and the ball just about went into orbit.

'What makes you say that?' I asked.

'She told me. She wanted to do it the week before we left. Can you believe that? I practically had to beg *her to wait.'*

'So now we all know, except Martin. That's nice,' I said. But

sarcasm just glances off Hugo. It's like throwing paper darts at a rhinoceros.

In the afternoon we carried on to Naples – Nina wanted to drive into the city to have a look, but without a street plan we got hopelessly lost and ended up in the seediest quarter imaginable: shabby, crumbling hovels, and narrow streets strewn with litter, and patrolled by gangs of grubby children, and emaciated dogs with distended udders dragging in the dirt. At one point we got stuck trying to execute a 23-point turn in a tight spot between hovels, and found ourselves surrounded by a gaggle of these urchins, all holding their mucky hands up to the window for money. They seemed very taken with our tiger mascot, and would have prised it off the front bumper if we'd been stationary long enough. In the end Hugo passed them a tin of golden syrup, but they didn't seem over-impressed with this gesture, and as we drove off one of them lobbed it at the back of the Land Rover, smashing a rear light. Hugo surprised us by sticking his head out of the window and delivering a torrent of obscenities in their native tongue.

'I didn't know you spoke Italian, Hugo,' said Nina, when we were on our way again.

'I don't,' said Hugo. 'But I took the precaution of learning to swear in all the necessary languages before we left. I've got some really offensive Arabic up my sleeve if it's needed. You wait.'

'Ever the diplomat,' said Nina.

It's evening now, and I'm writing this in the campsite, which is perched on the cliff overlooking rows of Aleppo pines and the bay beyond. I can just see the skirts of Vesuvius in the distance; the rest is in clouds. Tomorrow a new continent.

24

Nina sat in the back of the Land Rover, which was parked outside the *douane* in Souk Ahras, counting her insect bites and waiting for Hugo to return. They had been camped just inside the Algerian border for three days now, unable to advance any further, apparently because of a problem with their papers. Every morning Martin or Guy would drive Hugo the fifteen miles up the track to this customs office for another fruitless collision with local bureaucracy, while the other two stayed behind to guard the tent and its meagre contents. They had been warned by the man from the Royal Geographical Society that nothing – however trifling – was beneath the attention of thieves.

The crossing from Naples to Tunis had passed off without a hitch, and had, in fact, been very pleasant for the first few hours when the boat was almost empty and they had been able to sunbathe and even swim in the open air pool. At Palermo they had docked to pick up more passengers and within minutes the deck was swarming with homecoming Tunisians. Men, women and children – along with goats, chickens and mountains of luggage – poured across the gangplank until every chair, table and available inch of floor space was occupied and the boat was listing steeply to port, a position it maintained for the rest of the journey. At one point Nina ventured to find a toilet, but having picked her way over the prone bodies on the stairs and corridors, apologizing in English and then French as she went, she found three people already wedged tightly in the cubicle. There was no possibility of displacing them without someone at the other end of the boat going overboard, so she gave up and fought her way back to the deck unrelieved.

The customs officials at Tunis had waved them through with only the most cursory look at their papers, and without letting Hugo get more than two sentences into his carefully worded speech of explanation. And now here they were, stuck on the Algerian border in this infernal heat, with nothing to do but shift the tent from one ants' nest to another and wait for some official from ENEMA – *Entreprise Nationale Écologique et Météorologique d'Algérie* – to confirm their story.

A door opened, and through the film of dust and mashed mosquitoes on the windscreen Nina saw Hugo emerge and stride towards the Land Rover, scowling. He was wearing a pair of baggy safari shorts and a crushed khaki shirt, like an overgrown Boy Scout. He flung himself into the passenger seat. 'They want ENEMA to fork out £3,000 surety for our equipment – as if we're bail bandits or something. It's fucking highway robbery. They'll never pay it.'

'And what are we supposed to do in the meantime?'

'Just sit on our arses, I suppose. When they've finally established beyond any doubt that they're not going to be able to extort any money out of this situation they'll give up and let us through. God, it's such a waste of time.' Hugo's knuckles bulged white in his clenched fists. He looked as though he'd like to punch someone.

'Did you ask if we could at least camp outside to save driving back and forth each day?'

'Oh yes. You'll love this. We can park outside the customs office, but we aren't allowed to camp there. We can camp on that bit of waste ground opposite the *gendarmerie*, but we can't park there. Brilliant. Where's Martin?'

'Answering nature's call. He's been gone ages. Do you think they've kidnapped him?' As she said this Martin appeared from behind the *douane*, looking ashen. 'Well, I won't be awarding that the full three stars,' he said, climbing into the driver's seat. 'Any luck?'

Hugo shook his head. 'We can go and fetch the tent. I suppose that's an advance on yesterday.' They had left Guy at the border, guarding the camp and killing ants. 'Anyway, I'll be back in there at nine o'clock tomorrow morning, don't you worry. You can come and try out some of your French, Nina. I think my tact might have been getting lost in translation. But I'm starting to build up a sort of captor/captive rapport with the *douanier.* He actually made eye-contact today.'

That night they slept on the forecourt of the *gendarmerie*, in the open air. This compromise had been reached after the Land Rover was placed under arrest to prevent any attempt on their part to abscond. They arranged the tubular framed camp-beds in a square, and lay, listening to the rustle of cicadas, and looking up at the sky, low over their heads and strewn with a million stars. The sun had set suddenly, taking them by surprise. 'To think, they're always there, and we never see them at home,' said Nina, transfixed. Everywhere she looked shooting stars were leaving their glitter trails across the darkness, as if the heavens were disintegrating, piece by piece, before her eyes.

'Yes, thank you. Here are your passports. You are free to continue your journey.' The customs official pushed a manila envelope across the desk. The tiny office contained no other furniture, apart from a scratched metal filing cabinet and the wooden chairs on which the three of them were sitting. Above their heads a ceiling fan rotated at a sluggish pace, stirring the dust particles, which shimmered in the wedge of light from a barred window high on the wall.

'Terrific,' said Hugo reaching forward.

'But,' the official was too quick for him, placing the palm of his hand down on the package, 'you must leave your technical tools here and collect them on your way home.'

'What? Go on without any measuring equipment?' Hugo took out a grey handkerchief and applied it to his forehead. The sweat was pouring off his scalp. In spite of the early hour the heat was already formidable. Apart from a few beads of perspiration – or was it oil – on his moustache, the customs officer looked cool and unruffled. There were knife-edged creases in his brown uniform, as though it had just come out of a packet, and he smelled strongly of cologne. 'How are we supposed to conduct our research without it?'

This was answered with a shrug.

'As for picking it up on the way back, we're not even coming back this way – we're getting the boat from Oran.'

Another shrug.

'We are here at the invitation of your government,' Nina put in, even though Hugo had instructed her not to intervene unless called upon to translate something complicated. She was feeling the heat, too, in her long dress. Hugo had told her to cover herself up, and, from the way the *douanier* and the *gendarme* outside had looked her up and down, it was clear his advice hadn't been unwarranted.

'I've said all this before,' Hugo muttered. 'What do you imagine we're going to do with a set of ranging rods and an anemometer? Bring down the government?' This was clearly the wrong thing to say to a representative of that organization, as his thick black eyebrows gathered into a frown, and he drew the envelope fractionally towards him. 'You might sell them to the Moroccans,' he said finally.

'Hasn't the meteorological office confirmed our credentials yet?' Hugo demanded. His tone was growing less and less conciliatory. Nina had seen this pattern before. The next stage was outright belligerence, shouting and fist-waving, which would sabotage any advantage so far achieved.

'We are still waiting for the telex from Algiers,' said the man.

'We are effectively hostages,' Hugo announced, dramatically.

'Not at all. You are free to go.' The man lifted his hand from the passports.

'This is an outrage,' said Hugo, pompously, standing up and pulling Nina to her feet. 'Come on. We shall have to contact our embassy.' As they reached the door the man beckoned Hugo back. Nina, who had had enough of Algerian bureaucracy and Hugo's aggressive negotiating style, carried on across the road to the patch of waste land where Martin and Guy, watched by several local children, were playing a game of *pétanque* using four tins of golden syrup and a stone. They had attempted to set up a camp, but had been thwarted in their efforts by the hardness of the ground. Half a dozen bent pegs and a headless mallet lay alongside the sunken and swaying tent, the slack guy-ropes held down by rocks. Nina gave them a thumbs-down sign as she approached. Martin lobbed one of his tins high in the air in frustration, and it landed a few yards away, stoving its side in on a protruding flint, so that the lid burst open and a golden tongue of treacle flopped out into the dirt.

'They're still on about the equipment,' Nina said, watching the children pounce on the abandoned tins and start throwing them in the air. 'They seem to think we're going to spy for the Moroccans.'

Guy raised his eyes skywards. 'Typical of these paranoid third-world countries,' he said, kicking the dust. 'They've got nothing and they like to think everybody wants it.'

'Hugo doesn't exactly charm his way out of trouble,' Nina went on. 'You can see him winding the guy up until eventually he decides to keep us hanging around here just to be bloody-minded.' She stopped as Hugo himself appeared around the corner of the *douane*, smiling and shaking his head.

'Progress,' he called, as he came within earshot. This was greeted with raised eyebrows from the other three. 'Yes. He said they'll let us through *with* the equipment, provided he can sleep with Nina.' There was a moment's silence as they digested this.

'He actually said that?' asked Nina.

'Well, he said "the blonde". I assume he didn't mean Martin.'

'And what did you say?' Nina inquired, sweetly.

'I said I'd ask you.'

'You said what?'

'He's not unattractive,' Hugo wheedled.

'Tell me he's joking,' she appealed to the other two, who laughed at her indignation.

'Well, I must say I'm disappointed in you, Nina,' said

Hugo. 'Passing up this opportunity to help your friends out of a tight spot.'

'Of course he's joking,' said Guy, though he didn't sound completely convinced. That was the trouble with Hugo. He couldn't be relied upon to hold the orthodox opinion.

'Actually, I declined on your behalf,' Hugo admitted.

'Now what?' said Guy.

'More waiting. They'll give up soon. Now that they've established they'll get nothing from us. You'll see.'

'Do you know what the best thing about this trip is?' Nina said suddenly. The others looked blank. 'No, neither do I,' she said. 'I can tell you the worst thing though. Dehydration.' She crawled into the tent and returned with a bottle of orange squash, now hand hot and smelling strongly of Sterotabs. They had filled their water canisters from the tap at the *gendarmerie*. It had been marked *eau potable*, but they weren't taking any chances. She took a swig and passed it on, her thirst unquenched. However much she drank she still felt sick and depleted.

'Dehydration, frustration, constipation, and lack of copulation,' said Martin bitterly, and they had all laughed at that, even Nina.

'Do you think if we get ourselves arrested we'll be thrown into a nice, air-conditioned cell?' Guy asked later, as they skulked in a patch of shade behind the small kiosk, which served a lone petrol pump (out of order), next to the waste ground where the tent sat abandoned in full sunlight. They had removed one of the bench seats from the Land Rover, which was still impounded, and propped it against the kiosk wall, and now sat in a row, reading, like strangers waiting for a train. Guy was engrossed in an account of Scott's last voyage.

'Not exactly morale-boosting stuff,' Martin pointed out.

'I thought reading about frostbite might cool me down,' was Guy's explanation.

Nina had finished *A Glastonbury Romance* and was well into Hugo's copy of *The Doors of Perception*. She was a fast reader, and running out of books was a real concern. If Martin didn't hurry up with *The Seven Pillars of Wisdom*, she'd have to resort to Hugo's guidebook on Algeria, which would hardly offer the escapism she was seeking. She had only been in the country four days – and only just inside it, at that – and she hated the place already. The children, whom she had considered so sweet at first, with their huge dark eyes and skinny shoulders, and smooth, dusty skin, flatly refused to run along when instructed, and followed her everywhere, wanting to touch her blonde hair. Even when she went to the toilet – a dark, foul-smelling shack behind the *douane*, with a hole in the floor – they would trail along after her and peer through the gaps in the door, so that she almost fell over them when she emerged, gasping and beating off flies.

Occasionally some of the older villagers would saunter over to the camp for a good gawp. They seemed utterly unembarrassed to be caught staring, but would stand their ground and watch for ten minutes at a time, while the four travellers turned the pages of their books in a pantomime of concentration. It was Nina who bore the brunt of local hostility. On their first day in Souk Ahras she had been cursed and spat at in the street by a shambling old man. She had taken him for a lunatic, lost in dementia, but then it had happened again and again; wherever she went men looked at her with hatred or worse.

'Why me?' she wanted to know.

'Because they think you're a whore,' said Hugo, kindly. This, and the fact that she was now roasting in an ankle-length batik dress while the boys went around in nothing but shorts was beginning to get on her nerves. And now that revolting perfumed customs official wanted to sleep with her: it was enough to make her flesh crawl. She closed her eyes and tried to imagine England: green grass, hedgerows, gentle rain. She had already forgotten the drought they had left behind not more than a week ago. Come on, Nina, she urged herself. It hasn't even started yet. It was disappointing to discover how easily her thirst for adventure could be slaked. She was disturbed in her reveries by a nudge from Guy. The shade was on the march and he needed to move the bench seat. A bright sword of sunlight struck her across the eyes as she looked up. Hugo and Martin had disappeared.

'Are you feeling homesick?' he asked, when they had shifted the bench, and Nina had flopped back on to it with a sigh.

'Just sick,' said Nina. 'I haven't got a home.'

'You should take a salt tablet,' Guy suggested. 'Do you want me to get you one?'

Nina shook her head. 'Not on an empty stomach. Is that book any good?'

'Gruesome. Listen to this: *Sunday 18 March. My right foot has gone, nearly all the toes – two days ago I was proud possessor of best feet. These are the steps of my downfall.*'

Nina pulled a face. 'Go on,' she said. 'I'm starting to feel better.'

'Okay. What about the death of Oates? *He has borne intense suffering for weeks without complaint, and to the very last was able and willing to discuss outside subjects. He did not – would not – give up hope till the very end. He was a brave soul. This was the end. He slept through the night before last hoping not to wake; but he woke in the morning – yesterday. It was blowing a blizzard. He said, "I am just going outside and may be some time." He went out into the blizzard and we have not seen him since.*'

'What a terrible way to die,' said Nina. 'Alone and frightened.' She felt tears stinging the backs of her eyes. I mustn't cry, she thought. He'll think I'm a great big baby. 'Perhaps I will have one of those salt tablets,' she said, but as she hauled herself to her feet there was a whoop, and Martin appeared from behind the *gendarmerie*, climbed into the Land Rover and brought it bouncing across the track towards them. 'Get that tent down,' he called through the window. 'The telex has just arrived from Algiers. We're off!'

'So our friend at Customs never got his £3,000 backhander,' said Guy, when they had finally loaded up and were on their way. This exercise had been performed at great speed and without much care in case a fresh excuse to detain them was suddenly devised.

'And he never got to sleep with the blonde!' laughed Martin, one hand on Nina's knee.

Now that they were on the road again, with a warm breeze blowing through the open windows and the empty track winding before them up into the Atlas mountains, spirits were high, and all their old hostility to the country was forgotten.

'But the really good news,' said Hugo, reaching through the slashed vinyl of the passenger seat with one hand, and producing a small piece of crumpled foil from the tangle of springs and webbing, 'is that they didn't find the dope.'

This announcement was greeted with a stunned silence.

'You had better be joking,' said Nina at last, in her head-prefect-on-the-rampage voice.

Hugo replied with a dismissive laugh.

'He is,' said Guy. 'There'll be nothing in there but a bit of old chewing gum.' Nina leaned over and snatched the piece of foil. Inside was a brown cube of cannabis resin.

'You stupid wanker,' said Martin. 'If they'd found that . . .'

'They didn't find it though,' said Hugo, still wearing the fake grin of someone determined to brazen his way out of a tight spot.

'How dare you put us all at risk,' Nina went on. 'If you want to moulder away in an Algerian jail for years go ahead, but don't try and drag the rest of us with you.' It was his nonchalance that was so maddening – when she could already imagine herself raped and shackled in a filthy cell. 'You're not even sorry.'

'You're all acting as if we got caught,' Hugo complained. 'We didn't. Events have vindicated me.' He turned to Guy. 'You're on my side, aren't you?'

'No,' said Guy. 'I'm with Martin on this one: you're a stupid wanker.'

'Okay, you're all mad at me now,' Hugo said. 'But you'll be happy to share a joint later, I bet.'

Nina gave him a disgusted glance and looked away, and the argument was allowed to die there.

25

Guy's diary: 9th July
After the Souk Ahras experience we decided it would be better to camp in the middle of nowhere rather than in a town, so we only stopped in Constantine to take on petrol and water. Now we are camped by the side of the road in a field of fleas miles from anywhere. There is a strong smell of wild garlic in the air, but I can't see any growing. Hugo is ostentatiously smoking a joint: the rest of us are ostentatiously abstaining. Earlier, while Nina and Martin were putting up the tent and we were changing a tyre he said to me, 'Nina's being a bit short with me. Have you noticed? Do you think it's PMT?' I advised him not to suggest that in her hearing.

I've taken quite a few photos, usually through the Land Rover window as we hurtle along. I didn't know what to expect from the scenery – I suppose I thought it would be just sand dunes from the moment we crossed the border, but it's nothing like that. The Atlas mountains are rocky and barren with small scrubby trees on the low slopes. We've passed a couple of working farms – dry, stubbly wheatfields surrounding an arrangement of brown, thatched buildings. At one of these a bony horse was harnessed to some sort of threshing machine – trudging round and round in circles, poor thing, in a cloud of chaff and flies.

This evening, as Hugo was cooking up another of his famous tuna curries, a white saloon car crawled over the horizon from the direction of Constantine.

'Oh-oh. Les flics,*' said Martin, as soon as the car was close enough to be identified.*

'They probably saw us driving through the town and have come to leer at Nina,' said Hugo, at which point Nina, who had changed back into her bikini top and shorts outside Souk Ahras, gave a sigh and retreated into the tent.

'They're probably not even going to stop,' I said. 'Let's not get paranoid.' Directly I said this, of course, the car pulled up with a

screech of brakes, showering us with dust and grit, and two gendarmes *in dark blue uniforms climbed out. One of them had a gauze pad over one eye.*

'Leave the talking to me,' said Hugo, master tactician and diplomat. Martin and I shared a moment of eye-rolling.

'Bon soir,' *said Hugo.* 'Est-ce qu'il y a un problème?'

'English?' barked the one with the eye-patch.

'Yes,' Hugo conceded.

This established, he proceeded to address us in high-speed French, now and then pausing obligingly to translate anything self-evident – dangereuse, *for example – and leaving us to guess the rest. The gist, I gathered, was that this wasn't a good place to camp and they couldn't guarantee our safety. At one point the other bloke actually said '*Les voleurs*', and drew a finger across his throat with a 'tsk'. Just like a cartoon. They kept glancing over at the tent, against which the silhouette of Nina struggling into a pair of jeans was clearly visible. I wondered if I should go and tell her to turn the torch off. Anyway, we declined their offer to escort us back to Constantine, and after a burst of shrugging and head-shaking, they drove off the way they'd come and we were alone. Then night came down like a guillotine, and we sat under the stars eating curry and not admitting we were nervous. Martin got the guitar out and entertained us with a Bob Dylan medley until we begged for mercy.*

'That should keep the voleurs *away,' Nina said, and I said, 'No, it just means they'll kill us first.' And that reminded us all over again that we were stuck out in bandit country with nothing but a shovel and a set of ranging rods to defend ourselves.*

10th July

Up at the crack of a hot dawn, still alive and unmolested by voleurs. *Hugo, fearless, or just stoned, slept out under the stars with only the short legs of his camp-bed between him and the seething insect life below. Nina and Martin took the tent, although Hugo had made it clear at the outset that they weren't to expect what he called 'honeymoon facilities'. I didn't want to interrupt, so I slept on the roof of the Land Rover and felt quite safe and pleased with myself, as if I'd bagged the top bunk. I made the mistake of leaving my boots on the ground overnight, and when I gave them a shake this morning,* a little black scorpion dropped out. I didn't have the presence of mind to whack it – I just leapt back and watched it scuttle away into the wheat.

Hugo is the only one who seems to be coping with the heat; the rest of us are sick as dogs. The temperature inside the Land Rover when we got in this morning was 68°C. Even the wind is hot – Nina compared it to being stuck under a hood-dryer all day. Humidity must be zero. It's such a dry, enervating heat, you don't even enjoy the luxury of a good sweat. Every so often we had to pull over for a Vomit Break. We're drinking and drinking our water supply, which is warm and tastes of swimming pools, but I don't think any of it is getting as far as my kidneys.

In the afternoon we decided to stop for a chance to stretch our legs and take on water. We'd been driving across a scorched, featureless plateau for hours when we saw Ghardaia, lying like a pile of discarded pink and white boxes in the valley below. Marking the boundary of the town were plantations of squat, dusty palm trees, and it all looked very much less lush and inviting than the image of an oasis that I've been carrying in my head since school. Just another example of reality failing to deliver. We inquired about fresh water at the gendarmerie, and were pointed in the direction of a standpipe outside. Two emaciated mongrels, covered in weeping sores, were fighting over the minute puddle of mud that had formed at its base. Every so often one of them would jump up and lick the slowly forming drop of water from the end of the tap. This did nothing for our queasy stomachs, so we moved on.

There was absolutely no one about as we drove through the town, but given that the temperature was 46°, and the usual hairdryer wind was blowing, it wasn't too surprising. From every other window came the tinny twang of Algerian radio; you can't get away from it. We parked in the shade in a large, deserted square – the sort that the French would fill with pétanque players or market stalls – and ventured out to explore. Hugo thought we'd driven past a red Coca-Cola sign on the way and was keen to track down some cold drink. No sooner had Nina emerged from the Land Rover than half a dozen men materialized and sauntered past us and back again for a good stare. This is another thing I've noticed – you never see any women. The last time we saw a woman who wasn't Nina was back in Souk

Ahras when half a dozen black chadors emerged from a doorway, flapped down the street and vanished into another doorway.

After about ten minutes of dragging ourselves down the alleyways of Ghardaia, gradually accumulating a sizeable retinue of begging children, we found the shop with the Coca-Cola sign. It wasn't so much a shop as a room containing an Algerian with a fridge. Needless to say there was no Coke available, so we bought twelve bottles of the only thing on offer – an orange fizzy drink called Smack, which tasted like Old English Spangles, and was so sweet it made you thirstier than you had been to begin with. Satan himself couldn't have devised a worse torture: after three bottles each we were completely bloated and still gasping for water.

On the way out of town we passed the standpipe again. The rabid dogs had gone so we filled up our canisters and then took it in turns to stick our heads under the tap to cool off. Then we started to flick water at each other and it all got a bit raucous, until one of the gendarmes came out and started shouting at us in French, so we got back in the Land Rover quickly before we got ourselves arrested. I wasn't sure if it was the noise he objected to or the waste of precious water. Thoughtless of us, really. As we drove off a muezzin on a minaret began to wail, calling the faithful away from their radio sets to prayer.

We covered more than four hundred miles today, swapping drivers every couple of hours to relieve the monotony. It didn't work. The scenery changed gradually – far too gradually to be interesting, of course – from semi-arid farmland to completely arid rocky desert, with white sand and stones and brown xerophytic plants. If you had a pickaxe and the inclination you could dig rose sable out of the ground by the ton. For some of the journey the road ran alongside a north–south railway line linking the oil wells to the coast. We didn't see a single train though. Every hour or so we might meet another truck coming the other way and exchange a salute of headlights, but that was it. I think we only passed two roadsigns all day: One said EL GOLEA 200 and the other was a red triangle with a picture of a camel. Martin thought it read EL GOLEA ZOO. 'Why would anyone stick a fucking zoo out here?' he said. For some reason we found this hilarious, and for the rest of the day all anyone had to do if it went quiet was to start singing, 'We're going to the zoo, zoo, zoo', to set us off again.

We camped in the wilderness, about a hundred miles from El Golea, behind an outcrop of rocks. The ground was too hard to take tent-pegs, so we slept out. The night-time temperature falls to a blissful 30° – it's about the only time I feel comfortable. The penthouse accommodation on top of the Land Rover seems, without any discussion, to have become mine. I did gallantly offer it to Nina, but she said she was quite happy down on the ground with the sidewinders. I said that was no way to talk about Hugo and Martin, and she laughed. She's got a suntan already, and a little constellation of freckles on her nose. I didn't think blondes were supposed to tan easily.

None of us had any appetite for supper, but it's the only way to take on enough salt, so Hugo slaved over the primus and we had salty meatballs and Smash. I can't think of any other circumstances in which I'd be prepared to contemplate this culinary adventure, but afterwards I did feel slightly better.

11th July
Awoken by the now familiar dawn chorus of dry retching. Hugo has caught up with the rest of us at last. One thing is becoming apparent: none of us shares the heroic fortitude of Scott and Co. – in particular Martin, who is an arch-hypochondriac and whinger. He seems to think he is uniquely afflicted by heat exhaustion and salt depletion, and the fact that he moans loudest is proof of greatest suffering. I begin to sense an edge to Nina's expressions of sympathy. Honestly, listening to him complain, you'd think he was the only one producing shit the colour and consistency of Guinness.

Breakfast consisted of porridge made with powdered milk and golden syrup, a handful of salted peanuts and a mug of peppermint tea – which we have discovered by trial and error to be the only thirst-quenching drink that masks the taste of Sterotabs. While Nina and Hugo were preparing this and I was jacking up the Land Rover to change over to sand tyres, Martin was still lying in the shade, groaning and refusing to move. As soon as the work was done, I noticed, he seemed to revive and drag himself across for his share of the food.

It's funny how we seem to be taking it in turns to be the outcast. After the dope-smuggling incident we were all against Hugo. Now the tide of resentment has turned against Martin. I can't imagine Nina becoming the focus of bad feeling – but maybe I'm biased – so it'll probably be my turn next. Another scorpion in my boot this morning.

Today we had our first encounter with a sand dune, or barkhan, *as Hugo insists on calling them. Since we left Ghardaia the landscape has been changing from stony desert (*reg *– another of Hugo's words) to sandy desert (*erg*). I did query the likelihood of two parallel terms being anagrams of each other, but Nina and Martin assure me Hugo isn't making it up.*

On the road to El Golea – a straight strip of grey across an infinity of beige – we found our path blocked at one point by the progress of one of these advancing barkhans. It was only a few feet deep at its highest point, but still enough to rouse Hugo to a pitch of excitement not seen since our escape from Souk Ahras. Here was the raw material of his PhD in action. He immediately leapt out and started taking photographs from all angles, all the while enthusing about its perfect crescent shape, and the angles of its windward and leeward slopes. Fortunately we didn't have to resort to demolishing it with shovels in order to drive on as the ground at the roadside was firm enough to hold us, so a minor detour was all that was required. And, as if this wasn't drama enough for one morning, a few miles further on I saw a mirage: a shimmering disc of spilt mercury in the middle distance. Imagine my disappointment when everyone else claimed to be able to see it too; gradually as we approached, the image materialized into a roughly circular watering hole, cloudy white and about 150 feet in diameter, its cause and origin a complete mystery. At the far end a few wild camels were drinking, and it's a measure of our overheated state that we thought it would be a splendid idea to wallow around in it ourselves and cool off. The others had stripped to their underwear and were wading in, while I was still picking at the knots in my bootlaces. By the time I'd caught up, they'd reached the middle and found the water was warm and still only thigh deep. We had to be content with kicking water over each other until we were soaking wet, and Nina's brilliant-white bra and knickers had turned semi-transparent . . .

Then I looked down at my feet through the murk and noticed dozens of these tiny, bladder-shaped sacs floating up to the surface, and I thought of bilharzia and every other waterborne disease and made an undignified sprint for dry land. The others didn't seem to share my concern, and continued to frolic around, while I crouched in the minute sliver of shade alongside the Land Rover and watched the drops of water evaporating off my skin, leaving behind a chalky deposit, rather like the streaks on our shower curtain back home. Within a couple of minutes even my hair was dry and I was hot and prickly again. I thought about those curious floating creatures, and started absent-mindedly writing my own obituary for the UCL Alumni magazine. I'd only got as far as my performance as the donkey in the school nativity (age 5) when Hugo waded back out, looking ridiculous in a pair of purple underpants, his suntan stopping abruptly several inches above and below, describing the shape of his safari shorts in marble white flesh.

'What's up?' he said. 'Camel piss not good enough for you, all of a sudden?'

El Golea turned out to be an improvement on Ghardaia. In the middle of the town there was a 'luxury hotel' – not exactly five-star as we would understand it, but at least offering a bar area selling cold soft drinks, and somewhere to sit out of the sun, and a group of Londoners on their way north. Naturally, over a few bottles of Coke and that infernal Smack, we fell into conversation, and immediately bonded with them, in the way that you do in a foreign land with strangers from home. They had come all the way through Kenya, Cameroon, Nigeria and lately Tamanrasset, and were heading for Marrakesh. When we told them we were off to In Salah to measure dunes on the Great Western Erg they just laughed. 'You think it's hot here,' they warned.

I said goodbye rather wistfully: talking about London had made me feel nostalgic for home. The Test Match on the telly, Monty Python, country pubs, Beefeaters, the Bobby on his beat . . . Well, maybe not the last two. As a gesture of friendship we swapped one of our tapes for one of theirs, but when we came to play it, it turned out to be all this twangy Indian sitar music – not so different from the ubiquitous Algerian radio – so we jettisoned it pretty smartly.

Late this afternoon, about an hour the other side of El Golea – at least sixty miles from the nearest settlement – I was driving and

Martin and Nina had fallen asleep in the back, when Hugo suddenly said, 'Look!' and pointed out of his window. In the far distance, and quite alone, was a Tuareg in a blue jellaba and turban, striding across the sand.

'Where's he going?' I said.

'Where's he been?' said Hugo, and we kept glancing out of the window at his receding figure until it eventually became indistinguishable from the surrounding grains of sand.

'Perhaps we should have tried to wave him over,' I said. 'Offered him a lift.'

Hugo pulled a face. 'I don't think hitch-hiking is part of the nomadic tradition,' he said drily.

'How long do you reckon we could survive out there in this heat, just walking?'

'You and me? A couple of hours, maximum. Nina: half an hour. Martin . . .' he glanced over his shoulder to check they were still sleeping . . . 'five minutes.' I laughed, but didn't pick up this cue to begin the full-scale character assassination that Hugo would clearly have relished. The idea of talking about Martin while he was asleep didn't appeal: he might have been shamming.

Morale reached a bit of a low today. Meeting up with those other Londoners and watching them head off north while we turned south, deeper into the desert, didn't help. And the milometer on the Land Rover has packed up – probably got sand in it like everything else – so we can't tell how many miles we've done, or how much further we've got to go. Every time we reach a new crest in the road we keep hoping to get a glimpse of In Salah, but we never do. There's just more and more of this relentless moonscape – dust, sand, wadis, and endless empty road. At one point a mobile muezzin passed us in an open-topped jeep, broadcasting his eerie cries through a megaphone.

Around six o'clock I was starting to feel a bit sick again – early evening is always my worst time, so when Martin woke up I asked if he wanted to drive for a bit, but he said he was feeling 'a bit funny'. Nina said, rather sharply, 'I don't suppose Guy's feeling a hundred per cent either, Martin. That's why he'd like a break.' So we stopped for a quick puke and a changeover and Martin made a great point of heaving and hawking and wiping his eyes, so I felt like a total shit for asking him to swap.

I sat in the back with Nina amidst the luggage. There seems to be less and less leg-room every day. Originally whoever was responsible for reloading the Land Rover after breakfast would do it properly – stacking the food and utensils in boxes, and stowing the beds and rucksacks neatly away. Now it all gets hurled in loose with the sleeping bags stuffed in the gaps so there's no room to stretch out in comfort. I couldn't face tackling the job while we were still moving, so I just closed my eyes and was asleep almost immediately.

Something disturbed me a while later – I thought it was an insect in my hair, and I twitched violently and found that in my sleep I must have slumped over sideways and was now resting my head on Nina's knee. She was brushing my fringe out of my eyes.

'Sorry,' she said, swimming into focus as she withdrew her hand. 'I didn't mean to wake you, but it looked so uncomfortable.' I could have stayed there like that, pretending to drowse – she didn't move away – but as soon as I let myself think about it the muscles in my neck tensed up and I had to move slightly. That infinitesimal adjustment must have communicated my self-consciousness to her, because we both sat up abruptly and shifted apart. Perhaps I'm inventing nuances which weren't there. Perhaps she just had pins and needles. She certainly hasn't shown me any special favours, and if Hugo hadn't told me she was about to ditch Martin, I don't think I'd have guessed.

It was getting towards dusk at this stage and a suitable stopping place still hadn't presented itself. We couldn't pull too far off the road because we'd have been into soft sand and stuck, but there was nothing remotely serviceable in the way of shelter as far as the horizon. I think Hugo would have been quite happy to keep going all night, if necessary, until we reached In Salah. The closer we get to our destination the more he resents any delays. While the rest of us are wilting and dying he calmly sits in the front seat reading the Annals of the Association of American Geographers *and making notes in the margin. He doesn't even get car sick! I could tell Martin was keen to stop as soon as possible – he kept fidgeting and looking at his watch, and sort of* hissing *– but Hugo was absorbed in his journal and missed or chose to ignore these hints. Neither Nina nor I came to Martin's rescue. It wasn't pure malice on my part; more a lack of energy. I couldn't have swatted a fly. Finally Martin said,*

'I'm not going any further,' and just pulled up in the middle of the road.

Hugo put his book down and said, 'God, you people have got no stamina, have you? I didn't bring you on this trip for your looks, you know, Martin. Just drive the bloody Land Rover will you, or we'll never get there.'

'Why didn't you learn to drive yourself then, you lazy bastard?' Martin replied.

There was an awkward silence while he remembered exactly why it was Hugo had never learned: driving had killed his mother. Nina and I cringed on Martin's behalf, but Hugo didn't say anything for a while, and Martin drove on, staring straight ahead, white knuckled and rigid.

I left it to Nina to be the peacemaker. Women are so much better at that sort of thing. I'd have been tempted to recommend Hugo and Martin slug it out in a fist fight, or a Scrabble head-to-head. Anyway, she blethered on for a while about the need for us all to recuperate before we got too tense and irrational, and, without appearing to take sides, managed to negotiate a cessation of hostilities and an overnight stop without anyone having to backtrack or apologize. We pulled just off the road, far enough not to be obliterated by a passing lorry, but keeping to the compacted, stony sand so we wouldn't sink. We pitched the tent in the lee of the Land Rover to avoid being flayed alive by the hot, gritty wind, and sat on our sleeping bags, eating water biscuits and baked beans straight from the tin, and a bar of Toblerone which Nina had bought on the cross-Channel ferry and which had melted and reset several times since.

'I bet you're missing your haute cuisine, *Hugo,' Nina said, breaking him off a warped segment of chocolate, which was covered with a fine white bloom.*

He shrugged. 'I wouldn't normally choose to eat tinned *food.' Even the words seemed to leave a bad taste in his mouth. 'But I knew what to expect, so I don't complain.' He couldn't resist this little dig.*

I'm writing this in the Land Rover. Hugo and Nina are lying on their stomachs with their heads sticking through the tentflaps, enjoying the last cigarette of the night. Martin has headed off downwind for a squat. I can just see the torch beam swaying across the sand. Tomorrow, surely, we'll reach In Salah.

What a night. It's early: the others haven't moved yet and I'm taking the opportunity to get this down on paper before the usual morning scrum begins. I don't want to forget the details.

I couldn't get off to sleep last night – it must have been that afternoon nap. I sensed the others dropping off to sleep one by one. Hugo was the last, still trying to read Annals of the Association of American Geographers *by the light of a torch-pen. Then I lay there for at least another two hours, listening to their breathing and the rustling of the nocturnal insect life outside, trapped in that insomniac's no-man's land between alertness and exhaustion. I've never felt so lonely. I could have been the last man alive, or an astronaut lost in space. Rather than succumb to an attack of agoraphobia I pulled on my boots, and shuffled out of the tent in my underpants into the warm empty desert. Above me the sky was blue-black and sprayed with stars: fat blots and the fine white dust of emulsion flicked from a brush. They seemed to be only just out of reach, and yet at the same time receding, drawing me upwards. As I stood there, swaying dizzily, with my head tipped back as far as it would go, peering into infinity, I had what I can only describe as a religious experience – an overwhelming sense of joy, dissolution and perfect affinity with the creative force – God – whatever. It was palpable. It seemed to well up from beneath my feet like fire spreading through my veins. Tears leapt to my eyes, and at this great moment of epiphany I looked down and realized I was standing on an ants' nest. Hundreds of black soldier ants, half an inch long, were swarming over the rim of my boots and up my legs, attacking me with their acid-tipped daggers. I let out a yell and started dancing about, brushing and swatting in a frenzied attempt to dislodge them, and transferred several dozen to my arms in the process. The burning pain intensified: in sweeping the little fuckers away I had merely decapitated them, leaving their pincers firmly embedded in my flesh. My grunts and curses finally roused Nina, who emerged through the tent-flaps in a long T-shirt and clogs, looking scared. I could have been murdered out there and the other two would have slept through it. 'What is it?' Nina asked, strafing me with the torch beam.*

'Ants,' I whimpered, still cavorting.

Nina approached cautiously and started to swipe at my legs and arms with one hand. The other, in which she held the torch, was covering her nose and mouth and she was shaking.

'It's all right,' I muttered. 'You can laugh out loud.'

'I'm sorry,' she said. 'But you looked so funny leaping around. Like a puppet.' I called her a heartless bitch and that made her laugh even more. She began brushing her hand gently down the front of my thighs to sweep away the last few tenacious ants, and in spite of the pain I could feel the tweaking of an imminent boner, so I had to turn away quickly and concentrate on trying to picture James Callaghan with no clothes on – a trick which has worked for me since my teens. Nina didn't seem to notice anything amiss, but instead said, 'I've got a pair of tweezers in the Land Rover. I could pull those claws out. But I'm not sucking out the poison,' she went on, over her shoulder, and I followed her thinking James Callaghan, James Callaghan, James Callaghan . . .

Anyway, I lay on my stomach on one of the bench seats with the light on so Nina could see what she was doing, and she scrabbled around in the luggage for a while until she found the tweezers and then set to work to remove the pincers one by one, dabbing each puncture mark with TCP.

'I smell like a thirteen-year-old on his first date,' I grumbled, wincing as I felt the sting of torn flesh. 'Are you sure those are tweezers you're using and not a fish-hook?'

'You're in no position to complain, so I'd advise you to shut up,' she said firmly.

'I can't afford to lose too much blood, you know. Mine's a rare group.'

'What is it?'

'A.'

'It's not that rare,' said Nina. 'I'm A myself. We can donate to each other if necessary. What were you doing outside anyway?'

'Looking at the stars,' I said. 'I was in the middle of this transcendental religious experience. Now I'll never know whether it was the Holy Spirit or formic acid.'

'I don't understand a word you're saying sometimes,' said Nina. 'There.' She showed me a palm full of black ant fragments. 'All

done.' And she smacked my bum, hard, to indicate that she'd finished, and then blushed violently. 'Sorry,' she said, furious at her own discomposure. 'I thought you were someone else.'

26

Nina sat in the meteorological station at In Salah, listening to the hum of the iced-water dispenser, and watching the condensation run down the sides. A pile of white paper cones like dunce caps sat beside the tap to tempt the unwary. A treacly twist of flypaper, studded with corpses, hung from the ceiling. The man from ENEMA had left a note on the open door explaining that they could find him in Adji's bar, or make themselves comfortable until his return – not an easy option in a room with only two chairs.

Guy and Hugo had volunteered to track him down, while Nina waited behind in case he came back by a different route without having passed them. Martin, who had fallen asleep on the journey, was still slumped in the front of the Land Rover, which was parked in the shade of the courtyard. Nina had taken a photograph of him through the window, as peaceful as a baby. She was tempted to go and wake him now. The others had been gone half an hour, and she could picture them comfortably installed in a bar, cold Cokes in hand, while she sat sweltering.

'Don't touch that water, whatever you do,' had been Hugo's parting instruction. 'You'll have the screaming shits for a month.'

She gave a start as the door opened and Martin stood there, newly awake and disorientated, the red imprint of the seatbelt across his neck like a fresh scar. 'What's going on?' he asked, rubbing his eyes. 'Where are we?'

'In Salah,' said Nina. 'We've arrived. Guy and Hugo have gone to find our contact.' Martin made straight for the drink dispenser, plucking a paper cone from the top of the pile and filling it.

'Hugo said not to drink that,' she exclaimed, before he could put it to his lips. 'That iced water is meant to be the worst stuff of all.' As soon as she'd said it she knew it had been a mistake to attribute the advice to Hugo. A third-rate psychologist could have told her that wouldn't work.

Martin hesitated a second. He glanced down at the paper cone, and then at the liquid in the dispenser. It was crystal clear, almost blue, through the tinted plastic. 'Looks all right,' he said bullishly. 'I mean, they wouldn't put it here if it wasn't drinkable,' and before Nina could point out the fatuity of this line of argument, he had drained his cup with a gasp of pleasure. 'In for a penny,' he said, helping himself to a refill.

'You idiot. Don't come crying to me when you get amoebic dysentery,' Nina retorted, but her display of indignation was entirely trumped up. If she was honest she didn't care whether he made himself ill or not, provided she wasn't expected to nurse him. The sense of revulsion for him, which she had tried to communicate to Hugo before they left, had mutated into indifference and occasionally disdain. It seemed as though the further from home they travelled, the fainter her feelings had grown. He didn't even look like himself any more. With his tanned face and sun-bleached hair, coarse and matted from nearly a fortnight without washing, and the uneven beginnings of a fuzzy blond beard, he looked altogether wilder than the man she had set off with. Like John the Baptist, she thought. Or Stig of the Dump. The worst of it was that he appeared not to have noticed any change in the relationship at all: either she was a brilliant dissembler, or he was even less observant than she thought.

'So lovely and cold. I couldn't resist it,' he was saying, crushing the paper cone in his fist and looking around for somewhere to drop it. There was no bin, so he was left to pass it from hand to hand and finally tuck it into the pocket of his shorts.

'I'm thirsty too. I managed.'

'Ah, well, you've more self-control than me,' said Martin, sitting next to Nina on the only other chair and squeezing her thigh in a proprietorial manner.

'Evidently,' she said, coldly, moving her leg away a fraction.

'Mind you, in some respects I haven't done badly in the self-control department,' he went on. 'Do you think we've got time for a quickie before the others get back?'

Nina shook her head. 'They should have been here by now. I can't think what they're doing.'

'Well, maybe now we've got somewhere to stay there'll be a bit more privacy. I quite fancy doing it in the open air. Under the stars. Don't you?'

Yes, thought Nina, but not with you. 'It's an idea,' she said, non-committally, and was spared having to pursue this conversation by the sound of voices and footsteps outside heralding the return of Guy and Hugo. They were accompanied by a young Algerian in flared jeans and a tight cheesecloth shirt. In spite of his rather lush moustache he looked to Nina to be about eighteen. His skinny fingers were freighted with gold rings. The three men seemed to be great mates already.

'This is Hamid,' said Hugo, introducing Nina and Martin in turn. 'He's come all the way from Algiers to give us any help we need. Apparently we can camp in the courtyard, or sleep on the floor in here if we prefer.' Martin automatically glanced at Nina, who kept her head down, refusing to meet his eye. 'So, he's going to take me for a drive to look at barkhans. When I've found a suitable one we can set up the equipment and a rota.'

'What do we do in the meantime?' asked Martin.

'If you can fit in my car,' said Hamid, in only slightly accented English, 'I will take you to the palmery. You can wash and keep cool there – it's very pleasant.' He waited while the others hurriedly ransacked the Land Rover for towels, warm bottles of Coke, books, football, and other paraphernalia, and then led them out to his dusty blue Citroën. Hugo automatically took the front seat, but since he was much the fattest no one challenged him. They drove through the town's wide, dusty streets, between flat-roofed, brownstone buildings, past the industrial quarter – a yard stacked with piles of bricks and lengths of irrigation piping, and shops which were no more than windowless hovels containing nothing but bolts of fabric or a crate of melons. As they passed the post office, a newer, cream-coloured block in the same style as the meteorological station, Guy asked to be let out. He disappeared inside and returned a few minutes later holding a pale blue envelope bearing an English stamp.

'From my mother,' he explained, wedging himself back in between Nina and the car's rear door. '*Poste restante.* I knew she'd write.'

There were a few people out on the street – soldiers in khaki uniform, Tuaregs in blue jellabas, and a few men in Western trousers and nylon shirts – but they were outnumbered at least two to one by donkeys. There seemed to be one on every corner – placid creatures, standing like statues in the midday sun, enduring the torment of clouds of flies with infinite patience.

As they drove Hamid pointed out various landmarks – the mosque, the barracks, the *gendarmerie*, Adji's bar, as much it seemed for his own benefit as for theirs. It emerged in the course of conversation that he had grown up in In Salah, but had gone to university far away in Algiers and had not been back to visit his home town for some years. His apologies for its shabbiness and squalor were overlaid by a hint of protectiveness.

Nina complimented him on his English, but he waved this away with a laugh, his jewellery flashing. 'No. It's really ever so bad. I lived in Montpellier for one year as part of my studies. I shared a flat with one French and two English. At the end of the year we are all speaking English.'

'Well, that's typical,' said Nina. 'I don't suppose the others had picked up any Arabic.'

'Of course not,' laughed Hamid. 'Except some swear words. They thought that would be all they would ever need.' Nina pointed to the back of Hugo's head and nudged Guy and Martin to share the joke.

Hugo, badly misjudging the slant of this conversation and taking it as an opportunity to pick up a few more handy obscenities and tips on pronunciation, began regaling Hamid with his repertoire. Hamid looked genuinely uncomfortable, and then suddenly held up one hand, palm outwards, and said 'No!' rather forcefully. 'I'm sorry,' he said, in a more measured tone, 'that last thing you said. That's really very, very rude. Don't ever say that to anyone round here. It's different in the cities – but maybe even in the cities you shouldn't use that either. But here you would get into a lot of trouble.'

'Oh,' said Hugo. 'Sorry.'

'No need to say sorry to me,' said Hamid. 'I just had to tell you. So you know. We're nearly here now,' he went on, as Nina glimpsed a fringe of palm trees above the rooftops and caught the first trace of fetid water on the breeze.

The palmery was a shady area of date palms and other fruit trees, irrigation ditches and long, low troughs around which groups of local men sat, bathing their feet, smoking and passing the time. In one of the blackest and rankest smelling of these troughs a few women in billowing chadors crouched to wash laundry.

'In Salah means "the source of the salinated water",' Hamid explained, as he dropped them off. 'It's quite rich in minerals. You'll be able to feel the difference.'

'Enjoy yourselves,' said Hugo, waving paternally from the front seat. 'Make the most of your leisure time. It'll be all work from now on.'

'What did you say to him, for God's sake?' Nina heard Martin whispering through the window, while Hamid was unloading their clobber from the boot. 'Oh, I'm not sure,' came Hugo's reply. 'Something to do with mothers and camels. Obviously touched a nerve.'

One of the men by the troughs recognized Hamid and came across to embrace him. There followed a rapid exchange in Arabic, during which glances were thrown in the visitors' direction. 'I'm explaining that you've come all the way from London to study the barkhans,' Hamid said. 'My friend is very impressed.'

When he and Hugo had departed, Nina, Martin and Guy found a shady spot at a discreet distance from the main area of troughs and set about making themselves inconspicuous.

The fact that they had been introduced by Hamid had prevented them from being treated with hostility, but they remained objects of curiosity, covertly observed from afar. Martin stood half a dozen Coke bottles in one of the nearest troughs to cool, and having tipped water over his head, he shook himself like a dog and lay on his towel reading Hugo's copy of *The Doors of Perception*. Nina produced a child's sewing kit – the sort that comes on the end of a keyring – and tried to make repairs to one of her clogs where the leather was coming adrift from the sole.

Guy opened the letter from his mother: the blue paper gave off the faintest trace of her perfume – Yardley's lily of the valley. When he closed his eyes she was there before him in her usual navy skirt and high-necked blouse, a combination that had proved impregnable to the dictates of fashion over the years.

Dear Guy [he read]

I hope this finds you well. I wonder, in fact, if it will find you at all. I don't suppose the Algerian postal system is up to much. You have chosen a good time to be away: we are all suffering under this awful drought – temperatures in the nineties every day, and no sign of it breaking. They are talking of standpipes in the street next. Some counties are already using them. The garden has been absolutely devastated: we are trying to recycle our bathwater for the borders, but the lawn is in a very sorry state. Brown and parched. All the other gardens in the village look the same. The family in the New house have been using the sprinkler after dark, which is typical.

Some wonderful news: William got a First in his Mods. His name was in the Telegraph. *I've saved the cutting for you. Your father has some leave next week. We may go to Norfolk for a few days, and visit Mother on the way. I wonder if you've had a chance to send her a postcard yet. It would cheer her up so much. She isn't enjoying this heat – her feet have come up like balloons.*

I met Julian Pellow's mother in Marks & Sparks last week. Do you remember? He was head boy in the year above you. Apparently he's got a very good job with Proctor and Gamble –

earns an absolute fortune. I think her other boy's at the BBC, in charge of something or other. Anyway, she sent her regards.

When you come back I must get you to sort out all the clobber from your wardrobe. We're going to turn your old room into the guest room as it's got its own washbasin. And you won't be needing it any more. I've put everything in boxes in the garage for the moment, but that obviously won't do in the long term.

No other news. I must take Bones out for his run now (Mad dogs and Englishwomen . . .) and I'll post this on the way. Don't forget that card to Granny.

Love from Mums.

'Everything okay at home?' Nina asked, as Guy folded up the letter and replaced it in his back pocket.

'No change,' he said. It all seemed so remote, now, his parents' world: wilting begonias and Julian somebody-or-other's meteoric career, and his grandmother's pneumatic feet. Let them strip his bedroom if they wanted: his self-portrait in the style of Salvador Dali, and those Airfix model Hurricanes trailing their cotton-wool smoke. They could bin the lot as far as he was concerned.

'My parents aren't great letter-writers,' Nina was saying. She had given up on her sewing. The needle was too fine to penetrate the leather: she had succeeded only in bending it into an L shape and impaling her thumb on the eye. 'But they said I could ring from anywhere and reverse the charges.'

'I don't think my mum knows where I am,' said Martin. 'When I told her we were going to Algeria, she said, "Oh no! I've told everyone you're going to Africa."'

'Your mum's a sweetie,' said Nina. She had met Irene only once, some months earlier, at Martin's suggestion. They had all gone to lunch at the Carvery and eaten enough roast beef to immobilize them for the rest of the day. This was Irene's idea of Luxury and Value. Nina had taken to her straight away, because she was so generous and welcoming and unaffected. Nina's mother would have called her 'a good sort' – the implication being that she was not exactly their sort. Irene herself had been delighted with Nina, who was so pretty, and so intelligent, and moreover so good for Martin. Irene's inevitable disappointment was the only aspect of her plan to finish with Martin that was giving Nina any unease. 'She worships you,' Martin said. 'I can't imagine why.'

'Do you think I dare go and paddle?' Nina asked. Her clogs felt as hot and unyielding as a couple of clay ovens.

'You'll be all right as long as you don't flaunt yourself,' said Martin.

Nina plucked incredulously at her ankle-length, printed smock. 'Flaunt myself? In this tent-dress?'

Guy looked up from composing a card to his grandmother. He had got as far as *Dear Granny, the weather is very hot here in the Sahara.*

'Temptress?' he said, interested. 'Where?'

Martin started throwing up that evening. He had complained of stomach cramps during the drive back from the palmery and refused a plateful of Hugo's chickpea risotto at supper-time. Then, when the others had set up the camp-beds in the walled courtyard behind the meteorological station and were listening to Hugo's enthusiastic account of his discovery of a textbook barkhan ten minutes' drive beyond the oasis, he had suddenly leapt up and sprinted inside.

'Do you think he's all right?' Nina asked.

Hugo, who was about to embark on a detailed explanation of the fieldwork requirements of the next week – principally, who was to do what and when – was not to be so easily derailed and waved her down again. 'The plan is, we each spend two hours in turn out on the dune, taking readings from the anemometers every two minutes. There'll be a small tent there, with the recording equipment in. I'll show you exactly how to use it. You'll be dropped off and picked up by Guy or Martin, and the rota will run continuously, twenty-four hours a day, provided there's any wind, of course. I'm happy to do a double stint at night, but basically you've got two hours on, six hours off, so you should be able to grab some sleep between shifts. Any questions?'

Through the silence came the distant sound of violent retching. 'Uh-oh,' said Nina. 'I'd better go and investigate. I did warn him not to drink that iced water.'

'*What?* He drank some of the . . . He didn't!' Hugo exploded, almost dashing his head against the wall in frustration. 'That was the last thing I said! Oh Godalmighty.' He pointed a finger at Nina as if she was as much to blame. 'Well, we're starting work tomorrow, whatever.'

'Don't go overboard with the sympathy, Hugo,' Nina retorted, as she turned her back and strode indoors. She wasn't sure whom she was more annoyed with – Martin for being ill or Hugo for being callous and self-centred. Her anger with Martin evaporated as soon as she found him kneeling over the hole in the filthy toilet floor, streams of bilious sick erupting from his mouth and nose. This was nothing like the restorative Vomit Stops they had made on the journey down; this was something altogether more virulent. He looked up at her through watering eyes, his skin drained of colour, and gave her a weak smile before another spasm bent him double. Nina supported his forehead and felt him straining against her hand, until at last the retching stopped and he sat back on his heels.

'Oh God,' he said, wiping his face with his hands which he then smeared down his shorts. 'I think I'm going to die.' His teeth were chattering uncontrollably.

'Don't say that.' Nina helped him to his feet. 'You've just got a bug from that water. You'll be better now it's out of your system. You'll probably feel fine in the morning,' she said, with a voice full of optimism and a heart full of fear.

27

'Where's the nearest hospital?' Nina asked Hamid when he arrived the next morning. She had sat up with Martin most of the night while he thrashed from side to side, clutching his stomach and drawing his knees up to his chest with the pain. He had been sick half-hourly and was delirious with fever.

'Tamanrasset,' said Hamid, with a helpless shrug.

'How far's that?'

'Seven hundred kilometres.'

Hugo rolled his eyes in horror. Nina knew what he was doing: totting up exactly how long the Land Rover and both drivers would be out of commission.

'Hospital? That's a bit melodramatic, isn't it?' he said, his calculations complete. 'He'll pick up, if we just keep a close eye on him. Make sure he doesn't dehydrate. That sort of thing.'

They were sitting in the meteorological station, Nina and Hugo on chairs, Guy and Hamid on the floor, while Martin dozed on his camp-bed in the annexe – a small office-cum-storeroom next to the toilet.

'How are we supposed to do that when he can't even keep water down?' Nina wanted to know.

'There is a doctor in the town,' said Hamid without much conviction. 'We could call on him.' His tone of voice implied that this was best attempted only as a last resort. 'I can't guarantee his . . . expertise.'

'Well, it's something to bear in mind if Martin takes a turn for the worse,' said Guy. He felt oddly detached from the situation. Martin's health wasn't his problem, and neither was Hugo's PhD. In the teeth of such majestic indifference it was easy to be calm, judicious, unselfish. 'But I'll gladly drive him to Tamanrasset if it comes to it. No trouble.'

Nina gave him a grateful smile. He seemed to her infinitely

capable and rational – an ideal of maleness in this depressingly masculine country. In fact, she thought, he was the only good thing about the whole dismal, stinking half-arsed exercise, and if he hadn't been there to keep her cheerful she'd have bailed out long ago.

'Well then, what I propose is that Nina stays here with Martin; Guy, you drive me and Hamid out to the dune and I'll get everything set up and show you both how to take readings. I'll do the first two hours, then Hamid, then you, then Nina. Whoever's left behind looks after Martin.'

The others cautiously agreed to this. It still irked Nina to see how inflexible Hugo could be when anything threatened, even temporarily, to stall his research. Hamid offered to do Nina's shift for her but she refused. It was Martin, not she, who required special favours, and she didn't want it flung back at her later that she hadn't done her bit.

A faint groan from the annexe alerted them that Martin was stirring. He opened his eyes as Nina tiptoed in and knelt beside him. 'How are you feeling?'

'Like shit.'

'You look it.' Through his suntan his skin was grey and the blond fuzz of his beard had formed into crispy strands, fused together with dried sweat and vomit. The blue of his eyes looked even more intense than usual against their pallid background. 'I'm so cold,' he said, trying to nestle deeper beneath his sheet sleeping-bag. 'Are there any blankets?'

Nina laid the back of her hand against his forehead. 'You're not cold. You're burning up. Do you think you could keep a paracetamol down?'

'I'll try.' As Nina stood up he caught the hem of her dress in his hand. 'Don't leave me,' he pleaded. She smiled down at him, a reluctant Florence Nightingale in cheesecloth and clogs. Such babies, men.

'I'm coming back,' she promised, easing the edge of her smock from between his fingers. She didn't want it torn – not now that she'd crippled her only needle.

In the courtyard the three men were preparing to leave. Hugo had taken a frozen bottle of squash from the icebox of the mini-fridge and replaced it with a warm one from their supplies. 'Is he okay, then?' he asked, climbing into the Land Rover and slamming the door on her answer so that she had to wait until he'd wound the window down to repeat herself.

'I don't know. If I knew, I'd be a bloody doctor, wouldn't I?'

'Well, you do whatever you think,' said Hugo.

'I'll be back in half an hour,' Guy called across to her, sensing that Hugo's breezy abdication of responsibility wasn't quite what she wanted to hear.

'Well, go on then.' She could sense their agitation to be gone, to shake off the stale atmosphere of the sickroom. By the time she had returned to the annexe with the paracetamol and a glass of boiled water Martin had dropped back off to sleep. She found him curled up in the foetus position, a thumb resting against his lips. He was flushed with fever and his skin was hot to the touch. She had meant to wash him down and take his temperature, but it seemed a cruelty to wake him, so she crept out again and had a drink of the warm orange squash from the fridge, then made herself as comfortable as possible on the two chairs, and was asleep herself in minutes.

She awoke some time later to find the blackest man she had ever seen leaning over her. He was wearing a vivid purple shirt, and holding six bottles of Orangina. She jerked upright, her hands automatically smoothing down her dress.

'Adji,' said the man, nodding and smiling.

'Adji?' Nina looked blank. 'Oh, *Adji*.'

'I met your friends yesterday,' he went on, in what it took Nina a while to realize was French. 'I've brought you these.' He raised the glass gourds which dangled between his fingers by their necks.

'Thank you,' said Nina. 'That's very kind.'

He put them down on the desk beside the fridge, ducking past the flypaper and unceremoniously shoving aside files, papers and synoptic charts to make room. 'Where is Hamid?' he asked.

'They've gone to find some sand.' This was the best she could do in her schoolgirl French. The word for dune had never come up in her studies of Balzac and Racine.

Adji roared with laughter. 'We've got plenty of that. You've come to the right place.' He would still be slapping his leg and guffawing over it when he left. 'Tell him you're all coming to dinner tonight at Adji's. Cous-cous, goat, very good.'

'Thank you,' said Nina, wishing she could provide firmer evidence of her proficiency in French. She wondered if she should mention Martin, who wouldn't be going anywhere, but before she could frame a simple sentence of explanation, Adji said, 'Your friend is ill.'

Nina nodded towards the annexe doorway. 'Very sick.' She was almost embarrassed at this admission as if it showed them all in a bad light: pale, weak creatures, naïve and unprepared, constitutionally unfit for travel, but Adji didn't appear to hold it against her. Indeed he affected outrage that the doctor had not visited.

'Lazy dung-beetle,' he muttered, brushing aside Nina's protests that the doctor had not in fact been summoned and therefore could hardly be expected to . . . 'Leave it to Adji.' And he departed, leaving Nina with the uneasy feeling that she was being drawn into a private feud.

Outside in the courtyard Guy was sitting in the shade eating a large wedge of melon. 'I didn't want to wake you,' he said, wiping his chin, which was shiny with juice. 'This is lovely. Do you want some? There was a bloke selling them by the roadside.'

'Well . . .' Nina looked doubtful. After Martin's experience it was hard to feel confident about foodstuffs of such dubious provenance, but it was so long since she'd tasted fresh fruit. '. . . Go on then.'

Guy cut her a slice with his penknife and she sank her teeth inelegantly into its cool, green flesh. 'I've just met Adji,' she said, between mouthfuls. 'He doesn't look Algerian, does he? Not like the others.'

'He's *Touarega*, according to Hamid,' said Guy. 'I can't understand a word he says.'

'He's promised to cook us goat tonight.'

'Where would you graze a goat around here?' Guy wanted to know.

They were just debating whether to share the rest of the melon and dispose of the evidence, or save half for the others, when the side gate opened, and a young Algerian, smartly dressed in short-sleeved shirt and well-pressed trousers, came in. He was carrying a clipboard and pen.

'Hello,' he said. 'I've come to check the rain gauge.' His English accent was good – even better than Hamid's. He bent down to inspect the brass funnel contraption that was sunk into the ground. 'I have to do it every day,' he explained, smiling at their surprised expressions.

'How long is it since it rained here?' Guy asked.

'Seven years,' said the man, laughing. 'I'm just making sure it hasn't filled up with sand.' He checked the Stephenson's screen before he left, opening the white slatted door and noting down readings from the wet and dry bulb thermometers. 'Forty-three,' he said on his way out. 'Cooler than average.'

The next visitor to call was the doctor. They could hear his hacking cough while he was still half way down the street. It reached crisis point just outside the meteorological station. 'Médecin,' he called, hoarsely, rapping on the door.

'Where is the patient?' he asked, when Nina and Guy had let him into the office. He spoke the same brand of non-European French as Adji, requiring all Nina's concentration to decipher it.

'He's in there,' said Nina, pointing to the door of the annexe. It wouldn't have surprised her to learn that he had been recently roused from his own sickbed. Before he could advance two paces he had been seized by another paroxysm of coughing, and stood hawking and wheezing as if in the last stages of tuberculosis.

'Physician, heal thyself,' Guy muttered to Nina as the man staggered past them into the makeshift sickbay, where Martin, who had been woken by the commotion, lay shivering and groaning. A rancid smell of sweat and sick and exhaled air caught the back of Nina's throat, making her gag. She picked up the bucket, recently used, and rinsed it in the toilet, her eyes watering at the effort of keeping her gorge down.

'What's the problem?' the doctor asked, crouching beside the camp-bed. 'Any vomiting? Diarrhoea? Fever?' he asked, flipping open his black bag. The contents were revealed to be a single, primed syringe. Clearly, no matter what symptoms the patient had described, the cure was the same. He was getting whatever was in that syringe.

'Yes,' said Nina, replacing the bucket. 'All of those. And he gets quite delirious from time to time.'

'He needs to drink. Give him boiled water only. From a spoon if you have to.' He averted his face for another burst of lung-clearing. Within two minutes of his arrival he was on his way, having given Martin a jab in the gluteus maximus without committing himself to a diagnosis.

'I bet it's just a placebo,' was Guy's comment. 'Some of that saline water the place is supposed to be famous for.'

In the end dinner *chez* Adji had to be abandoned. Hugo would be out on the dune; someone – Nina – was required to stay behind with Martin, and Guy's halting French was not nearly adequate to sustain a conversation, however unambitious.

'No problem,' said Adji, when they broke the news to him. 'Another night. Dinner will keep.'

In this heat? thought Nina. She was not sorry to be spared a night of socializing. It was an effort just staying awake late in the evening, without having to act as interpreter and raconteuse. And her stint at the dune had wiped her out. Guy had warned her about the infernal heat in the tiny tent, and the grinding tedium of the task, but even he hadn't managed to articulate its full horror. A sense of spiralling panic had engulfed Nina the moment she had seen the dust from the departing Land Rover, and it didn't altogether recede until she was picked up again two hours later. The job of noting down wind-speed readings from the meter, which was wired to two anemometers at the horns of the dune, was not sufficiently interesting or challenging to provide a distraction from the heat (48°C under the canopy) and the nausea. On the contrary, it was checking the second hand of her watch to observe the two-minute intervals that taught her how very slowly unpleasant experiences pass.

She tried closing her eyes and imagining she was Captain Scott, holed up in a blizzard, with frostbitten feet, but it was no use; that sort of transcendental meditation couldn't be practised in two-minute slots. Then she tried singing 'In the bleak midwinter' but her voice sounded weak and alien, and besides it was a soprano's song – she'd never been able to hit the top notes. To crown it all, after carefully eking out her ration of iced squash for the first hour so that she wouldn't run short in the second, she had fumbled with the lid and dropped the bottle. Before she could snatch it up half the contents had leaked away into the sand. She had hit a high C then all right – a screech of fury that could have tripped an avalanche. It was the little things that sent people over the edge, she decided, as she wept stinging tears of rage. In facing tragedy and disaster, the human spirit had proved itself remarkably resilient, but it was no match for the perversity of inanimate objects. Nina herself would be the proof of this: when the real time of trial came, she would be stronger than any of them.

28

When Nina woke up in the dark and couldn't see the stars she panicked. Then she remembered: she had moved her camp-bed into the meteorological station so that she would hear Martin if he called out during the night. They had been at In Salah for four days now, and although Martin's condition had not deteriorated, it had not exactly improved either. The injection – whatever it was – had stopped the vomiting, but he was still running a temperature which only occasionally dropped to normal, had no appetite, except for boiled water, and was consequently as weak as a rag.

There hadn't been enough wind to ruffle a feather for the whole of the previous day, so work on the dune had been abandoned. Guy and Nina did their best to hide their relief, while Hugo stood in the courtyard staring at the paralysed anemometer and wind-vane on the meteorological station roof and making no secret of his frustration. 'Bloody, buggering, pisspot waste of a day,' he said, slamming a kick into one of the Land Rover's tyres. 'I'm going to Adji's.' The two men seemed to have hit it off. The friendship, greatly simplified by the lack of a common language, was based on compatible superiority complexes and a shared love of hashish.

Guy and Nina had spent the morning at the palmery and the afternoon back at base, playing Scrabble, drinking Coke, shoring up Martin's spirits during his waking hours, and reading five-year-old copies of *National Geographic*, which Guy turned up in one of the filing cabinets in the annexe.

'I've now read every single book we brought with us,' said Nina, closing *Scott's Last Voyage* with a bang so that a trickle of sand slid out of the spine. 'I shall have to resort to snooping through your diary.'

'I wouldn't advise it,' said Guy, shifting Scrabble tiles

around. 'It would probably send you into a coma with boredom. Did you know that Nina Osland is an anagram of LAIN ON SAND?' he mused.

'No, I didn't,' she said, watching him pull out the words UGLY and BORE from the letters of his own name.

'Besides,' he went on. 'You might come across a reference to yourself.'

'Really? In what context? My irritating little ways?'

'Oh no, nothing incriminating like that. I can't get it out of my head that one day someone or other might read it, so I've kept it incredibly bland. The other two might come in for a bit of flak now and then, but for some reason I don't find you nearly so annoying.'

'I think that's what they call "damning with faint praise",' smiled Nina, absent-mindedly forming the words GLUM BOY with one finger. All the same she was pleased. Guy wasn't given to idle flattery.

He gave a laugh of acknowledgement. 'There,' he pointed to his completed anagram, picked out in Scrabble tiles. BLOW MY ROGUE, it said.

'Blow it yourself,' said Nina, heading off to the fridge for more Cokes.

She ran through this exchange in her head as she lay in the dark waiting for the pummelling in her chest to ease off. It was unnaturally quiet indoors: she had grown used to sleeping through the rustle of insects and the racket of In Salah's youth, catcalling and practising handbrake turns in their clapped-out cars on the deserted market square. It was black as ink, too, without the moonlight. After five minutes only the faintest outlines began to suggest themselves.

Was it possible, Nina was wondering, to feel guilty about something one may never have the opportunity to do? Was it a rehearsal for the greater shame and remorse to come? She got no further with this line of inquiry because now that she was fully awake she realized just how maddeningly thirsty she was. Her tongue was fused to the roof of her mouth and had to be peeled away with one finger. It was no use, she'd have to get a drink. She swung her legs over the edge of the camp-bed, feeling the cool tiles under her feet, took two steps towards the fridge and blundered into the spiral of flypaper. Her shrieks brought Guy running in from the courtyard. Martin was practically comatose, and Hugo was sleeping the sleep of the stoned. A snort of laughter escaped Guy when he located the light switch and saw her there, writhing like a maggot on a hook. Her frantic attempts to free herself had only served to snag more of her hair. 'Oh dear, oh dear, oh dear,' was all he could say.

'Don't stand there laughing, you callous bastard,' she hissed, her eyes smarting at the indignity of it all. 'Do something.'

'I'm sorry,' he said, still chuckling, and walking around her to take in her predicament from all angles. 'But you're so funny.'

'And you're so smug and annoying!' she replied.

He tutted. 'I'm afraid you're in no position to complain, so keep still and stop whining. He was enjoying himself enormously. Revenge for the ant incident, no doubt, Nina thought. If only she'd stayed in bed. If only she'd stayed in England! Glancing up she saw a tiara of dead flies in her fringe and twitched violently, nearly scalping herself. 'Oh my God!' she yelped, gooseflesh breaking out on her bare arms and legs.

'I may have to shave your head,' Guy was saying, as he began, strand by strand, to disengage her hair, which was thick with glue and crushed insects.

'Why not just cut my head off?' Nina suggested, making a final bid to recover her sense of humour in the face of this monumental loss of cool.

'No, no, you'll never keep your sunhat on without it,' he replied. 'God, this is a horrible job. What's in it for me?'

'My undying gratitude. Is that good enough?'

'I suppose it'll do to be going on with. I wish I had a pair of chopsticks, like the nit nurse at school. This glue is revolting.'

'Do you think I'll ever get it out of my hair?' Nina asked as he freed the last clump, and she let it fall heavily against her neck.

'I don't know. Have you got any shampoo?'

'In my rucksack.' She hadn't had the opportunity to use it since leaving Italy.

'Come on then.' He helped wash her hair under the tap in the courtyard. Even the rattle of running water against the drain, and Nina's yelp of shock at the cold didn't wake Hugo. Guy had propped a flashlight in a niche in the wall beside them and a succession of giant moths, crickets and other winged insects battered themselves against the lamp and fell twitching at their feet. Hamid was right about the water. It did feel different – almost silky to the touch.

'You're being very thorough,' Nina said, as Guy massaged away at her scalp, working his fingers into the roots of her hair, so that creamy spilths of lather dropped on to the dust.

'It's the only way to get this glue out from under my nails,' he confessed. Afterwards they sat on Guy's camp-bed and shared a packet of strong Algerian cigarettes, while Nina took a comb to her hair and tugged the tangles out with a severity which made Guy wince.

'This is the nicest time,' he said, looking up at the stars, spellbound again by their sheer profusion. He would never get used to it. 'The temperature's just about bearable now.'

'It's a shame we're never awake to enjoy it,' said Nina, wrenching the comb through a particularly stubborn knot.

Another shower of meteors grazed the sky: Guy put his head back and stared into deep space. Try as he might, he couldn't recapture that sense of the divine that he had experienced out in the wilderness. 'It's almost enough to make you believe in God, isn't it?' he said, and then stopped, embarrassed, as though he'd just admitted to sucking his thumb, or some other infantile habit.

'Not for me,' said Nina. 'It's enough to make me not believe. I mean,' she made a sweeping gesture with her cigarette, taking in the Milky Way in an arc of rippling smoke, 'why would He bother?'

'I don't know. And the more I think about things, the less I understand. All I'm doing is uncovering vast new tracts of ignorance.' He ground his cigarette out in the dust.

'How can you say that?' laughed Nina. 'Here we are at the cutting edge of geological research . . .'

'Oh, don't remind me. We'll be back out on that sodding dune again tomorrow.'

'I suppose we'd better get some sleep,' said Nina, standing up to shake out her hair, which was silky and tangle free now, and already almost dry.

'Pray for another day without wind,' said Guy, lying back on his camp-bed, hands behind his head.

'But to whom?' asked Nina, as she turned to go back indoors.

Guy watched her departure with a smile. Who on earth still used the word 'whom' in the course of normal conversation?

29

There was no wind again. Hugo and Hamid climbed to the top of the dune and released a dozen or so helium balloons, one at a time, so that Hugo could study the spiral patterns of their ascent in the thermals, which he filmed with a cine camera. On their way down Hamid's boot had come off and he had tripped half a dozen paces without it and blistered his foot badly on the burning sand. Hugo had helped him hop the rest of the way back to Hamid's car and then, untutored, unlicensed and uninsured, had driven him back into town. Unable to walk or drive, Hamid was now resting at his cousin's attended by the tubercular doctor and effectively invalided out of service.

Fortunately this setback coincided with an improvement in Martin's condition: on the morning after Nina's skirmish with the flypaper he rose from his bed and took an unsteady walk around the courtyard. 'You look different,' he said to Nina, who was washing out some of her clothes in a bowl and pegging them on the guy-ropes to dry. Her hair, bleached blonder by the sun, and clean at last, was worn in two long plaits behind her ears.

'I am different,' she said, but didn't elaborate. 'You look better. Better than yesterday, anyway.' By which she meant that although his ribcage was more prominent than usual, and his hair was as dull and matted as the fringe of an old afghan coat, and there were shadows like bruises under each eye, he was at least vertical, which had to be considered progress.

He managed a bowl of porridge for breakfast and some plain boiled rice for lunch without relapsing, and even began to talk of putting in an appearance at the dune, at some unspecified future date. Nina was doubtful about the wisdom of this, but Hugo, whose impatience with each fresh obstacle to his schedule was growing daily, was eager to deploy him as soon as possible.

Hugo informed them that he was hoping to extend their stay in In Salah by a few days in almost the same breath that he broke the news of Hamid's accident. Nina and Guy were furious when they discovered that the first day's data, so painstakingly collected, was now redundant. 'It's continuity I'm after,' Hugo explained. 'Not random snapshots. Ideally I'd like an unbroken week's figures. I may have to settle for five or six days, I accept that.'

Nina looked mutinous. 'We're hostages to the weather, now, are we?' she grumbled. 'We could be here indefinitely if that's the case.'

'Listen: the longest continuous period of recorded sand-dune activity prior to this expedition is *six hours*. If I can get six full days' data I'll be able to rewrite history.'

'Geography,' Guy corrected him, earning himself a glare from Hugo who tended to lose his sense of humour when talking about matters close to his heart.

'I know it's all a pain in the arse,' he went on, through a mouthful of tuna kedgeree. 'But I'm not asking you to do anything I'm not prepared to do myself. You don't think I like sitting out there on my own in that heat writing down rows of numbers, do you?'

Nina didn't answer. It sounded to her precisely the sort of obsessive, anti-social activity he'd enjoy. Besides, quarrelling with Hugo was rather like trying to untangle a snarl of metal coat-hangers. It was impossible to stay calm, in spite of one's best intentions.

'I'll give you full credit when I publish,' he said, with his usual towering condescension.

Behind him Guy mimed puking.

It was during the early evening that the wind began to pick up again. Nina noticed the pages of her book fluttering and little eddies of dust gathering in the courtyard. She was rereading *A Glastonbury Romance*, regretting having skimmed it first time around. If she had known how heavily time would hang on her hands she would have been more thorough and made it last. Martin had gone back to bed after lunch, weakened by his morning's exertions, but insistent that he no longer required round-the-clock surveillance. The others were free to go out if they wanted: he had inconvenienced them enough. He would be up and about tomorrow, thought Nina, and that would be the end of her cosy chats with Guy. She was ashamed at how much this bothered her, and how readily she could view Martin's illness solely in terms of its inconvenience to her. But she couldn't help noticing how much more attention Guy paid her while Martin was out of the way. She had dropped off to sleep after the flypaper incident, in the comfort of a delicious certainty that Guy was interested. Patience was all that was required. And then, to compound her frustration at Martin's imminent recovery, she discovered that, on what might prove their last opportunity to be alone, Guy had chosen instead to accompany Hugo to Adji's. In a fit of pique, poorly disguised as a headache, she had stayed behind, to experience all the satisfaction of having punished no one but herself.

Jamming her feet into her clogs, she hoisted herself off the camp-bed, which had been backed into a corner by the advancing sun. The courtyard faced west, and soon there would be no shade left at all. The knickers and T-shirts which she had pegged out earlier were baked dry and swinging stiffly in the new breeze. They crackled as she rolled them up and stowed them in her rucksack. In the annexe Martin was still asleep. She was tempted to take a pair of scissors to his beard – the side she could reach, at least – but decided instead to drain the undrinkable iced water from the dispenser and use it to wash her feet, in the hope that the rest of her would be deluded into feeling cool and clean. She was standing in a bucket in the main office of the met. station, observing the unsightly phenomenon of a suntan that came to an abrupt stop half way down each foot, when she heard voices outside, and the door swung open.

'Wind's up. We're in business again,' announced Hugo, cheerfully, giving one of her plaits a playful tug. 'Why are you standing in a bucket? Don't you know the old saying – "pissing on his feet keeps no man cool for long."' He was in a good mood again, now that things were going his way. In the doorway she could see Guy trying not to smile.

'God, you're coarse sometimes, Hugo,' she said, stepping daintily out of her footbath and back into her clogs, leaving a pattern of prints on the tiled floor.

'Coarse I am,' he said, plucking the car keys off the table and tossing them to Guy. 'So who's going to volunteer, then? The twilight shift – very pleasant.'

'I'll do it,' said Nina, surprising herself.

'Excellent,' said Hugo, delighted to find her so co-operative. 'Don't forget you'll have to take the counter back and rewire it to the anemometers. Obvious, really,' he conceded, as Nina raised her eyes to the ceiling.

'Is your headache all right now?' Guy asked, when the two of them were on the road.

'What? Oh, yes, just a dull ache,' Nina improvised, having forgotten her trumped-up excuse for staying behind.

'You should have come to Adji's,' he went on.

'I didn't feel like it. Until about ten minutes after you'd gone,' she said, mollified by his concern.

'We could have done with your French,' Guy went on, unaware that in Nina's current mood this would be wilfully misread.

I'm just the interpreter, she thought. There was silence as the Land Rover bumped along the pitted track, heading south, leaving the squat brownstone bunkers behind them. In the west the sun was dropping towards the horizon; a huge globe of molten wax. The hard, bright landscape of the day was softened by the dusk, the dunes trailing long velvet shadows. Everywhere she looked Nina could pick out naked human forms: here a raised knee, there a shoulder, here the curve of a breast. In the distance, the tiny tent, fluorescent orange and angular, was the only aberration.

'You seem a bit preoccupied. Is everything okay?' Guy asked eventually, glancing sideways at her.

'Yes,' said Nina, snapping to attention. It was impossible for her to be natural with him now that she'd admitted to herself how desperate she was for his approval. I must be giving myself away with every gesture, she thought, her whole body feeling leaden and awkward.

'Oh look.' Guy pointed out of his window. Two Algerian soldiers, dressed in khaki, rifles on their backs, were walking across the dunes hand in hand. 'They do that a lot here, apparently. Men.'

'I think it's nice,' said Nina.

'I can't see it catching on in the British Army,' said Guy. He was thinking of his father, who had always found physical contact with his own sons uncomfortable, unless of course he was administering a walloping.

'It must be comforting,' Nina said. 'When there's just two of them in all this empty space.'

They pulled up alongside the road by the observation tent. Guy switched off the engine and they listened to its dying shudders being absorbed into the surrounding silence.

'Well, here we are,' said Guy, jumping out and fetching the digital counter from the back. Nina shouldered her raffia bag containing cold drink, cigarettes, towel, torch, book, clipboard and pen, and followed him over the sand, dragging her feet in the furrows left by his boots. 'No. Here I am,' she thought.

By the time he had wired up the anemometers and checked that the counter was working the sun had almost sunk out of sight. In a couple of minutes it'll be dark, thought Nina, fear tightening like a rope around her neck.

'I suppose I'd better leave you to it,' said Guy, hands in the pockets of his shorts, transferring his weight awkwardly from foot to foot. 'Will you be all right?'

Nina nodded, not quite trusting herself to speak. *Don't go,* she was thinking. She had spread out her towel in the cramped space under the canvas, with her book and her bottle, as though she was at the beach. 'You won't go off and get stoned somewhere with Hugo and forget to pick me up,' she said, staring down at her two-tone feet.

'Of course I won't.' Guy, who had taken a few steps back, now stopped.

'What if you have a puncture or break down or something?'

'I'll hijack a donkey.'

She couldn't help smiling at this, in spite of herself. 'Okay. I'm totally reassured. I don't know why I'm being so feeble. I think the heat has affected my brain.' She picked up the clipboard and wrote the time and date at the top of the page. *Don't go.*

'Bye then. See you in two hours.' He turned away with a wave, and walked back to the Land Rover.

'*Don't go!*' For a second she wasn't sure if she'd actually said the words out loud. She certainly hadn't meant to, but she heard them differently this time, from outside as well as inside her head. But Guy didn't stop or falter; he just climbed into the driver's seat and set off without a backward glance. She had simply imagined it after all. Just as well, she thought, blushing with relief at such a near miss. That would have been a Big Mistake.

She leant forward. The Land Rover had stopped about two hundred yards down the road. It was now reversing, fast and erratically the way it had come, churning dust from under the wheels. Yes! She was on her feet before Guy had even got the door open: before he had put a foot to the floor she was racing down the slope towards him, tripping and stumbling the last few steps of their downfall.

Afterwards Nina said, 'They'll wonder what took you so long. What will you tell them?' Her hands were still shaking as she lit two cigarettes and passed one across to him.

'I'll say I got lost.'

'It's a straight road.'

'I'll say I stopped to look at the stars and fell into a trance.'

'Be serious.'

'I am serious. In fact I may well do just that on the way back, then I won't even have to lie.'

At the thought of the deception and concealment that would now be necessary Nina's feeling of euphoria rapidly drained away. She was glad of the darkness now. It offered some protection against self-exposure and embarrassment. There was just the moonlight and the glowing tips of their cigarettes as they inhaled.

'You'll have to cook up some figures for Hugo,' Guy said, passing her the clipboard, on which he'd been lying. 'You seem to have neglected to take any readings.'

'Okay, I'll fill them in at the end.'

'Don't be too creative, though. We don't want future generations of desert morphologists barking up the wrong cactus.'

'I'm not actually like this,' Nina said. Her image of herself as a decent, honest, unselfish person was impregnable to occasional lapses of behaviour.

'I know. That's why I like you.'

'It's all Hugo's fault,' she burst out, cutting him off mid-compliment. All her life's trials and irritations could eventually be traced back to him, she was convinced. 'I wanted to finish with Martin before we left England. Now look at the mess I'm in.' What she really wanted to say was 'Where do we go from here?' but she thought that might be to presume too much.

'If being found out is what's worrying you, then you can rest easy. Martin will still be asleep, and Hugo's far too self-absorbed to suspect anything. All shall be well,' said Guy, taking a final drag on his cigarette and flinging the butt over his shoulder. 'All shall be well and all manner of thing shall be well.'

'That's probably how they start in the first place,' Nina observed, following the trajectory of the burning stub with her eyes. 'Like oysters with grit. Under every dune a single cigarette butt. Who said "All shall be well"?'

'Julian of Norwich.'

'Never heard of him.'

'Her. She was a religious nutter in the Middle Ages. Lived in a cell, cut off from all human contact.'

'Sounds eminently sensible to me,' said Nina with a sigh.

'Don't worry, your sordid secret is safe with me,' were Hugo's first words to Nina when, a little over an hour later, he took her place in the tent. Speechless, she gaped beyond him to where Guy, illuminated by the interior light of the Land Rover, was miming an apologetic palms-up shrug.

'Sorry, sorry, sorry,' said Guy, as Nina climbed in beside him, her face like thunder. 'He was waiting for me when I got back and guessed straight away. I tried to deny it but he just laughed.'

'Brilliant,' said Nina. 'Absolutely brilliant. That's the golden rule of discretion – blurt everything out to the first person you meet. Especially if it happens to be a tactless troublemaker like Hugo.'

'I did not *blurt*,' Guy protested. 'Anyway, Hugo won't say or do anything that would jeopardize his research. It's all he cares about.'

And what do you care about? Nina wondered, thinking for the first time how little she knew him.

30

At the time no one except Nina gave any thought to Hugo's story of the angry Arab on the donkey. It was just another anecdote to take home with them, richly illustrative of the oddness of foreigners, which would be exaggerated with every retelling.

Hugo had been working out on the dune in the afternoon when the figure of a man on a donkey had shimmered into view over the horizon from the direction of In Salah. Hugo had watched his approach with interest. It seemed likely that it was the observation tent, and not Tamanrasset – seven hundred kilometres further on – that was his destination: the donkey did not look especially fit.

'He said the Land Rover had been parked all day under his palm tree and he'd come to collect the rent,' Hugo explained to Martin and Guy, while Nina was working her shift. They were at the palmery, where the temperature was a degree or two lower than at the met. station, and where the Land Rover was indeed parked in the shade of the disputed date palm. All three were sitting on the edge of one of the water tanks, cooling their feet and smoking, like locals.

'So what did you say?' Martin wanted to know.

'Well . . .' Hugo was inhibited in his narration by the fact that Guy had already had a version of the story on the drive back and would therefore be alert to any embellishments. 'I told him it was impossible, because for part of the day, at least, the Land Rover was out on the dune with Guy. And secondly that I should like to see evidence of his ownership of the tree. And thirdly that I didn't recall entering into any rental agreement with him and had no intention of paying.'

'To which he replied?'

'To be honest his English was so hopeless I think the finer points might have been lost on him. But he must have understood the last bit because he pointed at my watch. I thought at first that he was asking the time, but he was actually suggesting I hand it over in payment. It was at that point that I started to lose patience.'

'Don't tell me you got into a fight,' begged Martin. That was all they needed – an international incident to stir up a bit of local ill will.

'No, no, nothing like that. I just told him to be on his way – words to that effect – and he started to rant a bit and actually said *you* had sent him to pick up the money from me.' Hugo's laugh tailed off as he took in Martin and Guy's frozen smiles. 'Did you?' he demanded.

'It was a joke. We didn't seriously think he'd trot off ten miles into the desert on his donkey,' Martin said.

Hugo turned on Guy. 'You never told me this on the way here.'

'You never asked. He came up to us here this morning and spun this yarn about owning the bit of shade we'd parked in, so we offered to move the Land Rover, but he said we still owed him for the time we'd already had. Then I said that we didn't have any money and he should discuss it with our leader, who lived in an orange tent on the road to Tamanrasset.'

'We were only taking the piss,' said Martin. 'We thought he was just the local wide-boy, trying it on.'

'That's exactly what he is,' said Hugo. 'He had a good old gawp at the measuring equipment as well, while I was talking to him. Probably wondering if he could nick that.'

'So how did you get rid of him in the end?' Martin asked.

'Well, he was shouting at me by this stage, not in any language I could understand, so I'm afraid I had to resort to that turn of phrase which so offended Hamid the other day.'

'You mean the one he said you should never say?' Guy asked. Hugo had omitted this detail in his original account.

'Yes, that's right,' said Hugo, oblivious to Guy's attempt at irony. 'I must say, Hamid didn't exaggerate the touchiness of these guys. Jesus. Talk about hypersensitive. I thought he was going to have a coronary. It did the trick though. He muttered something under his breath and rode off on the donkey, whacking it with a stick all the way.' And they all laughed, united for once in a spontaneous rush of xenophobia. 'Anyway, Martin,' said Hugo, noticing for the first time that the former invalid was up and about, apparently cured, 'since you're out of bed at last perhaps you'd like to do the next shift.'

❦

Nina, broiling out on the dune again, couldn't decide whether the fact that her fling with Guy coincided with Martin's re-emergence into society was a matter of good or bad timing. It meant that the opportunities for her and Guy to be together and indulge in potentially embarrassing apologies or declarations were severely limited. This was surely a good thing. But it also left the matter hanging, unresolved. It meant, too, that she was required to behave in a girlfriendly manner towards Martin, something which his recent isolation had spared her. She was finding the strain of acting unnaturally with both men hard to bear, and she tended to be withdrawn and silent to avoid giving herself away. But keeping silent was itself contrary to all her instincts. She felt as though somewhere, beneath these layers of pretence, the real Nina lay buried, awaiting excavation. On those occasions when she found herself in Guy's company, Nina noticed an electric awkwardness between them, which intensified to a high-pitched humming in her ears whenever Martin was also present. Sometimes Guy might say 'Are you all right, Nina?' and she would nod and say 'Yes, fine, fine', in a reassuring voice, perfectly pitched so he would know she wasn't suffering. Her dignity was still important to her. As for Guy, he was non-committal to a fault, asking for nothing and giving nothing away. Patience, Nina thought. In a few weeks' time we'll be home and I can tell Martin I'm moving out. 'All manner of thing shall be well.' She remembered Guy's words and repeated them, loudly and confidently, into the void.

31

The feeling of unease which Nina had been nursing since she had heard about Hugo's altercation with the man on the donkey condensed in a sliding sweat when she and Guy pulled up opposite the observation tent to collect Martin from his first shift and found it empty, the equipment missing, and Martin himself nowhere to be seen.

'Something's happened,' said Nina at once, panic rising in her throat like vomit. The sand at the opening of the tent was churned up with footprints and pitted with dark brown spots. On top of the dune and at the horns of the crescent, the anemometers whirled unchecked, their wires trailing on the ground.

For a moment they stood rooted to the spot with fear and confusion, entirely at a loss. How were they supposed to search in a landscape with no hiding places?

'MARTIN!' Guy bellowed through cupped hands, but the wide blue sky and parched ground failed to give back even an echo in reply.

'Let's go back and fetch the *gendarmes*. Something's happened to him,' said Nina, tugging at Guy's arm to shake him out of his temporary paralysis, but he was staring past her into the middle distance.

'What's that?' he said, squinting against the glare. 'There's something up ahead by the side of the road.' Nina followed the direction of his gaze and made out, through the trembling heat-haze, a distant streak of colour: denim blue. For the first time in weeks she felt icy cold all over; goose pimples sprang up on her skin and her scalp tightened. Then the two of them scrambled into the Land Rover without another word, the slam of the doors in the silence ringing out like gunshots. And they drove towards the scene that would always now be waiting for them whenever they closed their eyes, and that they would never be able to forget, even when they were old and confused and had forgotten almost everything else.

He had tried to crawl along the road for help – the very worst thing he could have done with his injuries. He had been beaten about the head with a stick and left in the sun to die: the motive, apparently, theft. The digital recording machine (useless without the anemometers and not, one would have imagined, desperately saleable with them) along with Martin's Woolworths watch and camera were the only items stolen. Martin had, in any case, set off in the wrong direction – away from In Salah – and the position in which they found his body, and the marks in the sand beyond it, suggested he had belatedly realized this and turned back again before collapsing.

It was Nina who got everything done. From the moment she saw him face down in the sand, his blond hair black with blood and flies, all normal emotional responses shut down and she felt herself overtaken by a robotic zeal to get him home to his mother. It was in this sub-human frame of mind that she was able to take on the sort of labyrinthine bureaucracy which, in other circumstances, would have overwhelmed her. It was she who persuaded Guy that they should take Martin's body back to the *gendarmerie* themselves, who contacted the British embassy in Algiers and made that terrible long-distance call to Irene in London. She gave exhaustively detailed witness statements in English and French to a succession of uniformed policemen, including Hugo's description of the angry rent-collector, to which they listened without much interest, and without taking notes. The official response to the tragedy had so far been to shout at her for moving the body and to confiscate passports. She, Guy and Hugo were only saved from being left in the cells overnight by the intervention of Hamid's uncle, who was apparently Somebody in Sidi bel Abbes. It had never occurred to them that they might be considered suspects.

The man from the embassy, Mr Aspinall, was kindness itself, explaining over a crossed telephone line the complex procedures surrounding a local inquest and the repatriation of a body in such circumstances, and offering to send legal representation should they become embroiled in a criminal investigation. He sounded very much like a younger version of Nina's father, whose name she dropped into the conversation in the hope that it might oil a few hinges. It turned out that the two men's career paths had indeed crossed in Kuala Lumpur. Mr Aspinall then promised to make the journey to In Salah himself to give them any assistance they might need, and the phonecall ended on a note of the utmost cordiality.

Nina's parents themselves, when she had finally run them to ground, holidaying in Rhodesia, were ready to fly out at a moment's notice, and Nina had accepted the offer with the proviso that her mother remain behind. If there was anything technical, legal, bureaucratic to be managed, her father and Mr Aspinall could do it. Her mother could not be relied upon to contribute anything more than tears, and Nina felt inclined to guard her reserves of consolation for the truly needy.

Oddly, it was Guy, who had known Martin least, who seemed to cope the worst. 'I've been such a shit,' he kept saying. Or, 'I keep thinking it's my fault', over and over again. Whenever she walked into the met. station on the way to or from yet another errand, he would be sitting on one of the chairs, staring into space, arms dangling, or slumped with his head in his hands, no use to her whatsoever. Hugo, who might have had firmer grounds for self-reproach, expressed no such qualms. Nina couldn't help entertaining the suspicion that his vengeful expressions of outrage and grief were as much for his sabotaged research as for the loss of a friend. On that first dreadful day, when she had been browbeaten by the *gendarmes* and treated like a nuisance, and no one had shown her a drop of human sympathy, she had caught Guy and Hugo clinging to each other and crying. For a second she had felt tempted to join them – to collapse into their arms and abandon herself to hysterics, but instead she had slunk away unseen. Then, later, Guy had come up to her as if to give her a hug – at least he had twitched his arms in her direction – and she had cringed away.

'You're in shock,' he said.

Perhaps he's right, she thought, as she lay on Martin's camp-bed in the annexe, wrapped in his grimy, sheet sleeping-bag. Perhaps that's where I am. She pictured it as a raft, drifting along a smooth, slow-flowing river towards a waterfall. It wasn't a bad place to be – a little lonely, perhaps, but peaceful, and infinitely better than what lay ahead.

No one was ever brought to trial for the murder, though it might be said that natural justice was served. A month or so after Nina returned home, her father received the following letter from Mr Aspinall.

Dear Charles

I'm sorry that our paths had to cross in such appalling circumstances, but it was nevertheless good to see you again. Some information pertinent to the case has just reached me, and though not entirely satisfactory, it may be of interest to Nina.

About a week ago a man was picked up in El Golea trying to sell Martin's watch and camera to a couple of German tourists. He confessed to the murder 'under interrogation' – I can only leave to your imagination what form this would have taken – and subsequently died in police custody. And there the investigation ends, I'm afraid. Not a triumph for law and order, but a conclusion, at least, to this tragic episode.

I hope you are well and that Nina is bearing up in spite of all.

Yours ever

Peter Aspinall

P.S. I will arrange to have the watch and camera returned to Martin's mother in due course.

Having fought off grief with such determination, Nina found herself unable to surrender to it when at last the opportunity arose. She didn't cry when her father arrived, with his money and his list of contacts, and held her tightly and promised everything would be all right. And she was dry-eyed when she said her farewells to Hugo and Guy, who would be driving the Land Rover to Oran and taking the boat to Marseilles. She had already consigned them to the past. It was much later that the tears came: at the second inquest in London, and when she saw Irene at the funeral, so dazed and ghostly, and yet so grateful for the huge turnout and the many testimonies to Martin's popularity – small crumbs of comfort, hungrily received. And then again, later still, when she found she was pregnant.

III

32

'He's there again,' the school secretary, Mary, said, parting the Venetian blind so that Guy could see the distant figure skulking by the gate. It was the third time he'd been spotted near the school premises. *Paedophile*, had been the immediate, unspoken fear, but he didn't look much more than a child himself, and had made no approaches to anyone entering or leaving the premises. The question was, what did he want? He didn't look nearly old enough to be a parent – not that that meant anything these days – and, besides, it was a staff training day and there were no children on site to be collected. Guy wondered whether he might not be an animal rights activist. They'd had some bad publicity over that plague of frogs, and a spate of angry calls when it was reported that a man from Pest Control had been called in to flush them out.

'Maybe he's an ex-pupil,' he said, releasing the blind with a twang. 'Revisiting an old haunt.'

'Well, in that case why doesn't he just come in and say hello?' said Mary reasonably. 'People often do.'

'I don't know.' Guy took another quick glimpse through the slats. The boy had sauntered a little way down the road and was leaning against a lamp-post. He was holding something black and solid and passing it casually from hand to hand. Of course one read of deranged students in America harbouring murderous grudges and running amok with guns on prom night. But this was Twickenham. 'Perhaps I'll stop on my way out and have a word with him,' said Guy, tucking his trousers into his socks.

Now that the weather was warmer he'd taken to cycling. It was no distance – walkable really, but he was in a hurry to get home today. He and Jane were going away by themselves to a hotel for the night – the first time since the children were born. He had booked a place on the river near Marlow which had a couple of stars in their eight-year-old *Good Food Guide*. Sophie and Harriet were going to tea and sleeping over with that peculiar friend of Jane's. Erica. This was the only aspect of the arrangements which gave him any unease. From his own interpretation of various casual remarks Jane had let slip, he had built up a picture of a slatternly alcoholic, devoid of domestic skills or maternal authority, presiding over a household of feral children – an impression not wholly dispelled by that one meeting with her. She was the type of woman, he imagined, who would serve the children food rich in additives and let them stay up until all hours and sleep where they fell – probably in front of post-watershed television; the sort liable to use the f-word freely, have a drink too many and leave cigarettes smouldering . . .

It was madness to pursue this line of thinking. They'd never get a night away. It was decent of her to offer, and in the absence of able and willing grandparents you had to accept all such help gratefully. And it was imperative that he and Jane have some time to themselves, before they lost the knack of confiding in each other altogether. It was almost certainly his fault, whatever 'it' was – something he'd said or done or failed to say or do, that had made her withdrawn and distant. A week ago they had even argued. It wasn't a blazing row, exactly, since they wouldn't permit themselves to shout in front of the children – more of a forty-watt affair. Still, enough to light up some dark corners.

It had started with a piece of ill-judged intervention from Guy in a stand-off between Jane and Harriet over a plate of uneaten cauliflower cheese.

'I don't like it. It looks like sick,' Harriet was saying, making gagging noises. She had pulverized it with her fork, so that it did indeed resemble something freshly regurgitated. The cauliflower had given up its liquid and the cooling, curdled cheese now swam in a watery slick. Beside her, Sophie, who had finished hers and moved on to bananas and custard, was giggling encouragement. Jane stood over them in her wipe-clean apron, simmering.

Guy, who had been brought up on his mother's frugal rations, and had to clear his plate just to survive, found this brand of misbehaviour the hardest to stomach. He had only that moment come back from a day-long conference, was still wound up from a crawl around the M25, and hadn't had time to climb down to the sub-rational, knee-high values of family and home. 'How dare you waste food when there are children starving?' he said in his stern, headmaster's voice, and, before he could stop to reflect, he had swiped the mangled remains of the meal from under Harriet's nose and tipped it into the bin. 'Now you can go to bed hungry like half the world and see how it feels.'

'Thank you, Guy,' said Jane with heavy sarcasm, over the noise of pounding feet and sobbing. Sophie, who tended to fall in with the prevailing mood, had followed her sister upstairs, also in tears.

In retrospect he could see that weighing in uninvited had been a mistake. He wouldn't have dreamed of undermining any of his staff in that way but, while the realization was still dawning, he felt bound to fight his corner. 'I had to do something. You were just standing there,' he said, aggrieved.

'It was my quarrel,' replied Jane frostily. 'I was dealing with it.' She snapped on a pair of tight rubber gloves, as if about to perform surgery, and began spraying the kitchen surfaces with disinfectant, pumping the trigger vengefully.

'Well, I'm sorry. But it drives me nuts to see food wasted.' It was himself as a hungry child that he was thinking of with such indignation, rather than the starving millions.

'I said she was to sit there until she'd eaten it all. I was carrying out a threat, for once, like they say in the books.' Jane was pointing the nozzle of the spray at his chest as if holding him at gunpoint. He resisted the impulse to raise his hands.

'I didn't realize that. I was just trying to defuse the situation.' There was a pause while Jane continued scrubbing the worktops. From the commotion upstairs it sounded as though something had been detonated rather than defused. His lips twitched, but Jane gave the determined frown of someone unwilling to relinquish the momentum of a good row.

'I'm going up to bed myself anyway,' she said, peeling off her gloves and leaving them inside out on the draining board like a couple of severed hands. 'I've got a thumping headache.'

Guy glanced at the kitchen clock. It was only seven o'clock and he hadn't yet eaten. 'You should go to the doctor about your head,' he said.

'I don't need to go to the doctor,' Jane retorted, popping two paracetamol out of their plastic bubbles and swallowing them dry. 'I know it's only my period.'

'Well, you could get that checked out while you're there.' Over the past few months he had become conscious of a phenomenon whereby Jane's periods were lasting longer and the intervals between them growing shorter, with acute PMT expanding to plug the gap.

'There's nothing wrong with me,' Jane said in a shrill voice. 'I'm perfectly normal. It's everyone else who's weird.'

'I'm afraid that's a contradiction in terms,' said Guy, his sense of logic offended. 'I mean it's a perversion of the word "normal".'

'Perversion,' said Jane in a triumphant tone. 'Exactly!' And she swept out, as if she'd tied him up in knots with her rhetoric.

Guy stared after her in astonishment. He honestly hadn't a clue what she was on about. He made himself a cup of tea and a banana sandwich and ate them alone at the kitchen table. When he went upstairs, taking with him a forty-page document from the local education authority, Jane was sitting up in bed reading *Jude the Obscure*. So much for that headache, he thought, and then felt mean. She gave him a lukewarm smile, indicative of a truce rather than forgiveness, but by the time Guy returned from the bathroom, in the mood to be conciliatory, Jane had already switched off her reading light and had her back to him, feigning sleep.

'I've got this report to read. Do you mind if I keep my light on?' he asked. It wasn't even dark outside yet: Guy could still hear the distant shouts of children playing in the street.

Jane sat up. 'Of course not,' she said, and proceeded to rummage in her bedside cabinet, finally producing a black sleep-mask of the sort handed out on long-haul flights. This was doubly bizarre as they had never actually been on a long-haul flight, but Guy was too taken aback to question its provenance.

'It's all right. I'll do it in the morning.' There was no way he'd be able to concentrate with her lying there next to him like Zorro. He moved to tap her on the shoulder, and noticed as he leant towards her a single coarse grey hair sprouting from her parting. It stuck out at an angle, as if shunned by the finer, glossier red hair beneath. It was at this point that he'd decided they had to get away.

It would be fine, he thought, as he locked his office and strolled across the car park to the bike sheds, giving a last wave to Mary in the office. The weather had been perfect – another scorcher – with cloudless skies and only the faintest suggestion of a breeze. Everyone was saying it was going to be a good summer. They would be able to go for a slow walk along the river, have a drink in the garden of some country pub, and watch the sunset. It would be one of those dramatic, flamingo-pink ones; he had it all planned. He would make her laugh as he used to when they first met, when every little thing that happened was the cue for a joke, when wit was a token of love, when mishaps were simply funny, valuable as anecdote fodder for the future.

Not long after they had started going out together Guy had taken Jane to see *Tosca* at Covent Garden. He wasn't a great fan of opera, and neither, as it turned out, was Jane, but he had an idea that it would be a Grand Night Out, and just the sort of thing to impress a new girlfriend. As her contribution Jane had brought a box of rose and lemon Turkish delight in icing sugar, which they ate with a tiny plastic prong, like a date fork. She had been most particular to choose something that could be dispatched silently, without crackling or rustling or drawing attention to them in any way. They never saw the final act: when the lights went up for the interval Jane let out a strangulated yelp: her black dress and Guy's best suit were dredged with fine white powder as if they'd been flour-bombed from the upper circle. Guy even had a clean, stencilled patch on his lap where the programme had been lying. They had laughed so much they'd had to leave, stumbling between the rows of seats, sniggering and apologizing, and leaving sugary hand-prints on the red velvet. That wouldn't happen now. It would just be dismay, embarrassment, recrimination. 'Look at my dress! That'll never come out!' 'How am I going to get this suit clean by Monday?' 'I knew we shouldn't have brought that stuff.' 'I don't even like it.'

Of course he didn't expect to live every day as though falling in love: it would be too much like suffering from prolonged vertigo, but it would be nice now and then to recapture that sense of dwelling carelessly in the present. Perhaps they would manage something like it tonight, if they made the effort. There was the scenery to be enjoyed, the food and each other, without responsibilities or distractions. He had even bought her a surprise present – outside birthdays and Christmas, something he hadn't done for years. It was a little silky thing from Marks & Spencer. He wasn't sure whether it was a slip or a nightie, but it had looked pretty on the hanger. In any case he hadn't liked to thumb through the entire range in case someone took him for a pervert – an irrational fear: most of the other shoppers were sheepish men. 'Can my wife bring it back if it doesn't fit?' he had made a point of asking the sales assistant. She probably would, too, he thought. Exchange it for something shapeless in heavy-gauge khaki. Anyway, she would be pleased that he'd bothered.

A saying, long forgotten, sprang into his mind as he cycled down the tree-lined path to the gate. 'All shall be well and all shall be well and all manner of thing shall be well.' He couldn't remember now who had said it or to what it referred, but he liked its ambiguity. The reassurance was weakened, wasn't it, by the repetition?

The road into which Guy now turned, usually choked with badly parked cars and women with pushchairs at this time of day, was quiet and empty. Apart from the boy, who was sitting on the wall opposite, listening to a Walkman, legs dangling.

'Are you waiting for someone?' Guy called affably, encouraged by the fact that what he'd imagined in a moment of paranoia to be a gun, was just a mobile phone.

The boy looked up warily from under his baseball cap. 'No . . . Yes . . . Are you the headmaster here?' He slid down off the wall as Guy approached, now wheeling the bicycle. Behind Guy's head a sign like a For Sale board on a stake read *St Anthony's C of E Primary School. Headteacher: G.J. Bromelow, M.A.*

'Yes I am,' he said. 'Can I help you?' The boy looked oddly familiar, though Guy was positive they'd never met.

'You might be able to. My name's James Osland.'

To Guy's eternal shame, even the name Osland didn't ring any bells at first. He had a sudden idea that he was going to be someone from the local paper wanting a quote about the frogs. Or worse, an irate frog-lover.

'You're not one of these animal rights people, are you?' said Guy, glancing at his watch. He'd give him five minutes, maximum.

'No,' said the boy, looking bewildered by this accusation. 'I think I'm your son.'

33

Jane sat in Erica's sitting room, trying without success to muster the concentration required to play chess with Gregory, while Erica made tea.

It hadn't been that hard to leave home: her overnight bag was packed in preparation for the trip to Marlow and the girls were already installed at Erica's, building a camp in the bunk-beds. Harriet had burst into tears when she saw Jane on the doorstep, afraid that she had come to take them home. 'Go away, Mummy. We don't want you,' she had cried, but Jane was too dazed to register the slight.

Guy's voice had sounded strange and constricted on the phone: '*Jane*?' She had known it was bad news from the first syllable. She had felt disaster, like the blade of a guillotine, hanging just above her head, and then he'd said the words and it had come rushing down, severing her past from her future, so that nothing would ever be the same again.

'You missed a good move there,' Gregory said. 'You could have had my castle.'

'Oh, sorry,' said Jane, whose thoughts were elsewhere.

'Jane.'

'Mmm.'

'Does fuck actually mean what they say it means?'

'Er . . .' Jane appealed to Erica, who was just coming in with a tray of tea and cake. She was wearing a black T-shirt and a pair of wide, white linen trousers, which bore the marks of past encounters with food, drink, non-washable pens and grubby infant hands.

'Yes, more or less,' Erica said serenely.

'Oh, *gross!* I'm not saying that any more,' said Gregory, pretending to retch.

'Good. Now why don't you clear off and play with your

computer and leave Jane alone,' Erica suggested, distributing the tea.

'Check,' said Gregory, ignoring her.

'It's all right, really,' said Jane, politely. 'I need a distraction.' She had only managed to blurt out a summary of the catastrophe on the threshold while Erica was silencing the doorbell with a mallet, and then the kids had come swarming down. She had been forced to relate the details piecemeal, between interruptions. This wasn't the sort of matter that could be discussed in front of an eight-year-old. Particularly an astute and inquisitive eight-year-old. An astute and inquisitive eight-year-old who was a pupil at Guy's school. She slid her queen forward into the jaws of death.

'Checkmate,' said Gregory, pouncing.

'Oh dear,' said Jane, trying to sound disappointed.

'Don't worry,' he said, kindly, 'there are loads of easier games we can play.'

'I can hear water running,' said Erica, inclining her head to listen. 'Go and see what Will and the girls are up to,' she instructed him. 'I don't want another flood.' He slouched out, lower lip jutting.

'So Guy didn't know anything about this boy until today?' Erica said, sweeping a pile of comics and lidless felt pens off the couch so that she could sit beside Jane. Yorrick was sitting in what looked like a dog basket at their feet, banging saucepans with a wooden spoon.

'No. He said not.'

'And you believe him?'

'Well, yes. He wouldn't have been able to keep something like that secret all these years. He's just not a good liar.'

'But he's convinced the boy's genuine?'

Jane nodded. 'He didn't seem to be in any doubt. He did have a one-night stand with the mother when they were students. The timing fits. We didn't talk for long. He called me from James's mobile phone – that's his name, James.'

'Where are they now?'

'I don't know.' Jane raised her voice slightly. Yorrick was becoming more proficient with his wooden spoon. 'He wanted to bring James back to meet me, and so that they could talk some more. I said, "Fine, come home, but I won't be there."' She took a mouthful of scalding tea and gasped as it tore at the back of her throat. 'I just can't believe something like this can happen to me,' she said, her eyes streaming with the pain. 'I mean, he's had this whole other family longer than I've even known him.'

'Well, it's not quite like that,' said Erica. 'It's not as if he's a bigamist.' She stopped abruptly as Sophie and Harriet bounced in, almost tripping over each other. 'Can we have a biscuit?' they chorused, addressing Erica and ignoring their mother's presence.

'Not before dinner,' Jane said automatically.

'I'm afraid biscuits may well *be* dinner tonight,' Erica said, following them out. She took a tin of chocolate bars upstairs and tossed handfuls through the open bedroom door, as though feeding sea lions.

'What's a bigger miss?' Harriet could be heard asking.

'What am I going to tell the children?' Jane was thinking aloud as Erica came back into the room and shut the door.

'Well, I suppose that's something for you and Guy to work out between you,' said Erica. 'If you don't make a big deal of it, they won't. And as they grow up, they'll forget they ever didn't know.'

Yes, thought Jane. They'll grow up and the world will intrude more and more, with all its ugliness, and they'll forget what innocence felt like. 'My whole marriage has been based on a mistake,' she said, absent-mindedly dunking a piece of cake in her tea and watching it collapse to the bottom of the mug. From above their heads came the unmistakable sound of innocent children bashing each other. Seconds later there was the thump of feet on the stairs and Harriet appeared in the doorway with a tear-streaked face, her little shoulders heaving. 'Sophie called me a stinky cat!' she blubbered.

'Ignore her,' said Jane, offering open arms for a cuddle, but Harriet, apparently inspired by this advice, took off back upstairs at a run.

'What was I saying?' Jane asked, shaking her head. It was

impossible to marshal her thoughts into any sort of order with these continual stoppages.

'I can't remember,' Erica admitted. There were more clamorous voices and Harriet and Sophie burst in, jostling and shouting accusations.

'She hit me!' Sophie wailed, holding out a bare arm to reveal a pink slap mark.

'Why did you do that, Harriet?' Jane demanded. 'I told you to ignore her.' The two sisters had drawn apart and were glaring at each other, a pair of frowning trolls in little girls' clothes. 'Well, I don't know what ignore means,' said Harriet.

'Listen, why don't you go and play in the garden,' said Erica gently, taking both girls by the hand and leading them from the room, 'while I hide some treasure in the house for you to find.' Within seconds of Erica throwing open the back door and ushering them outside, all their sorrows were forgotten. A moment later they were joined by Will and Gregory, who set about dismantling the rusting pile of bicycles, scooters, stilts and pogo sticks which sat out on the lawn in all weathers like pieces of modern sculpture. Erica's garden was not large, but it was well stocked – indeed, crammed – with play equipment picked up from boot fairs and jumble sales, plus a few dangerous home-made items, like a tyre on a rope, which hung too close to the fence, and a slide made from a salvaged piece of motorway crash barrier. In the one flowerbed forget-me-nots and Californian poppies bloomed alongside various non-botanical specimens: punctured footballs, plastic frisbees and pieces of roller skate. The lawn itself was parched from the recent spell of hot weather.

Jane, who was watching from the dining room window as Harriet and the boys swarmed up to the top of the climbing frame, while Sophie flicked earwigs out of the sandpit with a spoon, couldn't help smiling at the scene. Like many fastidious people, she found untidiness rather bracing provided it was not on her own territory. 'I shouldn't have come here,' she said, when Erica came back indoors. 'You've got enough to do.' In fact she couldn't think of anywhere else she could have gone at such short notice. She still hadn't decided whether or not it was possible or even desirable to keep the whole thing quiet.

'It's no problem,' said Erica, twisting her hair up to expose the grey, and securing it at the back of her head without pins. She was holding a mesh bag of chocolate pennies wrapped in gold foil. 'I'll just scatter these around for the children to find later. Keep them happy. Then you'll have my full attention.'

She's got such patience with them, Jane thought enviously. Nothing rattles her. She wandered back into the sitting room to rejoin Yorrick, and idly inspected the bookshelves while she was waiting for Erica's return. The collection consisted largely of nineteenth-century English and French literature, Big American Novels, and modern crime fiction. When she had first met Erica, Jane would have taken the opportunity to have a good snoop, looking for clues to Erica's personality and habits. Her taste in books, music and soft furnishings would have been subjected to exhaustive analysis. But as she had got to know Erica, she had given this up as futile. You couldn't know a person from their things. There were no shortcuts to friendship.

'Right.' Erica appeared, eating a chocolate penny. She flipped the last one to Jane. 'Your tea's cold so shall we move on to wine? I think there's some in here.' She delved in a corner cabinet and produced a bottle of red *vin de table* which still had a raffle ticket stuck to it. 'I'm not a big wine buff,' she said.

'The thing is,' said Jane, accepting a dusty glass and wiping it on the hem of her dress, 'I'm really angry with Guy. I want to rant and scream at him. But he won't let me. He'll just parry all my abuse with common sense. I know him. In a way I think I'd prefer it if he had known about James all along. Then I'd have an excuse to hate him.'

'The way things stand you can't very well blame him for anything,' said Erica, who was having trouble with the cork. 'Except having had sex before he met you. And I don't suppose you thought he was a virgin when you met him at – what was it?'

'Thirty-two,' said Jane.

Erica put down the corkscrew and picked the foil off the bottle neck to reveal a screw-top lid with a neat hole through it. 'Do you know the woman?' she asked, filling their glasses at last. 'Have you ever met her?'

Jane shook her head. 'She's much older than me,' she said, with unnecessary spite and then remembered that Erica herself was nearly forty. 'Guy says he only slept with her once. On this field trip to the Sahara when he was a student. Her actual boyfriend was murdered. It was all pretty horrendous.' The moment she had put the phone down on him she had ransacked the boxes in the loft and fetched down his photo album. There she was: slim, blonde, tanned, pretty: some ridiculous outfits she had on, but it was 1976. Jane felt a surge of anger and hatred towards this two-dimensional woman who had lain dormant so long between the pages of an old album and had now risen up to torment her. Now she came to look at the pictures carefully, through newly suspicious eyes, it was clear that there were many more of this Nina woman than of the other members of the expedition, even the poor dead one. Of course, Guy couldn't have known at the time that he was going to be killed, that much Jane had to admit. But still.

'The question is,' said Erica, balancing her wine glass on the arm of the couch, so that it wobbled every time she moved, 'what, if anything, does she want from Guy?'

'Money probably,' said Jane. 'Apparently she's been passing this James off as the son of the murdered boyfriend all this time.'

'She sounds completely unscrupulous to me,' Erica agreed.

Jane nodded, not really listening. She was trying to calculate what a backdated claim for eighteen years of child maintenance might look like. She would have to go back to work – at a lower grade, naturally – and take in ironing at weekends. They would never be able to afford holidays; the girls would have to be clothed from charity shops. They would have to sell the car. Jane's eyes began to smart. Until now she hadn't even considered the financial implications.

The boy was probably just off to university, grantless and broke, and requiring regular handouts. 'I wonder if we could countersue her if she asked for money. For denial of access or paternal rights, if there is such a thing.'

'Do you think it's likely to come to that?' asked Erica, unaware of the way Jane's thoughts had been running.

'Who knows? Nothing would surprise me any more.'

'Put it this way: I don't think she'd have a case in law,' said Erica. She stooped down to the baby, whose drumming was getting harder to ignore. 'Too noisy, darling,' she admonished, removing his wooden spoon. He immediately let out a series of piercing shrieks, his chubby face turning scarlet with indignation. 'Oh no, that's even noisier,' said Erica, hastily handing it back. As his yells modulated to whimpers, the distant sound of a telephone became audible. Jane stood up and then sat down again.

'If it's Guy I don't want to speak to him.'

'Up to you,' said Erica, withdrawing. A moment later Jane could hear her saying, 'Hello . . . yes . . . yes, she is . . . yes, they're fine . . . Okay, I'll tell her. Bye.'

'Didn't he want to talk to me?' Jane asked, unable to keep a note of disappointment from her voice.

Erica shook her head. 'He was just checking to see where you were. He said he wouldn't bolt the front door tonight in case you decided to come back.'

'I'm not going back tonight. I can't.' Jane's heart quailed within her at the thought of confronting Guy face to face. They might have the sort of argument in which unforgivable things are said – an exchange of home-truths from which no relationship could recover. 'I'm sorry to be such a nuisance. I know there aren't enough beds. I'll sleep on the floor.'

'Absolutely not. You and the girls can have my bed. I'll sleep with Will on the bottom bunk and Greg can have the top. Yorrick will be in his cot. Plenty of room.'

Jane glanced down at Yorrick who was starting to nod over his saucepans. She picked him up and sat him on her lap where he gave a few experimental wriggles of protest and then nestled against her chest, thumb in mouth, and presently closed his eyes. A proper boy, Jane thought, cradling his solid little body and feeling its warmth. Such chunky hands and feet. And she sank back against the balding velvet upholstery of the armchair and thought of that other woman with her long blonde hair and cheesecloth smocks, who must have rocked Guy's son to sleep in just this way.

Erica insisted on putting the children to bed herself, while Jane lay pinioned beneath the baby. She called them in from the garden where they had been taking it in turns to bury each other in the sandpit, and they tore through the house like dust-devils in their quest for the hidden chocolate pennies, ignoring Jane's frantic signals to keep quiet near Yorrick.

'Oh, don't worry about him,' said Erica, herding children towards the stairs with the aid of a Kenyatta-style fly-whisk. 'He can sleep through a stampede. It's only tiptoeing that wakes him.'

A few moments later the whoops and cries were muffled by the roar of the shower, and all over the house pipes began to clank and groan. Jane shut her eyes, grateful that she'd been spared the bathtime ritual. She stroked the soft skin of Yorrick's legs and rubbed her cheek against the fluffy down on his head. He smelled gorgeous: pure and unpolluted. Jane allowed her knotted muscles to unclench and the tension fell away like chains. The baby gave a sudden shivering sigh as if he'd sensed this transference of energy, and Jane felt a surge of tenderness towards him, for being so defenceless and trusting, and moreover a part of Erica that she could legitimately hold and love. Surely, surely, she thought, if I can feel this way about a baby who isn't mine, I ought to be able to find a grain of affection for this boy who is half Guy.

When Erica returned, one leg of her white trousers transparent from a recent drenching, Jane had reached a state of deep relaxation. 'I stood them in the bath and hosed them down with the shower, but I got caught up in the backwash,'

Erica explained. 'I've left them fighting over the beds. I expect they'll all be crammed into the top bunk when we go up.'

From overhead, like a parody of frenzied lovemaking, came the sound of bedsprings creaking violently.

'No trampolining on my bed!' Erica bellowed at the ceiling. Yorrick, sleeping peacefully not five feet away, didn't even flinch. The creaking stopped momentarily while the bedroom door was closed, and then resumed at a slightly reduced pitch.

'Thanks for taking us in,' said Jane, too mindful of Yorrick to speak much above a whisper. 'You're so kind.'

'It's no big deal. You'd have done the same for someone in need.'

Would I? thought Jane, conscious that spontaneous generosity – especially to those outside the immediate family – was not one of her special virtues. She remembered with some shame her uncharitable reaction to Guy's offer to accommodate the homeless, jobless, wifeless Hugo. Here was Erica giving up her own bed, while she, Jane, begrudged the loan of a spare room – a room used merely for storing boxes. I've become a selfish, petty-minded, suburban drudge. No wonder my children hate me. No wonder Guy spends so much of his time hiding in the loft. I never used to be like this. 'No,' she said to Erica. 'There's a mean streak running right through me. I never put myself out.'

'Course you do. You came to my rescue in the park that time. And you lent me your library ticket.'

'Yes – and then regretted it a moment later.' She didn't add that these instances didn't count because they weren't indicative of her real nature. It was only Erica who could elicit this sort of behaviour. Just being in her presence made Jane a nicer person. She wanted to say something along these lines, but couldn't compose a reply that didn't sound embarrassingly needy and intense, so said nothing instead.

'And you're so good with your kids,' Erica was saying. 'Raincoats, boots and umbrellas when it's cloudy; sunblock and hats when it's not. Nothing left to chance. And you clean their teeth twice a day, and cook them real food using real ingredients. And you probably read the Classic Children's Literature at bedtime.'

Jane laughed at this portrait of herself. Only Erica could think it was flattering. 'And I name and date and file all their drawings, and rotate their best paintings on the kitchen wall, and hand-sew Sophie's ballet costumes, and polish their shoes every night. All the mechanical things that don't matter.'

Erica whistled, impressed. 'They do matter. God is in the detail. Every night, though, Jesus. I don't think I've ever polished a shoe. I was only thinking the other day that I never change the boys' sheets unless they're actually sick or wet the bed. Fortunately this happens reasonably often,' she added hastily, aware that Jane or her children might, after all, be sleeping on these sheets. 'Here, let me have that baby.' She peeled Yorrick from Jane's chest to reveal a sweat patch on the front of her dress. 'Into your cot,' she said, carrying him from the room. She came down a moment later to report that the girls were in the double bed and the boys in the bunks. Only Gregory was still awake, playing computer chess behind the curtain. 'It's a devil getting him to sleep on these light evenings,' she said. 'I think he's photosensitive. It's ever since I dropped him in a tray of developing fluid when he was a baby.'

Jane smiled. She was beginning to realize that Erica was mostly joking, although she was still not sure about those sheets. It occurred to her that she hadn't thought about her problems for at least ten minutes.

For supper Erica produced a selection of cheeses, some slightly bendy celery and a granary loaf. 'Homemade: I got it in the market,' she said, as pleased as if she'd done the kneading herself. In between mouthfuls she encouraged Jane to review her predicament from any unexplored angles, but Jane had had enough of the subject. 'I'm sick of talking about it. Sick of thinking about myself. Sick of *being* myself.'

'I know what'll take your mind off it,' said Erica, putting down her plate. 'Something physical.' For a moment Jane thought Erica was going to lunge at her, and was ashamed to find the idea wasn't wholly unappealing. But instead Erica leapt to her feet and beckoned Jane after her. 'This way. Not afraid of spiders, are you?'

Jane, who was, put down a wedge of Camembert untasted and followed Erica into the hallway, where she was rolling back the rug to expose a wooden trapdoor. This is a bit spooky, thought Jane. 'You're not going to kill me and cut me up?' she asked.

'No,' said Erica. 'Not in these white trousers.' She lifted the trapdoor and clumped down a steep flight of steps into the darkness. By the time Jane had joined her at the bottom Erica had located the light switch.

Two bright, wall-mounted spotlights illuminated a generous-sized cellar, about seven feet high, containing nothing but a table-tennis table, two bats and a ball.

'Can you play?' Erica asked, chopping the air experimentally with one of the bats.

'I used to,' said Jane, who had always preferred sports on a miniature scale. 'I haven't played since I was about fourteen, but I always preferred this to hockey.'

'Brilliant. I hardly ever get a game nowadays with Neil away. Greg's not quite old enough to take me on.'

They patted the ball back and forth across the net. The distinctive tick-tock sound, amplified by the cavernous surroundings, immediately transported Jane back in time – to the school gym, youth club, campsite games rooms: all places where she'd been young and happy. After a few minutes' warm-up Erica suggested they start scoring. She had the advantage of more recent practice, but Jane soon picked up. You never entirely forgot childhood skills – they were all there, waiting to be reclaimed. After a few games, won by Erica, Jane suddenly began to laugh.

'What's so funny?' Erica wanted to know.

'I'm just picturing Guy's expression when he asks me how I spent this evening and I tell him about this. He'll really think I've lost it this time.' She realized she had inadvertently committed herself in her mind to reconciliation and return. 'He already thinks you're a bit eccentric.'

'Me?' said Erica, astonished.

'Oy,' said a voice. 'What's going on here?' And Gregory's head appeared upside down through the trapdoor, his hair falling into a halo of spikes.

Nothing much, thought Jane. Just two middle-aged women playing ping-pong in a cellar.

'Go away, I'm winning,' said Erica.

'The baby's crying.'

'Oh b . . . blast. All right, I suppose we'll have to call it a day.'

As they emerged from the vault Yorrick's wails were clearly audible over the chiming of the hall clock. 'I had no idea it was so late,' said Jane, checking the time on her watch.

'I'll probably have to climb in with him to shut him up,' said Erica. 'If I'm not down in ten minutes, feel free to go to bed.'

Jane replaced the oval rug and washed and dried the supper things. She made an attempt to put them away, but the cupboards seemed to be booby-trapped with avalanches of crockery, so she retreated. After a quarter of an hour there was still no sound from upstairs, so Jane turned all the lights off and tiptoed up to bed with her overnight bag. She peeped round the door of the boys' room. Gregory was in the top bunk; Erica was asleep on the bottom, still fully clothed, with Yorrick beside her, and Will was wedged into the cot, his arms and legs extruding through the bars.

In the bathroom Jane opened her bag to find the wrapped present that Guy had hidden there before leaving for work. She pulled off the tissue paper and held up a tiny oyster silk nightdress with spaghetti-thin straps and a lacy, semi-transparent bodice. She put it on, smiling. It was touching, really, that he still considered something like this appropriate for her raddled 31-year-old frame. She cleaned her teeth at the sink, which was already generously daubed with toothpaste, and looked round for a towel, before resorting to wiping her face on the grey bathrobe hanging on the door.

Occupying Erica's double bed, in a depression in the slackest mattress Jane had ever seen outside of a French hotel room, Sophie and Harriet lay curled like prawns in the bottom of a wok. Jane clambered gingerly over the wok edge, afraid of rolling on top of them. The bedclothes were tangled underneath their skinny limbs. Jane managed to extricate a miserly corner of duvet, beneath which she would shiver in her skimpy nightdress until dawn. The sheet felt strangely gritty against her skin, and on further investigation she discovered she was lying on a fine layer of sand.

34

'That's him,' Nina said to herself, as Guy walked across the car park of the Windmill on Clapham Common. She watched him pause at the door to hitch his trousers up and re-tuck his shirt, and then glance round self-consciously before ducking inside. Shorter hair, but otherwise just the same, Nina thought, aware that time hadn't dealt so kindly with her. She didn't have long hair herself any more, but the blonde was now naturally highlighted with grey, and he would find her fatter too. After having James, she'd never recovered that flat-stomached, willowy look she'd had as a student. From within the driver's mirror a pleasant, lightly freckled 39-year-old face stared back at her. Tiny pin-tuck creases appeared at the corners of her eyes when she smiled experimentally, and didn't altogether disappear when she stopped. Nina snapped the mirror back into position irritably. She was sitting in the front seat of her old car, which Kerry had kindly loaned her for the night. Ever since Nina had offered to take Kerry out for driving practice at weekends in preparation for her test, relations between them had undergone something of a thaw. It was fortunate, for the continuation of this trend, that Kerry had so far been too busy to take up this offer, as Nina was an exacting passenger, unlikely to inspire confidence in a nervous learner.

On the seat beside her was a small photograph album, carefully compiled, showing James's progress from nought to eighteen. She would let Guy keep it if he expressed an interest, though it would be hard to part with some of the best pictures. James, digging on the beach at Bournemouth, in a funny pith-helmet; in his over-large school uniform, aged four; holding Moriarty, his pet guinea-pig, now deceased. The poor creature had been abducted from an insecure cage by a fox. The lies she had had to tell to cover that one up. *Moriarty has run away to the railway cutting to live with the other guinea-pigs.* James had cried so much he'd had to have the day off school. She was tempted to slip that photo out and keep it, but that would leave a gap, which would need explaining.

In the most recent shots he wasn't smiling – it wasn't the done thing apparently. You just had to face the camera down with a good, hard stare. In some ways he was a typical teenager, in others, not at all. Nina had been astounded and humbled by his reaction to her recent confession. He had been dazed and a little disbelieving at first, to think that the man whose grave he had been made to visit all these years, whose absence was such a feature of his childhood, was not in fact his father. And he had fidgeted uncomfortably in his seat when Nina had been obliged to refer to her sexual history. But he hadn't raged or stormed over the deception, or reproached Nina in any way. A daughter would never have been so forgiving, Nina was sure. Once he'd heard her out she had left him alone in the restaurant to digest all her excuses and explanations, and waited for him in some trepidation at the tube station. Ten minutes later he had caught up with her and simply said: 'So am I ever going to meet this guy, Guy, or what?'

'It's up to you,' she'd said, overcome with relief that he'd forgiven her, and not imagining that he would make such quick and efficient steps to track Guy down. For a moment she had worried that his equanimity might be a front for inner turmoil; perhaps he was saving his angst for Kerry. But she hadn't been able to sustain this anxiety for long. With James there were no hidden depths – the waters were transparent and unpolluted.

Five minutes. Guy would have had time to buy a drink and find a table by now. She checked her appearance once more, for smudged mascara and lipstick-on-teeth, before getting out of the car and following Guy into the pub.

From the vantage point of her own car, Jane watched the new arrivals, trying to guess which one was Nina. Those old photographs weren't much help – unless she turned up in batik and clogs, which was unlikely. Most people seemed to come in twos and threes, anyway, or were indisputably students or teenagers.

The plan, arranged by telephone the night before, was for Guy and Nina to meet somewhere on neutral territory to discuss James and any matters arising. Once the ice was broken and initial embarrassments smoothed over, after an hour and a half, say, Jane was to join them for a drink. 'I don't want to come,' she'd said, knowing all along that she would have stalked him and lurked in bushes just to get a look at Nina, but feeling that a show of mature incuriosity was required.

'I want you to be there,' Guy insisted. 'Just so it's clearly understood where my priorities lie.'

'Which is where?' It was only the Sunday of the aborted weekend away, the day after Jane's return from Erica's, so certain issues were still smouldering.

'With you of course. And the girls. And then with James.'

'She'll think I'm being possessive, or nosy, or both.' And she'll be right, thought Jane. She would never have believed herself capable of jealousy on this scale until now. She had thought all such stormy and irrational passions to be beneath her. It was most confusing. I must love him more than I know, a still small voice inside her kept saying, while more clamorous voices talked of rage and revenge.

'No, she won't,' said Guy. 'Anyway, who cares what she thinks? It's what we think that matters. And we're facing this together, aren't we? Isn't that what we've agreed?'

'Well, yes, all right,' Jane admitted, grudgingly. 'But you can go in first and get all the awkward stuff out of the way.'

A woman was making her way across the car park. She had blonde bobbed hair topped with a pair of sunglasses, and was dressed in a stone twill skirt with buttons down the front, and a pink polo shirt. She was carrying a purse and a small, flip photo album. That's her, was Jane's immediate thought. Size fourteen, minimum, was her next. Then, relieved to discover that Nina was nothing like the femme fatale she had been expecting, and in fact resembled an ordinary woman, a working mother, a pillar of the tennis club and PTA, Jane settled down with Erica's copy of *Jude the Obscure* until it was time to make her entrance.

At his corner table in the Windmill, Guy sat back, one arm along the top of the banquette, in a pantomime of relaxation. In fact he was sweating profusely: every so often he would take a pad of tissues from his trouser pocket and apply it to his forehead and neck to mop up some of the run-off. He was grateful for the foresight which had made him put on a white cotton shirt which wouldn't show the huge, soaking patches under each arm. He picked up a discarded *Evening Standard* from the floor and fanned himself, and then, under cover of the table top, discreetly took his pulse. 128! He'd keel over and die in a minute if he didn't calm down. His blood pressure – borderline at the best of times – would be off the scale. He'd been feeling sick all evening. He didn't know if it was anxiety or that piece of day-old salmon quiche Jane had given him for tea. 'I think I've just eaten something that's off. You try it,' she'd said.

He belched behind his hand and tried to turn it into a cough. 'Come on,' he thought, looking at his watch. 'Let's get this over.' It was the anticipation he couldn't stand. When James had accosted him outside the school without warning he had coped fine. It was much better to be mugged by bad news than tortured slowly. Not that he considered James, in himself, to be Bad News. He was, in fact, pleasant, intelligent, well-mannered: exactly the sort of son Guy would have wanted in other circumstances – that, on occasions, when he saw some young boy kicking a ball to his dad in the park, he still did want. They had talked and talked that Friday evening, once Guy had recovered his powers of speech. James had told him about his early childhood, looked after by Irene – Martin's mother – while Nina went out to work. Guy had related his version of the desert trip: how close they had all been, and then how suddenly Martin's murder had caused their dispersal and estrangement. Nina had been rescued and brought home by her father; Hugo had stayed on in In Salah, refusing to abandon his unfinished project, and he, Guy, had driven the Land Rover himself the hellish journey to Oran, picking up hitch-hikers wherever possible, en route, for company.

They discovered some features in common. James was planning to study Economics at university – though not so far with a view to primary teaching. Both were keen armchair sports enthusiasts, with a particular interest in cricket. While Jane and Erica had been playing ping-pong in a cellar, they had traded occult cricketing lore and statistics. *Q. Who is the only Nobel Laureate to be mentioned in Wisden's? A. Samuel Beckett.* Guy had promised to take James to Lords.

It seemed possible that from this shattering experience something intrinsically good and worthwhile might be salvaged: a father-son relationship that was free from the constraints of discipline on the one hand, and rebellion on the other.

A sudden gust of fresh air made Guy look up: there was Nina, framed in the open doorway, just as she had been that time at the flat when he'd brought Hugo home, stoned. Her features were instantly recognizable, though they seemed smaller – or was it just the rest of her that was bigger. This was the woman he had followed across two continents, and who had seemed an ideal of beauty when he was twenty-one, but her entrance today caused no heads to turn. It gave him a pang to see how ordinary she had become. He half rose to his feet and then sank back again, pinned between table and seat, and she gave a quick nod of acknowledgement, and made her way towards him, a smile frozen to her face.

'Hello.' She extended her right hand across the table as though they were business associates, or strangers, and then gave a yelp as Guy reciprocated with one of his firm, headmasterly handshakes, of the sort usually reserved for visiting dignitaries and overbearing parents.

'Sorry,' he said, aghast at his own strength, as Nina flexed her crushed fingers. There: exactly what he'd promised Jane he wouldn't do – start on an apologetic note, as if Nina, not he, were the wronged party.

'Bitter?' asked Nina.

He was about to deny this vigorously, when he realized she was pointing to his empty glass.

'Oh. Yes, thanks. Just a half.' He hadn't intended to down the first pint so quickly. He wasn't here to get boozed after all. While Nina was buying the drinks he moved around the table so that they would end up sitting adjacent to one another, rather than directly opposite, which all those management courses had taught him was off-putting and confrontational. He had rearranged his office at school on just the same principles, and could no longer open the window without clambering on to his desk.

'You haven't changed,' she said on her return.

'Neither have you,' he replied, adopting the convention.

'Hah!' She laughed derisively. 'Well, cheers. Here's to tact and diplomacy.' They raised their glasses, slopping beer – a result of full measures and slightly shaky hands. 'I know I owe you an apology,' Nina went on. 'Several apologies. I've probably wrecked your life. James tells me you've got two little girls.'

'Yes. Sophie and Harriet.'

'That's nice.' She took a sip of her Guinness, leaving a pair of tiny foam tusks at the corners of her mouth. 'I'm sorry if I've caused any upheaval.'

'Yes, well, we're still getting used to the idea,' said Guy.

'You know, I felt guilty all those years for not telling you, and I feel even worse now I've told you.'

She was urging him to say, oh it's okay, don't worry, what's another kid between friends? but he wasn't going to let her off that easily. 'It would have been better if you'd said something earlier. I mean right at the beginning, before he was born,' said Guy, as if thinking it out, rather than issuing a direct rebuke. But would it really? he thought. He probably would have stuck with Nina and never met Jane, something it pained him even to consider. And he couldn't wish his own daughters unborn. His sense of regret remained annoyingly unfocused.

'I wanted to tell you. I would have done, but I was staying with Martin's mother, Irene, at the time, and she guessed I was pregnant, and I couldn't deny it. But of course she assumed it was Martin's, and she was *so* happy. I couldn't tell her the truth – the thought of the baby was the only thing keeping her going.'

'But how could you sustain a lie like that for so long? It would have been on my mind the whole time.'

'It seemed the lesser of two evils. I searched my conscience, I honestly did. I prayed and prayed for a miscarriage – I even decided to have an abortion and tell Irene I'd miscarried. I got as far as my appointment at the clinic, but when I went up to the desk to check in, or whatever you call it, I could see my file on the top of the heap. It had the word STOP written across it in big black letters. I thought it must be some sort of sign. I was already in a state anyway, but when I saw that I just burst into tears and ran out of there as fast as I could and never went back.'

'How awful,' said Guy, ambiguously. He was thinking what a narrow escape James had had.

As if Nina had read his mind, she said, 'I've never told anyone that before. Please don't tell James, or anyone.'

'Of course not,' said Guy, though he was making no promises not to tell Jane. In his view their marriage vows invalidated all subsequent oaths of secrecy.

'It was only much later that a friend who works in a hospital told me that STOP just stands for Surgical Termination Of Pregnancy. So it wasn't a sign after all.'

'Oh, I think it was,' said Guy. 'They're everywhere.' Hadn't James himself come to him in answer to a prayer? Though not, of course, the answer Guy had been expecting, but wasn't that always the way?

'It certainly seemed like it at the time,' Nina admitted. 'You do understand why I couldn't be honest. It wasn't for my benefit. It was for Irene. She was looking forward to the birth so much. She was the one who looked after James while I did my finals, and then went out to work. My own parents weren't all that supportive. Well, they weren't even in the country. They thought I was being irresponsible and throwing away my future. They wanted me to have the baby adopted. But Irene really loved James. And once I'd decided that Martin was going to have to be the father, it wasn't that hard to believe it. I mean there was no scientific evidence that he wasn't. I suppose there's an *outside* chance he might have been.'

'What do you mean?' asked Guy. 'What makes you so sure James *is* mine?'

Nina was swilling the last inch of Guinness around the glass, leaving a tidemark of froth. 'Well.' She leaned forward a little, so that the uncomfortable subject of sex wouldn't have so far to travel, and addressed her remarks to the buttons of Guy's shirt. 'I wasn't actually sleeping with Martin on that trip. Because we were never alone, and I didn't want to anyway. And before that we'd always used precautions.'

Guy nodded sagely, trying not to look as though he was remembering their own recklessness. He tried to imagine what it would have been like to be Nina, bereaved and pregnant, and locked into a deception which could only have been remedied by causing pain. He found himself inclined to believe and pity her.

'You know,' she said, examining her bitten nails. 'I think if you'd got in contact or come to see me when you got back from Algeria I probably would have cracked and told you then.'

Guy's sympathy evaporated. He wasn't about to have the responsibility for eighteen years' duplicity thrust back at him. 'Well, if I'd known you were pregnant I certainly would have done,' he said with some asperity. The truth was, Martin's death had made it impossible for Guy to make any further approaches. It would have been like dancing on his grave. A similar feeling of guilt and self-disgust had gripped Nina, too: he'd seen it in her eyes when she'd said goodbye before leaving In Salah with her father. He knew then that they would meet at Martin's funeral as fellow mourners and nothing more. And he was almost ashamed of how quickly he had got over her once he was home, even though he had dreamed of her every night of the long journey back overland. It wasn't shallowness on his part but a form of self-preservation. Martin, Hugo and Nina had dropped into his life and out again, like characters in a dream. They had had no mutual friends; in Guy's circle their names never even came up. England was just as he'd left it – unchanged, indifferent. People had been interested in hearing about the tragedy, of course, but Guy had no wish to satisfy morbid curiosity. He'd been torn between telling everything – the whole story of the trip, detail by detail – and saying nothing at all, and it was generally easier to do the latter. After a time even his memories of Algeria seemed to take on a dreamlike quality. Only his diary and photos, shut up in a box and never re-examined, were proof that it had all happened.

'I'm sorry,' Nina said again. Then, 'You know, it wasn't Irene's death that set this off. It was Hugo. You've heard he's coming back, I suppose?'

Guy nodded. 'We're meant to be putting him up. I've phoned and faxed him from school, but there's no reply. I don't know exactly when he's coming.'

'I haven't even returned his calls,' said Nina. 'I'm not desperate to see him, to be honest, but I know he'll track me down in the end. My first thought when I heard his message was, Shit. He'll meet James and work out the dates and put two and two together. That was when I decided to tell James myself. I didn't want either of you to hear about it from Hugo of all people.'

Guy acknowledged that this wouldn't have been a pleasant scenario. 'It must have been hard for you, bringing up a baby on your own,' he said. He wanted to tell her she'd done a good job, that James was a credit to her, but he'd never been good at delivering straightforward compliments. They always sounded phoney to his ears.

'I wasn't on my own. I had Irene. But, no, it wasn't easy.'

A silence settled over the table as Guy realized he had

inadvertently lapsed into his apologetic manner. 'Anyway,' he said, hauling himself back on to the level, 'the important thing is James. What can I, we – Jane and myself – do for him?'

'I don't want money, if that's what you mean,' said Nina quickly.

'But he'll be off to university soon – he'll need funds for that. They don't get grants any more do they?'

'No,' said Nina. 'But he'll be okay. Irene left him a couple of thousand.'

'That's hardly the point. I'd like to contribute, however belatedly, to his education.'

'I don't know.' Nina shook her head. Her bobbed hair, neatly blow-dried and lacquered, moved as one piece. 'It's something I'll have to think about. I'm not sure a handout would be at all appropriate.'

'Perhaps one of those deeds of covenant?' Guy suggested. He'd been through the figures in bed this morning while the household was still asleep. It would be a pinch. They could wave goodbye to the idea of getting decorators in, and the car would have to limp on through another few MOTs, but they wouldn't starve. And Jane always rose brilliantly to the challenge of thrift. 'I'm not the sort of person to dodge my financial obligations,' he finished, a trifle stiffly.

'I'm glad to hear it,' said Nina, sliding her glass across to him. 'It's your round.'

There was quite a crowd at the bar by this stage of the evening and it took Guy a while to be served. They were both on soft drinks now. Nina had explained her predicament with regard to transport, in which she was obliged to borrow back her own car for the evening, from which Guy deduced, incorrectly, that she could no longer afford to run it. While he was waiting for the woman beside him to finish reeling off her order he caught sight of his appearance in the mirror behind the bar. His hair and the front of his shirt were limp with sweat and his face was pink and greasy like a ham left out in the sun. He looked as if he'd just staggered off a squash court. He glanced at his watch. Jane would walk in any moment now. At the thought of brokering this particular introduction Guy's guts began to churn ominously. He abandoned his place at the bar and made it into the Gents with seconds to spare.

Outside in the car park, Jane put down *Jude the Obscure*, marking her place with a pay-and-display ticket from the dashboard. The book was obviously an old school edition, misappropriated by Erica years earlier, as it had St Philomena's stamped on the endpapers and its margins were richly defaced with doodles, exclamation marks and cryptic annotations in different hands. *Irony, Symbolism, cf. J.S. Mill, good quote*, someone had signposted at intervals throughout the text, while the less scholarly offerings included *A.T. is a Big Lezzie*, and a pencil drawing of a penis.

Jane locked the car and made her way towards the pub, smoothing the creases out of her T-shirt. She had dressed down for the occasion – some might say belligerently so – in faded jeans and trainers, in order to signal that she considered the event of no great moment. When she saw Nina, alone at the table, apparently reading a book, she hesitated. But before she could retreat Nina looked over, straight into her eyes, so she was forced to keep walking. 'Hello, I'm Jane,' she said, sliding into the seat recently vacated by her husband. 'Where's Guy?'

'At the bar, I thought,' said Nina, closing her photo album. 'But he's been gone rather a long time. I'm Nina. It's nice to meet you.' They began, tentatively, to extend right hands, and then stopped half way, laughing at the oddness of the gesture. The ice broken, Jane allowed her smile to unclench.

'How did you know I was me?' Nina was asking.

'I watched you come in,' Jane confessed, no alternative explanation leaping to her mind. 'You were the only person who fitted the bill.'

'Resembling one's reputation,' Nina said, shaking her head in despair. 'What a thought!'

'I didn't mean . . .' said Jane, who wasn't quite sure how to take Nina. She had expected coldness, resentment, not repartee.

'It's all right,' said Nina. 'At least you didn't mistake me for her.' She indicated a ravaged-looking woman by the door with a brittle perm and a plunging top which exposed a tanned and leathery cleavage.

'Imagine,' said Jane, faintly.

'Where are your children tonight?' Nina went on.

'Staying over with a friend,' Jane replied, always glad of an excuse to invoke Erica, even tangentially and in front of a total stranger. It was only the second time they had stayed away from home but they had romped down Erica's path in their pyjamas and slippers, toothbrushes in hand, without a backward glance.

'It goes so quickly,' Nina said, her hand straying to the photos again. It was a moment before Jane realized she meant childhood.

'When observed from above, it does. My own seemed to last for ever. What have you got there?' she added. 'Pictures?'

'Just shots of James growing up.' She started to turn the pages.

'He's like you,' said Jane, leaning towards her and scrutinizing the images for traces of Bromelow genes. A pleasant face – not Hollywood material, but intelligent and interesting. He had brown hair, like Guy, but the features were pure Nina. Jane felt a sense of relief at this, but wasn't sure why. It didn't change anything.

'I must say, you're taking all this . . . very well,' said Nina.

All this shit, Erica would have said.

'Well,' said Jane non-committally. At last, she thought, something I'm good at.

When Guy emerged from the Gents not long afterwards, having flicked cold water in his face and dried his hair under the hand-dryer, he looked marginally cooler and less overwrought. He went to wave at Nina to reassure her that drinks were on their way, when he saw with a jolt that Jane had joined her at the table unannounced. There they sat, in one place, the mothers of his children, their heads bent together, like old friends, over the pages of a photograph album.

35

A week or so after this encounter in the Windmill, Jane was in the kitchen with Harriet, making pastry for a chicken and ham pie. Cooking with actual ingredients, Erica would call it. Harriet had her own piece of dough to maul and was rolling out a long, greasy snake while Jane lined the pie-dish. From the dining room came the jangle of a commercial radio station: a continuous spool of adverts, pop music and chat. James and Kerry were in there wallpapering – an arrangement devised by Guy and Nina to dignify an awkward transfer of funds. 'I'd rather he worked for the money,' Nina had said. 'And if there are jobs around your house that he could do it would be a good way of keeping him busy this summer.' His attempts to find orthodox employment had been unsuccessful. He had chucked in a Saturday job at Sainsbury's before his A levels to give himself more time to study, and the temp agencies had nothing for a school-leaver without experience or special skills.

'This is the ideal solution,' Guy had said, when Jane expressed doubts. She didn't relish the prospect of having someone, especially this someone, in the house all day wanting cups of tea and snacks and supervision, and generally filling up her space. 'James gets work and we get the dining room decorated. You know you've wanted something done about that damp patch since we moved here.'

'I'll feel uncomfortable with him under my feet all day,' she protested, but not too forcefully, because she did, after all, want the job done, and they wouldn't now be able to afford a proper decorator. But she wanted it duly noted that she was the chief victim of the scheme's shortcomings.

'What if he turns out to be hopeless? DIY isn't everybody's thing,' she said, pointedly. Guy had a modest selection of power tools, still in sealed boxes in the garage, and a slightly larger collection of blunt, rusty, lethal hand-tools such as might be found in a provincial museum of Victorian life. His home improvement projects tended to be characterized by vaunting ambition and minimal competence, and inevitably foundered before a finger was lifted. If the aptitude was inherited, went Jane's reasoning, all was lost.

Her fears on this score proved to be unfounded. James was in fact reasonably diligent and painstaking. As he was being paid by the job, instead of by the hour, Jane had rather assumed he would dash the work off and be gone as quickly as possible, and was nonplussed to find him, a week on, still on the doorstep at eight every morning. He had begun by sanding down the floorboards – a noisy filthy job from which the dust was still settling. Each new day there would be a fresh fall on the window sills and picture rails. He had applied several layers of varnish to the floor which was now finished, dried and buried under layers of polythene sheeting. The rambling rose wallpaper and contrasting borders had been steamed and scraped off the walls and the room was starting to look clean and bare. All this was in sharp contrast to the rest of the property, which was having to accommodate the dining room furniture and now looked full and cluttered. The Welsh dresser was in the hallway, occluding the porthole window, along with two carvers and a granddaughter clock. The living room was playing host to an extra table, four chairs and a piano, while the contents of two shelf units were stacked at the end of the marital bed. The spare room was not available. It was no longer spare: Jane was sleeping there. Ever since she had come back from her night at Erica's she had insisted on separate rooms. It was only a case of enacting physically the sort of mental disengagement she had been feeling for months, but this new revelation of Guy's had provided her with the perfect pretext.

'Please don't do this,' Guy had begged. 'We need each other more now, not less.'

'Don't think I'm trying to punish you,' Jane said. 'It's only temporary. I'm still having difficulty with this whole business.

I need a bit of thinking space where we're not . . . on top of each other.'

'You don't love me any more is what you mean,' said Guy.

'This isn't about you; it's about me,' Jane replied, ashamed to find herself repeating an expression she'd heard recently on an American mini-series. She prayed Guy wouldn't recognize it.

'What will Sophie and Harriet think? They'll think we're about to divorce. Perhaps we are,' Guy added, tragically.

In typically half-baked fashion, Jane had agreed a compromise whereby she would set her alarm for 5 a.m. – assuming she was not already awake and brooding – and creep back into bed with Guy in case Sophie or Harriet should come romping in at daybreak, as frequently happened. It was understood, without being discussed or negotiated, that this concession did not signal a weakening of Jane's resolve, or an imminent resumption of intimacies. It was simply a matter of protecting the children. As Jane's mini-series heroine might have said: 'This isn't about us; it's about them.'

'I've made a willy,' said Harriet, pointing to the pastry snake and then suddenly and violently flattening it with her clenched fist. Jane jumped at the noise and then blushed when she saw James standing in the doorway. What must he think I've been teaching her? she wondered. But he just laughed and ruffled Harriet's hair – a liberty which even Jane was not permitted.

'Can I get some more water?' he asked. 'This is a bit gluey.'

Jane took his bucket and refilled it at the sink. 'Can I help?' Harriet asked James, abandoning the pastry and sliding off her seat. In only a few days she had developed a fixation for James and would happily shadow him all day unless Jane intervened. She was often like this with older children, boys especially. At Erica's it was Greg she followed and pestered, even though it was Will who was her own age. James, to his credit, did not discourage her attentions, put up with her insatiable questioning, laughed at her unintelligible jokes, and forbore from snapping at her when she climbed up the stepladder behind him, or wandered off with the scissors, or whatever else he had momentarily laid aside. Both he and Kerry seemed to find her cute and hilarious – adjectives which Jane only applied to Harriet in exceptional circumstances. More commonly she was apt to describe her – to her face – as difficult, stroppy, disobedient, etc.

'No, darling. Don't bother James. Stay and help Mummy.' Jane laid a coronet of pastry leaves around the crimped edge of the pie and let Harriet paint the surface with beaten egg. 'Don't gouge,' she instructed, her hands itching to snatch the brush away and finish the job herself. Then, leaving Harriet happily absorbed in a messy task, Jane put her head around the dining room door to check on progress and offer the workers a sandwich. The pie would not now be ready in time for lunch.

'Would you like . . . oh!' Jane stopped. They were standing in the uncurtained bay window, in a deep embrace. James was holding the back of Kerry's head and kissing her as though eating a large, overripe peach. They broke apart with an audible pop. 'Sorry,' croaked Jane, paralysed with embarrassment at this display of adolescent passion under her own roof. She flapped her hand feebly. 'Carry on.'

'We were . . . er . . . just having a break,' said James, wiping his mouth on his sleeve. 'Papering's nearly done.'

Jane glanced at the fireplace wall, stripped and sanded and mapped with a tracery of dried polyfilla. The rest of the walls were covered with lining paper, still wet in patches, with the odd blister showing beneath the surface. James, following the direction of her gaze, said, 'Don't worry about those air bubbles. They'll pull out.'

'Oh, yes,' Jane agreed. She'd be back later with a brush to make sure.

They accepted her offer of a sandwich, but when she checked the bread bin it was empty. Guy must have had the crust for breakfast. 'I'm afraid we're out of bread,' she called. 'I'll have to go round the corner.' She rescued the pie from further damage by Harriet's aggressively *pointilliste* brush-strokes, and slammed it into the oven. 'Come on, Harry, you'll have to come too.'

'I want to stay here,' said Harriet, who was now slapping beaten egg over her mangled pastry penis.

'Well, you can't,' said Jane, thinking how much quicker and easier it would be if she could.

'I'll look after her,' said Kerry, appearing in the doorway. She was wearing a black sports bra under white, knee-length dungarees, and clicking her tongue stud against her top teeth. A nervous habit, Jane decided, though no less revolting for that. Harriet was at Kerry's side in one bound, taking her by the hand and dragging her towards the stairs.

'Well . . .' It was too good an offer to refuse. Jane had frequently felt the temptation to sneak out on some brief but pressing errand while Harriet was engrossed in a game, rather than drag her along, scuffing and whining. She'd never dared, of course. More often than not the errand would be left undone in the interests of harmony. It wasn't as if James and Kerry were strangers, she told herself. They had been in and out of the house every day for a week now without showing any sociopathic tendencies. And he was, after all, Harriet's brother.

'If you're sure. I won't be too long.'

'Don't hurry. We'll be fine,' said Kerry, languidly, allowing herself to be led up to Harriet's room to see the doll's hospital.

'They've all got chicken pops,' Harriet was explaining, as Jane slipped out, childless and unencumbered into the sunshine.

It was only a further five-minute jog from the baker's to Erica's house. Kerry had told her not to rush. Jane bought an extra doughnut and trotted on up the hill. She often dropped in unannounced, usually with some sort of edible gift, which she would then leave on the doorstep if Erica was out, like an offering at the shrine of an idol.

Just a quick glass of water and a How are you? and I'll go, she promised herself, her pace slowing to a limping walk as she turned into the cul-de-sac. Five years of plodding along at infant pace seemed to have wasted her leg muscles. It was only when she had occasion to break into a sprint that she realized she no longer could.

Erica's house looked different, even from a distance. As Jane approached she saw what it was: the straggling privet hedge behind the front wall, which formerly reached the top of the ground-floor windows, blocking out most of the natural light from the sitting room, had been savagely pruned, so that it was perhaps a metre high and now displayed more twig than leaf. In the front garden, in place of the usual loose clutter, were five full black refuse bags, and as Jane opened the gate, now back on both hinges, the front door flew open and another black sack was ejected and rolled down the steps on to the path. Erica followed, staggering under the weight of a cardboard box, loaded with empties.

'Hullo,' Jane called, to ward off further missiles.

'Oh, Jane, give us a hand with this,' said Erica gratefully, allowing the box to slip forward into Jane's chest.

'What have you got here?' Jane asked, conscious that the bread bag was now squashed against her ribcage.

'Just some junk for the tip. If you can walk backwards we might get it in the car. *Mind that!*' she added, as Jane side-stepped the lethally placed garbage bag and nearly landed in the hedge.

'What's going on?' Jane asked, once the box was safely stowed in the boot alongside piles of broken garden furniture, and she had brushed herself down and peeled the fused doughnuts from the side of the loaf.

'I've been having a bit of a clear-out,' said Erica. 'You wouldn't believe some of the crap in that place.'

Oh yes I would, thought Jane, but instead she handed over one of the crushed doughnuts, and said, 'What's brought this on all of a sudden? It's a bit late for spring cleaning.' Before the words had even left her lips she knew the answer. It hit her like a bucket of icy water. She stood there, drenched and gasping, while Erica, noticing nothing amiss, took a bite of doughnut and between munches, said, 'I've got some people coming to look at the house tonight.'

'You're moving.' It was a statement rather than a question.

'Not selling, just letting. It's all such a botched, spur-of-the-moment thing. Neil's contract has been extended for two more years, so we're going over to Kuwait.'

'Kuwait?' Jane repeated, as though trying to familiarize herself with the name of a newly discovered planet.

'Yes.' For a moment Erica appeared ill at ease, as if she had an inkling of Jane's dependence on her. 'Look, why don't you come in? We don't have to stand here in the garden,' she said, still chewing. 'I've got some iced tea in the fridge.' She led the way into the front room which, clear of junk and bathed in sunlight, was unrecognizable as the crepuscular hovel of previous visits. Jane sat down heavily in one of the armchairs, while Erica clattered around in the kitchen. She reappeared moments later with two cans proclaiming themselves to be *Traditional Long Island Diet Iced Tea.* And for a second Jane had almost imagined Erica making the stuff herself. 'Kuwait,' she said again, her forehead crumpling into a frown.

'I know.' Erica grimaced, popping open her can and catching the erupting foam on her tongue. 'It's been such an agonizing decision – taken in the course of a ten-minute phone call, naturally. We never expected the job to run on, and we certainly hadn't envisaged being apart for longer than eighteen months. I don't think it's good for the boys being away from their dad all that time. So it was either a case of turning it down, or us moving out there *en masse.* He did think of refusing, but it's so ludicrously well paid. Two more years and we'd be able to buy a decent-sized place when we come back. Neil could start up his own business . . .'

Erica rattled on about the short-term domestic upheavals and the long-term economic advantages while Jane listened dumbly. She felt breathless, winded, as though all six of those fat black refuse sacks – full of things, like Jane herself, for which Erica no longer had any use – had come bowling down the steps and squashed her flat. 'When will you be leaving?' she managed to ask in a conversational tone.

'As soon as we can manage it. During the summer holidays, ideally, so Greg can start at one of the international schools in September. Which is why I'm trying to make this dump habitable for tenants. The letting agent was unbelievably scathing.'

'Well . . .' said Jane, whose sympathies lay with the prospective tenants. 'If you need a hand. Cleaning and so on . . .'

'Oh really? That'd be great. I've kind of let things build up,' said Erica, crushing her empty can between the palms of her hands, tossing it at the waste-paper basket, and making no move to retrieve it when it missed.

'You're taking it all very calmly,' said Jane, who didn't feel the least bit calm. 'Considering you could be gone within a month.' She'd noticed before that Erica wasn't a worrier or a moaner, and was suddenly conscious and ashamed of the huge fuss she'd made over their own relatively slight relocation, from one part of South-East England to another.

'I can't get myself worked up about little things,' Erica said. 'I reckon I could live anywhere. Two years is no time at all, is it? When I come back nothing will have changed. Most people won't even notice I've been away, I bet. And even people who do will get along just fine without me . . .' She didn't meet Jane's eye as she said this.

Will I? thought Jane. Regular phonecalls to Kuwait were out of the question, and something told her that Erica wouldn't be a fanatical correspondent. It would be unreasonable to expect someone who mislaid phone numbers and library books and occasionally her own children to answer letters promptly. 'You'll be busy from now on,' she said, thinking aloud.

'Oh, not really,' said Erica, with her usual refusal to be fettered by responsibilities. 'There's one thing we must definitely do before I go, and that's go out for the day. To the seaside, or somewhere quintessentially English. Preferably without the kids.'

Kids. Jesus. Jane shot out of her chair, still clutching her unopened can of *Traditional Long Island Diet Iced Tea.* Ohmygod. I've got to go. I left Harriet with James and Kerry. I was only supposed to be nipping out for two minutes. I've been ages.'

'I'd offer you a lift, but Yorrick's asleep upstairs and the car's full of junk.'

'Don't worry, I'll walk. Run,' Jane corrected herself. 'I'll call you,' she added, from half way down the path. Then she took off, without waiting for a reply and without the bread, down the road, past the shops and the church, along the lane, the thin straps of her sandals biting like cheese-wire, and arrived home to find the kitchen full of smoke and James, Kerry and Harriet alive and well and inspecting the charred crust of her home-baked pie.

36

This was always going to be the worst part, thought Guy, waiting in the lobby of his mother's club behind Marble Arch, like a naughty boy outside the headmaster's office. Even worse than telling Jane, and that had been bad enough. In fact this was going to form the basis of his defence: *if my wife can accept it, surely you can*, though he wasn't going to elaborate on the qualified nature of Jane's 'acceptance'.

His mother had been surprised and suspicious when he had rung to propose an unseasonal solo visit. 'Is everything all right? You haven't lost your job?' She sounded almost disappointed at his denials. She had never thought it much of a job anyway.

'I was just thinking it would be nice to see you,' he lied. He wasn't going to be drawn into discussing the matter by phone. (Why not? Jane wanted to know. A phonecall had been good enough for her.) 'Jane and the girls are busy this weekend – I'm going to be in their way.'

'Well, I'm coming up to town for the sales. I could meet you for lunch.'

'Oh.' Guy had not so far considered the possibility of tackling his parents singly, but this had obvious strategic advantages: they would be on neutral territory; he would not be outnumbered. His mother would be forced to rely on her own opinions, rather than simply reinforcing her husband's. This last might not work in his favour, of course: it was hard to predict which way her prejudice would fall. Would genetic snobbery triumph over outraged moral sensibility, or not?

'Okay then. Lunch.'

'We'll go to my club.'

Guy's heart sank. An oversized rest-room full of malicious

eavesdroppers: a less congenial venue for a disclosure of any sensitivity could scarcely be imagined.

'All right.'

'I know what she'll say,' said Jane, as she watched his preparations to leave. '*Are you sure? Have you had tests?*' she brayed, in a passable imitation of Mrs Bromelow's thoroughbred vowels. She was not so inclined to be deferential these days, and Guy made no attempt to rise to his mother's defence; he merely grimaced as he straightened his tie.

'I'll probably be disinherited,' he said, combing his hair neatly and then raking his fingers through it to untidy it again.

'Don't build my hopes up,' was Jane's send-off.

The lobby door opened and his mother stood there, her handbag slung diagonally across her large chest to foil muggers, and various expensive, rope-handled shopping bags over one arm. Her free hand was bandaged to the wrist and held up in a sling made from a Liberty's silk scarf.

Guy sprang to his feet to divest her of her luggage but was beaten to it by the liveried attendant.

'I'm in a state of collapse,' she said, offering Guy her floury cheek, and then disappearing into the Ladies.

'What have you done to your arm?' he asked, five minutes later, when she emerged, repowdered and lipsticked and smelling more strongly of lily of the valley.

'I fell out of the golf cart,' she explained, as they followed a waiter to a table in the plush, silent dining room. 'There's quite a slope at the tenth and it started to run away with me, so I stepped on the brake rather hard and the whole thing tipped over. It's just a sprain.' She waved the injured limb at him. 'I've got some lovely bruises, too.'

'Poor you,' said Guy, trying to banish the image of his

mother tumbling down the fairway before it set him off. 'But if you will play these dangerous sports . . .'

'That's more or less what your father said. The Club Secretary drove me to the hospital and they X-rayed it. There's nothing broken. It's an awful nuisance, though, trying to do the sales with one arm.'

'It must be,' said Guy sympathetically. 'All that pushing and shoving to reach the bargains.'

Mrs Bromelow ignored this remark – her usual policy with humour or sarcasm, which she regarded as impediments to sensible conversation, and vastly overrated. 'It's the carrying, and writing cheques,' she went on. 'And of course public transport is out of the question, so I'm having to take taxis everywhere.' She managed to imply that this was a matter of gross inconvenience. With her good arm she signalled to the hovering waiter. 'Have we decided? I have,' she said to Guy, who had barely glanced at the menu.

'Oh?' He skimmed the contents in search of something hearty: a fat steak or some venison perhaps, but the fare seemed to be predominantly fish – aimed, no doubt, at a clientele with modest appetites and impaired digestion.

'I'll have the sole, no potatoes,' said Mrs Bromelow. 'Could you manage some wine? I couldn't.'

'No thanks,' Guy obliged. He ordered lamb with creamed potatoes, which appeared the most promising in terms of bulk. He'd decided earlier that he would get the meal and an exchange of news out of the way before mentioning James. 'How's Dad?' Guy shook out his large, starched napkin and spread it across his knees. It sat there, awkwardly concertina'd, like an unfolded road map. Beside him the waiter poured out their two glasses of tap water with a flourish.

'Oh, fine. We're tackling the hall at the moment. He's got a boy in.'

So have we, thought Guy.

'No, actually, he's started attending these political lectures in London: Whither the Right? – that sort of thing. It's given him a new lease of life. The only trouble is he comes back and wants to discuss it all with me. And I'm simply not interested.'

'Ah.' Guy tried to remember what it was that did interest his mother. The house and its contents. The dog. The garden, in summer at least: the rest of the year it was left to the devices of another 'boy'. His younger brother, William, the New York banker. She sat on committees, he recalled; occasionally turned them upside down like the golf cart.

'Anyway, how are Jane and the girls? Harriet still giving you trouble?'

'Fine. Harriet's okay. She's just bright beyond her years and gets frustrated easily.' He was shocked to find himself sounding like a parody of deluded parenthood. He had heard this spiel so often at parents' evenings. In any case he wasn't aware of having confided that they were having problems with Harriet. It wasn't the sort of admission Jane would make to her mother-in-law. It must be something she's observed, he thought. 'Sophie's doing well at school,' he went on. 'And she was in a little show with her ballet group. Did you ever get the photos?'

His mother looked blank. 'Er, I believe I did,' she said, evasively. 'Very nice.'

They were interrupted by the arrival of their main course. Mrs Bromelow had declined an hors d'oeuvre and Guy had politely followed suit. Now he looked down in dismay at his meal: one thin lamb cutlet sat on top of a dollop of glossy mash. Two mouthfuls at best. Around the edge of the mash, but not touching it, ran a dribble of apparently unrelated gravy. One small stuffed tomato and a lattice of carrot matchsticks comprised the vegetable accompaniment.

'How delicious,' said Mrs Bromelow, eyeing her sole, which at least covered a fair proportion of her plate. 'They certainly know how to cook here.' She slipped her bandaged hand from its sling and set to work, her filleting skills to all appearances unaffected by the recent injury. 'He's started writing his memoirs,' she said at last, having parted flesh from bone and then laid down her fork as though exhausted or full.

'Who?' asked Guy. He'd been thinking of James, for

whose existence he would soon have to be apologizing.

'Your father. He's written about fifty pages and he's not even got himself born yet. I've told him it'll have to run into twelve volumes like that biography of Churchill.' Her face looked suddenly wary and Guy realized she was staring over his shoulder at a new arrival – a short, plump woman with jet-black bouffant hair. 'Oh *God*. Mavis Dudley. What does she look like? She's on her own. We don't want her with us, do we?' she hissed.

'No, no,' said Guy, horrified. An uninvited guest was the last thing he needed.

'Hello-o, Mavis. Nice to see you,' Mrs Bromelow cooed, as the unloved acquaintance was installed at a nearby table. The two women waggled their fingertips at each other and then dropped eye-contact sharply.

'Is this autobiography business with a view to publication?' Guy asked, in a slightly lower voice, now that there was someone within earshot. He had disposed of the tomato and half the mash in one mouthful and was toying with his bread roll to spin things out.

'Oh, I very much doubt it. I expect the market for that sort of thing is very limited nowadays. But it will be interesting for you boys to know a bit about your background.'

'Wasn't he doing the family tree when we last spoke?' Guy asked. Strange how everything kept coming back to genealogy today – not the best springboard for his confession. 'Whatever happened to that project?'

'It foundered somewhere in the eighteenth century with nothing terribly significant having come to light,' his mother said, picking at her Dover sole.

By 'significant' you mean *titled*, Guy thought.

'Still, it was rather fun, nosing around old churchyards, looking at the headstones. We came across some lovely little villages. Whereas this writing business just keeps expanding to fill up all our free time. I was hoping to go to Lugano this summer . . .'

'We might be going away at the end of August for a week,' said Guy. Apart from the stripped lamb bone his plate was empty, polished to a high shine by his last piece of bread.

'Oh? Anywhere nice?'

'Pembrokeshire.' They wouldn't now be able to afford anything more exotic. 'In a tent.'

'Oh.' This, he knew, would be his mother's idea of hell. She was not especially interested in dramatic scenery, unless it was visible from the terrace of a good hotel. Even when she was younger and fitter nothing would have induced her to put on a pair of walking shoes and go out and meet it half way. 'Well, as I say, I don't know if we'll get away at all.'

The waiter, who had been hovering discreetly for some time, removed Guy's clean plate and his mother's virtually untasted sole.

'That was delicious,' she said, pre-empting any inquiries. 'No dessert for me. Just a black coffee, very weak, with a dash of cold water.'

Guy refused to capitulate this time, scanning the menu ravenously for a stodgy pudding, but again finding his appetite confounded. It was all syllabubs and sorbets and – ugh – champagne jelly: nothing that would make any impact on his hunger. 'I'll have the ice-cream,' he said, a touch self-consciously, like a small boy, out for a treat with Mummy. His hands, unoccupied with the business of eating, fluttered and fidgeted at the edge of the table. Any minute now he would run out of conversation and be forced to ask after his brother, William. He would have to listen to news of his latest triumphs on Wall Street, the size of his annual bonus, the cost of interior design work on their Manhattan apartment, the acreage of their country retreat. Guy didn't dislike or resent his brother, and he had no time for envy. It wasn't as if William had ever made an effort to curry parental favour. It had simply rested upon him, unasked for and unearned, like God's grace. But still, one could only take so much.

Across the table his mother had brought out her shopping list and was making deletions with a thin gold pencil. It wasn't a list of items needed, but of shops to be visited, with Harrods and Harvey Nichols at the top.

'So did you find any bargains this morning?' Guy asked.

'Oh, the reduced stuff is all absolute rubbish. I've picked up some lovely things that weren't in the sale though.'

This twice-yearly ritual visit to the sales in order to spurn the half-price goods had always mystified Guy. He congratulated himself on having married someone without these absurd and costly pretensions.

The waiter reappeared, bringing the coffee and a golfball-sized scoop of ice-cream decorated with a coronet of spun sugar and a single pistachio nut. Guy allowed a little hiss of disbelief to escape him. Even the infants' school dinners came in more generous measures than these.

'So not much happening your end?' said Mrs Bromelow, beginning to stow her pencil and paper back in her handbag.

It was now or never. Guy took a deep breath as though preparing himself for a high dive. 'Well, in fact . . .'

'Oh!' His mother gave a sudden loud whoop as her rummagings turned up a blue airmail envelope with a US stamp. 'How *could* I forget? I've thought of nothing else for days. We've just had the most marvellous news from William.' She wafted the letter at Guy as if he might be able to divine its contents. 'Caroline's pregnant at last!' she declared in a voice that carried to all four corners of the room. 'Isn't that wonderful?'

'Yes,' said Guy, deflating slowly. 'Great news.' His carefully rehearsed speech of annunciation died on his lips. How could he possibly follow that. Instead, he said, 'Have they known long?'

'Seventeen weeks. They didn't dare tell a soul until they got past the tricky stage. Anyway. She's had her second scan now, and guess what? It's a boy. I'm going to have a grandson.' She raised and lowered her shoulders in a gesture of girlish excitement.

You already have a grandson, Guy thought. Though not the kind you'd want to put on the family tree. It had been unintentional, no doubt, but the tone of her last remark felt like a slight to all of them – himself, Jane, Sophie, Harriet and James. 'Excellent,' he said calmly. 'Give them my congratulations if you speak to them before I do.'

'I will. I'll be ringing them tomorrow evening.' Mrs Bromelow finished her coffee. 'Anyway. What was it you were going to say?'

'Nothing,' said Guy, pushing his pudding away untasted. 'Shall we get the bill?' He would never tell her now. It had been an insane idea to think that anyone could possibly benefit from such a revelation. There would be nothing but mortification all round. She had her grandson-in-waiting; the Bromelow name was secure; she would have no interest whatever in James. He bitterly regretted the whole enterprise, not to mention the squandering of a precious Saturday.

Mrs Bromelow hailed the waiter with an imperious wave of her bandage and then looked at Guy's untouched orb of ice-cream, now collapsing in the afternoon sunshine like a cartoon snowman. She closed her eyes with the expression of one gathering reserves of patience.

'What a waste,' she sighed.

37

Nina sat in a folding deck-chair on the patio of Kerry's father's house in Crystal Palace, drinking Bucks Fizz and watching feeble tendrils of smoke from the barbecue. It looked ominously dormant to Nina. The coals were still black, and when she put her hand above them she could only feel the faintest trace of warmth. Not enough to melt a knob of butter, never mind cook a kebab. From the kitchen came the crashing and clanging and ostentatious whistling of Kerry's father, Bob, preparing food in a mild state of panic.

Nina glanced at her watch with growing annoyance. 'Be early,' she had told James. 'I don't want to arrive before you.' She had been looking forward to and dreading this event in equal measure, ever since the invitations had been issued.

'Dad said do you want to come over for a meal next Friday?' Kerry had said on her way out one evening. 'It'll just be the four of us.'

'Oh, well, thank you. Tell him I'd be glad to. Would he like me to bring something? A pudding, perhaps?' She was already working out how feasible it would be to take a dish of poached pears in Marsala on the bus.

'Na-a-o,' said Kerry in her usual drawl. 'He'll do the food. It won't be anything flash.'

At first Nina had welcomed this opportunity to observe Kerry *en famille*, and to gain admittance to this magic circle which had enclosed her son. He had often remarked that Nina would get on well with Bob; that they had plenty in common.

'Such as?' Nina wanted to know.

'Your jobs for one thing.'

'I don't follow.' She had a feeling that a policeman and a social worker would not be natural allies.

'Well. Quite large sections of the public really hate you.'

'Oh, I see.'

'Plus, you're both the same . . . generation. And you're both alone.'

'I didn't think I was alone,' said Nina, bridling at this notion of herself as middle-aged and, moreover, unloved – as both an individual and a type. 'I thought I had you.'

'Yeah, well, you know what I mean.'

Later, recalling this exchange, she had started to feel anxious. Will I be able to make conversation? Will I be an embarrassment to James? What should I wear? It was hopeless to look to the young for guidance in the matter of dress. Weddings, funerals, job interviews, parties: one uniform did for all. When she was a girl her mother had always taught her it would be social death to show a bra strap or an inch of petticoat. Nowadays Kerry seemed quite comfortable going out in nothing *but* a petticoat.

In the end she settled on a red linen pinafore, which looked smart on the hanger, but would be crumpled and casual by the time she had fought her way from Tooting to Crystal Palace on public transport. She took the precaution of arriving twenty minutes late – much against her instincts – to find the barbecue still unlit, no sign of James, and Kerry's father threading chunks of partly frozen chicken on to wooden skewers.

He had refused all offers of assistance and installed her in the garden with a drink and a bowl of olives, where she now sat alone, overlooking neighbouring gardens to either side and a former psychiatric hospital – now luxury apartments – to the rear.

From inside came the sound of voices. Nina strained to listen. 'Why don't you go outside and say hello to James's mum? She's all on her own out there.' This was Bob. 'Nah.' A male voice, early teenage, was followed by pounding footsteps and the slamming of a door. Presently pop music erupted from an upstairs window.

Bob came to the back door holding an empty bottle of sauce and looking harassed. He was slightly overweight, Nina noticed, but balding gracefully, and not entirely unattractive – apart from a green polka dot apron, which reached a couple of inches below the hem of his shorts and gave him from the front the appearance of a pantomime dame.

'This stuff says marinade for 24 hours. I thought it said 2–4 hours. Do you think it'll matter?'

'I doubt it,' said Nina. In her experience the subtleties of herb and spice were lost on food incinerated over coals. Generally one was lucky to be able to identify the meat.

'Good.' He pointed upwards to the source of the music. 'My son,' he said, apologetically. 'He's going out in a minute. Do you want another one of those?' he asked, picking up her empty glass from beside a small cairn of olive stones.

'Yes, please. Perhaps without the orange juice this time.'

'I'm nearly done in there,' he promised. Then, betraying precisely her own anxiety, added, 'I wonder where the kids are. They're not normally late.'

I wouldn't know, thought Nina. They never eat with me. Deep inside she felt jealousy beginning to stir. She pictured it as a sinuous, fast-growing plant – bindweed, perhaps – which always left a tiny piece of root behind, however hard you tried to eliminate it, and if left unchecked would flourish and spread and choke the life out of everything beautiful and cultivated. She had felt it in relation to Jane and Guy, too: the cosiness of their set-up. And now thanks to her belated attempt to do the right thing by everyone she was lonelier than ever. All the time he wasn't at Bob's, James was over in Twickenham with Guy and Jane prettifying their house, while if she, Nina, wanted anything done around the place she had to do it herself . . .

She beat back an advancing thicket of bindweed and stood up. Any second now Bob would emerge from the kitchen with a rack of raw – possibly not even defrosted – chicken, to find the barbecue had gone out and she had made no attempt to save it. A couple of the coals closest to the firelighters had begun to glow orange at one corner. Nina bent down and blew on them, recoiling as a flurry of ash and grit flew up into her face.

'Everything all right?' asked Bob, reappearing with her glass of sparkling wine.

'Oh!' said Nina, conscious that her face must be streaked with soot. 'I was just trying to ginger it up, but I think I've put it out altogether.'

Bob picked up a pair of tongs and gave the charcoal a vigorous stir. 'No, you're right,' he conceded. 'That's dead, that is. This is going to set us back a bit. Are you starving?'

'No,' Nina lied, fractionally too late.

'I wonder if I could use my blowtorch.'

'To cook the chicken?' asked Nina, experiencing a sudden loss of appetite.

'To relight the barbie. I've got one tucked away somewhere.'

'I don't know. I've never done it. I thought men were supposed to be experts at this. I thought it was inborn.'

'Yeah. Like map-reading,' said Bob. 'I'm no good at that, either.'

Nearby a telephone rang. Bob put his arm through the kitchen window and brought out a cordless phone into which he spoke, all the while maintaining eye-contact with Nina. She found this disconcerting, if not ill-mannered. It reminded her of a former colleague from her days at Camden Council who used to do something similar. If Nina ever knocked on his door while he was on the telephone he would beckon her in and gesture for her to wait while he talked on and on, occasionally throwing her a grimace, as if to pretend she was part of the conversation.

'Yes, she is,' Bob was saying. 'What do you mean "going to be"? You're already late.' He started to tap his foot in mock impatience. 'Good. Well, as long as it looks nice . . . Maybe some charred bits and pieces. Love you too.' He snapped the aerial into place and posted the phone back through the kitchen window.

'That was Kerry. They're going to be late. They only had a little bit left to do on the wallpapering and they wanted to get it finished. In case the paste went thick overnight or something. So they're just setting off now.'

'From Twickenham?' said Nina in dismay, bindweed swarming around her ankles. 'They'll be ages.'

'Hours.'

'Well, I suppose it will give us a chance to get this charcoal alight.'

Bob gave a derisive laugh and vanished indoors again, in search of the hidden blowtorch, Nina presumed. She was therefore somewhat disconcerted when he returned a few minutes later having discarded the apron and changed into a pair of smartish trousers.

'Do you eat Greek?' he said.

For a moment Nina thought he had said, 'Do you *read* Greek?' and was about to reply that she'd studied the subject briefly at school, but didn't consider herself proficient, when the penny dropped and she was able to say, 'Yes. Why?'

'There's an okay Greek restaurant five minutes from here. Come on.'

'What about James and Kerry?'

'When any of my children are late for a meal I don't sit around waiting for them. Do you?'

'Yes,' Nina admitted. In fact, now she came to think of it, she spent an awful lot of her time waiting, attending other people's pleasure: solicitors, judges, clients in particular, who would think nothing of keeping her stranded for an hour on their doorstep in some crumbling tenement, even though her good opinion might be crucial in deciding their fate.

'It's a bad habit,' Bob advised, pocketing wallet and keys. 'People take advantage.'

'James never used to,' said Nina. Until he met your daughter, she refrained from adding as she followed him indoors. What a waste of an evening, she was thinking. If she had known there was a chance that James wouldn't be there she would never have come. She had a sudden, ghastly suspicion that he and Kerry had planned the whole thing – as a piece of prurient teenage matchmaking. Nina felt her cheeks flame at the thought that she'd been set up in this absurdly ill-judged manner. It struck her that if James himself was casting around for someone, anyone, to take her on in his absence, then she must have been displaying a pathetically needy and dependent streak which she would do well to curb. I'm not that person, she thought. I'm a confident, successful woman with inner resources. I don't need a man – or a boy – to complete me.

'I'll leave them a note. They can join us if they want,' Bob was saying. He picked through a jam jar of pens on top of the fridge, discarding one after another until he found one that worked, and scribbled a message directly on to the fridge door, which was already defaced by lists, instructions and reminders in different hands. 'You won't know what to do with yourself in September when he's off to university, will you?'

'He'll be back in the holidays, I expect,' said Nina, remembering too late that this wasn't the reply of a confident, resourceful woman with wide-ranging interests. 'I'll adjust. It won't be so different. He's never in now as it is. Anyway,' she went on, 'I might take in foreign students. Or a lodger.' She said this casually, though the idea had only that moment occurred to her. Already she could see herself cooking Full English Breakfasts for svelte French girls and tall, homesick Germans. 'I'll be all right. I like my own company. Don't worry about me.'

38

Jane parked outside Erica's house and sat listening to Vaughan Williams's *Lark Ascending* while she waited for her friend to appear. It was 9 a.m. and she was already tired and irritable from the protracted negotiations and preparations which had brought her to this state of readiness for one day out without children.

It had been arranged that Guy would take Sophie to school with him early, and be responsible for her once lessons were over at 3.15. 'Well, all right,' he'd conceded, when Jane had proposed the idea. 'But I'll be in a meeting until five. I can't entertain her.'

'So she can sit in your office and do some colouring, or a jigsaw or something,' said Jane. 'Or she could come to the meeting and hand round the biscuits.' Guy rolled his eyes at that. 'Why the hell not? You're the head – you can do what you like.'

'I don't see why you can't go at a weekend when I'm here to look after the children properly.'

'Because it's easier for Erica with Greg at school and Will at nursery. She doesn't have to impose on quite so many people.'

'What's so special about this trip anyway?' Guy wanted to know. He was beginning to feel a sense of kinship with the Imposed Upon.

'Erica's going abroad in a few weeks' time. For two years. We thought it would be nice to have a day out at the sea before she goes. Somewhere typically English, to remind her of home. Pub lunch, stroll along the beach, look round the shops, that sort of thing. You know how difficult it would be with children tearing around.'

'I have two hundred children tearing around me all day,' Guy said, loftily. This was dangerous.

'Are you saying I shouldn't go?' Jane demanded.

'No, of course not. You go. You obviously need a break,' he added. 'What are you going to do about Harriet? You're not suggesting I take her to school too?'

'Well, she's the problem.' As usual, Jane thought. 'I wonder if your mother would have her for the day. I could drop her off on the way down to Worthing and pick her up on the way back.'

Guy raised his eyebrows. Since their dismal meeting in London he no longer felt inclined to ask his mother for any favours. She had never exactly been an enthusiastic grand-parent. She observed birthdays and Christmas, but tended to find pressing reasons not to babysit.

'You'd think she'd be glad to have her once in a while,' Jane remarked.

'Try her and see,' was Guy's advice. 'You might catch her off-guard and startle her into being generous.'

This was precisely what had happened. Jane had telephoned early one morning and put the question without any preamble, wondering what Mrs Bromelow would produce from her arsenal of excuses, and was surprised when, after some huffing and tongue-clicking, her mother-in-law had agreed. The only proviso was that Harriet was to arrive germ-free. 'We don't want any sniffles brought in, thank you. I've only just thrown off the most shocking cold. Everything goes straight to my chest nowadays.' Jane had accepted this condition and everything seemed settled. Harriet was elated. Sophie was sulky at first at the thought of what she might be missing, but was soon bought off with the promise of biscuits and grown-up talk at Daddy's meeting.

Then, last night at bathtime, just as all the details had fallen into place and the weather forecast promised that the hot dry spell showed no sign of abating, Harriet had complained of a sore throat. Jane had sent her to bed with a pre-emptive dose of that cure-all syrup from the medicine cupboard and prayed that the soreness was merely the result of too much shrieking, and not the early stage of a virus.

The following morning Jane's hopes were dashed: Harriet

came tottering into her parents' bedroom just minutes after Jane had made her regular 5 a.m. transfer from the spare bed.

'I've got a snotty nose,' the child wailed, her face awash with mucus and tears. Jane cleaned her up with a wad of tissues and let her climb in between herself and Guy. Harriet snuggled up to her mother gratefully and was asleep in seconds, while Jane lay there, trapped uncomfortably between Harriet's jutting elbows and knees and the precipitous edge of the bed, and wondering why it was that her youngest daughter only craved physical affection when she was carrying something contagious. A few hot, stinging tears of frustration gathered in her eyes and slid down into her hair. All her carefully laid plans were ruined now. Leaving Harriet with Guy's parents was out of the question. Jane would have to bring her along or cancel the trip. She had looked forward to it so much; even the idea of a postponement was more than she could bear. She cursed Harriet for her lousy timing, and Guy, who was never inconvenienced by childhood illnesses, and was moreover enjoying an untroubled sleep in well over fifty per cent of the bed, and her own unlucky stars, and was still awake and fretting at seven when the alarm went off.

'What are you going to do with her?' Guy asked on his return from the shower, as they stood over Harriet's limp form, looking in dismay at her watering eyes and runny nose.

'Take her with me, I suppose,' said Jane, at which point Harriet showed signs of rallying and began to bounce up and down on the bed with excitement.

'I don't know,' said Guy, laying his hand on Harriet's forehead with all the tender solicitude of one about to escape the sickroom by departing for work. 'I'm not sure she should go out in the cold. We don't want her to catch a chill.' Jane glanced out of the window at a cloudless blue sky. The temperature was already in the twenties and climbing.

'I'll do my best to make a sensible judgement,' she said, drily, as Sophie appeared in the doorway, already washed, dressed, and trying to tie her own plaits.

'What a good girl you are,' Jane said, coming to her aid.

For being quiet and sensible, and for not succumbing to inconvenient colds, she thought.

'Am I good?' asked Harriet, who had slumped back on to the bed surrounded by a nest of used tissues. As she spoke she pulled another tissue from the box, screwed it into a tight ball with both hands, dabbed it ineffectually in the delta of snot on her top lip and then dropped it on to the heap.

'Occasionally,' said Jane, still harbouring the irrational suspicion that Harriet had made herself ill on purpose. In a moment she would have to ring Guy's mother to break the good news, very probably waking her up in the process. The Bromelows were not early risers.

'Have fun!' was Guy's parting shot as he left for school on foot with Sophie. Jane was having the car: a fortnight after the grand clear-out, Erica's car was still packed with trash and effectively out of commission.

Jane dressed herself and Harriet, phoned her mother-in-law, and was dithering over whether to call Erica and cancel the outing when she saw James loping down the path to the front door. He had his Walkman on as usual, head lolling in time with the music. She had forgotten he was coming. He caught her gawping through the front-room window and waved.

'Hello. You look smart. Are you going somewhere?' he said, as Jane let him in. His mother had brought him up to be chivalrous, but Jane had in fact chosen her clothes – grey silk trousers and a black sleeveless shirt – with especial care. She always did when she was seeing Erica. This was illogical in the extreme, since, although Jane had a pretty good idea how to dress to please a man, she hadn't a clue what was likely to impress a woman – particularly a woman like Erica, who showed no interest in clothes and often looked as though she'd slept in hers.

'Thank you,' said Jane, thinking, not for the first time, what a nice boy James was, and how much she would have been able to like him if only she'd known him under different circumstances – as just the son of a friend, for example. 'I was going out, but now I'm not.' She put the kettle on and related the story of her sabotaged plans. 'I wish I was eighteen again,' she finished. 'Make the most of your freedom.'

'What freedom?' James protested. 'I'm not free. I'm either studying for exams, or working in some crappy job.' There was an uncomfortable silence while Jane poured the coffee and wondered whether repainting their spare room in preparation for the (still unconfirmed) arrival of Hugo was one of the crappy jobs to which he was referring. She hadn't before considered their relationship in terms of tyrannical employer and mutinous employee.

'I wasn't talking about you by the way,' he said, reading her thoughts. 'This job's okay.'

'No, you're right,' she replied, smiling. 'We're none of us free.'

'I am. I'm free-and-a-half,' said Harriet, walking in, nibbling an apple.

'Where did you get that from?' Jane asked. 'I hope you're not going to waste it.'

'They don't grow on trees, you know,' James admonished, in a fair imitation of Jane's voice at its most hectoring.

She had the good grace to laugh at herself. 'I'm not always such a nagging old witch,' she said. 'You've caught me at a bad time.'

'Look. Why don't you leave Harriet here with me for the day?' James suggested. 'I'll look after her.'

'Oh, no, I couldn't,' Jane said automatically. Already, though, she could see the advantages of the scheme, and could picture herself setting off, alone, with the sun roof open and the wind in her hair.

'Yes. I want to stay with James,' Harriet begged, hopping up and down, delightedly.

'I thought you wanted to come to the seaside.'

'No, I don't. I want to stay here. I'll be good.'

'Oh, I don't know.' Jane was experiencing twinges of maternal solicitude. What did an eighteen-year-old boy know about the care of small children? 'It's not fair on you. It's harder work than you think.'

'We'll be fine. She can help me paint the walls. We can always resort to the TV.'

'Is Kerry not coming today?' Jane asked. She would feel happier if there was a female in attendance, even one as inert as Kerry.

'No, she's got her driving test.'

'Ah.'

'Look, you can take my mobile phone if you like,' James offered. 'If there's any problem I'll call you.'

'Do you promise to be good and do whatever James tells you,' said Jane, fixing Harriet with a stern look.

'Yes, yes.'

'And not to sniff,' she added, wiping Harriet's nose with a vigorous twisting motion which made the child squirm.

'Yes,' she said.

'All right then,' said Jane, coming round to the position which she had known all along she would take. 'I owe you, James. And I'll bring you back a present if you're good, Harriet,' she said, bending down to kiss her daughter, who, recognizing these as exceptional circumstances, suffered the embrace without complaint.

Vaughan Williams had given way to Thea Musgrave, who didn't have nearly the same calming effect on Jane and was therefore switched off. Erica was still indoors getting ready, and when she finally emerged, Jane saw to her surprise that she was carrying, in addition to a large canvas bag, Yorrick, a car seat and pushchair.

'Sorry about the extra passenger,' Erica explained, lashing Yorrick into the back of Jane's car. 'The friend who was supposed to be having him has got chicken pox in the house.'

'It's okay,' said Jane, thinking that at least Yorrick wouldn't answer back or throw tantrums or plague them with endless questions. All the same, she thought, we're not free. 'We very nearly had Harriet with us.' And she explained her predicament, and James's providential arrival.

'Your in-laws aren't particularly doting, then?' said Erica.

'Far from it. Though they're quite excited about Guy's brother's foetus.'

'Oh, I see. Like that, is it? Do they know about James?'

'No. Guy was supposed to tell his mother last week, but he decided against it.' Jane started to turn the car around. Before they had even left Erica's road the phone rang. 'Oh God, what's happened?' Jane said, picking it up and letting Erica take the wheel and steer them into the kerb. 'Hello?' she said anxiously.

'Who's that?' said a woman's voice in surprise.

'Jane Bromelow. Who are you?'

'This is Nina. I'm looking for James,' said the voice.

'He's at home. My home, I mean. I've just borrowed his phone for the day.' It hadn't occurred to her until now that this would involve taking all his calls, too.

'Oh really?' said Nina, sounding a trifle put out at the familiarity implied by this arrangement. 'Well, I'll try him there, then. Goodbye.' And she had hung up.

'False alarm,' said Jane, with relief, slamming the phone in the glove compartment. 'We're off. What's that you've brought?' she added, jabbing her thumb in the direction of Erica's hand-luggage, which sat on the back seat beside the baby.

'My camera. In case I see something. Oh, look out.' On the windscreen, perched or trapped on one of the wipers sat an exquisite butterfly, its orange and blue tissue wings mapped with the finest of black lines. Intending to free it, Jane instinctively hit the wiper button and watched in horror as the rubber blades swept up, mashing the creature against the glass.

'Oh my God!' said Jane, hysterically.

'Shit,' said Erica. 'What did you do that for?'

'I wasn't thinking! Poor little thing.' Jane leapt out of the car and removed the mangled corpse with belated gentleness, and then pumped the windscreen washer repeatedly to clean off the smears. It was only when she had set off again that she noticed a tiny scrap of orange wing still fluttering on one of the wipers like confetti. In spite of herself, her eye kept returning to it.

Beside her in the front seat Erica was polishing her sunglasses on the cuff of her T-shirt, which she was wearing with cut-off jeans. Cut off by Erica herself, evidently, as one leg was slightly shorter than the other, and no attempt had been made to turn up a hem. There was a bag of chocolate limes on her lap. Every so often, without being asked, she would unwrap one and pass it across. Her skin was tanned and freckled from the recent sunshine. Jane suspected she must spend hours out in the garden, though there was never any evidence of gardening having taken place. Probably she just sits, doing the crossword or reading, thought Jane, who tended to view her own garden in terms of a list of pending chores rather than as an oasis of relaxation.

'Will you have a garden in Kuwait?' she asked, prompted by this train of thought.

'No. We're in a flat. I suppose there must be parks. I haven't investigated. If you've got the space for any of our outdoor equipment, you're welcome to it.'

'Well,' said Jane, not committing herself to harbouring any of Erica's lethal home-made slides and swings, with their protruding nails and fraying ropes. With children you had to put safety first. 'Sophie might like the pogo stick.'

'Done. And I'll throw in a barbecue and a sand-pit if you've got room in the shed.'

Jane nodded. 'I'd offer to keep some of your stuff in our loft, but we haven't got a loft. It's Guy's observatory.'

'Don't worry,' said Erica, crunching on a chocolate lime. 'We're shipping most of our belongings out to Kuwait and the leftovers can go in a boot sale. I'd be happy just to take a suitcase, myself, but Neil says the flat is a bit under-furnished for a family.'

'It's funny,' said Jane. 'Just as you move back in with your husband, I'm moving away from mine.'

'You're not leaving him, are you?' said Erica, nearly choking on a shard of sweet.

'No, no. Nothing like that.' Jane explained about the new sleeping arrangements. She half expected Erica, who wasn't normally given to seek or offer confidences of a deeply personal nature, to change the subject, but instead she said, 'That's nothing. I didn't sleep with Neil for at least a year after Greg was born. He couldn't get near me. I always had a baby attached to my tit.'

'Really?' said Jane, suddenly feeling more cheerful than she had in weeks. 'So you don't think it's terminal then?'

'No, not necessarily. I think all relationships have these . . . patches. I bet it's more common than you think.'

'But what can I do about it?'

'I don't know. Wait for it to pass, I suppose, like this drought.' Erica looked out of the window at a backdrop of baked flowerbeds and grass verges in different shades of brown. Even the petunias in the municipal hanging baskets had wilted and died. 'It can't last for ever,' she murmured.

'According to the experts – you know, doctors, magazines, books – I'm a freak,' said Jane. 'In dire need of a cure.'

'Well, I think in personal matters you don't want to listen to what other people advise.'

'That's your advice, is it?' said Jane, smiling.

'Absolutely. Ignore all recommendations. Especially mine.'

'I can see the point of reproduction,' Jane conceded, pondering aloud, 'but I can't see much point in purely recreational sex. Or, at least, I can't see why it should be given precedence over other hobbies.'

'You'd rank it alongside stamp-collecting and ping-pong?' Erica inquired.

'Well, why not? I mean, supposing I wrote to an agony aunt and said, "Dear Flora, I used to enjoy playing ping-pong, but now I've gone right off it, in fact I don't mind if I never pick up another bat in my life." She'd say: "Give it up then and do jigsaws instead." She wouldn't tell me to try playing it by candlelight, or in high-heeled shoes, or up against a wall instead of on a table.' Jane was getting quite carried away, unaware that Erica was shaking with laughter.

'But what about your unfortunate ping-pong partner, who

still enjoys the game?' Erica said at last. 'Wouldn't he be entitled to find someone else to have a knockabout with?'

'I suppose so.'

'The real question is: do you want Guy to play ping-pong with anybody else?'

Jane admitted that she didn't.

'Well, there you are.'

'You're as bad as all the other "experts",' Jane grumbled. 'Advising me to try harder.'

Erica held her hands palms up in a gesture of surrender. 'I've advised nothing, except waiting,' she said. '*Patient endurance attaineth to all things*, as the nuns at school used to say.'

'Now I'm having to take sex tips from nuns,' Jane sighed.

'Do you want to play Barbies?' Harriet asked James. They had done all the puzzles in the toy cupboard, eaten all the biscuits in the barrel and played five games of picture dominoes, of which Harriet had won the last four. When James had seen what a bad loser she was he had taken care to rig all subsequent games in her favour.

'Not really, no,' he replied. He couldn't quite believe how slowly time was passing. He kept shaking his watch in case it had jammed. 'Why don't you watch a video while I make us some lunch' – it was only half-past ten – 'What about *Dumbo*?'

'Too sad.'

'*Snow White*?'

'Too scary.'

'Well, what about . . .' he squinted to read Jane's tiny handwriting on the label, '. . . *Miscellaneous Educational 1* or *Miscellaneous Educational 2*?'

Harriet pulled a face. 'Can I do homemade playdough?'

'What's that?'

'You use flour and water and pink,' Harriet explained.

'No, I don't think so,' said James, imagining what a combination of flour and water and 'pink' would do to Jane's clean, white kitchen. Come on, Kerry, he thought. She had promised to come over straight after her driving test: to celebrate if she'd passed; to be comforted if she'd failed. He did like Harriet, but she was a little overwhelming. He could see why Jane was always so tense and cross; she was never off your case for a minute. Even when James was in the loo Harriet stood outside, with her toes right up against the door, and continued to interrogate him, or regale him with surreal made-up jokes. *What do you call a deer with no eyes? A badger.*

'I know. Let's go out in the garden,' James suggested. 'The sun's shining, the birds are tweeting, and you can show me how you ride your tricycle.'

'I want the paddling pool out.'

'I can't fill it up. There's a hose ban.'

'Mummy uses buckets.'

'Anyway, you shouldn't get wet. You've got a cold.'

'I could have hot water. Mummy lets me.'

'On second thoughts, go and get those Barbies. And blow your nose while you're up there.' He didn't really want to be outside in case the phone rang. Jane might be checking up on him, and if she got no reply would probably panic and come straight home. He was beginning to regret his attack of generosity, but Jane had looked so pale and miserable this morning. Now he could see why. It hadn't even occurred to him to think of Jane as a person before today. As a species, over-thirty-year-old mothers of small children were generally invisible to boys of James's age. She was just Guy's wife, someone to whom he wasn't related, and who could make no demands on him. It was only something Kerry had said that had put him on this track and prompted him to look at her properly.

'She must hate having you around the place, but she hides it well,' she'd said, one evening as they were walking away from the Bromelows' house, watched by Harriet and Sophie.

'Why should she hate me?' James wanted to know. 'I've never done anything to her.'

'Yes you have: a) got born, and b) turned up. That's enough. I feel sorry for her. She's sleeping in the spare room.'

'How did you know that?' asked James. 'Is this the fabled feminine intuition, or did she tell you?'

'Of course she wouldn't *tell* me something like that. I've hardly spoken to her. But when she showed me which bits of the spare room needed doing, I noticed the bed had been slept in.'

'It might have been one of the kids.'

'And there was a book on the bedside table. And a pair of earrings.'

'Are you saying you think they're going to split up. Because of me?'

'I don't know. I was just saying.'

'It never even occurred to me,' said James, bewildered by these intimations of female complexity. 'She's always so friendly, I just assumed she liked me.'

'I love you, James. You're so uncomplicated.'

James, waiting in the front room for Harriet to bring down her dolls, and looking at the photographs on the mantelpiece of a younger, happier Jane and Guy, was thinking of this conversation again. He'd assumed Jane liked him: from her behaviour it wasn't an illogical assumption, but now here was Kerry, who probably had a better eye for these things, saying she hated him. From overhead he could hear the bump-bump of a toybox being dragged down the stairs, and then from outside came the insistent hooting of a car horn. It was Kerry. In the driver's seat. Alone. He punched the air. Yes! It was going to be a good day after all.

Erica had retuned Jane's ancient and temperamental car radio and was now singing along to a pop station. She seemed to know the words to all the songs. Jane would never be able to get Radio Three again. From now on it would always default to this channel, and every time she got in the car she would be reminded of this day.

They had crossed the South Downs and Jane was on home territory now and completely at ease. She loved the Sussex landscape: the gentle hills, with their chequerboard pattern of green and gold; the grey turrets of Lancing College; hay bales like cotton reels in the fields, and every so often, in the blue distance, a flattened triangle of sea. There was nothing dramatic or extreme about the scenery: it was this modesty that appealed to Jane. Only those with a truly discerning eye were admitted to its subtle beauty.

They had lunch early at the Royal Oak in Worthing; it had been Jane's local when she was a teenager. They sat outside at the last free table and Erica fed Yorrick some grey mush from a jar, while they waited for their meals. He had slept for most of the journey, and was now sitting up in his pushchair, alert and interested. His chubby hands kept lunging for anything within reach – handbag straps, wine glasses, wasps. It was hard for Erica to bring the spoon anywhere near his mouth without his flailing arms batting it into orbit. Jane began to fear for her silk trousers.

'Will you be sad to leave?' she asked, shifting out of the line of fire and spreading a paper serviette over her knees. What she meant was 'Will you be sad to leave *me*?' but hoped that Erica might answer the unasked question at the same time.

'Not sad,' said Erica, pausing with an outstretched spoonful of sieved vegetables. 'Everything will still be here, just the same, when I get back. Anyway, I don't get attached to places. We moved house a lot when I was a kid.'

'Well . . .' It had been Jane's intention all along to speak frankly today. She was determined that Erica should not escape to Kuwait without hearing what a difference her friendship had made, and how dull life would be without her. This wouldn't be easy. Erica tended to head off anything that looked like turning into a compliment. Nevertheless Jane was resolved. She was hesitating between 'I'll miss you', and the less personal 'We'll miss you all', as a way in, when Yorrick knocked the whole jar of mush into Erica's lap, and in the confusion and swearing that followed, the moment for openness was lost. Later, Jane promised herself. Somehow I'll work round to it.

After lunch they strolled down to the seafront, past the

cream Victorian villas alongside the green. On the promenade a man was selling fresh fish at a stall. Beside him a fox terrier was lying fast asleep on a table in the sun. Erica's hand strayed to her camera bag, but then she thought better of it, distracted by the beach itself.

'Just look at all that seaweed,' she exclaimed. It lay in huge drifts like autumn leaves on the sand. 'You'd think they'd compost it or something.' Young children in swimsuits were dodging around the heaps on their way down to the sea, which looked an intense shade of postcard blue through Jane's sunglasses; nothing like the slate-grey waters she had swum in as a child. 'Wait here a moment,' said Erica, abandoning the buggy and clattering down the shingle to take a picture of the pier, a curious mixture of well-preserved Victorian and crumbling Art Deco. She returned a minute later, disappointed. 'I can't fit it all in.'

They abandoned the buggy on the stones and carried Yorrick down to the water's edge. The seaweed was unexpectedly spongy and yielding underfoot. It reminded Jane of her night on Erica's mattress, but she desisted from making the comparison out loud. Instead she took off her sandals, rolled up her trousers, and felt the wet rippled sand and wormcasts massaging her bare feet.

Erica was paddling in the warm incoming tide, and trying to persuade Yorrick to get his feet wet. Every time she lowered him towards the water he drew up his fat little legs, refusing to be dunked. 'What's that place?' Erica asked, looking east along the coast to the white hotels and glittering tower blocks in the distance.

'That's Brighton,' said Jane, laughing at her ignorance. 'That was the Big City when I was growing up. When the girls in my class – the real no-hopers, I mean – were asked what they wanted to do when they left school, they'd say: "I'm not sticking around in this dump. I'm going to *Brighton*." As if it was the Promised Land, or something.'

'I would have been one of those girls,' sighed Erica. 'I couldn't wait to leave school. I tried to get expelled, but the bloody nuns kept forgiving me. I didn't even go to university until I was twenty-two. I worked in the local dry-cleaners. That's how much it put me off education.'

'Why did you hate it so much?' asked Jane. As someone who had shone at school, but felt herself growing progressively dimmer ever since, she had nothing but fond memories of the place.

'Oh, I don't know. I've got no respect for authority, I suppose. I think there are people who like order and rules and discipline . . .'

'Like me,' Jane interrupted.

'Yeah, like you,' Erica agreed. 'And people who hate being told what to do and automatically rebel. Even now if a law strikes me as illogical or stupid, I'll break it. Your Sophie – now she's a natural respecter of rules. She'll have a tidy bedroom and neat writing. Harriet – she's more like me.'

'An anarchist, you mean?'

'Well, if I could have a girl, I'd choose a Harriet any day.'

'That's one of the nicest things anyone's ever said to me,' Jane replied. 'You're the only person who's ever actually admitted to liking her. Except James and Kerry, who think she's cute. But they've got nothing to compare her to.'

'You know the worst thing about having all boys,' Erica said, kicking water into the air and watching the arc of crystal droplets catch the sunlight. 'None of my experiences will be of any use to them. I've got nothing to pass on.'

'Perhaps that's what Guy feels about the girls. He's never said so. Perhaps that's why he likes having James around the place. So he can pass something on.'

'I certainly feel as though there's a big part of me that will go to waste,' Erica said.

'You can be Harriet's moral and spiritual guardian, if you like,' said Jane. 'Then I can blame you when she goes off the rails.'

'Thanks,' Erica replied. She had edged deeper into the water. Jane, who was standing further back, had rolled her trousers above the knee.

'Or you could try for a fourth,' Jane suggested. Although she had found two children more than plenty, she often found herself urging other people to increase the size of their family. Like an anorexic pressing everyone else to second helpings.

'I might do that,' said Erica, holding Yorrick up in the air and nuzzling his tummy until he squealed. 'I've often thought I might pop one more out before I'm forty. There'll be nothing better to do in Kuwait.'

'What if it's a boy?'

'It would be. It would probably be twin boys. You can't cheat fate. Oh!' She gave a gasp as a wave rode up over her knees, soaking the bottom of her shorts. 'I wish I'd brought my swimming costume now. I didn't think I'd fancy going in.'

'You could just strip. I'll look after Yorrick and your clothes,' said Jane, without so much as a smirk.

Erica shuddered. 'It's not a nudist beach.'

'No, but you're a rule-breaker and an anarchist, remember.'

'Yeah, well. Even we anarchists like a day off now and then.'

'Speaking of days off, I wonder if I should just ring James to check that everything's okay,' Jane mused, slipping her handbag from round her neck and ferreting for the phone. 'Blast. I forgot to take it out of the car. Now I won't know if he's been trying to ring me.'

'A Freudian psychologist might say there's no such thing as accidentally forgetting,' Erica said, retrieving her shoes from the breakwater, and following Jane back up the beach.

'You think I subconsciously want to be unobtainable?' asked Jane. 'Maybe there's something in that.'

'I don't think anything,' Erica replied. 'I didn't do psychology.' She strapped Yorrick back into his buggy and flexed her aching shoulders.

'What was it you studied?' said Jane.

'I did English and Fine Art at one of the humblest establishments in the country. When I told my father-in-law where I got my degree, he said, "Oh yes, I always think of it as the last stronghold before the polytechnics." Neil and I still laugh about that one.'

They walked back to the car, where Jane discovered she

had left the phone switched off. 'Brilliant!' she muttered, punching in her home number. 'That's odd,' she said, having let it ring and ring. 'No reply.'

'They'll be out in the garden,' said Erica, who was, as Jane had noted before, not a worrier. 'It's a beautiful day.'

'Kerry, Kerry, I winned at picture dominoes,' said Harriet, dancing up and down on the doorstep as Kerry sauntered down the path towards her.

'Did you? I winned at my driving test,' she replied, taking Harriet's hands and lifting her off the ground.

'Congratulations, I knew you'd do it,' said James, side-stepping Harriet to give Kerry a kiss. 'What did he ask you?'

'Stopping distances, parking restrictions. All the things you tested me on. Do you want to come for a drive?'

'I can't. I'm babysitting.' James pointed downwards at Harriet, who had interposed herself between them to frustrate, or join in with, their cuddle.

'Where's Jane?' Kerry asked in surprise. After the incident with the burnt pie-crust she hadn't expected them to be left in charge again so soon.

'Gone out for the day. She can't take Harriet to her in-laws because they'll die if they catch a cold or something.'

'Why? Have they got AIDS?' Kerry wanted to know.

'I don't know. Anyway, I'm looking after Harriet.'

'Yes, and you've got to play with me,' announced Harriet.

'She can come in the car with us, can't she?' said Kerry, ignoring this. 'We'll strap her in the back. Just a quick spin round the block.'

'Yes, me come, me come,' Harriet cried, turning excited circles like an untrained puppy.

'Okay,' said James, glancing at the telephone. 'We'll strap you in the back.'

Erica changed Yorrick's nappy in the boot of Jane's hatchback. 'Very handy for this sort of job,' she said, approvingly. 'I can never use mine because it's always full of garbage. You know I've had a FOR SALE sign stuck to the back windscreen for two weeks now and I haven't had a single call.'

'Maybe it would be more saleable without the garbage,' Jane hinted. 'Anyway, if you can't sell it before you leave, I'll do it for you.'

'Really? You are a mate. There's nothing wrong with it. It's never given me a day's trouble. And the mileage is quite low. For its age.'

'You don't need to talk it up for my benefit,' Jane reminded her. 'I'm not buying.'

'Anything you make on it you can keep,' said Erica. 'Or you can take it to the knackers' yard. Whatever.'

'Done,' said Jane. They had walked back to the promenade by now, where Jane stopped to buy two soft, whipped ice-creams and Erica launched a tirade against a particularly ugly example of sixties architecture, in the form of a featureless concrete block alongside a row of elegant Regency hotels. 'Who could possibly have thought it would be a good idea to put that there?' she ranted.

They turned inland, having exhausted the possibilities of the beach itself, and strolled through the precinct, looking in shop windows. Yorrick, lulled by the movement, dropped off to sleep with his thumb in his mouth, his free hand holding his earlobe. Erica went into a jeweller's to get a new battery for her watch, which had stopped some weeks previously. While she was being served, Jane scanned the trays of jewellery, hoping to find something that might do as a parting gift. It had to be unusual, tasteful and interesting, but not too expensive. She didn't want to embarrass Erica into reciprocating, and besides, now they were paying James there wasn't much spare cash around for luxuries. She settled on a small gold lapel pin – or perhaps it was a large nose-stud – in the shape of a question mark. The shop assistant polished it with a scrap of silk, before dropping it into a tiny velvet pouch.

'What are you buying?' Erica asked, peering over Jane's shoulder as she signed the credit card slip.

'Nothing. Just a present for you actually.' Jane handed it over, as casually as possible, as if offering a bag of sweets, and watched Erica tip the tiny stud into the palm of her hand and examine it for a second or two before clipping it on to her shirt collar. Jane was relieved. Only a truly ostentatious person would have worn something that size in their nose.

'It's lovely,' said Erica. 'The question is, what is the question?'

Jane smiled. 'It's just a general expression of uncertainty,' she explained. 'I should have got one for Guy: he could swap it for his crucifix whenever he has his attacks of Doubt.'

'I've got something for you,' Erica said. 'Or at least I will have. But you've got to work for it,' she added cryptically. 'Come on.' She led a puzzled Jane through the precinct and back to the beach, and this time they carried Yorrick's buggy like a sedan chair over the stones so as not to wake him.

'Where are we going?' Jane wanted to know.

'Just sit there, against that breakwater,' Erica ordered, pointing to a section of wood, worn almost smooth, and bleached white as bone. 'Perfect.' She unzipped her camera bag. 'Now, just look out to sea and ignore me while I sort myself out.'

'Oh, I don't take a good picture,' said Jane, reluctant, self-conscious and flattered, all at the same time.

'I'm taking the picture,' Erica corrected her, producing a small Olympus camera, and crouching down on the shingle. Jane had expected her to own something bigger, flashier, with an armoury of light-meters and giant lenses, and was nonplussed when Erica presently stood up and packed the camera away.

'No good?' she asked.

'Yes, all done,' said Erica. 'I'll get them developed when I get home and let you have a copy. To remind you of today.'

'Thanks,' said Jane. 'That was quick.'

'Well, you have to work fast with people, before they start getting all rigid and uncomfortable.'

That's right, thought Jane, staring at the sodium glow of sunlight on the water. Work fast: avoid discomfort. 'Erica,' she said out loud. 'I do love you.' The blood in her ears sounded like waves crashing on rocks and when she looked up black and red blobs shimmered and swam before her eyes. Erica was dancing up and down on the stones, twitching her arms and legs, as if possessed by seven demons.

Oh my God, thought Jane, paralysed with shame and regret. What did I say that for? Her heart gave several loud knocks as if asking to be let out.

'Bloody wasp flew down my shirt,' said Erica, giving it a final swipe before coming to rest. 'Die, you bastard! Sorry, what did you say just then? I missed it.'

'Nothing,' said Jane, faint with relief, the red snakes still seething in her line of vision. Her cheeks were burning with the shock of her brush with certain humiliation. 'Nothing,' she said again.

'Ssh,' said Erica. 'What's that noise?'

Through the booming in her ears Jane could make out the feeble, but close, metallic trilling of a telephone.

39

When the call came Guy was in his office looking at plans to replace the two mobile classrooms with an L-shaped block, which would enclose the playground. There were architectural drawings all over his desk; somewhere beneath them the phone buzzed like a trapped insect.

It was Nina, fated again to be the bringer of bad news, who called to tell him about the accident. She had heard it herself from Bob. Kerry had been the only person in the car carrying any identification, so he was the first to know. It was only when Nina and Bob arrived at the hospital that they discovered there had been a third person in the car – a small girl. Nina had realized instantly whose child she was.

'She's alive. Yes, yes, she's alive,' Nina had assured him, over and over again.

'But is she all right?'

'She's going to be all right,' Nina said. 'She's in the High Dependency Unit. They're looking after her.' These were just platitudes. Nina had no idea what was happening: the doctors had told her none of the details of Harriet's condition.

'How am I going to reach Jane? I don't know where she is?'

'I've rung her. She's on her way,' Nina assured him.

It was only towards the end of the conversation that Guy thought to ask after James. His anxieties about Harriet had driven out all thoughts of his unofficial son. 'Is he . . . ? Is he . . . ?'

'He's in theatre at the moment,' Nina said, in a choked voice. 'His spleen or something. They don't even know. I can't talk any more.'

'I'm coming now.'

Guy had rushed out of school, on foot, and was half way

down the drive when he remembered he had another daughter, still in her classroom and for whom he was responsible. Like the shepherd who abandoned the flock to go after the lost sheep, Guy's thoughts were all for the one in peril. He swung round to see the school secretary, Mary, running after him as fast as her high heels would allow, waving a bunch of keys.

'Take my car,' she said, stopping to shake the grit out of her sandals.

'What about Sophie?' Accustomed as he was to giving orders, he felt confounded by the simplest decision.

'I'll look after her: you go.' She had to push him in the direction of the car park.

Mary's Volvo was an automatic. It took Guy several attempts to get going. She's okay, she's okay, she's okay, he kept telling himself, all the way, as if it was only his confidence that was keeping her alive. There was a sick, vacant feeling in his stomach and sweat was streaming down his back, even though he had the windows open and the airflow was cool. When he stopped in traffic, he tried to wriggle out of his jacket, but the lights changed before he'd worked himself free, and he had to drive on, one arm and shoulder still caught up, and a yard of wool gabardine bunched behind his back.

At the hospital he joined the queue of cars crawling around in search of a parking space. If it hadn't been Mary's he would have dumped the thing in a towaway zone and taken a chance. Just ahead of him a blue Metro was indicating to pull out. The driver in front began to reverse, but must have caught sight of Guy, hunched grimly over the wheel, pressing forward, and thought better of it, as he presently screeched away.

Guy tossed aside his crumpled jacket and sprinted for the main block, following Nina's garbled directions to the High Dependency Unit, which was in a dead end off a long, highly polished corridor. The double doors, like most of the doors Guy had passed, were locked and operated by a combination keypad, and there was no one about. A sign on the wall alongside read: *Authorized personnel only beyond this point. Please ring for assistance.* He pressed the bell and, hearing nothing, pressed it again, harder. A moment later the door was snatched open and a nurse stood there, a look of impatience on her face. 'Yes? Can I help?' she asked crisply.

'My daughter's in there,' Guy said, identifying himself.

'Ah. Right. She's with the doctor at the moment,' the nurse replied, more kindly, now that his impatience could be explained. 'If you wait in the relatives' room' – she pointed across the corridor – 'she'll come out and see you in a minute. Five minutes,' she corrected herself.

'You mean she's up and about?' said Guy, with a great surge of joy, which subsided instantly as he caught the nurse's expression.

'I meant the doctor,' she said, mortified.

'But . . . but . . . Harriet is okay?' Guy had a sudden, terrible suspicion that she was already dead and no one wanted to tell him. 'She's alive, isn't she?'

'Oh yes,' said the nurse. 'Yes.' Her relief at being able to offer this grain of encouragement was palpable. 'The doctor will be with you soon,' she added, retreating.

She doesn't want to make any false promises, Guy thought, pushing open the door to the waiting room. He would have preferred to leave it open, but it was on a stiff spring and slammed shut behind him, cutting off the sounds of the hospital and leaving him standing in a room about eight feet square. It was furnished like the lobby of a cheap hotel chain or conference centre, with six upholstered curved-backed chairs and a glass-topped coffee table, on which lay copies of the *Spectator* and *Ideal Home*. On the walls were a series of watercolour prints of wild flowers – blown up versions of cheap birthday cards. In the corner stood a Klix machine and a cold water dispenser in clear blue plastic. Looking at it Guy was suddenly reminded of the meteorological station in In Salah, and he sat down, dizzily, and wiped his forehead on his shirt cuff. How anyone could be expected to drink coffee, much less read a magazine at a time like this he couldn't imagine.

Five minutes passed; then ten. This is my fault, he thought. Jane will hold me responsible. It was my idea to have James and Kerry in the house. Jane never wanted them there. He took his pulse: 130. They'll find me in here dead, he thought, standing up abruptly and crossing the room in two paces. He poked his head around the door, intending to waylay the first passer-by. A cleaner in a plastic overall, pushing a floor-polisher, was vanishing round a corner. From the same direction a trolley, hung with drips and tubes and accompanied by a cavalcade of medics, swung into view. The patient was a middle-aged man. Guy shrank back into the waiting room as it sped past him and disappeared into the High Dependency Unit. Even in his mood of desperation he couldn't bring himself to flag down another casualty. In the silence of the pale green hospitality suite Guy sank to his knees and prayed.

Please God, forgive me for doubting you. Please don't take Harriet from me. Please let her be all right. I will never ask for anything again. I will never have another petty thought as long as I live. Oh, and please let James be all right too. And his girlfriend. Whatshername. Amen.

Guy was still on his knees when the doctor – a tiny Asian woman – walked in. When he scrambled to his feet he towered over her. She spoke so quietly he had to bend down to catch every word. 'You are Harriet's father?' she whispered.

'Yes.' Guy clenched and unclenched his hands at his sides to stop them from shaking.

'You can see her now, but it will be quite distressing for you. Her face is very bruised and swollen, and she has had some stitches in her scalp.' She patted the left side of her head. 'So a patch of hair has been shaved off. She has a small fracture to the skull. That's not necessarily as bad as it sounds. Her brain scan is clear, there's no sign of any damage, so that's good. But it looks alarming when you first see her.'

'But is she going to be all right?' Guy asked, for what seemed to him the hundredth time. He would go on and on asking different experts all the time Harriet lay in hospital until someone came out with an unqualified Yes.

'Well, as I say, there's no obvious sign of damage to the brain,' said the doctor. 'So there's no reason why she shouldn't make a full recovery. But we always take head injuries seriously, especially with children, so we're monitoring her very closely.'

'Can she talk? I mean is she awake.'

The doctor looked perplexed at his naivety. 'No. She's not talking at the moment. The painkillers have left her very woozy. But you can sit with her. Ready?'

Guy nodded, bracing himself for shock, and followed the doctor through the locked double doors.

In another wing of the hospital Nina paced the corridor outside Theatre Two. There was nowhere to sit – loiterers were not encouraged – but she wanted to see James the moment the operation was over. Just a glance would be enough for her to tell – with a mother's instinct – whether it had gone well.

The Senior House Officer who had assessed James's condition on his arrival in Casualty had explained to Nina that they needed to operate. Internal injuries were suspected. He had taken her aside into a curtained-off cubicle to give the illusion of privacy. Beneath the curtain hem on both sides Nina could see feet and ankles, not a metre away. 'It may be a ruptured spleen,' he had said. 'In which case they'll perform a splenectomy.'

'Is that a dangerous operation?' Nina asked. 'Do most people, you know, survive?'

'Any operation carried out under general anaesthetic involves an element of risk,' the doctor replied, with what Nina soon came to recognize as standard-issue professional caution. 'But, no, it's not *especially* dangerous.'

'He's got a donor card,' Nina said, in a dull voice. She didn't want to be asked about it later, when she might say No. The doctor escorted her back to the waiting room, his hand hovering near but not quite touching her back. 'There's no reason why it should come to that,' he said. 'But thank you.'

Nina stared at the closed doors of Theatre Two, willing them to open. She would have prayed, but she didn't believe in God: the more she knew of the world the less likely it seemed that there was anyone in control. Instead she prayed to James himself: to be strong, to fight, not to leave her. She made extravagant bargains with destiny. *If James comes through this I will never be jealous or clinging or protective or bossy as long as I live. I will devote my life to helping Others.*

She opened her eyes and glanced down at her watch. An hour, the doctor had said. Almost no time had passed since she last checked. Presently the anguish of hoping overcame her and she began to weep, silent streams, which collected in the lines on her face and dripped off her chin. This lasted a minute or two and then the tears ran out – as if a tank had been drained. Nina dried her burning face on a fresh tissue, feeling marginally better. Crying seemed to have released a build-up of pressure inside her skull. She thought of Irene, who had lost her only son and lived another eighteen years in the shadow of grief, and was profoundly grateful that she had been spared this day. And in that brief moment of deep concentration it came to her with absolute clarity that in giving Irene a share of James she had done the Right Thing. She had never been perfectly convinced until now, even when trying to explain it to herself, but this new sense of justification would stay with her for ever.

Jane drove as fast as the speed limit would allow, occasionally faster if the traffic permitted, her eyes fixed on the road ahead. Apart from initial expressions of dismay and sympathy Erica made no attempt at conversation, intuiting correctly that Jane had no desire to talk. From the back seat Yorrick babbled and laughed, oblivious to the change of atmosphere.

This is all my fault, Jane was thinking, chewing mechanically at the skin on the inside of her cheek. Harriet will die because I left her behind. Guy will never forgive me. This is my punishment for wishing her out of the way. The feeling of nausea deep in her guts was a combination of fear of losing Harriet and fear of facing Guy. How would she drag herself through the rest of her life under the weight of so much sorrow and grief? She gripped the steering wheel and locked her arms to stop herself from slumping forwards, already feeling the pressure on her shoulders like a sack of stones.

In the seat beside her Erica flinched. They were too close to the car in front. Jane braked sharply. Concentrate, she told herself. Just get there. She gave Erica an apologetic glance and noticed the gold question mark on her collar flashing as it caught the sun.

'Oh, I never got Harriet a present!' she cried, remembering too late her parting bribe. Another rock of betrayal for the sack.

'She won't hold it against you,' said Erica. 'Anyway, there'll be a shop at the hospital selling teddy bears and things like that.'

'I said it would be something from the seaside.'

'She won't mind where it's from. Don't upset yourself.'

But Jane refused to be consoled, preferring instead to torture herself all the way home with the thought that her last words to Harriet had been a broken promise.

Guy sat beside Harriet's bed holding her limp hand. The nurse had positioned the chair on her good side where the bruising to her face was less shocking. All the same Guy was shocked. He had expected at least to recognize Harriet, but with her black eye and swollen cheek and jaw, so raw and purple, and her curly hair combed straight back off her forehead, around a gauze dressing, the resemblance to his beautiful girl was not even passing. She looked so small, too, in the wide white bed; she hardly made a bump under the sheet. He concentrated on watching her breathing: the gentle rise and fall of the hospital gown was infinitely comforting.

The only other occupant of the unit – the middle-aged man who had been wheeled past him earlier – was on a ventilator. Guy could hear its mechanical sighs. He tried talking to Harriet while she dozed, and reciting those bits of *The Jumblies* and *The Owl and the Pussycat* that he could remember, just to let her know he was there, but his voice sounded strained and artificial, and more likely to communicate anxiety than reassurance, so he had stopped. Occasionally Harriet's good eyelid flickered, and she made a faint mewing noise in the back of her throat and, once, she opened one eye and closed it again, but she seemed reluctant to wake up fully.

Just five more minutes, thought Guy, and then I'll go and phone Mary, and tell Sophie that everything's fine. And then I must find Nina and James. He was torn between his duty to James, who was, from Nina's account, more seriously injured, and his desperate desire to be with Harriet when she woke, and, if possible, to intercept Jane on her arrival. He was surprised and a little ashamed to find how clearly and naturally his priorities had declared themselves; his sense of responsibility and goodwill towards James was nothing beside the anguished love he felt for his girls.

'I've just got to go and find out how my son is,' Guy explained to a nurse who was adjusting dials on the bank of monitors at the head of the middle-aged man's bed. He felt bound to make a point of his departure so that they would know that Harriet was now unattended.

'We'll keep an eye on her,' the nurse promised, catching on.

'I'll be back soon,' said Guy, tapping his watch face.

'Just ring. I'll let you in.'

He made his way down the cul-de-sac into the long straight corridor which formed the hospital's main artery. Two doctors passed him at a brisk pace, their white coat tails flapping. Porters with trolleys criss-crossed the passage and disappeared into lifts. A pregnant woman in a dressing gown was feeding coins into a pay phone. A woman well past retirement age pushed a jangling tea-cart from ward to ward. And then for a second the corridor cleared, and Guy saw the figure of his wife, silhouetted against the glass doors in the far distance, staring up at a bewilderingly comprehensive directory.

'Jane!' he bellowed, in violation of all accepted protocols, and causing several heads to turn in annoyance. She looked up, startled, and her face seemed to melt with relief, and she ran to meet him, dodging and apologizing as she went.

'She's all right,' he said, as soon as she was comfortably within earshot, and this was so exactly the right thing to say, and at that moment the only words Jane wanted to hear, that she threw herself at him and hugged him gratefully. He could feel her arms around him, pressing against the damp fabric of his shirt.

'I'm sorry,' they both began, and then stopped, surprised to be on the receiving end of an apology.

'Never mind,' said Guy, keeping one arm around Jane as he led her back to the High Dependency Unit, telling her everything he knew about Harriet's condition on the way. Just outside the double doors he stopped. 'Her face is very distorted. You can hardly recognize her,' he warned. 'But they say she won't be disfigured. It's just bruising.' He heard Jane's sharp intake of breath as she approached the bed.

'My little baby,' she whispered. He couldn't know it, but at that moment Jane was experiencing the outrush of yearning love that she had never felt at Harriet's birth or since, until now. She leant over and kissed the unblemished, downy skin of her ear.

Guy noticed that Harriet seemed to have moved since he had left: the sheets were disarranged. As Jane sat back and pressed the heels of her hands into her eyes to stop the tears forming, Harriet twitched and opened her good eye: the other was hidden beneath a seam of puffy flesh. For a second it seemed as though she hadn't seen her parents, but then the eye widened and she turned her head to bring them both into view.

'Darling,' they both said in cracked voices. Jane squeezed the tiny hand on top of the bedclothes, willing her to give some sign of recognition. It had occurred to both of them separately that she might have amnesia and be unaware who or where she was. Harriet licked her dry lips. Jane and Guy swayed forward expectantly to catch whatever words might escape.

'Mummy,' said Harriet hoarsely, and Jane's heart leapt. My little girl, she thought. My precious.

'Mummy. Did you get my present?'

40

It was left to Kerry to provide an explanation of the circumstances of the crash. She was the only one of the three who remained conscious at the moment of impact. Apart from bruising to the chest from the steering wheel she was uninjured. It had been the passenger side which had taken most of the punishment. James could remember nothing of the accident or the events leading up to it and Harriet was a highly unreliable witness. Over the forthcoming weeks she would occasionally claim that *she* had been driving.

What had in fact happened was this: Kerry had strapped Harriet tightly in the back on the passenger side, unwittingly using the faulty seatbelt which Nina had neglected to mention in her original sales pitch. There were a couple of graphite tennis rackets on the front seat. Before she found out they were babysitting, Kerry had envisaged a game in the park. James sat in the front with the rackets between his knees, handles uppermost. They had been driving down Kingston Hill, quite fast, when the driver of a van, badly parked on the brow of the hill, had flung his door open. Kerry swerved to avoid it, nearly colliding with a minicab which was belting up the middle of the road, then veered back to the left, mounting the kerb and burying the car bonnet in the trunk of a sturdy horse-chestnut. Her final piece of bad luck had been to hit the accelerator instead of the brake as she came out of the second swerve.

The force of the crash caused Harriet's seatbelt to burst open, flinging her against the car door and knocking her out. If she had been any taller her head would have gone through the window. As it was she was hit by a piece of flying glass from James's shattered window which left a three-inch cut across the top of her head and contributed to the gruesome spectacle she had presented to her parents in hospital.

James, in the worst seat of all, was showered with fragments of glass and struck the side of his head on the seatbelt casing, causing him to black out. His worst injury, however, was inflicted by those tennis rackets. (This confirmed what Nina had always maintained: that all sports were dangerous.) The compression of the front nearside had, in addition to breaking his big toe, driven the graphite shafts up into James's abdomen, breaking his bottom rib and rupturing his spleen. His rescuers had been obliged to use the very latest cutting equipment to free him: the rackets were now in pieces. Which was a shame, Kerry said later, since they were new, but then neither she nor James would be playing much tennis for the rest of the season.

Nina had no reason to disbelieve Kerry's account. The girl had made no attempt to exonerate herself: on the contrary she blamed herself bitterly. Her test certificate was still somewhere in the wreckage of what had once been the glove compartment: she had no intention of trying to salvage it.

'I'll never drive again,' she promised Nina, not histrionically, or like someone wanting to be dissuaded, but in a matter-of-fact tone.

They were sitting on either side of James's bed the morning after the accident, talking across him while he lay wreathed in a fog of post-operative pain and nausea, trailing tubes like the suckers of some rampant weed. He wasn't asleep but his eyes were half-closed as if he could only admit so much reality. Every so often he would emit a low groan. Nina had commandeered the extra chair from the neighbouring bedside. The patient, an elderly man, said: 'Keep it. I won't be needing it. I don't get any visitors.'

'That's a shame,' Nina had replied, inadequately. There wasn't so much as a card, a book or a newspaper on the top of his formica unit. His hands lay slackly on the sheet, unoccupied, and once this exchange with Nina was over he continued to gaze into the space where she had formerly stood. Poor man, she thought, as she drew the dividing curtain between them to give Kerry some privacy while she relived the events of the previous day.

It was the detail about the defective seatbelt which made Nina's heart miss a beat. The very next time she saw Guy she would feel compelled to abase herself and confess. She would go on to confess to Kerry, Bob, Jane, the doctor who was treating Harriet, and anyone else who would listen. This was the worst of agnosticism: your sins were always with you.

'Don't try and take all the blame for this, Kerry,' she said. 'No one's angry with you.'

'I'd feel better if I was more injured myself, if you know what I mean,' Kerry said. 'When they were doing my chest X-ray I was secretly hoping they might find a broken rib or two. Because the bruises hurt like hell anyway, but it sounds better. Stupid, isn't it?'

Nina agreed that this showed a lack of logic, not to mention self-esteem, which was quite understandable in the circumstances. In view of her own act of barbarous negligence, Nina was willing to forgive Kerry anything – even the fact that her name had been the first word uttered by James on his emergence from anaesthesia. (He had in fact been having a nightmare that Kerry was trying to hit him with an iron bar, and had called out her name through fear rather than desire, but Nina would never know that.)

'As far as I can gather, everyone seems to be feeling guilty. It's infectious.' Her attempt at penitence hadn't gone quite as planned: Guy, Jane and Kerry were all as dismissive of her part in the disaster as they were anxious to protest their own complicity. Kerry chewed this over for a minute. 'Well, in my view if you feel guilty, you are guilty,' she said at last in her ponderous way. 'I mean if you can't trust your own conscience, who can you trust?'

Nina looked at her with new respect. In all their encounters Kerry had never before expressed anything resembling an 'idea'. I wonder how long she's planning on staying, Nina wondered, and then it dawned on her that Kerry – and very probably James, too – was waiting for her to leave. She stood up suddenly. 'I'm going to get myself a cup of coffee,' she announced, brushing the creases out of the clothes which she had slept in. 'You sit there.'

On the way out of the ward she met Bob coming in, holding a bunch of grapes. 'You look terrible,' he said, bluntly, after he had inquired about James. 'Did you spend all night here?'

Nina admitted that she did. 'I lay across three chairs in the reception area for a while, but I didn't sleep.' They stood back as an empty trolley was wheeled past. 'I would have paid good money for one of those by three in the morning,' she said, staring after it.

'Let me take you home. You can have a sleep.'

Nina shook her head. 'I feel I have to be here. Haunting the place.'

'You could get . . .' Bob worked it out, '. . . four hours or so. Then I'll pick you up and bring you back this evening. How's that?'

'But you've only just got here.'

'I only came to see James. I know Kerry's all right. I'll poke my nose round the curtain and say hello, and then I'll be with you.'

The thought of her comfortable bed and cool cotton pillow was almost too tempting. She was already looking forward to collapsing. Then she remembered that the new, self-reliant Nina no longer threw herself on the mercy of others – particularly when it might be misread. She didn't want Bob thinking she had any interest in him personally. 'I will go home, but I don't need a lift. I'm in your debt already,' she said. 'That Greek meal the other day.'

'Do you think of all your friends in terms of creditors or debtors?' Bob asked. 'Do you keep the running totals in your head?'

'It's not like that. It's just that I'm not supposed to be accepting any more favours. I'm committed to helping Others now.' She explained the substance of her Agnostics' Prayer.

'Well, isn't that what you're doing all the time in your job?'

Nina thought for a moment. Her most recent case concerned a twelve-year-old girl, pregnant by her sixteen-year-old boyfriend. It was Nina's job, as guardian ad litem, to advise the courts whether the child would be better off living with her mother – a recovering alcoholic – or in care. 'I suppose so. Though most of my clients don't seem to see it that way.'

'Perhaps you should start with the old boy in the bed next to James,' Bob advised. 'The poor bloke can't even see the TV from where he is. He's just lying there bored to death.'

'You're right. I'll take him some newspapers,' she said. 'Get him doing the crossword.' She already had him marked down as her next project.

'I bet you will too,' he laughed, absent-mindedly starting to eat the grapes as he took Nina's place in the ward.

41

Guy carried a sleeping Sophie from the car indoors and straight up to her bed, stepping over a pile of unopened post on the mat. Even the jolting she had taken when he had tried to unlock the front door without putting her down hadn't roused her. He pulled off her shoes and socks and gently extricated her skinny arms from her cardigan and then looked around in the half light of the curtained room for a pair of pyjamas. He hadn't a clue where such things were kept: Jane had her own mysterious system, which he'd never cracked. In any case, he hadn't a hope of removing Sophie's summer dress which was buttoned up the back and tightish, without disturbing her.

She looked so peaceful that he decided to let her sleep in it just as she was. It would be simple enough to iron out the creases before school in the morning. If he could find the iron. He felt a pang of conscience about her teeth, recently sluiced in lemonade at the hospital café. Jane would never let a child of hers go to bed without brushing their teeth: it was like a religious observance. Well, these were exceptional circumstances, Guy thought. It wasn't surprising that standards were slipping. They hadn't even had time to look at their mail. Besides, he had more important things on his mind, and he was knackered himself: the hospital routine was starting to exact a price. Generally Jane took the day shift, while Guy was at work. He would bring Sophie to see her sister straight after school, while Jane dashed home to shower and change. On her return, Guy would look in on James and give Sophie tea in the hospital café before bringing her home to bed. Once Harriet had been moved into a paediatric ward Jane was able to stay overnight beside her on a Zed Bed. The minimum level of comfort and relaxation necessary for sleep was just about achievable. All the same, Jane looked exhausted. 'I want to be there in case she has a nightmare,' Jane insisted, when Guy had expressed concern about her own health. 'I'll catch up when she's better. It won't be long.'

It was true that this state of affairs was not likely to drag on indefinitely. Harriet was greatly improved – eating, drinking, playing with toys, chattering to the nurses – and paediatric beds were much in demand. She would probably be turfed out before the weekend. The swelling to her face had diminished considerably and the discoloration was less livid, or so it seemed to Guy. The skull fracture would heal itself in time without any medical intervention, and Harriet didn't appear to have suffered any lasting damage as a result of the injury.

There was a difference, though. He and Jane had both noticed it. She was calmer, more subdued, less prone to fits of rage.

'It's not surprising,' said Guy, when they'd discussed it, in a busy corridor, out of Harriet's hearing. 'It probably hurts if she starts tossing her head around too much. She's just protecting herself.' He stepped back as the distant 'whump' of double doors heralded the passage of another trolley.

'I don't like it,' said Jane. 'I want her back the way she was.' Through the doorway they could see Sophie and Harriet sitting in bed together, giggling. Harriet was pretending to feed one of her dolls, pressing its head to her chest.

'And another thing,' said Guy. 'She's enjoying being the centre of attention. We're ready to do her bidding day and night. She's got no reason to be temperamental.'

'Maybe,' said Jane, dubiously. 'I just hope you're right, and it's nothing permanent.'

'But you've always wanted her to be more docile,' Guy protested. 'You did nothing but complain about her tantrums and her bad behaviour.'

'I know,' said Jane. 'I was horrible and selfish and wrong. I've been a bad mother to her: it's me who needs to change, not her.'

'That's not true. You're a good mother,' Guy protested, hating to see her put herself down. 'And a wonderful wife,' he added, kissing her between the eyes and tasting salt tears on his lips.

She laughed at this. It was months since they'd made love, weeks since they'd slept in the same bed, days since they'd slept in the same building. 'I'm sorry I've been so . . . distant lately. I don't know what's the matter with me.'

'Don't worry. Once Harriet's home we'll sort everything out. We'll talk about things. We'll make each other laugh like we used to.' He put two fingers in the corners of his mouth and two up his nostrils and pulled a grotesque face, to the astonishment of a passing nurse. Jane laughed, out of gratitude more than anything. 'Perhaps we could go for a long weekend somewhere, just the two of us,' he said, getting carried away now.

'I'm not leaving the children,' Jane said quickly.

'No, no. Of course not. We'll take them with us. As soon as term ends we'll drive to Pembrokeshire. I'll book up a cottage.'

'But it's the money . . .' Jane tailed off. In his enthusiasm Guy had forgotten this detail. All major expenditure had been cancelled to pay James for the trumped-up decorating work.

'Something will turn up,' Guy insisted, Micawber-like. 'We'll bung it on a credit card for now. By the way, your friend rang last night. Emily.'

'Erica,' said Jane. 'I wondered if she'd call.'

'I told her Harriet was doing well and all that. She said she's off soon, and cheerio, that sort of thing.'

'To Kuwait? So soon?' Jane wondered aloud. 'I never said goodbye. I was in such a panic.'

'She said something about going up to Scotland to see her parents first.' He wished he'd been paying more attention. There had been a piece of bacon under the grill when she rang and he'd been trying to cut things short before the smoke alarm went off. 'And something about her car which I didn't quite catch.'

'Oh yes, I'm getting rid of it for her. I'd forgotten that.' In truth she'd hardly given Erica a thought in the last few days. Their brief friendship and the strange, unreturned infatuation that Jane had experienced seemed as remote as her teenage crushes on Trevor from Cheshunt, or Séverine, the hairy French *assistante*. It was her own family who commanded all of her attention and emotional energy now. There was nothing left over to sustain any sort of fantasy life. Guy had been so brilliant, providing endless reassurance, and never a word of reproach. And he had leapt to her defence when his mother had criticized her over the telephone for leaving Harriet with 'some boy you hardly know'. They had called her from the hospital with news of the accident. 'Jane isn't to blame,' he had said, in the hard voice that he seldom used at home. 'She feels bad enough as it is, without you sticking your oar in. You might just as well blame yourselves for not looking after Harriet that day.' And his mother had been shocked into spluttering out a retraction. It was the first time Jane had ever known him to argue with his parents, and as she stood in the booth beside him, listening, she became aware of an unfamiliar sensation: the faintest stirring of sexual desire.

It was James that Guy had gone to see next, while Jane returned to the girls, who were now trying to crayon the same page in Harriet's colouring book, elbows and nibs clashing.

He found the patient sitting on top of the bedcovers wearing a white T-shirt and a pair of gaping boxer shorts. Guy had observed on previous visits to hospitals that invalids often lost all sense of modesty. James's catheter, drain and drip had been removed, and he looked moderately healthier. Even so there were dark shadows under his eyes, and his skin, formerly as pallid as tinned lychees, was only just beginning to recover its flesh tones. His plastered foot bore the imprint of a heavily lipsticked kiss. He was listening to a Walkman, in the absence of any visitors: Kerry had a follow-up outpatients appointment, and Nina was off somewhere, buying provisions. James pulled off his earphones as Guy approached.

'How are you feeling, then, Jimbo?' Guy asked, adopting

the hearty avuncular tone that he always used for talking to Young People over a certain age.

'Shitty,' James replied. 'Really wiped out.'

'So you're saying you won't be finishing that bedroom ceiling tomorrow?' Guy smote his forehead in mock exasperation.

James gave a twisted smile and shook his head. His one shaved, stitched eyebrow fixed his face in an expression of permanent inquiry.

'Bloody typical,' Guy muttered. 'The youth of today . . .'

James ran a hand around his neck and chin, which were patchy with stubble and raised red spots. 'Mum bought me an electric razor to use in here,' he explained. 'It's useless – just chews your face up. How's Harriet?' He blushed at the sequence of his thoughts.

'Okay. Better than you. She should be home tomorrow or the day after.'

'I can't even go and see her,' James said.

'Have you done much walking yet?'

'I shuffle to and from the loo. That's about it.' He let his head fall back against the pillow as if even the notion of movement wearied him. For a second he reminded Guy of someone. He had a look of . . . Guy wasn't sure whom.

'Is there anything I can bring you?' he asked, feeling that practical assistance was more his department than uplifting bedside conversation. Nina could provide that – round the clock if necessary.

James thought for a moment. 'I don't think so. Mum brings me loads of snacks and newspapers every day. I'll tell you what though.' He indicated his Walkman on the sheet beside him. 'I'm getting a bit sick of listening to music. I wouldn't mind some of those audio-books. If you've got any.'

Guy hadn't. He had always harboured the suspicion that they were designed for people too lazy to turn pages. 'I'll bring you some tomorrow,' he offered. 'But I don't know what you like. Or what you've already read.'

'Oh, anything,' said James. 'Whatever you think. It doesn't matter if I already know it.'

'Right,' said Guy, racking his brains to try and remember what he had enjoyed twenty or so years ago. George Orwell and D.H. Lawrence. But hadn't they rather fallen out of favour lately? He could see that this particular commission was going to expose all too clearly how little he knew of the tastes and interests of the modern teenager.

'Oh-oh. What's she got now?' said James.

Guy looked up to see Nina come into the ward, laden with magazines, newspapers, books, biscuits, fruit, flowers. She was even carrying a chess set and a 500-piece jigsaw puzzle of a Beefeater.

'I said "No puzzles",' James remonstrated, but, ignoring him, Nina approached the neighbouring bed and addressed the elderly occupant.

'Good afternoon. My name's Nina. I've brought you some things.' And she started to unpack her pile of goodies, placing the basket of flowers on the top of the unit, and arranging a pyramid of bananas, peaches and grapes on a paper plate.

'Wh-what are you doing?' the man protested, roused from his torpor to a state of anxiety, and failing to recognize Nina from their previous encounter. 'I didn't order these.'

'That's all right.' Nina smiled encouragingly. 'It's a gift. Now do you prefer *The Times* or the *Mail*? Would you like me to read to you?'

'Are you one of these religious people?' the man demanded.

'Oh no, I'm . . .'

'I said I didn't want any religion when I came in here.'

Guy and James, watching this scene, started to laugh.

'I'm sorry, I should have explained,' said Nina, refusing to be intimidated by this unexpected show of resistance. 'I'm not a professional visitor, or anything like that. I'm James's mother.' She pointed across the divide. James gave an apologetic wave. 'I noticed you didn't have much in the way of entertainment and I thought you might like some reading matter and so forth.'

'Oh.' The man sounded slightly mollified by this explanation. 'So you're just giving them away?'

'Exactly.'

Once it was established that he was not expected to pay or convert, the man cheered up considerably. 'Well, that's very kind of you. I'll have a look at the *Mail* if you don't mind. The big papers, they're all doom and gloom.'

'I hope you're taking note of this so you can pick up tips on how to embarrass Sophie and Harriet in public when they're older,' James whispered to Guy.

'Mmm,' Guy replied, with the non-committal grunt of someone whose attention is elsewhere. He had picked up the clipboard from the end of the bed and was browsing through James's medical notes. There were the temperature and blood-pressure charts, and dosages of painkillers administered, along with a slip of paper recording the details of the transfusion he had had at the time of his operation: serial number, blood group (AB) and quantity (500ml). Guy looked at it, frowning. There was something odd here, unless his memory was deceiving him. And then it struck him who it was James had reminded him of, fleetingly, as he lay on the bed bemoaning his state of infirmity: Martin.

Guy closed the bedroom door on Sophie and fetched the loft ladder down from its trapdoor on the landing. The aluminium steps chimed beneath his feet as he climbed up into the darkness. He threw the switch and the room was filled with flickering light from the neon strip on the ceiling. Either side of his desk the china alsatians sat, unsold, gathering dust. From its tripod beneath the skylight the telescope stared at him with its one blank eye, and for the first time he felt no inclination to share its secrets. It was selfishness, he now realized, to annex a whole room for the pursuit of an occasional hobby. He had spent too much time gazing up at the stars while neglecting what was underfoot. It would make a perfect playroom for the girls: its low, sloping ceiling would be fine while they were still small. All their toys could be kept here, liberating the living room and hall from the tyranny of Barbie and her million fragile accessories. Jane would be pleased. And if he sold the telescope they might be able to afford to go away somewhere nice after all. He'd get to work at the first opportunity. In fact he'd make a start now by getting rid of those dogs. Procrastination was pointless: the children were growing bigger every day; there were only a few years of innocent enthusiasm left before they became moody teenagers, and soon after that they'd be off to college or wherever, like James.

James. With a sinking heart, Guy remembered what it was he'd come up for. He located his diary for 1976 in the cardboard box, marked *Nostalgia*, in the corner, and sat down to read, alternately skimming or becoming engrossed as his eye caught a reference to some long-forgotten incident. He kept having to recall himself to his task, searching, searching. After half an hour he shut the book and laid his cheek on its faded vellum cover. It was all there, of course, as he'd known it would be. James wasn't his; and he didn't know whether to laugh or cry. Instead, he climbed down the ladder, threw himself on his bed and lay staring at the moving shadows on the ceiling for a long time, until the sky outside was quite dark. He would have slept there where he'd landed – in his clothes, like Sophie – but he remembered he hadn't locked up downstairs and the porch light was still on, so he stood up, too quickly, and swayed dizzily as a kaleidoscope of snaking lights and floaters swirled before his eyes.

There was the mail on the doormat. He picked through it with one hand while sliding the bolts home. Several large, colourful envelopes, instantly proclaiming themselves to be junk mail, went in the bin unopened. Two bills, a bank statement and a begging letter from a children's charity were put in the rack for later. Guy had almost thrown out the charity letter, but something in the reproachful gaze of the bruised child pictured on the envelope reminded him of Harriet, so he had kept it back. That left a pale blue aerogramme, postmarked Sydney, and addressed to Guy in the unmistakable, microscopic script – unchanged since schooldays – of Hugo. A printed address label announced his metamorphosis into *Dr H. Blanchard-Etchells*. Guy tore it open, obliterating most of the first paragraph. Piecing it together, he read:

Dear Guy

Repeated attempts to telephone you have confirmed my suspicions that you are Never In, and thanks to your refusal to engage with the modern world and buy either a fax or an answering machine I have had to resort to this primitive form of communication. I only hope it arrives.

I'm afraid I'm going to have to turn down your kind offer to put me up this summer: there has been a major change of plan. Contrary to my earlier gloom-laden projections, the Geography Faculty here has caved in at the eleventh hour and renewed my contract for two years. It was obviously my calling their bluff that did the trick. And on the domestic front Anne-Marie and I are back together and giving things another try. Again, I think it may have been my threat to relocate to London that swung things in my favour. Anyway, we'll see how it goes. So, all in all, it doesn't look as though our Grand Reunion is going to take place. Unless, of course, you're planning a trip to Oz. I never did hear back from Nina, so perhaps you'll explain my non-appearance. That's if you have any contact these days. Incidentally, I came across this acknowledgement in a book on desert geomorphology the other day: 'I am indebted to H. Etchells and others for their work on aeolian processes in dune initiation (1976).'

There: didn't I promise you everlasting glory.

I hope all is well with you and yours, and that you haven't been put to much inconvenience on my behalf.

Yours ever,

Hugo

Guy shook his head. Good old Hugo. Unreliable to the last. He refolded the letter carefully and put it in his wallet for safekeeping. He and Nina would be able to laugh about it later; especially the acknowledgement, and the notion of 'inconvenience', whose many ironies Hugo would never begin to suspect.

42

On a seat under a beech sapling in the hospital grounds sat Nina and James, lost in a moment of private reflection. It was one of those hexagonal benches surrounding the tree trunk, designed so that even those desiring intimacy are forced to face away from each other.

Presently Nina spoke. 'It was the blood group thing that got him thinking. He saw you were AB, and he remembered from a conversation we'd had in Algeria that we were both A.'

'So there's absolutely no way . . .'

'Apparently not.'

James gave a dry laugh. 'Just as I was beginning to get used to the idea.'

'I know. I'm sorry. I'm as bewildered as you are.' What she didn't tell him was that Guy had also in his diary found references to herself and Martin alone together. That time on the beach north of Naples when she had, reluctantly, followed him into the woods. And the first night away from Souk Ahras, when the two of them had shared the tent, while Guy and Hugo slept out in the open. She had told Guy in the Windmill that such opportunities had never arisen, but now she remembered. Her amnesia had not been entirely accidental: it had been preferable to imagine James conceived in a moment of passion, than as a result of a perfunctory screw.

'At least I never called him Daddy.'

'That's funny,' said Nina. 'He said something very similar.'

Guy had rung her early in the morning, catching her just as she was leaving for work. She had arranged a ten o'clock interview with the pregnant twelve-year-old and her perpetually slewed mother, in their tenth-floor flat in Elephant and Castle. It hadn't been a difficult decision to phone and request a postponement. She wouldn't have been able to give them anything like the attention their plight deserved.

What had surprised her, almost as much as the news itself, was Guy's attitude. He had relayed his findings haltingly and with many apologies, like a doctor delivering an unexpectedly poor prognosis. After he had begun his fourth sentence with the word 'unfortunately', or one of its fellows, Nina had interrupted. 'If you don't mind my saying, you don't sound particularly thrilled with your own discovery.'

'To be quite honest I don't know how I feel,' Guy had replied. 'I suppose Jane will be relieved not to have to explain everything to the girls. I don't think she'd ever have accepted it comfortably.'

'But she seemed to take it so well. When I met her in the pub that time. And James says she's been very good to him all the time he's been at your place.'

'Oh, she'll always do the right thing,' said Guy. 'But not with her whole heart. Our relationship . . .' he hesitated, as if regretting this drift towards the confessional, '. . . did hit a rough patch.'

'I'm sorry about that. All for nothing, as it turned out.'

'So it appears. Although . . .'

'What?'

'I can't help feeling a bit, I don't know, disappointed. I do like James, you see. I thought I'd felt a bond there, a biological bond. Genes recognizing genes. But it was just imagination. He probably didn't even feel it. He never could call me Dad.'

Nina recalled herself to the present as James eased himself up from the bench, wincing. He had acquired the habit of holding one hand protectively in front of his scar, as if to catch anything that might burst out. 'Let's walk a bit,' he said, picking up his crutches. The physiotherapist had been round earlier with some frightening statistics about the percentage of muscles wasted by one week's bed-rest, and he was eager to start moving again.

Nina helped him up on to his good foot and they performed a slow circuit of the outpatients unit, past the pathology labs and the ultrasound department and the creche. In spite of the early hour, the steam from hundreds of boiling potatoes rose through the kitchen grilles, with the smell of wet dog. 'Mash for lunch again,' said James. At one of the back doors a man was unloading bales of clean laundry – monster decks of cards – from a van. A motorized trolley clattered past pulling its cargo of Foul Waste for incineration, and in the distance came the whoop of sirens as ambulances arrived and departed from Casualty. The sound made the skin on the back of Nina's neck prickle. We're the lucky ones, she thought, grasping for reasons to feel cheerful. In a way this morning's audience with James had been even harder and more uncomfortable than her original, mistaken, confession. As if it wasn't bad enough that she'd had to admit to being promiscuous and dishonest in the first place, now she'd proved herself incompetent – a fool. Her unnecessary intervention in Guy's life had very nearly cost him his marriage, if she'd understood him correctly, and James was fatherless once more, except this time with a jaded view of his parents' relationship, and a fresh sense of what he'd missed.

'I know I don't come out of all this very well,' she said, looking down at her suntanned hands and long, ringless fingers. 'If you're angry with me I quite understand.'

'I'm not *angry*,' said James, after a pause in which he seemed to have been trying out various moods to see which one suited. 'I mean, it's not as if you've been doing this to annoy me.'

'No,' said Nina. 'Of course not.'

'But next time you come up and say "James. There's something I must tell you", I think I'll have a prior engagement.'

'You'll be glad to get away from me,' Nina said, with half a smile. And James smiled back, but didn't deny it. 'But that's good – all as it should be,' she went on bravely. 'You need to move out' – she looked at him, hobbling beside her – 'spread your . . . crutches.'

'Stand on my own foot,' James agreed, and they grinned at each other.

It wasn't only James's reaction that was an issue for Nina. From a practical point of view there was the ticklish problem of money. Out of a sense of belated financial responsibility Guy had offered to pay James an immoderate amount of money for a very modest amount of decorating – work which would in all probability never be finished. Now that it was clear no such responsibility existed, how could the subject possibly be broached without embarrassment, Nina wondered.

'Would you mind going a bit slower?' James pleaded, as Nina, preoccupied with these troubling thoughts, began to lengthen her stride.

'I'm sorry,' she said, falling back into step and taking his arm again. 'I was trying to outrun my worries.'

'Why should you be worried? Everything's finally sorted out.'

She marvelled again at his nonchalance. So few things bothered him. 'I feel guilty. And, as Kerry says, if you feel guilty, you are guilty. I've interfered in someone else's life, and I've managed to deprive you of a father – twice.'

James disengaged his arm from Nina's and put it round her shoulder, heavily, something he'd been in the habit of doing ever since he grew tall enough. 'I've always known who my real father is,' he said, giving her a squeeze.

She looked up at him, puzzled, and at the same time thinking how handsome he was, in spite of his zippered eyebrow and the shaving rash on his neck. 'What do you mean?' she asked, failing to catch on.

'You are,' he said. And this time the skin on the back of Nina's neck tingled with pleasure at the compliment, and some of her present gloom evaporated.

43

Early on the day Harriet was due to be discharged from hospital Guy was standing by the entrance to Mortlake Cemetery waiting for Nina. He was holding a large bunch of white chrysanthemums, which he'd bought from the roadside stall for what he thought an indecent amount of money. Term had ended the day before and he still had the twitchy, supercharged manner of someone who has not yet disconnected himself from the rhythm of work. He kept fidgeting and looking at his watch, putting the flowers behind his back and then under one arm, alternately humming and sighing. He often complained of having no time in the day to stop and draw breath, and yet here he was, with an idle fifteen minutes, and not a clue how to spend them.

He had promised Jane he would be back home by midday in time to celebrate Harriet's homecoming, and then to pack. His secretary, Mary, was lending them her cottage on the Gower peninsula for a fortnight.

A white minicab drew up alongside, bristling with antennae, and Nina emerged, flustered and apologetic, and also bearing floral tributes – a fern and a cactus in full bloom.

'Must cost you a fortune, all these cab fares,' he observed, stepping forward to kiss her cheek.

'I know. I'm through with public transport,' she said. 'I'm going to have to go back to owning a car.' They started to walk through the cemetery, Nina leading the way.

'Jane's supposed to be selling one,' Guy offered, conversationally. 'An estate, I think. Nice big boot.' He'd been thinking of the luggage requirements of their family holiday, quite forgetting that Nina would have other criteria.

'What would I need one of those for?'

'Oh. Taking hedge clippings to the dump?'

Nina pulled a face. 'A two-seater would be ample for me.

Or do you think I'm too old for a sports car?'

By way of reply Guy hummed a few bars of 'The Ballad of Lucy Jordan'.

'Yes, well,' said Nina. 'I've never driven through Paris in a sports car – though we did drive through Naples in a Land Rover, remember.'

'It's not too late,' said Guy. 'Do you think that's what you'll do when James is off your hands. Travel abroad?'

'No, I had a vague idea I might get abroad to come to me. Take in language students.' Nina took a path off to the side between rows of graves, Guy following a deferential pace behind.

'Does it pay well?'

'I haven't a clue. I'd be doing it for the company, not the money.'

'Speaking of money,' said Guy, 'I haven't forgotten what I owe James for the decorating.' He patted the bulge of wallet in his back pocket. 'I've got it here.' He lowered his voice as they passed an elderly woman who was on her knees with a scrubbing brush, cleaning bird-droppings off a headstone. The plot was beautifully tended, laid out like a miniature garden with immaculate, green turf, evidently regularly watered, and a tiny flowerbed. Alongside it neighbouring graves stood neglected and overgrown.

Nina put up her hand as if to ward off further blows to her self-esteem. 'Oh, please. He didn't even finish the job.'

'That doesn't matter. The guest room isn't a big priority any more. Our guest won't be coming.' He handed over Hugo's aerogramme. 'Read that.'

Nina took it from him, shaking her head over the microscopic handwriting. She laughed at the acknowledgement. 'Typical Hugo,' she said. 'I see he got his PhD in the end.'

'And he's gone double-barrelled,' Guy said, pointing out the address label.

'What a fraud. You know, if he hadn't got back in touch none of this might have happened.' She passed the letter back.

'That's a thought,' said Guy. He wasn't sure whether it was

a pleasant or unpleasant thought. He would rather not have gone through the events of the last month or so, but he couldn't regret having met Nina again, to say nothing of James.

'There's one thing I'm grateful for,' said Nina. 'Just imagine if I'd told Irene that James wasn't her grandson.'

Just imagine if I'd told my mother he was, thought Guy.

'Anyway, speaking of fraud, I really can't let you part with any money. I feel bad enough about all the trouble I've caused you, without obtaining money under false pretences.'

'It's James I'm paying, not you,' Guy pointed out. 'Anyway, I'm adamant, and so is Jane. The paternity issue is irrelevant.'

Nina considered. 'I think I'd be more scared of an adamant Jane,' she decided.

Guy laughed. 'I know she seems aloof, but it's just shyness. She's very rewarding if you make the effort.'

'You make her sound like one of your Special Needs pupils,' said Nina. 'Perhaps we could do a deal over that car of hers. James could use it for learning to drive. Here we are.'

She had stopped beside a white marble stone, which rose as cleanly as a new tooth from its brown grassy bed. Guy read the inscription:

Martin Anthony Shorrocks
Born 6 March 1955
Died 18 July 1976
A beloved only son
Gone but not forgotten

Guy automatically bowed his head before this strange, cold object, which conjured up nothing of the Martin he'd known. At a distance of nearly nineteen years it was hard even to visualize his face with any clarity. He tended only to see Martin as he appeared in the few group photographs that were now in the box in the loft. 'Forgive me for not coming before. Amen,' he murmured, conscious that Nina was looking sideways at him with an expression of curiosity. 'I should have done this years ago,' he offered, by way of explanation, then he tore the paper off the chrysanthemums and threaded them one by one into the holes in the top of the sunken vase. As a child he had mistaken these metal grilles for air vents – precautions against untimely burial – and had found them slightly unsettling ever since.

Nina unwrapped her potted fern and swapped it for the withered remains of its predecessor, which had been frying in the heat for weeks, unwatered.

'We used to come often when James was little,' she explained. 'And it was a place of pilgrimage for Irene, right up until her illness.'

'I suppose it's a comfort to have something to visit,' said Guy, trying for a second to imagine what it might feel like to be grateful for such meagre comforts, and quickly retreating from the images summoned.

'It doesn't mean much to James now. Maybe when he's older. With kids of his own.'

Guy nodded. 'Genealogy isn't a teenage thing, is it?' He thought of his own father, trawling parish records and dusty archives in vain for some sign of distinction. 'They live in the present.' Guy straightened up, his flower arranging complete. For all his efforts, the chrysanthemums stood stiffly in serried rows.

'Well,' said Nina, folding the polythene plant holder and pocketing it. 'His life is still measured in terms. He's no need to look too far forward or back.'

'So is mine,' said Guy. 'Terms subdivided into the four-weekly intervals between paydays.' He cursed himself for this remark: he hadn't intended to bring up the subject of money again in case Nina took it as a glancing reference to James and the unpaid debt.

Fortunately Nina's thoughts had taken a different route. 'Will Jane go back to work, do you think, when Harriet starts school?'

'I don't know.' Guy shrugged his shoulders. 'I don't like to suggest it in case she thinks I'm putting pressure on her. I'd be quite happy for her to stay at home. But she might see that as pressure too.'

'Did you tell me she used to be a nurse?'

'No, a health service manager. She has a troubled relationship with work, Jane does. It's her perfectionism. She's never satisfied with her own performance. That's why she's so hard on herself as a mother.'

'I know that feeling.' Nina held up the flowering cactus. 'I must leave this for Irene,' she said, as though Irene herself might be popping by later to pick it up. She made her way to a distant corner of the cemetery which consisted of more recent grave sites, most too fresh to be marked by a permanent stone.

'You know it's quite right what you said about Jane,' Guy went on, when he caught up. 'She does have Special Needs.' The idea had never occurred to him before, but it seemed obvious now. Things that more robust people took in their stride – like moving house, or the temporary absence of a friend – she felt as personal tragedies, and yet in the face of calamity, such as they had just experienced, she was strong and brave. 'You know, the weird thing is,' he went on, 'when I told her James wasn't mine I expected her to dance around with relief. But she didn't. I mean, I could tell she *was* relieved, but one remark really struck me. She said, "That doesn't mean we'll never see him again, does it?"'

Nina set the pot containing the fat, prickly cactus down on the parched earth of Irene's grave, its one red bloom a tongue of fire against the dust. 'It's not very beautiful,' Nina admitted. 'I only bought it because I thought it would last in the heat better than cut flowers. But then I was listening to the radio in the cab on the way here and the forecaster said the dry weather's coming to an end.'

'Not too soon, I hope,' said Guy. 'We're off to Wales on Monday.'

'No. After a week or so, the man said,' Nina backtracked. 'I think you'll be safe.'

'Perhaps James might come and see us some time when we

get back,' Guy suggested. 'Once he's up and about. Only if he wants to. Don't pressurize him.'

'As if I could,' said Nina. She thrust her hands deep into the pockets of her shorts, dragging the canvas fabric tight across the dome of her stomach. 'He does actually like you. You've converted him to D.H. Lawrence, by the way, for which I'm not sure I thank you.'

'Oh?' Guy laughed, pleased to think that his selection of tapes had hit the mark. In an attempt to demonstrate as broad a range of tastes as possible he had, after careful deliberation, settled on *Sons and Lovers*, an early Terry Pratchett, and *Beloved*.

'I hope you don't think this is a cheek,' said Nina. 'But I was going to ask if you and Jane wouldn't mind being sort of unofficial godparents. I mean I don't believe in God, myself, but . . .'

'But I do,' said Guy, surprised at his own vehemence. 'I'd be honoured. Really.'

'Perhaps you ought to talk it over with Jane. I mean obviously there's not much to be *done*, now he's eighteen – I mean for God's sake don't get him a silver napkin ring – but I'd like to think he could turn to you, as a man . . .'

'Of course,' said Guy. 'Not that I'm any sort of role model, heaven knows. Still – in the important things like cricket and real ale . . .' He was already planning that trip to Lords.

'Good. That's settled then.'

They had reached the cemetery gates. Guy paused, wondering whether to buy Jane a bouquet from the stall and to hell with the price. But what sort of person brought flowers away from a cemetery? She might take him for a grave-robber. He decided to stop on the way home and get chocolates instead. 'Do you want a lift anywhere?' he asked, quite forgetting that Jane had the car.

'No. I'll make my own way,' said Nina, and she turned with a wave and walked back down Mortlake Road, like a confident woman, of infinite resources, with somewhere important to go.

44

'Will you be happy to be back home?' Jane asked, as she drove Harriet away from the hospital having witnessed a protracted farewell, in which all the nurses on the ward had been kissed and hugged goodbye at least once.

'A little bit happy and a little bit sad,' said Harriet, after giving the matter some thought.

'Why sad?'

'I liked the dinners. And the big television.'

'What was so good about the dinners?' Jane wanted to know. Even the smell of the food trolley had made her want to heave.

'They were nice and cold,' Harriet explained. She was firmly strapped in her car seat, and holding a helium balloon in the shape of a dolphin – a gift from Erica, which had arrived boxed and gift-wrapped on the ward with the message, 'a present from the seaside'. It kept straying into Jane's line of vision, blocking the rear window, but she had promised herself she wouldn't nag, today of all days.

Guy and Sophie would be at home waiting for them by the time they arrived; Jane had bulked out the reception committee with a few of Harriet's favourite dolls and teddies, placed on the stairs under a homemade banner saying WELCOME in Sophie's careful script. Jane had made an unintentionally macabre cake in the shape of a bed in which a marzipan Harriet lay pinned beneath a white icing sheet, 'like a corpse on a slab', as Guy pointed out.

They would save the champagne for later, when James was out of hospital and well enough to visit. Now it was established that he wasn't Guy's son and had no special claim on his affections, she felt much more inclined to be friendly. In fact, when it occurred to her that James himself might have no particular reason or desire to pursue the acquaintance, she found herself unaccountably depressed, and prone to invent excuses for maintaining contact. Even Nina appeared in a new and more sympathetic light. Jane realized with some shame that until now she had allowed jealousy and mistrust to stifle any natural impulses towards friendship, despite sensing, in that very first meeting in the Windmill, how much she could like Nina if she let herself. It wouldn't be easy to make amends inconspicuously – Nina would no doubt be sharp enough to interpret correctly this sudden thaw. Still, if she had half the insight Jane credited her with, she would understand and forgive.

As she turned the car into their road her reveries were interrupted by a squeal of delight from Harriet. 'Look, that's Erica's car!' Sure enough, the familiar form of the unwashed red estate was parked directly outside the house.

'You're right,' said Jane, marvelling at Harriet's ability to distinguish between similar makes and models of car. It was obviously a recent phenomenon of Western culture – the equivalent of the Inuit's legendary classification of snow.

'Have they come to play?' Harriet asked, swivelling round in her seat as Jane drove on up the road in search of a parking spot.

'I don't know. We'll see.' They ran back the fifty yards towards Erica's car together, Jane holding Harriet's small suitcase, Harriet tugging her dolphin balloon behind her on its string. The front window had been left open, and on the driver's seat was a large, hard-backed envelope addressed to Jane in black marker. Jane put her arm through the window to retrieve it, noticing with relief that the car's interior, though not exactly clean, was at least free of junk. Along with a set of keys and registration documents, the package contained a photograph and a brief note from Erica, written on the back of an unpaid parking ticket.

Dear Jane

Sorry to have missed you. We fly up to Scotland to stay with my parents for a week, then we're straight off to Kuwait. We've been thinking of you all, especially Harriet. I spoke to Guy on the phone and he told me she was doing well. Give her a hug from me and tell her to keep asking awkward questions.

You won't want any reminders of that day, but here is the photo I took of you on the beach, to redress the imbalance on your mantelpiece. It's nice, don't you think? One of my best.

I'll try to drop you a line with our address when we're settled – though I'd be the first to admit I'm the world's laziest correspondent. I didn't even write a proper letter to Neil all the time he was away! Perhaps you'll let me know how you're getting on some time. Not that I have any doubts – you were always much more capable than you realized. Memories of our many conversations and the thrashing I gave you at table tennis will sustain me during my exile.

The car is yours to keep, sell or scrap as you please.

With love, Erica

The photograph, A4 size, showed Jane in crisp focus, perched delicately on a breakwater, straight-backed, hands between her knees, looking out to sea. Beside her, but out of her line of vision, stood a seagull, with the same erect pose, staring in the same direction. Behind them both were the blurred struts of the pier. The foreground was a collision of textures: coarse, shaggy seaweed and glossy, ruffled hair; pebbles pitted as though with woodworm, and wood smooth as stone, all picked out in the deepest blacks and the most luminous whites with a million shades of grey in between. Jane was delighted: Erica had made her look not just pretty, as she had hoped, but *interesting*, and who could ask for more from a portrait? She would put it in the sitting room alongside the one of Guy with the glasses and the grin, where it would serve as a talking point and a reminder of her absent friend.

'Come on, Mummy,' urged Harriet, who had skipped down the drive and was climbing on to the edge of a large terracotta pot of geraniums to reach the doorbell. Her fingers scrabbled, millimetres from their target, and then she slipped backwards into the geraniums. There was the crunch of tender stems snapping, and a squeal as Harriet lunged for the door handle to save herself, and let go of the balloon.

'My dolphin!' she wailed, as it soared skywards, clearing the fence and taking off up the road, propelled by tiny gusts of wind.

'It's all right. I'll get it,' said Jane, dropping the suitcase and photo and vaulting the front wall. The balloon was a few days old now and had lost some of its gas: otherwise its trajectory might have been more vertical, and Jane would have had no chance at all of catching its trailing ribbon, which was even now skimming the tops of the shrubs in the neighbouring gardens. She flung herself after it – Jane, who would never compromise her dignity by running for a bus in case she missed it – over fences and front lawns, oblivious to the rules of trespass and road safety, but the balloon seemed possessed by a demon. Every time she came within arm's length the ribbon-tail would be twitched out of reach. Harriet's cries of 'Run faster, Mummy', grew faint in her ears as she reached the bend in the road.

I'm not going to do it, she thought, as she watched the dolphin bump and nudge its way over a garage roof and out of sight. She felt suddenly limp with disappointment at the thought of facing Harriet empty-handed, and was seriously considering jogging ever onwards until she found a shop that sold its kind. Where had Erica bought it? Arbroath? Aberdeen?

As Jane stood contemplating her inglorious return, the dolphin reappeared a few houses down, bobbing and swaying as if enjoying the game, and then suddenly and miraculously came to a halt as its ribbon snagged a standard rose bush. It hovered there, bent-backed, like a giant comma in the air, giving Jane the crucial few seconds to swoop and reel it safely in.

'Clever Mummy!' Harriet called joyfully, as Jane approached the house, dishevelled but triumphant.

'Come and see what we've got for tea,' said Sophie, dragging Harriet indoors. Within a few moments the prized balloon would be abandoned as they set to arguing over who would eat the coveted marzipan cadaver from the top of the cake.

Guy, who had heard Harriet scrabbling at the front door, had watched the pursuit from the end of the path. If he was surprised to see his wife crashing through hedges like a hound after a fox he gave no sign of it. He held up Erica's photograph, which he had retrieved from the dusty pavement where Jane had dropped it. 'What's this?' he asked.

'It's me,' said Jane. 'Erica took it.' She found her eye drawn to the black dustbins by the gate. In each one sat a china alsatian, its muzzle resting on the rim, the lid balanced on its pointed ears.

'It's lovely.' He turned it away from the light to stop the sun's glare bursting off the gloss. He squeezed her hand. 'You look like somebody . . .'

'That's because I am Somebody.' Jane smiled, returning the pressure, and they followed the girls back into the house.

Later, while he was reading Harriet and Sophie a bedtime story, Guy could hear Jane padding about on the landing. When he came out to see what was going on he found her moving all her bits and pieces from the spare room back into their bedroom. She was filing them away neatly in drawers and wardrobes where they belonged. A pair of cream satin pyjamas which he'd never seen before lay on the bed.

'These are nice,' he said, stroking the material with the back of his hand. 'Are they new?'

She gave a guilty smile. 'The nightie you bought me was a bit chilly. These are more me.'

'That's okay.' He was so pleased to have her back. 'Anything that's You is fine by Me.'

A commotion outside drew him to the window. A group of children, a little older than Sophie, were roller-blading on the pavement below, deliberately crashing into one another and shrieking as they went over. Kids from his school. He tapped on the window and pointed at his watch face. It took them a second or two to realize who he was, and then they scrambled to their feet and skated off, terrified, staggering on their skinny foal's legs.

Jane came up behind him and put her arms around his waist. As he felt her cool hands inside his shirt – not passionately, but lovingly, comfortingly *there* – he dared to feel a sense of optimism, and to picture a future in which, with patience, all manner of things might be well.

'I see you've put the dogs out,' Jane said, pointing at the bins. 'They might get nicked.'

'Why? Even the dustmen won't take them,' said Guy, and they started to laugh, the sort of dangerous uncontrolled laughter that can easily turn to hysterics and start to hurt. 'No. What we need is an exorcist.' His shoulders shook.

'We'll have to drive to Beachy Head and chuck them over the cliff,' said Jane, wiping her eyes.

'That's going a bit out of our way. What about the Severn Bridge?'

They stood there at the open window for some time, arms around each other, enjoying the silence of the house, with the girls both safely asleep in the next room, and looking out at the evening sky which was feathered with high cirrus clouds – the first, unmistakable signs of a change in the weather.